Unexpected Beginnings

Samsara - The First Season

Volume One – Book Two

JL Martin

Time Travellers Publishing House PTY LTD

ALSO by JL Martin

FICTION

SAMSARA- The First Season

That Fated Night- A Short Novella of Love and Loss

The Golden Glow

Unexpected Beginnings

Torn in Two

Loss of Innocence

Unconditional Love

Returning Home

Letting go

Soul Connections

Healing the Heart

Legacy and Love

Leo- Back to me!

Lilith- Utopia

SPAWNED OF SIN- Trilogy Series

Through Windows in the Sky I Fall

Tainted Blood, Poisoned Soul

The Ties That Bind Behind Me

Unexpected Beginnings

THE FIRST SEASON

J. L. MARTIN

Published by Time Travellers Publishing House Pty Ltd 2021

The series is written in British English, as the Author is Australian and the books are based in Australia. My American friends will find U's where they have no right to be, Z replaced with S, and so many double L's you may feel like throwing the book against the wall. I apologise in advance, and hope one day we can all live in harmony...

National Library of Australia

Cataloging-in-Publication data

Martin, J L, 1971-.

Unexpected Beginnings

Samsara-The First Season

ISBN Print: 978-1-925852-22-6

ISBN Ebook: 978-1-925852-21-9

Cover design by Thea Atkinson

Editing and text design by Marianne Delaforce

Printed and bound in Australia by Ingram Sparks

A Note from the Author

IN READING THE SERIES 'Samsara-The First Season', I ask you to consider the era in which this work of fiction is set. In these more enlightened times, elements of this story may be considered homophobic, racist, and outright morally corrupt—along with being barbaric and downright ignorant. However; in 19th century Australia, they were not. Themes throughout the series are reflective of the times and are an accurate account of the attitude, bias and outright hate a large majority of society held towards the LGBTQI+ Community and our First Nations Peoples. In saying this, we no longer consider it appropriate for a fifteen-year-old girl to marry—forced or not—but 130 years ago, it was not uncommon.

The character of Leo is based on a real person. As outrageous, inappropriate and politically incorrect as he is—I love this soul. It is not my intention to stigmatise him or cause offence to anyone—only to remain authentic in my best effort to honour and immortalise a very dear man who left a significant imprint on my life—and who unfortunately was born without a filter and lacks all sensibilities; and can be very, very badly behaved.

Please be aware there are themes of violence, racism, and homophobia throughout this series; however, I have been mindful to write these scenes as sensitively as possible and with the utmost care.

I truly hope you enjoy 'Samsara-The First Season' just as much as I enjoyed writing it.

Dedication

To my darling girl, Aurorah Michelle.

You, sweetheart, changed my life when you made me a grandmother
for the first time, and my love for you only deepens as each day passes.
Nothing you could ever do could diminish my love for you. Love
without limitations and always, always, be kind.

Chapter One

The breeze from Port Phillip Bay was colder than I expected, the seasons opposite to Scotland. The Captain had advised all passengers last night we would arrive just in time for our first Australian winter, apparently much milder than back home. At the end of what I now knew to be Railway Pier, I stood in the seaside suburb of Emerald. I had only said goodbye to Hamish moments before, and I already missed him. Polly, Bessie, and Mary followed me towards the road. Leonardo skipped ahead to the older man loading our large carpetbags into a carriage, the sign he had been carrying with my new surname now discarded on his seat. Before I could speak, he bowed to me, Leonardo mockingly bowing back before I pinched him on the leg.

'Mr Ian McPhee sent the Melbourne office coach for ya to have at your disposal until ya catch the train in the mornin'. We'll have the larger trunks freighted to Geelong an' transported to ya home in time for ya arrival. I've placed ya overnight bags in the carriage, Miss Delmont.'

'Thank you. What's your name, Sir?'

'Me name is Geordie McGovern. I drive for ya solicitor, Mr Ian McPhee, when he's in Melbourne. You can call me Geordie. McGovern sounds too posh for the likes of me.' He gave me a toothless smile, his grey eyes sparkling in the daylight, his hair pure white. It pleasantly surprised me to find a faint golden aura surrounding him.

I provided Catherine's address in Bourke Street and asked him to take us there, before he assisted us into the carriage, including Leonardo.

The carriage moved through the working-class suburb. We passed many tiny workers' cottages nestled between the occasional grand residence before the carriage turned into a wide road leading to the town's busy centre. I watched the carriages and carts that moved ahead of us, then turned back to stare at those following behind, along with people on horseback; most of them men, while a horse-drawn tram passed us, going in the opposite direction.

Bessie and Mary quietly chatted between themselves while Polly reread the love letters Angus had written to her throughout the journey. I stuck my head out of the open window, taking in the river below as we crossed a large bridge, the dust from the road catching in my throat and causing me to cough. Mr McGovern pulled the horses up at an intersection to wait for passing carriages and carts that slowly ambled down Flinders Street.

A large square building, the train station I noted, stood to our left and, across the road, a bluestone pub—Young and Jacksons—and I decided there and then we must visit while in Melbourne. The carriage jolted forward, continuing ahead into Swanston Street, passing St. Paul Cathedral on our right. My eyes widened as I gazed up at The Delmont Hotel, standing proudly beside the church. The grand building stood on the corner of Collins and Swanston Street, looming above the many shops that appeared busy, while we slowed for a horse-drawn tram that had stopped to collect passengers.

The sights and sounds of the busy town overwhelmed me, Leonardo's excitement contagious as he waved to anyone who was unfortunate enough to even glance in our direction. I realised I must send word to the Melbourne law firm to request they arrange our accommodation for the night and advise our driver not to bother returning for us, as it was not far to walk back to the hotel where I assumed would be our lodgings for the night.

We came to an abrupt halt in front of a large, double-story building in Bourke Street, jolting me back to the present. I stepped down from the carriage, thanking Mr McGovern for his help, then turned to stare up at the unique shop. It surprised me to find the building was ten times larger than I had imagined, the shop below appearing expensive and quite exclusive. Two immaculately dressed women stepped outside, their servants carrying several large packages as they followed behind.

'Geordie, do you mind speaking to Mr McPhee regarding our accommodations for the night, please? I am uncertain what they have arranged for us.' He nodded, Bessie, Polly and Mary staring open-mouthed into the window at several of the dresses on display, while Leonardo was more interested in the grocery shop next door. I thanked him profusely for taking the time to collect us before bidding him farewell. He gently slapped the long reins on the horses' rounded rumps, moving them forward as he waved farewell.

I approached the shop, then pushed open the door; Bessie, Mary and Polly close behind, while Leonardo lingered on the street for a moment. The bell tinkled overhead as we stepped inside, carrying our overnight bags, finding Catherine at the back of the shop waiting on a customer. The woman appeared well to do and dressed like a princess. A princess with an exceptionally sour face. She glanced at us in disdain, causing Catherine to turn her head to see who had dared offend her habitué.

Catherine screamed, excitement overwhelming her as she ran to me, deserting her customer. The lady angrily abandoned the fine material she had been perusing and stomped out of the shop in a very unladylike manner, causing me to laugh aloud as she slammed the door behind her. Catherine rushed into my arms, embracing me tightly, the golden glow surrounding her somewhat brighter than I remembered. The sight of her filled me with joy and pleased me greatly to find her looking so well. Her blonde hair was now thick and glimmered in the light, her eyes sparkling, her face radiant, while she had put on a healthy amount of weight and no longer looked drawn and anxious.

She hurried to the front of the shop, locked the door, placed a sign in the window, advising her customers she would return within the hour, and then ushered us to a back staircase. We obediently followed her, stepping through a large door at the top of the stairs and into the sitting room, finding Nanny sitting with Beatrice, who played silently with a dollhouse.

'She still doesn't speak,' Catherine remarked as she guided us through the room. 'The screaming has nearly stopped, but she won't talk to anyone, not even Nanny. Father and Mother have just about given up on the poor little thing.' She tousled Beatrice's hair as we walked past, and I kissed her hello, although she ignored me before I embraced Nanny. Then, finally, we entered a smaller room where William sat in a high-back chair near the fireplace, reading the newspaper.

'Well, well, well, you still insist on exposing us to the undressed and the unwashed, don't you, Abigail?' he remarked casually, gazing across at Leonardo, whose clothes had seen better days. His shirt and pants, along with his thick coat, were clean and well kept; and I thought William rude to say such a thing. He continued to look Leo up and down in disgust, making no attempt to hide his displeasure, infuriating me.

'William, I see nothing has changed regarding your manners,' I snapped. I was beyond angry, rage rising inside me, and I had only been in his company for thirty seconds. Catherine laughed nervously, pulling me into another tight embrace before indicating to sit on the lounge or the chair next to William. While Polly sat down next to William, I chose the lounge, Leonardo quickly planting himself down beside me.

'I have missed you so much, Abigail; even you and William arguing is music to my ears.' She giggled as she ushered Mary and Bessie back to meet the kitchen staff, the correct etiquette taught to her by her parents, as you did not sit and socialise with your servants in the Montague home. Polly and Leo remained, given he was no servant to anyone—at least, not in the traditional sense, and Polly was family to me and would serve no one unless by choice. An awkward silence hung over the room until Catherine returned with a tray of refreshments, placing them on the table in front of us. She sat down heavily beside me, taking my hand in hers.

'I adore it here, Abigail. The weather is warmer, and there are far fewer people than on the streets of London.' She squeezed my hand, her face shining. 'Everyone is so much friendlier, and my father is now allowing me to design dresses to sell at a lower price for women who want to save money or cannot afford his designs. I am receiving quite a bit of attention from the ladies who mix in my parents' circles; although, they are the ones who can afford to pay what my father asks, which confuses me.'

'I am so pleased for you, my dear friend. I would love to see a sample of what you have created since you arrived.' She nodded, rising to her feet, then pulled me to mine, leaving Polly, William, and Leonardo to their own devices as we made our way back down the stairs to the shop. She led me to the back of the shop and into a large storeroom to show me her work, which I examined carefully.

'These dresses are unique creations, Catherine. They're works of art.' I asked Catherine to design several to suit the Australian climate; besides, it would give me an excuse to see her more often if obligated to attend Melbourne for fittings.

We returned to the parlour to find William still reading the news-paper and Polly and Leonardo sitting in silence while devouring the Madeira cake and warm, freshly baked biscuits with milk.

'I am so delighted you and Abigail found each other again, Polly.' Catherine smiled warmly before offering her another piece of cake, Polly thanking her as she took another slice. 'You were all she could talk about and of all the memories you share, having grown up together. I feel as if we're already acquainted.' She rose and embraced a surprised but clearly happy Polly.

'I've heard all about you, too, Catherine, and I feel the same way,' Polly replied shyly before returning to her seat.

'Hello? What about me? No one is talking about me,' Leonardo exclaimed loudly, startling me. 'Do any of you feel you know me? Of course not, because Abigail didn't tell you I am her new best friend, and you two little dirty birdies are on the way out.' He waved his finger at Polly and Catherine, Polly glaring back silently while Catherine giggled. William glowered at Leonardo, shaking his head in disbelief, as people usually did when first exposed to his outrageous opinions on anything.

'Well, tell us about yourself, Leonardo,' Catherine probed kindly, causing me to cringe. He crossed his legs and rested his chin on his hand, appearing ready to chat for hours—as long as the attention remained on him.

'First, call me Leo. I only force people I don't like to refer to me as Leonardo.' Catherine giggled again as he relaxed back in his seat and puffed out his chest. 'Back to me. All eyes here,' he called out, pointing to himself dramatically. 'When it comes to me, I'm a humble person and don't enjoy talking about myself much.' I laughed loudly, tears streaming down my face as he turned to scowl at me before continuing. 'Abigail has no clue she has befriended the most renowned chef in the world. You only have to smell my food to agree with me. Blessed with physical beauty, I'm possibly the most handsome man that currently walks the earth, but I'm sure you're aware of that.' He stopped, leaning forward to pick up his glass of orange juice, taking a small sip before turning to William. 'I am normally a dapper dresser, and I will be again, mark my words. I'm not a rich puttana like you appear to be, living on daddy's money; however, I will be soon, and then you will no longer look down your more-than-handsome nose at me.' He widened his eyes at William for a moment, turning away and dismissing him with his hand. 'I am blessed with the ability to make anyone fall in love with me. Abigail is only one example of thousands.' I rolled my eyes, discreetly elbowing him in the ribs in the hope he would stop talking. 'Don't look at me like that—thank you, William. I've heard all about you, too, and from what I know, you're not an amiable person, unlike everyone else in the room. Hands up if you're a nasty and bitter human. Go on, William; raise your hand. No one else here needs to. You have been awful to my butter face, Abigail, and I don't appreciate it one bit. Your clothes may be finer than mine; however, my disposition is finer than yours, you wicked wee cockroach.'

Catherine choked on her juice as I smothered a smile, taking great pleasure from the look on William's face. He turned his attention to me, frowning, as though this entire situation was my fault.

'The company you keep doesn't surprise me at all, bringing filth like that to our door,' he snapped, roughly folding his newspaper up and throwing it down on the floor beside him. 'The fine clothes you now wear have not turned you into a lady, Abigail. It does not differ from painting a pig's lips and dressing it in one of my father's creations; it is still a pig. You have offended my family by bringing these servants into our home and expecting us to serve them morning tea and socialise with them as if we are equals.' I raised my eyebrows, my mouth twitching as I smothered a smile. 'This is not something to laugh at, Abigail, so stop it now and take me seriously. Do you think I cannot see what he is, or should I say she? A Mary, through and through. Next, you will expect us all to meet you for a gin in a Molly house.'

Polly watched silently, wide-eyed, while Catherine appeared confused. At that moment, I wanted to rip William's blonde head off. To call Leo horrible names—including Mary, a derogatory term used for homosexual men—made me physically sick.

'Sweetheart, you can call me Maria and braid my hair, but unlike you, I'll never have to worry about being called a funt, which, I must add, is Abigail's favourite word. It is not one I use personally, though. I feel it would be quite appropriate, but alas, there are ladies present.' The blood drained from William's face as Leo turned, pointing to my chest. 'I agree sugar lips here is no lady; however, she is far from the interesting pig you speak of who enjoys dressing up. Be aware—I will train her to be that lady you so clearly expect her to be, and she'll kick your firm backside to kingdom come for insulting her in the company of her friends—who, by the way, believe she resembles a giraffe with large breasts, rather than your fascinating painted pig whom I would dearly like to meet.' He looked away for a moment, deep in thought, while I used every drop of strength in me not to punch him in the face, although he was genuinely trying to defend me. 'I bet you've never had her go after you like I have when you've done something wrong, have you?' He leaned forward, focussing his attention on William, who appeared unable to speak. 'I'll give you a tip for free; Abigail may be small-boned, but she is as strong as three men when she gets wild, and she can seriously hurt a man the size of you, William. She was ready to kill me when I dangled her over the side of the ship by her ankles. She overreacts more often than not, so watch yourself.' I could have murdered him the day he had hung me over the railing of the ship, feeling I was about to die. I had been furious with him for days afterwards. Eventually, I had forgiven him, knowing he was just an overgrown child who acted in ways no other person would, no matter what their inclinations or sexual preference.

William jumped to his feet, stomping across the room, before stepping through the door and slamming it behind him. An awkward silence hung over the room yet again until Catherine turned to me and smiled weakly.

'I do apologise on William's behalf. He has just started his first year at Melbourne University, studying law. He has told us he enjoys it very much, but I do not believe him for one moment.'

'Oh, do not give it another thought, Catherine. Tell us more of what you have been doing since you arrived,' I replied, holding her hand in mine.

'I work all week now in the shop and spend my evenings drawing my next creation. I have every intention of opening my own business when I am of age, with my parents' blessing, God willing.' I believed she would do well wherever she opened her shop. From what I had seen so far, her gowns were stunning and far superior to anything I had in my wardrobe, despite it all being brand new.

Catherine invited us upstairs to the rooftop garden for luncheon, the time flying by so fast it was four o'clock before we knew it. Mr and Mrs Montague were away in Sydney, meeting with potential employees required to manage a recently established store in Sydney town. Mr Montague intended to make his creations in a range of sizes, then ship them to the Sydney store, ready to be fitted by the seamstress. It sounded like a good idea to me and would make them a great deal of money.

Catherine asked to join us at the hotel for the night, feeling she was not ready to say goodbye just yet. Given William had not reappeared, we farewelled Beatrice and Nanny and filed out onto the street. We walked along Bourke Street, turning into Swanston Street toward the grand Delmont Hotel, talking and laughing, finally feeling excited to be here.

I felt my stomach lurch as we approached the imposing hotel that carried my new name. It was enormous compared to the buildings surrounding it. Stopping outside the entrance, I stared up at it in awe, the grand building casting a dark shadow across the side street. It was plain and grey, with a tiled roof overlooking St. Paul's Cathedral and Flinders Street Station, and the wide river. Yet, to me, it was the most majestic building I had ever seen. The detail the stonemasons had applied to the exterior was art in and of itself.

I stepped into the reception area, my friends behind me, where a tall man stood behind the marble counter waiting to attend to the guests. I approached him and identified myself before looking up, admiring the ornate ceiling high above.

'Abigail, this is even more elaborate than the London Delmont. Look at the lighting,' Polly remarked, staring above us at the grand ceiling. The room was at least three stories high, with an enormous chandelier that sparkled high above.

'Oh, it's not that fantastic. I have seen much better myself in my travels all over the world,' Leo replied smugly; although he too stared around the impressive room, wide-eyed, as I tried to smother a smile.

'You couldn't have possibly seen anything like this. How does a man of your means get to travel as often as you have?' Catherine asked curiously. I could tell she found him interesting, although very different from anyone she had ever met.

'Abigail, Polly, Catherine, Mary, and Bessie, look at me. No! All of you look at me now.' He clapped his hands loudly, causing the other guests to stare. 'Come, sit on the settee and I will tell you all something for free, which doesn't happen often.' He clapped his hands again, leading us away from the reception desk. I reluctantly followed, sitting down with them in an oversized, comfortable lounge; while he loomed over us, looking down as if he were our teacher and we were his pupils. 'Now girls, listen to Uncle Leo,' he ordered, clapping his hands again to get our attention. 'You can't just hitch your horse to any wagon. If you choose the wrong one, you will drag a heavy load of manure behind you for the rest of your life, which will take all your energy and make you all old, ugly, and fat before your time. What you must do is *be* the wagon, not the horse. You want a big, strong, wealthy horse to hitch himself to you and take you through life in comfort. Do not go shagging—yes, I learnt that word from Hamish, Abigail, so don't look at me like that. What I was saying before Abigail rudely interrupted me with her look is, don't go shagging a wagon, shag a horse.' We stared blankly up at him, his eyes wide and eyebrows raised as he waited for someone to respond.

'That has to be the worst metaphor I have ever heard,' I snapped, shaking my head in disbelief. 'There are times I seriously doubt your sanity—and I certainly do not understand how your brain works. You make no sense at all.' Confusion crossed his face as I rolled my eyes, ready to stand and push him to the floor.

'What, Abigail? I am only explaining things to help you secure a wonderful future for yourselves.'

'So, you tell the girls to shag a horse, which explained nothing to us, and only showed us what a shit you are. I'm fighting the urge right now to punch you square in the face, or strike you with significant force in your soft parts. You are so rude sometimes.'

'Not sometimes; he is rude constantly, day in, day out. There is no rest from his idiotic behaviour or means of escape,' Polly snapped. I stood and marched across the room, leaving Bessie and Mary, along with Catherine, giggling as I hurried away. Leo flopped down on the lounge beside them to gossip, causing them to laugh harder at whatever the clown was saying. Finally, the manager approached me as I waited patiently at the desk, his eyes twinkling.

'You seem to have become distracted by your boisterous friends over there, Miss Delmont. I have your suite ready, as instructed by Mr McPhee. Here are the keys, and I will escort you to your room,' he said politely, stepping around from behind the large marble counter that ran the length of the room. I walked beside him while the others followed, laughing as they all talked. I advised him I would not take the elevator, following him as he guided us to the staircase, climbing flight after flight until we reached the top floor, where the manager led us into the balcony suite.

Three bedchambers adjoined a spacious sitting room overlooking Swanston Street below. Each contained a double bed and was large and luxurious. Catherine immediately asked to share with me, given we were parted for what felt like years. Polly and Leonardo reluctantly agreed to share, with Leo forcing Polly to vow not to touch his dangly bits, as he liked to call them, while he slept. Before anyone else, Bessie and little Mary had already decided they would like to share a room, having become close friends during our voyage.

I left them in the suite to find Dana and her girls. I closed the door quietly behind me and made my way down the stairs and through the wide hallways until I found her room. She screamed when she opened the door to her suite, embracing me tightly before ushering me inside. I hugged Charlotte and Victoria, inviting them to dinner; however, they politely declined, advising me they were all feeling tired. I kissed them all goodnight, promising to visit in the morning before we departed, their musical voices calling out farewell as I returned to the stairs.

We dined at Young and Jacksons on the corner, as no one was eager to walk too far, and I felt the hotel restaurant was too fancy.

'So, we're all finally here and back together,' I remarked as I smiled, looking at each of them around the table, feeling pure love. The publican forced us to eat in the saloon, forbidding us entry to the public bar where the men frequented. They had rooms upstairs they rented out at a reasonable cost compared to The Delmont. The small black-and-white tiles on the floor were elegant, as was the gleaming wooden bar where the server had gone to collect our meals.

'Yes, and isn't it wonderful?' Catherine said. 'Our group of friends has expanded already, and I'm so happy to have met each of you today. I was so concerned about leaving Abigail in London, with only her solicitor and his family to care for her, while she stayed alone in that enormous hotel. I cried every night on the ship, worrying about her and, of course, Beatrice, who did not cope with the voyage well at all. She would scream so loudly, we had other passengers complain about her. They treated us better when we explained she was only a ten-year-old, traumatised child, and from then on, the complaints stopped. It was good to stand on solid ground when we arrived; however, our parents are so busy they give Beatrice no attention and seem ashamed of what happened to her. It is as if they blame her, as though she caused the attack, which has left me feeling extremely resentful towards them.' I reached across and held her hand as she broke down, discreetly handing her a clean handkerchief.

I embraced her while she sobbed, not caring or noticing the inquisitive patrons who looked on and whispered behind their work-roughened hands. She calmed herself within several minutes and regained her composure, the patrons' slowly losing interest in our table.

Leo quickly changed the subject, entertaining us with tales of far-off lands and lovers, the server bringing our meals to the table. We ate in silence as we listened to his beautiful voice, with only a soft lilt of an Italian accent, as he spoke of the wonderful times he had shared with friends, now long gone, his eyes shining. He had allowed me to tell the girls of his inclinations, as he believed if I trusted them, then he could, too.

'I suppose Hamish will be at his home in Geelong now.' I sighed deeply, missing him already as our server placed my dessert in front of me.

'When will you see him again?' Catherine asked. She had pulled herself together and eaten her meal, accompanied by two glasses of wine.

'As soon as he attends my solicitor's office to get my address. He will visit me then, I'm sure. Of course, he will have to settle first himself, so I imagine it won't be for a few days.' I wondered if he would stray or would stay true to his word. We finished dining and walked back to our suite, arm in arm in the twilight. 'What happened with Danny last night before you parted?' I asked Bessie as we crossed Swanston Street, her face glowing under the gas streetlight high above us.

'We said our goodbyes.' Her eyes sparkled, her brown hair pulled back tight at the nape of her head as we took our time. 'I knew we wouldn't find each other today with everything being so busy. He plans to go to your solicitor's office tomorrow to get our address so he can call on me, if that is acceptable, Mistress?'

'Of course it is, Bessie. He is welcome wherever we are, as long as he makes you happy.' I slipped my arm around her shoulder as we climbed the four wide steps to our hotel and strolled through the grand reception room. The manager at the desk smiled politely as we passed him while I left the others at the elevator, laughing and teasing me as I hurried away. I climbed the stairs with Polly, discovering the Otis did not enthral her either. We arrived at our suite gasping for breath, pausing in the wide hallway to catch our breath. I pushed the door wide, allowing Polly to enter, before closing it behind me.

'Well, Mary and I are off to bed. This is the first day I haven't had to chaperone horny goats that won't stop chewing on each other until I stand between them with a great big stick.' Bessie sighed deeply, my hand going to my mouth as I smothered a smile, laughter rising in me I quickly pushed down. 'I need a break to recover from the voyage I believed was going to be a break from all that shite.' I threw my head back and laughed aloud while she smiled slightly, rolling her eyes, before saying their goodnights and disappearing to their room. No doubt to gossip for hours.

'Thank you for all this, sweet cheeks,' Leo said as their door clicked shut. 'You really do take care of me. I know I make light of nearly everything; however, you are very special to me, Abigail. If I didn't have you as my friend, supporting me until I can find a job, I could starve; and I don't think I would enjoy it much. You are the sweetest woman I have ever met, despite being so unfortunate looking. So, I have overlooked that part and remain your friend.' He stooped to kiss me while I rolled my eyes, shaking my head in disbelief.

The closer Leo and I became, the more I understood he unfortunately said whatever came into his head without realising, or caring, how it sounded to those around him. He rarely meant to offend anyone on purpose, and it upset him greatly if he did so unintentionally. I opened my arms and stepped forward, Leo pulling me into a warm embrace. He was a large man and broad; however, not nearly as big as Hamish. He stood six feet tall and was handsome, his tanned complexion, dark hair and eyes only enhancing his beauty. He was attractive, but unfortunately, he knew it and paraded around like a peacock. I kissed Polly, who embraced me, whispering in my ear that Leo would be lucky if he survived the night and she didn't smother him in his sleep. I giggled to myself as I made my way to my room, readying myself for bed with Catherine's help. We had a big day tomorrow, and I wanted to talk to her alone. Before slipping into my own and climbing into the big, soft bed, I handed her a spare nightgown.

'I have missed you so much, Abigail,' she said as she slipped in beside me, arranging the feathered pillows behind her head. 'Polly,

Bessie, and Leonardo are lovely, although Mary, your maid, is extremely shy. I am certain it will not take long for you all to draw her out of herself.' She turned to face me, propping her head upon her hand. 'So, tomorrow is the big day. You must write to tell me what happens. I'm dying to know.'

We turned off the light and lay together, speaking in hushed tones for the longest time—with me doing most of the talking. I told her about Hamish and the ocean crossing, of finding Polly shortly after she ran away, starving and begging on the street, and how Bessie, Mary, and Leonardo had serendipitously crossed my path. I felt a little hoarse before I drifted off to sleep, dreaming of friends, the ocean, and a home built of bluestone in a place I did not recognise.

Chapter Two

I WOKE EARLY, AWARE we must meet the first train to Geelong sometime this morning. Catherine, still sound asleep beside me, snored softly in the silent room. I gazed across at her, a smile touching my lips. She was a beautiful young woman with her wheat-coloured hair and fine bone structure. She was not as tall as me; however, she was the tallest of most of my friends, who all averaged around five feet at the most. Dana and her girls were the exceptions, all roughly my height, allowing me to feel normal when I was with them.

I quietly slipped out of bed, cautious not to wake Catherine, threw on my dressing gown, then tip-toed out of the suite and down the hallway and stairs to Dana's suite. I wouldn't have any spare time other than this moment to say goodbye. Once everyone was up and ready, we were required to depart almost immediately. I knocked quietly on their door, knowing I would wake them. I waited for a moment, hearing movement inside. Finally, the door opened, and Dana stood before me in a gorgeous red nightgown. She smiled, wiping the sleep from her eyes before she yawned.

'Hello, my sweet girl. Come and crawl into bed beside me so we can talk. It's far too early for me to be up and standing, or upstanding, whichever way you want to look at it.' She embraced me tightly before she led me into her bedchamber and climbed into bed. 'I hate goodbyes, so we're not doing any of that rubbish this morning.

Instead, we can say we will see each other again soon.' She took my hand in hers as we lay next to each other.

'Have you decided where you will settle?'

'I know you want me as your next-door neighbour in Geelong; however, I need to give things a chance here in Melbourne first and stay for a while until the girls and I decide where we want to live. I truly believe we will end up where we are meant to, whether it's here or in Geelong near you.' She squeezed my hand before continuing. 'I am so proud of how you are managing your relationship with Hamish. Even a blind man can see how much he adores you and how well you get along with each other. I know you love him, Abigail, but guard your heart for a little while longer. His father was extremely inappropriate yesterday morning on the docks, and the way he looked at the girls, and myself, was salacious at the very least. I certainly found him rude, given his wife was standing beside him when I bid her farewell. Harriet appeared quite humiliated. She is not a stupid woman. Sons sometimes follow their father's ways, and I would hate for you to be hurt.'

I kissed her on the cheek, thanking her for her sincerity. We chatted for close to an hour before I reluctantly rose to my feet, Dana following me into the sitting room. I kissed Victoria and Charlotte, who appeared to have just woken only minutes before, then hugged Dana, feeling my eyes sting slightly as they waved from the door in their nightwear, calling out after me we would meet again soon. I returned to our suite to find everyone dressed, a feeling of urgency and excitement filling the crowded room.

'And where have you been, and roaming the hotel in your nightgown, too, I see?' Leo teased. 'Only you would behave this way, proving you're no lady, my little Delilah-No-Shame. I bet you'd run around here naked just because you own the place, you little minx.'

'No, that would be you.' He laughed aloud as I strode past him, drawing my dressing gown tighter and refastening the belt discreetly.

Although I was perfectly respectable, he was perfectly right. If anyone had seen me, they would have been beyond offended, and there would have been a scandal—ladies did not roam corridors in their nightwear or let anyone see them in a state of undress. I had enough self-respect to never flaunt my body; however, I could see nothing wrong with being among my friends in a dressing gown. In reality, it covered me more than some of my dresses.

Bessie followed me into my bedchamber and helped me to dress quickly, packing away my nightwear in my overnight bag. The hotel maids served our breakfast at the large dining table near the window overlooking the busy streets below. I joined my friends, hurriedly eating a plate of scrambled eggs with crispy bacon, along with toast, and then pancakes.

'You are such a greedy guts, Abigail—and don't use the excuse of the orphanage,' Leo remarked, arching his brows at me wickedly. 'Polly and Bessie were raised in one, too, and they eat a quarter of what you shove into your mouth. Then we must address the fact you continue to talk with your mouth full, and I have told you a million times already to stop it. Do you have any idea what a scrambled egg looks like in your mouth when it's wide open?' I smacked him on the arm, and he squealed, Bessie glaring at me for a moment before turning back to her food.

Everyone seemed in good spirits, looking forward to what the day would bring. My stomach had been in knots every time I would think about meeting with this new solicitor, Mr McPhee, and of what would come of it. I hoped it would be good news, but had been considering my options if it were not. Whatever happened, Mr Malcolm would ensure no harm came to me, as he had given me his word. I was confident they would provide enough money to me each year to support myself and my family and live a modest life, as that was all I had ever wanted.

We stood near the entrance to the grand reception room, ready to leave the hotel, when I excused myself to run one more errand before we boarded the train for Geelong. I walked Leonardo down to Swanston Street to a men's clothing store and stepped inside, pulling his hand firmly and forcing him to follow. Several smart day suits in dark hues hung in the window, while expensive tailcoats and trousers, along with frock coats, morning coats and lounge coats were displayed on racks throughout the expansive shop. Leonardo turned to me, his eyebrows raised as he ran his hand along a pair of lightweight pantaloons.

'Who can afford any of this, Abigail? Other than those who have pounds and pennies falling out of their backsides? Unlike you, some of us must wait to buy even the smallest of items, no matter how important, until we secure new positions here in this prison without walls.' His face flushed, and he appeared embarrassed for the first time since we'd met. Winking at him while trying to make light of the situation, I pushed him forward towards the tailor.

'Well, you won't get work looking like nobody owns you, so let's get you some new breeks and a couple of shirts to begin with—you can pay me back when you are able.'

'Well, I think something in magenta velvet would suit me,' he remarked thoughtfully, slowly gazing around the room at the comfortable daywear, screwing up his face in disdain before stepping away to examine the dinner jackets, waistcoats, and vests. I laughed as I politely asked the tailor for assistance, the man nodding silently. He was a small chap, who must have been at least seventy; however, I could tell as I ran my fingers over the stitching of an expensive woollen cape, the tiny man made exquisite clothing, while unable to look away from the thick coats and jackets hanging nearby.

'Do you think my wife is attractive or hideous?' Leo suddenly asked the tailor, who appeared startled but continued to take Leo's measurements. I could have smacked him as I watched the poor wee man swallow hard, remaining silent. 'Well, which do you think? I haven't decided yet. You see, I was forced to marry the cold-hearted icebox by my parents. They thought she was a nice girl, but, oh, my lordy, lordy, if they knew what I had to live with, they never would have arranged this marriage. She spends money like a drunken sailor and takes everything I earn every payday, leaving not a penny in my pocket for slaving away seven days a week. She also curses like a trooper and has the foulest vocabulary anyone has ever heard on a supposed lady. I don't know how she can eat with that mouth. So, tell me? Hideous or passable?' He persisted, continuing to harangue the patient man, while I closed my eyes for a moment, wishing the ground would open up and swallow me.

'Your wife is lovely, Sir,' was all he would say. Leo smirked at me, a villainous look in his eye.

'I am sorry,' I interrupted with as much decorum as I could muster. 'If we can just look at anything you have already made in his size, he can try that, as we leave Melbourne this morning, and have little time before our train departs.' The tailor appeared relieved and scurried into a back room to see what he could find. 'You are an evil wee man, Leo.' I glanced out the window before turning back to him. 'You need to learn when to shut up and stop making up stories with me in them, thank you very much.'

We left the shop with a pair of breeches and two pairs of trousers, three shirts, a woollen cape, along with a fancy frock coat in magenta velvet that hung elegantly to his knees as he strutted along beside me, appearing quite the dandy, while holding a pair of green pantaloons under his arm. They were hideously tight and had fallen out of fashion, and favour, decades ago; however, he adored them and that was all that mattered. I carried a large brown paper bag containing undergarments, socks, and a pair of sturdy boots, while he proudly strutted along beside me, a flamboyant cravat he had chosen tied around his neck, then tucked inside his new shirt. He stood out like a nun frequenting the local tavern—with a glass of whisky in each hand and a look of lust in her eye—compared to the bustling crowd dressed conservatively in bland, dark clothes as we weaved and dodged past them. All the fine clothes he now possessed were paid for, of course, by his wicked wife, who spent all his hard-earned money. He looked distinguished and handsome in his new clothes as he paraded like a peacock, glancing in the shop windows to admire his reflection as we passed by.

I had asked the tailor to discard the old garments, as they were in a terrible state and weren't fit to be seen. Bessie would wash them at night and invisibly repair every tear and hole, so talented with a needle and thread many brought their clothes to her for repair, and paid her a fair price for it too. Hamish had given Leo a shirt and a pair of breeks that were far too big for him, for dear Leo to wear while his clothes were drying, ensuring he wasn't confined to our suite naked or wrapped in a blanket.

We arrived back at the hotel to find my friends, sick of waiting for us, had all returned to the suite. It had taken much longer than I intended, and now we were running late. I ran up the stairs, taking two at a time. Leo met me on the top floor, calm and composed, having taken the elevator, while I was out of breath and sweating. We rushed in, and I waved my hands, urging them to hurry.

'Is everyone organised to leave?' I asked, my heart slowing as I caught my breath. Polly was conducting a last-minute check of her room while everyone waited impatiently, eager to get to Geelong.

We made our way downstairs again, each carrying a bag filled with our belongings. When I reached reception, I walked over to the desk to return the keys while the others stepped outside onto the busy street to wait for me. I asked the manager to allow Dana and the girls to stay as long as they liked as my guests, advising him they were not to be charged for their room or meals. He agreed immediately, bowing and scraping and humiliating us both as far as I was concerned. I didn't want people to know of my connection to the hotel or believe I thought myself better than them, preferring the attention to be on someone or something else.

I thanked the staff and bid them farewell before hurrying outside to join the others. We walked in silence, dodging and weaving through the crowded street to Flinders Street Station to find our train, hoping we hadn't missed it. Once there, I stopped a young lady carrying a large carpet bag over her arm. I could not take my eyes from her and asked if she knew where we could find our platform. She smiled brightly, noticing how flustered I had become with such an enormous crowd of people milling around, her face kind as she gestured for us to follow.

'Oh, that is excellent luck. I am going to Geelong to start my new position in a very grand house, so you can walk with me.' Relieved, we followed her to the train while she continued to chat about how excited she was about moving to another town before we hurriedly boarded and found our compartment.

I relaxed back in my seat next to the window and wondered what this new solicitor would be like. I hoped as kind as Mr Malcolm and his family, and competent enough to explain everything to me and honestly handle any money I had coming to me. I would finally find out exactly what the conditions of my great-aunt's Will were, and the thought of it had given me knots in my stomach. The journey passed uneventfully, except for Bessie and Mary's excited shrieks. They had never been on a train before and sat with their faces pressed against the window, exclaiming at each new and unfamiliar sight; while I closed my eyes and drifted off to sleep.

The train slowed, pulling into a small station before coming to a stop, the whistle shrilling loudly as I yawned before standing and picking up my bag. We stepped off onto the extended, roof-covered platform.

'So, what do we do now?' Polly asked, handing me a boiled sweetie as I shrugged my shoulders.

'I suppose we walk out and see if they have sent a carriage. No doubt they have,' I replied, breathing in what would have been clean country air except for the locomotive smoke that intermittently choked me. We made our way from the platform to find a coach was indeed waiting. The driver was standing at the side of the road next to the carriage, *McPhee and Sons, Barristers & Solicitors,* boldly written in yellow paint on the side. He appeared to be in his mid-forties and had a rowdy-but-friendly demeanour.

'Good morning to you all,' the man called out, breaking into a wide smile. He waited for a time as we stood silently, staring back at him. 'My name is Conor Ryan. Please don't go calling me no mister, either. Everyone calls me Ryan, and I'd be very pleased if you'd do the same. I drive for the McPhee family here in Geelong. You'd have met my colleague, Geordie McGovern, who drives for the Melbourne office?' he asked, his smile widening. I nodded, smiling back at this pleasant man.

'Yes, he was very nice,' I replied politely, although we had only met that driver once.

'Well, we aim to please, Mistress. If you'd like to get in, I'll take you to the office of Mr McPhee.' He cheerfully helped each of us up, except for Leonardo, who missed the last step and stumbled, before straightening up and screaming in frustration. I grabbed his hand

and assisted him inside, my mouth twitching as he made himself comfortable next to me.

'Thank you for the clothes today, Abigail,' he whispered, Polly glaring at him as she strained to listen. 'No one has ever done anything so nice for me before unless they were getting something back from me if you know what I mean?' He took my hand and kept it wrapped in his until the carriage came to a stop, everyone inside eager to get out.

'I want to buy soft, pink lip paint,' Bessie said, gazing in the window of a nearby shop selling make-up, toiletries, soap, along with a range of creams and potions for the body and hair. I opened my purse and handed her a five-pound note.

'If you don't mind, Bessie, please buy what everyone needs in the way of toiletries so we're prepared when we arrive at our new home.' She smiled and nodded, taking the money discreetly from my hand.

I wistfully watched my friends walk away to explore the shops, then turned to stare at the modest shop that contained Mr McPhee's law practice. The double-fronted building—with pane glass along the top of the windows and heavy drapes, now pulled apart—sat proudly in the central part of the main township. Geelong was larger than I expected and beautifully clean, next to a bay, often filled with trade ships. The buildings impressed me as we travelled through the streets, finding such a variety of shops and thriving businesses in the bustling seaside town. I had not needed to bring a thing, after all.

I took a deep breath and pushed open the door. A small bell tinkled overhead, alerting a woman sitting at a tidy reception desk. She appeared to be in her sixties, with grey hair tied up in a bun at the back of her neck, while her plain, grey dress was immaculate. I noted that a kind face offset her severely understated appearance. I approached her, smiling as brightly as I could, despite my fear and worry.

'Good morning, my dear,' she said, smiling back. 'You must be Abigail Delmont. We have been expecting you. I am Mrs McPhee, and it is my husband who will look after you. Unfortunately, he is currently busy with another client, but he told me as soon as you arrive, I am to take you to his office.' She quickly rose from her seat and led me down a dark corridor flanked by several doors, which I assumed were to other offices. 'Now, you sit down here, my dear, and I will get you a nice cup of tea,' she told me kindly before scurrying off. The fact she had a golden aura had not surprised me at all. Since leaving the orphanage, I had come across so many that possessed the unexplainable glow I almost expected it to surround every new friend or acquaintance I made.

I gazed around the small office, the room silent as I waited for her to return. There were many books, which appeared to be standard in a solicitor's office, while a large walnut desk with a brown, high-backed leather chair sat empty opposite me. I could not see the top of the desk for all the papers and documents strewn around. I hoped he was more organised in handling my affairs as, looking at the desktop, I would not know where to even start. Mrs McPhee returned with my cup and attempted to find a space on the desk to set it down. She glanced at me apologetically, murmuring to herself before fixing her attention back on the desk.

'I'm not allowed to move anything because he knows exactly where everything is. It looks like chaos to me, but he insists it's organised chaos.' She shifted a document slightly so she could place the cup before me. 'I know of your situation, and I'm that sorry for it,' she continued, her voice kindly. 'We have two sons and six grandchildren, and I couldn't bear the thought of them abandoned to be raised by strangers. I do not know what Isabelle was thinking. She was always such a generous person who would give all she had to prevent any soul living in misery—and then I find out she's gone and done this in secret to her own blood. I'm ashamed of her. We were close for many years, but once she returned to England, I never heard from her again. I received word from a friend of Isabelle's soon after she passed—a Dowager, no less—who knew of our friendship and was kind enough to write. It was only then I became aware Isabelle was upset with me because of my connection to the Chirnside family.' I exhaled slowly, the blood rushing to my face as I swallowed hard, feeling terribly uncomfortable. 'On the bright side, you're here safe and well, and everything can only get better.' She smiled brightly at me again, although sadness reflected in her eyes. I liked her very much. She possessed a gentle face creased with lines, resulting from laughter and joy, sadness, and pain. 'Have you seen your new home yet?' I looked up at her, excitement overwhelming me.

'Not yet, no. Please, can you tell me what it's like?'

'Now, that would be tellin' tales. You will see it when you have finished your business here.' She smiled at me as if I were a petulant child, crossing the room to the bookcase and slipping several books back where they belonged. I couldn't believe I was finally here. Soon I would know where my future lay, whether I would remain in Geelong or return to Scotland for a time to be near Sister until I made other plans. The palms of my hands were perspiring, and I discreetly wiped them on my orange dress. My heart raced and felt as if it would burst from my chest.

Mrs McPhee politely bid me farewell before returning to her desk, leaving me alone. I wondered how my Hamish was and if he missed me as much as I missed him. I pondered how long it would take him to find me. He had my solicitor's name and address, so he knew how to contact me. I also wondered if he had met any other women since he had arrived and if I bored him yet.

Just as I was thinking the worst of Hamish, Mr McPhee stepped through the door. He was a stern-looking man of average height and build, with hair that had once been black but was now sadly losing the fight with the grey scattered through his thick mop. He shook my hand, a lump in my throat rendering me unable to speak as I stared at the grey aura swirling around his body like a storm cloud.

'Miss Abigail Delmont. It is an honour and a privilege to be at your service, and I plan to be at your service day and night, anytime you need me,' he advised loudly before walking behind his desk and taking his seat.

He was the complete opposite of Mr Malcolm in appearance and manner. I was uncertain if I felt comfortable with him given his demeanour, his grey aura unsettling me greatly as I thought of Sister Monica.

'You must get paid a great deal of money to make yourself so freely available to a person you have never met before today.' He glanced at me sharply before clearing his throat.

'Henry warned me you're a feisty one and that you're far from a simpleton. Yes, I am paid two pounds a week as agreed with your

Aunt Isabelle.' He smiled coldly while shuffling some papers, then looked closely at his desk. 'Did my wife move anything on here?' He frowned suspiciously, and I tried to suppress a smile.

'Yes, just this one, when she put down my cup of tea.' I pointed to the paper, smothering a smile as he grimaced.

'Ah, yes, this one,' he said to himself, moving it back into place. 'I know well that you are not here for my good looks or my wit and charm, Miss Delmont. I think we will begin.'

He made his way over to a small cabinet with the name Delmont engraved on a strip of silver and fixed at the top, appearing to hold only my documents. He opened a drawer and pulled out a wooden box, not unlike the one sent to the orphanage, placing it on his desk; only this was much larger.

'There are documents in here even I have not been privileged to, as they're addressed to you. Your aunt was clear that if I ever opened them, she would haunt me from the great beyond, and I know beyond doubt she would keep her promise. I cannot tell you what these contain; however, we will start with your house.' He appeared nervous as his eyes darted around the room, looking at everything but me. 'Lady Isabelle Delmont purchased a property of two-thousand acres many years back, just out of Geelong town. Over twenty-years ago, several outbuildings and homes for the workers were built—and they established a stud soon after. They have only completed the main house in recent times after over fifteen-years of construction. Willow Grove, as it's so named, is a grand estate like you would see back in England. I know of no other home in Australia built to the proportions and quality—or possessing the grandeur and luxury of this property—although I am aware of a similar home in Werribee and have since confirmed that with my own eyes. Although the construction of the building begun while your great-aunt was still among the living, she was of advanced years and quite sensibly made provisions in her Will to ensure they completed the building to the standard she expected if she passed before it was finished—and believe me, that woman expected an enormous amount from those around her.' His eyes closed for a moment as a memory crossed his face before he opened them again, the emotion passing within moments. I could not tell just what emotion he felt towards my great-aunt, as it appeared he disliked her very much; however, his face remained like stone. 'My father acted on her behalf for many years until the day he took his last breath, God rest him. He truly was a tolerant man. That woman was difficult to deal with no matter how gently you handled her and would test the patients of the heavenly father himself.' He glanced up from his papers, studying my face for a moment, before dropping his gaze and focussing on a document that lay on the desk in front of him, clearing his throat nervously. 'Lady Delmont had all her ducks in a row, though, and I do not wish to speak ill of the dead. I met with her often over the years when she lived here, and everyone else considered her a wonderful, vivacious woman who had great plans for the property and the bloodlines of the horses she was bringing into Australia.' He coughed into his handkerchief before picking up a glass of water and taking a long drink. 'Anyway, back to the Will before we get lost in memories and nostalgia. Willow Grove is now in your possession to do with as you please; however, it may not be sold or transferred for the next fifty-years.' I nodded and attempted to smile; however, I failed miserably. The thought of living on a horse farm horrified me. The beasts terrified me, and the thought of being around them made my stomach turn. 'Here is a sealed document Lady Delmont asked me to give you. I've no knowledge of what it contains,' he snapped abruptly, handing me an envelope with a large wax seal on the back that was unbroken. The envelope was of high-quality, and whatever was inside was quite thick. I tucked it away in my reticule to read later when I was alone. 'Then there is the matter of the Delmont Hotels,' he went on briskly. 'There is a hotel in London, as you are very much aware, and now one in Melbourne. All profits from the Melbourne hotel are deposited into your trust fund here, which started out modestly compared to its current value. Your aunt left a significant sum of money to you now invested in trust at the Mercantile Bank. After we have deducted our weekly fee and costs, I will transfer a percent of the interest earned from the principal sum to a private account in your name, to do with as you will. It will pay for your servants and workers—and anything you want or need to maintain the highest standard of living money can provide.' He looked across at me as I stared blankly back at him.

'I heard the London and Melbourne Delmont are not the only hotels bearing the name.' He rolled his eyes before clearing his throat, his irritation obvious.

'I will confirm two more Delmont Hotels are currently under construction in Paris and New York under my supervision, which, on completion, I will hand over to Henry Malcolm for his office to manage. The profits will go directly into your London trust fund until you attain the age of thirty-years. That is your primary trust fund, which Henry will continue to manage. The fund here will provide for your every want and need without accessing the London fund, or any of the profits from your hotels based in countries outside of Australia. Do you have questions?' I took several moments to respond, my heart pounding hard.

'Yes, I do. You said before I would have servants. What do you mean by that?'

'Well, you have the farmhands, of course. Some of them have worked and lived on the property for over two decades. You also have the stablehands, or grooms as some like to say, who are there to look after the horses and the breeding of them—turning quite a profit, I understand. Then, there are the inside servants. Only yesterday, my Melbourne office advised me you had employed a ladies' maid, but failed to mention you also took it upon yourself to employ an extra maid—oh, never mind. I will find a place somewhere for her even if it's in the laundry, where most refuse to work,' he told me efficiently, my head spinning. Expecting a house barely big enough for the five of us, not one with strangers living there, I felt panic rising in me as my stomach lurched.

'Just how many house servants must I have? I hate even saying that word.' I felt overwhelmed, finding this man challenging to communicate with and unable to find one nice thing about him.

'Hmm, let me think. You have the new cook I hired, Miss Pickering, and several kitchen servants to assist her. Then there is a butler, along with a head maid with several housemaids under her, and a scullery maid—plus the footmen.' His face revealed nothing as my eyes widened, and I shook my head in disbelief.

'I don't want all those people in my employ. I don't need all those people.' Anger replaced panic as I struggled to control my temper. This great-aunt Isabelle—who I wouldn't have recognised had I walked right past her in the street with a sign around her neck—seemed intent on controlling all aspects of my life. Forcing me into a life she seemed to want for me, not once considering the one I wanted for myself, I resented her deeply even though I had never met her or even known of her existence until recently.

'You haven't seen the house yet, Miss Delmont, so hush your mouth, please. I have employed only the servants I know you require to run the estate efficiently, though I'm confident you will need many more in the future, something I will leave to your own discretion. You must give it a chance before you dismiss the idea altogether. That is all I ask.' he snapped, his voice stern, his expression perplexed. I could see my questions were preventing him from moving on to the next matter of business, his frustration clear, but I couldn't have cared less.

'I will at least try, as you say, before I come back to you and request changes. What is next on the list?' His eyes widened slightly at my tone before he again averted his gaze, then shifted in his seat, appearing uncomfortable.

He leaned back in his chair and placed his hands behind his head, remaining silent, giving me the impression he didn't know where to start, and he didn't really want to.

'Miss Delmont, you will not like this next condition—but let me explain the full story before you get upset with me.'

I watched as his left eye twitched, then twitched again. My heart pounded hard in my chest, my hands trembling as I tried to appear relaxed and unaffected by his abruptness. My mind raced, filled with a thousand thoughts of all the things it might be, but unfortunately, my options were limited without that money if I stood and walked away. It was no longer just about me. Now I had others depending on me to provide them with their livelihoods and a roof over their heads.

'How many conditions are there?' I asked suspiciously as he narrowed his gaze, now composed but clearly angry with me for a reason I was unaware of.

'Well, if you showed some patience, I could tell you,' he snapped, holding up his hand to prevent me from speaking. 'Around sixteen-years ago, in Edinburgh, your great-aunt befriended an Irish fisherman from whom she bought her daily seafood,' he began, glancing across warningly as I went to interject. 'When she heard he was struggling to feed his family and lived in a two-room shack, she offered her help. Your mother was pregnant with you, I believe.' He paused, clearing his throat again, his left eye twitching uncontrollably. 'Your aunt made a surprising, and I must say, quite startling, offer. I should hold my tongue, but it did not surprise me as I knew the woman well, and she was as mad as a cut snake. I digress, though. If this fisherman—a stranger to her, mind you—agreed to immigrate to Geelong with his family, she would purchase a fishing boat and land in his name, and offered to help secure their financial future, giving them a significant amount of money they were not required to repay. That figure is still unknown to me to this day.' He shook his head in disbelief and rolled his eyes again before continuing. 'In return, he promised in fifteen-years' time, his son would marry a young lady christened Abigail. That's how certain she was you would be a girl, the old witch she was.' I felt as if my heart had stopped, and I couldn't breathe as I clutched my hands together in my lap to stop them shaking.

'I will be forced to wed a stranger just to ensure I have a roof over my head? Doesn't that make me a hedge creeper of the worst kind, a glaikit hoore?' I spat, feeling revolted and trapped. I crossed my arms, leaned back in my chair, and stared at him. I knew this wasn't his fault; he was only the messenger, but I needed somewhere to direct my anger. He did not flinch, nor did he appear as if he would back down. I glared at him and jutted out my chin in defiance.

'I must warn you, Miss Delmont. If you do not comply with the conditions as stipulated in the Will, you give up all rights to any inheritance from the late Lady Isabelle Delmont. You will not receive a penny.'

'What are the rest of the conditions, you munter? Does she stipulate how many children I'm to have and whether they are to be boys or girls?' His eyes went wide before he shook his head in disgust.

'No, I assure you, young lady, that is the last of the conditions. And I am aware just what that word means. Your great-aunt also possessed a vile mouth I see you have sadly inherited.' He shook his head again, but it was me who rolled my eyes and groaned in frustration. 'Back to the remaining conditions. Other than the one stating you may access both trust funds once you attain the age of thirty, there is one last line that says to live happily ever after.' He forced a polite smile as I grunted.

'I doubt that, Mr McPhee. I cannot marry a man I have never met—and I have someone—someone who loves me.' I started to cry at the thought of Hamish and fumbled in my purse for my handkerchief. Mr McPhee quickly handed me a clean one from his pocket, attempting to show me some sympathy, which I doubted was genuine.

'I do not expect you to marry him tomorrow; just give it a chance,' he murmured soothingly. 'He will court you for a time to see how you get along. Then, we can meet again in two weeks, and you can tell me what you have decided.' I stared back at him, jolting backward in my chair as if he had slapped me.

'Two weeks. That's all you are giving me?' I exclaimed, frozen in disbelief.

'Well, yes, but we can reassess this again at the end of the fortnight. There is no need to worry. I have invited the lad and his father here today to meet you. Would you allow me to bring them in?' This was clearly not a request, rather a statement of fact. I nodded reluctantly, slumping back miserably in my chair, feeling defeated before we had even begun. He forced a smile as he stood and left the room, closing the door behind him. How would my poor Hamish take this news? I knew he was a jealous man; he wouldn't stand for someone else paying me any attention, let alone courting me. He would throw me over and would be off chasing the next pretty woman he saw. I had assumed he would be the one to ruin our budding relationship, never once entertaining the thought it would be me.

I heard heavy footsteps, and my body tensed. I turned toward the door to see the solicitor ushering two people into his chaotic office—two very tall men—my heart ceasing to beat as they stepped inside. It was not the fact they looked so much alike that rendered me speechless and unable to breathe, but the incredibly beautiful golden glow surrounding them both.

Chapter Three

IT TOOK ME A moment to compose myself as I stared up from my seat at the younger man, an awkward silence filling the room before I rose to my feet.

'This is Mr Gavin Cavanaugh and his son, Aaron. May I present Miss Abigail Delmont.' I glared hatefully at Mr McPhee before turning to the older man, who reached out his hand and clasped mine warmly. I then turned to Aaron and politely offered him my hand while nodding my head in greeting. He grasped my hand in his enormous fist, sending a jolt through me, the same hot pins travelling up my arm and into my body as it did under Hamish's touch. I sat back down heavily and averted my gaze. 'Miss Delmont has expressed some uncertainty over the matter and has asked for several weeks to consider her situation before she decides. She has a young man courting her, and I expect it will take her some time to settle things in her own mind. We don't want to rush things, do we?' Mr McPhee smiled at Mr Cavanaugh, quietly asking if he could step outside with him for a moment. The door closed behind them, leaving Aaron and me alone. I glanced sideways at him, avoiding his stare. Nice body, strong and tanned by the sun, with sandy, blonde hair streaked with light coloured strands, sun-bleached more than likely from the time he spent outdoors. He possessed a handsome face, with blue eyes the colour of the ocean, while he appeared friendly and harmless enough.

'How long have you lived here?' I asked, feeling awkward. His eyes lit up as he grinned broadly, revealing a beautiful set of teeth.

'Fifteen-years now. We arrived here in Geelong when I was knee high to a grasshopper. It's a beaut place to live—nothin' like the old country—so I hope ya not too disappointed if that's what you're used to. Why any mug would wanna live in a dirty, overcrowded city that overflows with shit house humans who would cut ya throat for a shillin' has me buggered.' His eyes twinkled kindly—his handsome face lighting up as a mischievous grin touched his lips. Although he had a roughness about him compared to Hamish—and I imagined he would join in a fight at the local tavern if pushed—he had a calmness about him that had eased my anxiety ever so slightly just by being in the same room. He was clearly a "man's man", as Mr Malcolm would call him if he were here. This man—a stranger to me despite feeling so familiar—was as big as Hamish and just as handsome. They were opposite in appearance—one dark as night—the other light as day. Mr McPhee and Mr Cavanaugh stepped back into the room and sat down, looking pleased with themselves.

'Aaron will call on you later in the day, Miss Delmont. Is there anything else we need to discuss?' Mr McPhee was undoubtedly trying to get rid of us—dismissing me with his hand before turning back to Mr Cavanaugh.

'Yes, I have something to say—no disrespect to you, Aaron.' My emotions got the better of me again, my eyes stinging as I fought back tears. 'How can you and Mr Cavanaugh sleep at night, trying to push us into this betrothal? We don't know each other—and neither one of us has asked for this—nor wants it. I'm sure you are a perfectly nice person, Aaron, but aren't there other women who hold your interest? I could make your life a misery and you mine, and no one else seems to fecking well give a fat rat's arse. For Christ's sake, the old woman is dead. What does she care who I marry now?' My body trembled, my voice becoming louder as rage spilled over, engulfing me. 'Why does anyone give a braw ballock about what I do or how I choose to live my life? What has anyone to gain by pushing us together? What satisfaction does anyone get?' I had lost control, my screams filling the room as I struggled to my feet, not caring in the slightest what they thought of me. I stamped my foot, jutting my chin out in defiance. 'You cannot force us to marry, you funt. You can't! Damn you all to hell.'

I struggled to remain upright—sobbing loudly while they stared at me—all the while remaining silent, the shock clear on their faces I had dared curse in their presence. Mrs McPhee opened the door and hurried to my side, embracing me tightly. My body trembled while I felt my legs would go from under me. She gently eased me back in my seat and pulled out a fresh handkerchief, wiping my tear-stained face.

'There, there, it is not all as bad as that, I'm sure.' She gently patted my back while murmuring soothingly, glancing across at her husband and giving him a look only married people understood.

'Before you take me to task, Beth, I have been very gentle with her.' He remained firm, although was far less aggressive when his wife was present. Mr Cavanaugh gazed across at me sympathetically, appearing concerned for my well being. I placed my head in my hands as I sobbed while Mrs McPhee went to make me another cup of tea. Mr Cavanaugh and Aaron stood to leave, again peering down at me with deep sympathy.

'Miss Delmont,' Mr Cavanaugh said, shifting uncomfortably from foot to foot. 'Just want to say for the record, me an' my mob thought you'd been told of the arrangement. I wanna apologise to you on behalf of the drongos who are lookin' after your best interests—but I see with my own eyes they're as reliable as a two bob watch.' I wiped my face and tried to smile at him, sniffing loudly. I knew this wasn't his doing. He was given an opportunity by this controlling, now-dead blaigeard, and had taken it with both hands and bettered his life, just as anyone would if it meant the survival of their family.

'Hey, Abi. I'm sorry, too,' Aaron added, his voice kind. 'I hope ya don't think I had anythin' ta do with the bulldust they've fed ya. Some people would make a blowfly sick, I tell ya. I'm gunna shoot through with me old man a'd give ya some time ta yourself to get over the shock of it all. I'll drop 'round ta have a cuppa with ya without the earwiggers.' He smiled reassuringly, nodding his head discreetly towards his father and Mr McPhee. Turning around sharply, I caught them listening before turning back to him and smiling weakly.

'Does earwigging mean gossip?' I felt my face flush, aware he may think me uneducated and feeble minded.

'Nah, not quite, but I wouldn't put it past these two to run their mouths more than they should when bendin' the elbow down the pub. An earwigger is someone who enjoys earwiggin' in on someone else's conversation without bein' invited, the rude buggers.'

'Listening in?'

'Yeah. Won't take ya long ta speak like the locals. You'll be an Aussie before ya know it.' He was perceptive and had noticed I was uncomfortable with his father and my new solicitor present, and I appreciated he seemed to feel the same way. After they had departed, Mr McPhee sat across from me once again and waited for me to calm myself.

'My advice, Miss Delmont, is to go home and get settled in and allow him to court you as you did this other young man. Then, give it some time. In a fortnight, you and I will meet again to discuss how things are coming along. How does that sound?' I could see he was trying extremely hard to control his frayed nerves and fractured ego.

'Fine, but I will not agree to anything until I'm sure of what I'm going to do,' I said defiantly, glaring back at him. He nodded his head and smiled.

'Well, it was a pleasure to meet you, and I will attend Willow Grove tomorrow to introduce you to the servants and explain the workings of the farm, if you feel ready after such a long journey?' I nodded my consent and stood to leave before he raised his hand to stop me. 'You know, it may not be all that bad. From what I know of the boy, he is a good lad—a bit of a larrikin, but a kind and decent bloke. There is a bit of rough and tumble in him, as is the way of some men here in Australia, but he is honest and loyal and comes from good stock, as they say here. He isn't hard on the eye either?' His physical beauty was the first thing I had noticed, and it made me feel I was betraying Hamish; and I was, in a way. Even considering this proposal was preposterous. I was so confused I forced myself to push it all to the back of my mind until I was better prepared to reflect on all that had occurred once alone.

Mr McPhee bid me a polite farewell before I stomped down the hallway and out onto the street, joining my friends, who were waiting outside the shop next door, unable to contain their excitement. Bessie proudly showed me several of their purchases, which looked interesting, to say the least.

'How was it?' Polly asked quietly, her forehead creased with concern. Despite mustering all my strength to hide my feelings, she could see straight through me.

'Just business and money matters, mo luaidh. Nothing to worry about,' I replied, smiling brightly at her. She stared at me suspiciously but let the matter drop, much to my relief. I felt there was no point in worrying my friends when there was little they could do to help. Mr McPhee had told me no one, not even Aaron, knew I would lose my inheritance if I didn't agree to marry him and this information was strictly confidential. I decided to keep it to myself for now and not give it another thought until tomorrow. It was time to see our new home, and I wanted nothing to ruin that.

The horses trotted past the estate's elaborate gates, the bluestone lodge assigned to the gatekeeper built long ago standing at the entrance of the property, appearing empty. Our carriage continued on down the long driveway lined with mature oak trees, the horses coming to an abrupt halt in front of a grand, sprawling manor, just as I had dreamed months ago. The imposing renaissance mansion reminded me of several grand buildings I had observed while in London, a two-story central block with a dominant tower and an arcade surrounding three sides of the building that held just over sixty palatial rooms. The mansion was at least three times the size of Emiliani House, once a grand castle too in its day. I couldn't believe it was ours to live in, feeling this all a dream I would soon awaken from.

The property was located outside of Geelong, where the farms took over the landscape, stealing it away from the city and towns, and it was peaceful. I could hear the brightly coloured rosellas singing in the trees dotted around the immaculate lawn surrounding the house, where masses of pure white rose bushes stood proudly with lavender planted among them. The flat open pastures beyond contained scattered river-red gums, lightwood and she-oak, while a post and rail fence enclosed windbreaks of Monterey cypress and pine, sugar-gum trees and an orchard. An English hawthorn hedge stood behind the freestanding stone laundry house, the five room building larger than most homes where the middle classes lived.

I took the key with a trembling hand and unlocked the elaborate front door. I called out, making our presence known, but no one answered, so I entered with the others in tow.

No one had uttered a word since we arrived; they appeared just as stunned as I felt this was ours—for the moment. We stepped into the richly decorated entry hall, the Minton encaustic tiled floor leading to a grand staircase and providing access to the reception rooms.

The elaborate staircase made of marble curved its way up to the second floor, splitting off in opposite directions at the landing halfway up; a large chandelier hanging from the centre of the double story ceiling taking my breath away. To the left was an enormous ballroom that led to a formal dining room, a large door allowing access to the garden and a swimming pool just visible through a sparkling clean window. I looked at the others in amazement.

'What would we do with a ballroom?' I started to giggle as Polly joined in.

'Well, we do know how to dance now,' she teased, taking my hand in hers and squeezing tightly.

Within moments, we were all in fits of laughter. The five of us—who hadn't a penny between us three-months ago—were now living in the fanciest mansion we had ever seen. Everyone was excited, deciding we should split up to explore the house before meeting back in the ballroom.

I assumed the manager of Willow Grove had taken our trunks to the bedchambers allocated to each of us yesterday when they arrived, while Bessie and Mary's rooms were in the servants' quarters—or staff quarters as I now referred to the large wing discreetly set aside at the back of the mansion. Bessie led me down a dark hallway to show me around, and, as I walked through the large, modern kitchen, I observed at least a hundred orphans could live here with no one feeling crowded. I followed her from the kitchen and through the door to the staff quarters, stepping into a large sitting room to find an enormous wooden dining table in the centre of the room, along with several comfortable lounges lining the walls. We walked through the room to a hallway from where the bedchambers were situated. Bessie's room was quite spacious and appeared comfortable, I noticed, as she invited me inside. It held a single bed with a nightstand next to it, a table with two chairs, and a small lounge next to an adequate wardrobe with drawers and a small fireplace. She looked pleased as she turned to me.

'So, do you like it, Bessie?'

'Oh, Mistress, I think it's wonderful. It's even better than the room I rented in London. I've never had such a beautiful place of my own, decorated with so much care. Look at the quality of the furnishings. And the bed is magnificent. I feel like the Queen of Australia.'

'They don't have their own kings or queens. They have the same as us, as England thinks it owns Australia.' I giggled, and she laughed as she rolled around on the bed.

'England thinks she owns every bloody country, including Scotland,' she replied through her laughter. She was right. England had invaded so many countries and, having devoured a few history books while still living at the orphanage, I understood they were quite brutal in their methods. 'What do you think of your bedchamber?' she enquired, bringing me back from my daydream and a time long ago I had only read about.

'I haven't looked closely yet, just a glance, but it seems nice. Is Mary happy with her room?' I already knew she would be after seeing this room. Decorated in pinks and yellows, which I thought would be a dreadful combination, it looked so pretty and suited Bessie's personality perfectly.

'Oh, yes, Mistress, she's in there now unpacking. She is beyond excited.' She gracefully rose from the bed and straightened her dress. I could soon have Mary fitted for new uniforms and day dresses, and now we were here, I was certain I could convince Catherine to make anything we needed, thanks to her kind offer. Leonardo pranced in excitedly and threw himself on Bessie's bed, sighing in delight. She spun around, her eyebrows raised at him invading her private space without invitation, then stepped towards him.

'This house is remarkable. I have seen nothing so grand. We will have so much fun here, Abigail. Think of all the mischief we will make and the adventures we will go on.'

'Get your arse off my bed this instant before you feel my boot up your backside,' Bessie threatened as he giggled and bounced up and down.

'Now, if you were a beautiful African man saying that to me, maybe I wouldn't ignore you; however, given it's you, I will pay your whining no heed. I am choosing to exit the room of my own free will—and it has nothing to do with me being terrified of you, thank you very much.' Giving one last bounce, he jumped up and pranced back out of the room, much to Bessie's relief.

'Oh, Mistress, doesn't he drive you mad? He is making my head hurt. Sometimes I could murder him in his bed with my own bare hands. It's as if I am now obligated to look after a mischievous two-year-old spawned from the loins of Lucifer himself. That man has the devil in him, and mind, you are no better when you're in his company. I have known men like him—attracted only to other men—but I never saw either of them behave the way he does, or say out loud the horrendous and offensive tripe that comes to his mind. I'm watching you both very closely now. This property is enormous, and there are far too many hidden places for you to get into trouble with the mischievous imp.'

'I honestly don't think he would behave any differently if attracted to women. He is unique in every way, but I do love him despite how awful he can be.' I kissed her before leaving her to straighten the bed, continuing on down the corridor to find little Mary, knocking several times on her door.

'Come in,' I heard her sing out. Her room was just as lovely, with furniture just like Bessie's, only decorated in mauve tones with cream, which I found calming.

'How do you like your room, Mary?' I made myself comfortable on the chair near the fireplace, the tapestry upholstery of the highest quality. Mary stopped unpacking and stood in front of me at her full height of four feet and six inches, just like a miniature soldier about to go to war.

'I have never seen anythin' so grand. I can't believe this is mine, and I don't have to share it with anyone,' she whispered, her voice barely audible. 'I've never had me own private space, havin' to share with me siblings all me life, then a cabin with three other maids on the voyage across. Tonight will be the first time since I took me first breath I get to sleep alone. It's the most overwhelmin' feelin'. I'm all scatty brained and can't even find the words to express how I feel, Mistress.' I nodded, feeling pleased for her as a smile touched my lips.

'I'm glad you're happy, Mary, and if ever you are not, I hope you would trust me enough to seek me out to tell me.' It overjoyed me how fine the staff quarters were. There were so many rooms leading off the hallway, I hadn't had time to count them yet.

I soon departed, leaving Mary alone to continue unpacking. I always hated keeping her too long. She was very formal in front of me, and I wanted her to relax, which she refused to do in my presence. Outside her door, Leo came rushing to my side, excitedly grabbing me by the arm and nearly knocking me off my feet.

'Abigail, you must come through the servants' entrance onto the verandah and see the gardens.' I nodded, Leo pushing me along and out through a door.

We strolled through the manicured garden that surrounded the mansion, arm in arm. I had never seen so many white roses in one place. I noticed a house in the distance and wandered over to see if anyone was there. The two-story building, also made of bluestone, with an attic above the second floor, and, although not grand compared to the main house, it was large and roomy and could house several families. I had the keys in my pocket, Leo urging me to hurry and open the door. We stepped inside and roamed from room to room, finding four bedchambers and a small staff quarters, along with a kitchen, sitting room, library, parlour, a study, and dining room. I could have happily lived here. In fact, it was more to my liking. Furnished elegantly, it appeared as if no one had lived there for a long time. They had covered the heavy wooden furniture in sheets, and there was a thick layer of dust on all the surfaces. Nevertheless, I liked the cottage and was reluctant to leave as Leo pulled me by the arm towards the front door. Finally, we let ourselves out and walked back towards the house.

'Where do you think the farmworkers are?' I asked, his arm comfortably draped around my shoulders.

'Probably out working the farm, Abigail. I can't wait to see them myself, come to think of it. I'm sure there will be something to my liking. Of course, I will have my pick, as they will all immediately fall in love with my good looks and charm.' I laughed aloud as we walked toward the impressive stables. Polly, Bessie, and Mary joined us soon after, all cheerful and very excited. We paused outside the enormous stable doors, the bluestone building even larger than the cottage we had just left.

'I'm not going in there,' I informed them loudly. 'You go inside and look.' I pushed Leo forward, but he backed away, not too keen himself on the frightening beasts.

'Not me. I was once in a carriage accident everyone blamed on me because I was driving, but they were wrong and still owe me an apology to this day. It was that brutish beast's fault who bolted when I slapped his lard arse with the reins. But, of course, the fact I had never driven a carriage didn't help either when I think of it,' he remarked thoughtfully, causing me to smile.

'They are your stables, Abi. You'll have to go in there sometime,' Polly pointed out, giggling as she tried to push me forward again.

'Well, not today. I will do it another day.' I backed away, not trusting any of them.

'Why are you so scared of horses, Abi? I've never understood it,' Polly remarked, casually leaning against an obvious hitching rail for the beasts.

'I have never been close to one, except for Tipple and the carriage horses, and they're at the front of the carts and carriages, tied up tight in a harness, thankfully. These are roaming free.' A beguiling black horse grazing in the stable paddock caught my attention, its shiny coat rippling over solid muscles. The beast had a magnificent body and was the largest horse I had ever seen. Although it appeared calm, I was far too scared to get up close—but maybe tomorrow.

Just then, a tall man with a kindly face stepped out through the stable door. My eyes went wide, immediately noticing the golden glow surrounding his body. A soft glow, the outline only a shadow slowly brightening around him, he possessed lovely dark hair and eyes, with a tanned, weathered face, still handsome for a man of some four decades, his eyes striking as they twinkled, while his face appeared kind.

'Good afternoon, Mistress. My name is Harry Black. Pleased to be at your service.' He addressed me formally, bowing deeply for a moment before straightening up, a lock of dark hair falling across his eyes before he quickly smoothed it back into place.

'What do you do here, Mr Black, if you would pardon my prying?' A warm, familiar feeling descended over every part of me. I felt as if I had met him somewhere before, but for the life of me couldn't recall where.

'I've been livin' here at Willow Grove for well over twenty-years in the employ of Lady Delmont, even though she's been with the angels for a long time now. I'm responsible for the breedin' program for the nags.' He smiled, proudly pointing towards the stable. 'Stablemaster, or foreman, I like to be known as—an' I oversee the property an' tend to the care an' trainin' of the beasties if no one told you.' He followed my gaze, smiling to himself. 'They're Martarinos. Lady Delmont brought 'em over from England—but they don't come from there—originatin' in Romania. Never heard of the place myself before arrivin' here, but sensibly took Lady Delmont at her word.' He chuckled to himself before continuing. 'We've been breedin' 'em since your aunt settled here at the property in 1868, but she owned this land decades before, an' came here often. They sell for a pretty penny, these horses do, as the affluent among us want 'em for their carriages an' to ride around town an' flaunt their wealth an' status. They're the gentlest giants you'll ever meet, an' I believe they're the loveliest-lookin' steeds I've ever laid me eyes on, in my humble opinion.' He looked proud of his charges, and I smiled at him.

'There is no need for you to bow to me, Mr Black, and please call me Abigail.' I already liked this man and felt I could trust him, despite having no reason to, being a stranger in a strange land surrounded by strange people who I knew nothing of.

'Can you call me Harry, then? It's just the other blokes will think I'm behavin' all self important an' the like if you go 'round addressin' me as Mister.' I nodded, smothering a smile as he gazed at me, his face breaking into a wide grin.

'I understand. Harry, it is. Do you know the whereabouts of the house staff?'

'No, Mistress... uh, I mean, Abigail. It doesn't feel right at all me addressin' you by your Christian name.' He paused for a moment, studying my face intently. 'I was told they come the 'morrow with Mr McPhee.'

'Thank you, Harry. I was uncertain if anyone remained from my aunt's time here. Do you mind telling me where the workers live? I understand the house staff will live in the staff quarters, but where do you all sleep at night?'

'I can show you if you like?' He seemed like an amenable man, and appeared quite casual and laid back, not appearing concerned in the slightest that I had been intrusive in my manner. Harry led us down the side of the enormous building, guiding us out behind the stables, then ushering us up a small hill. When we reached the top, I immediately noticed a number of two-story terraces in the distance nestled in a small valley, a dozen or so from what I could see from such a great distance. Joined and built in two rows facing each other across the paved road, it was as if a quaint little street in a charming little village had been picked up and transported here in one piece.

Harry enthusiastically led us down the undulating paddock towards his home, and once we arrived at his door, he warmly invited us in. There were two rooms downstairs—a kitchen and small sitting room, and an outdoor privy in the small yard out back. Upstairs were three bedchambers. I peered around and, although sparsely furnished, the home seemed well-built, comfortable, and spotless, with a fireplace in each room. Now I was closer, I had counted seven homes on each side of the street. They all had private backyards, and their front gardens appeared well maintained. Cast-iron railings surrounded the first and second-story balconies and resembled buildings I had seen in storybooks as a child. As we stepped out onto the street, I noticed a building still under construction further down the paved road.

'What is that meant to be?' I enquired, curiosity getting the better of me.

'Oh, Lady Delmont had given her approval to build a pub of our own once they finished the main house. The blokes started it, but stopped soon after when we heard word of your intention to settle here, wantin' to wait an' see if the new owner approved. We believed it'd be a waste of time to build it if we ended up with an employer who'd tear it down as soon as they arrived, as you would understand, Mistress. Pardon me—Abigail.' He appeared embarrassed. For what reason, I had not a clue. There was one thing that I knew for certain. I was going to get sick of being called Mistress.

'I will advise Mr McPhee tomorrow I am not opposed to the employees having their own pub, as long as you are all willing to run it—and don't get too carried away on Saturday nights and have us all arrested.' I felt excitement at the thought of a pub close to my back door. He smiled, then thanked me profusely on behalf of the other men.

While we slowly strolled back towards the main house, Harry talked of his life here at Willow Grove Farm. He had arrived when he was nineteen, straight off the boat from England. Raised on a farm and possessing a wealth of knowledge and years of experience tending to animals—both large and small—it was his love of horses, for which he had an affinity, that had kept him here long after most others had left. He had met Lady Isabelle Delmont on the ship after she had heard of his horsemanship through her maid, who had befriended him. Flabbergasted when, one night down in steerage, he looked up to find a striking woman standing over him where he sat at a table, demanding to know his name. Remembering little of what they discussed in those first few minutes so long ago now, he recalled she soon lowered herself into the chair beside him and asked what he knew of breeding horses. He wasn't an expert, but he impressed her enough that she offered him employment as a stable hand, and because of his dedication and hard work in the years to follow, my aunt promoted him to foreman. He now managed Willow Grove in its entirety, from what I could tell.

Harry never married and had remained at the property ever since. He believed he would die here and his bones would turn to dust in the soil of Willow Grove, and he seemed satisfied with that. As we prepared to part outside the stable, I asked if I could meet with him tomorrow to discuss a matter of business, to which he generously agreed. We returned to the house, the initial shock and confusion abating a little since first arriving. Standing in the kitchen, it surprised me how palatial the room was. Within moments Leonardo stood by my side, while Bessie and Mary went on to their rooms to rest.

'What are you doing standing here, Radgie Gadgie?' He gently shoved me away from the stove and towards a table, but I resisted.

'Did you just mean to call me a bad-tempered old man, or are you listening in on conversations of which you have no business?' I enquired, watching him nod enthusiastically.

'Yep, that one.' He winked at me before continuing. 'You know once the servants arrive, you're not allowed in here. This kitchen table is for them to take their meals in peace and escape your judgemental stare and constant demands. You, my dear, have that enormous dining room fit for royalty. Have you even taken the time to look inside? The table seats over thirty people, and if you squashed them up together, you could fit double the amount of handsome men around it. So, why are you just standing in here like a statue, anyway?'

'I was only wondering how all these things work. When I was growing up, we were cooking over a fire with only a small stove mainly used to boil water for the Sisters tea.' I gazed around the modern kitchen with its double ovens and a tall, wide black contraption I had never seen before, finding out from Leo it was a new type of oven released in the last year but was almost impossible to get—and if you were lucky to find one, the cost was exorbitant. We examined the combustion stoves with enthusiasm, while running my hand along the unused cook-tops. I slowly crossed the room to the large workbench in the centre of the kitchen—a substantial wooden table with matching chairs placed off to the side in what appeared to be a spacious dining room, still close but set apart from what I was certain would be the busiest room in the house. I noticed a large woodpile near the door, assuming they had placed it close by for convenience, making it easier to heat these grand appliances, and keep them burning, stacked full of wood and kindling.

'I would love to cook here. This is the most modern kitchen I've ever seen. It's of the same standard as the kitchens I've worked in, and we all know how exclusive they are. It's making me so excited I could widdle down my own leg. Please, Abigail. Can I be your chef?' He beamed down at me as I shifted from foot to foot.

Dumbfounded, not knowing what to say, I turned away and strolled over to a buffet holding expensive looking china. What looked like genuine gold rimmed the plates and bowls, a family crest printed underneath. Leo and I were friends, and I didn't want friends working for me in any capacity—it would feel uncomfortable having them bow and scrape like the others. It worked well with Bessie and Mary; however, I had initially met them as workers and not friends. Leo and I had started as friends and were even closer now, and I couldn't imagine ordering him around or having him at my beck and call. Nor did I believe he would listen, anyway. Bessie and I were just as close, but she would never take advantage of my friendship, and I knew that. I didn't believe Leo would, either, but then again, you never really could predict how he would behave.

'You will need to convince me, Leo. I think it's a terrible idea to employ my friends.' I smiled up at him as he slipped his arms around my shoulders.

'First of all, Abigail, you will eat the best food in Australia every day—breakfast, luncheon, and dinner—or tea, as the Australians call it. I only found that out last night, you know, and I'm what you would call cultured.' Laughing aloud as he led me over to the large window that looked out onto an enclosed courtyard, he smiled down at me. 'I know how much you love to eat. And I will work seven days a week and cater to all the fabulous parties you will have here, where we can admire all the interesting men you'll invite. Besides, you know the way to a man's heart is through his stomach. How else will you catch a husband without me? It won't be for your unfortunate looks or mind-numbingly boring personality—and you can't cook to save yourself.'

I had told them of the betrothal, and of my meeting with Aaron Cavanaugh and his father, but I hadn't told a soul I would lose everything we had if I didn't marry him. I needed a clear head to work this out myself without everyone whispering in my ear, giving me well-intentioned but unwanted advice.

'Leo, if I employ you as our cook, there are some issues we need to sort out. For example, where you will sleep, how much do you expect to be paid, and what hours will you work?' I still felt uneasy and that this might not be the brightest idea for either of us. He stood for a moment, deep in thought, then gazed directly into my eyes.

'Chef, not cook.' I rolled my eyes and sighed, shaking my head. 'All right, I will take a room in the servants' quarters with Bessie and Mary, and I will cook all your meals. I don't care how many hours I work, and you can pay me what I was earning in London.' He stared at me defiantly, silently challenging me to refuse him. 'Come now, Abigail. You need a chef, and I need a job. It also means I don't have to leave you. I can see you every day, and we can talk and play so long as I prepare the meals on time. I would miss you too much if I left.' He gazed at me, pretending to look sad, then whimpered.

'All right, we will try it, but you will only work from Monday morning through to Friday luncheon. I will use the cook Mr McPhee hired to work on the weekends. I will pay you more than what you were earning at the hotel, as I'm going to increase everyone's wages so you each can afford some luxury, too.' His face broke out into a gorgeous smile, and he grabbed me by the shoulders.

'Oh, Abigail, you make me happier than eating chocolate for breakfast.' He giggled as he embraced me so tightly I was struggling to breathe. 'I love you, my fat wee haggis. You are sweet as sugar, and I will admit, if I did like women and their ugly bits, you would be my first choice. Aye, yer a divine wee bowl of bonny parritch.'

'You need to stop trying to be Scottish. You don't seem to know the meaning of the words you speak.' I rolled my eyes as he picked me up off the floor and swung me around the kitchen, then promptly set me down and raced off to tell the others. I sighed. It thrilled me he was so happy about the job, but if there was even a hint our friendship was souring, he would revert to being a houseguest. I would not allow this to ruin the love we had for each other. It meant a great deal to both of us.

I planned to take Mary, and now Leo, into Geelong tomorrow to have several uniforms made, and order day clothes for church and their days off. Then I could organise proper uniforms for everyone through Catherine as soon as she could get here in the next few weeks. I could see I would be busy just making sure the souls who worked here had what they needed. Maybe it would be easier if I moved into that empty, dusty cottage and left them all to it in the main house. I was confident I would enjoy the serenity of living apart from everybody, including my friends and the house staff.

I was still uncomfortable with the thought of so many people working for me. Why we needed a footman was beyond my comprehension and left me feeling incompetent yet again. Dana would know all this, and it made me miss her all the more, leaving me wishing she were here to guide me. It was all too formal for me, but I would attempt to work things out with Mr McPhee tomorrow.

I walked into the staff quarters, which still surprised me with its sheer size, and again wondered how many workers it would take to run a house like this. The wing was enormous and would easily sleep twenty people occupying a room each, when most grand houses placed two or even four people in one room. The main room held a fireplace spanning the entire length of one wall, a long wooden dining table, and buffets around the walls, along with two large lounges and several sideboards. I followed the long corridor down to Bessie's bedchamber and knocked. She opened the door and welcomed me in again. Little Mary was sitting on the bed and quickly stood up when I entered.

'Please sit, Mary. I'm not the Queen of England, for God's bloody sake.' I immediately felt ashamed of myself, cringing as she quickly sat down again and lowered her head, avoiding my gaze. 'Mary, I'm only teasing. It's just that you don't have to stand up for me when I enter a room, even when you are working. That's something you like to do from what Bessie said, so I'll leave it alone. I would just like you to relax around me, that's all. I promise you, I will never bite your head off.' Mary raised her head, still appearing terribly uneasy as I smiled at her apologetically.

Bessie had chosen the last bedchamber in the wing, only so she wouldn't have others passing her door during the night. Mary had picked the one right next door and had already unpacked her meagre possessions. Leonardo was off choosing a room for himself where he could settle and practise the new Scottish words he had somehow learnt since arriving, causing me to shake my head in amusement. We were all finding our way and taking our places in this fanciful journey together, and right now, it was about securing the most important things money could never buy—our home and our ragtag family.

Chapter Four

L EO WAS BUSY IN the kitchen, preparing a late lunch with vegetables from our own gardens and groceries sent over by Mr
McPhee. I stood at the back door, looking out over the luscious
green lawn, when I saw a rider come around toward the stable and
dismount. Assuming he was a farmhand, I turned and made my way
across the room, the scent of parsley and butter filling the kitchen.
I sat down at the large wooden table on one of its lovely carved
chairs, the brown leather padding soft on my backside. It was so
comfortable, I could have remained there for the rest of the day.
Then, within moments, there was a knock at the front door. I could
barely hear it from where I sat, and I wondered how we would ever
settle comfortably into a place with such grand proportions.

I hurried through the enormous house to the foyer, where I felt
tiny standing in front of the towering double doors. I opened one
side to find Aaron standing before me, hat in hand. He was dusty
from the ride over and carried some flowers that looked the worse for
wear. I took them from his hand, and he grinned at me. I thanked him
and invited him in. He followed me to the kitchen, where I found a
vase in a cabinet and placed the flowers in water, setting it down on
the table. Aaron joined me just as Leo started bringing over plates of
food and setting it down before returning to the bench for more. He
sat down beside me and leaned in close, lowering his voice.

'How ya goin', Abi? Have ya recovered from the shock?' he asked quietly. 'I mean, I'm lucky 'cause I've known about ya ever since I can remember.' My gaze met his for a moment. He had the most astonishing eyes, the colour of the ocean that seemed to change with his mood, from what I could tell. They were bright blue now and sparkled as they looked deeply into my own.

'Yes, it was a shock—and still is—but you mustn't like it any more than I do?'

'Ahh, don't ya be worryin' yourself about me. I'm accustomed to the idea—an' I'm as happy as a possum up a gumtree now we've met. I'll tell ya a secret, though.' He leaned closer and lowered his voice, cupping his enormous hand to the side of his mouth. 'Me biggest fear was you would be short, plain, an' fat. When I turned twelve, I'd avoid goin' to me bed 'cause I'd have these terrifyin' nightmares—me head chock-a-block full of pictures of sea hags comin' to marry me by force—all goin' by the name of Abigail.' He chuckled, a deep, melodious sound to my ears, and I couldn't resist returning his smile. Despite my loyalty to Hamish, I felt drawn to him and the more we talked, the more we seemed to get along. I told him of my fear of horses, and he winked at me. 'You're as game as Ned Kelly—with a filthy mouth on ya to match. In no time, you'll be runnin' rings around the willy beasts,' he remarked, reaching across and picking up a roasted carrot before taking a large bite. 'Ya can't live on a farm an' not ride a horse. I'll teach ya every day till you're confident. By the time I'm finished with ya, Abi, you'll be a highly competent horsewoman.'

'But I'm too scared to even stand near them, let alone touch them.'

'I give ya me word. I won't push ya too hard. We'll get ya standin' next to a gentle mare first, an' then take it one step at a time. Will ya agree to at least give it a go?'

I nodded, but hoped he might change his mind and release me from my promise when he saw me quaking in my riding boots. I'd noticed Aaron had a healthy appetite and could eat more than I could, which surprised me, as even Hamish couldn't do that. Feeling terrible just being here with Aaron, and knowing how Hamish would react if he knew, I tried to push the thought to the back of my mind. There was also the dilemma I didn't find Aaron distasteful at all, which could muddy the waters. Bessie stepped into the kitchen, humming to herself as she crossed the room to join us. I glanced sidelong at him, eating and talking with Bessie as if he had known her for years. Aaron seemed like an easy-going man and was undoubtedly attractive, but different to Hamish. While Hamish was dark and brooding and preferred to keep me to himself, Aaron seemed to enjoy everyone's company, not only mine, and he was funny. His banter with Leo and Bessie throughout lunch made me laugh uncontrollably. He didn't seem nervous at all around me, putting me at ease. Once we finished our meal, he turned to me, his face creased in a broad grin.

'Will ya agree to come for a walk with me after lunch, Abi? I'd like to talk to ya alone,' he said, reaching over and lightly squeezing my arm. All I could feel were hot needles where he'd touched me, sending fire down into my belly.

'Of course, I would be happy to,' I replied, giving him what I hoped was a noncommittal smile. Bessie stared across at me knowingly, then excused herself, leaving us at the table with Leo. He scrutinised Aaron for a long time, while Aaron silently returned his stare, smiling all the while.

'Well, I'm not sure yet if I like you or not. You may or may not know by now, but Abigail doesn't do or agree to anything without my consent, me being her best friend and all.' Leo smirked wickedly before leaning back in his chair. 'They built you like a brick shithouse, didn't they? A solid, pleasant looking structure a wealthy person would shit in, not the peasant's dunny. I will admit you're handsome enough, I'll give you that, but it means nothing in this situation, as I am forced to overlook your prepossessing facial structure and burningly warm body. No, I'll have to ignore how you look and the things you make me want to do to you. You know you will have to court me to get to her, don't you? I mean, it's only fair, and why should cinnamon bum be the only one having fun?' Aaron sat back casually in his chair and chuckled, my face becoming warm as I grimaced.

'I'm not gunna argue the toss with ya, Leo. I'm tryin' to make an impression on Abi here by impressin' her friends. So tell me—how would ya like me to court ya? Flowers? Chocolates? Rum?' His blue eyes twinkled with amusement and I couldn't help but giggle. I admired how he was managing Leo already and felt such relief he seemed to have noticed he wasn't in any competition with him.

'Well, I'm not quite sure at this present moment, but I do have a predilection for chocolate. Maybe a romantic stroll around the property later might warm me to you a little, but you must hold my hand,' Leo replied thoughtfully, and we both laughed at him.

Aaron stood and took my hand, leading me out through the back door after thanking Leo for the meal. We strolled through the garden, admiring the flowers, until we found a stone bench with carved griffins on the arms and sat down. The autumn sky was bright, although the air was crisp and the temperature cool; the trees dotted around the property shedding their leaves and creating a brown, orange, yellow, and green carpet below.

'I wanted to speak to ya alone an' check how ya travellin' an' make sure you're all right after this mornin's muck up. We thought ya came here knowin' about the arrangement. I'm sorry ya experienced such a shock.' He appeared concerned as he gazed out over the paddocks, his thoughtfulness touching my heart. The poor man didn't know me from Ethel, and he was being placed in the same predicament as I was through no fault of his own.

'Yes, I will be all right. It's just a lot to think about,' I replied softly, although my mind was racing.

'I need ya to tell me about this other bloke I'm competin' with.' He grinned again as he sat back and waited, a blade of grass between his lips as he chewed, not taking his eyes from me for a moment.

'No. I do not feel comfortable speaking of him. I'm sorry.' I shook my head before staring up at the native birds chirping in the gum tree above.

'No worries, Abi. I'll tell ya about myself—as I'm a late ring in, an' this bloke is miles ahead of me—an' I plan to catch up.' He chuckled loudly, while I felt a little disturbed by the way he was talking, as if he were going to catch me and I would have no choice in the matter. 'I've told ya some of me life, but there's a great deal more to me than what people first choose to see,' he began, his tone quiet but confident. His accent was like none I had ever heard, a hint of Irish brogue, combined with a soft lilt I could not identify—although I only understood half of what he said, as many of the words scattered throughout his sentences were foreign to me. 'I'm the son of a fisho—a fisherman—an' I work the boat with me Da, an' three brothers every mornin' to earn our livin'. Me Ma looks after us—cookin', cleanin', an' tryin' to get us married off—so far with little luck. Since I was five, I've known about ya—an' I sensed me future was always predetermined—leadin' me towards ya since the day I took me first breath. Somehow, I sense it's been the same for you, if ya know it now or not. I've never asked a girl to step out with me—or even kissed a woman—'cause I've been waitin' for ya. Mark me words, Abi. You'll fall in love with me an' wanna be me wife. There'll be no force needed—if there were, I wouldn't pursue ya an' would politely back away. I wanna marry for love, an' for me wife to love me as much as I love her. I already feel deep within my soul it'll happen with you.' It startled me, although I did everything I could to hide my emotions and how I was feeling. He certainly spoke his mind with conviction, but I could see he was a man who was not easily moved once decided. There was a quiet determination about him, which I admired, and, despite my feelings for Hamish, I felt it wouldn't hurt to get to know him better. I liked he wasn't desperate to win my approval, and if he disagreed with me, he honestly told me so and why. I loved honest people and only wanted to be around them. 'What do ya say, Abi? Will ya at least give me a chance? Get to know me before ya run off an' marry this other bloke, whose name ya won't even speak?' He smiled confidently, drawing my eyes to his charming mouth. 'May I ask how long you've known him?' I felt his sincerity deserved an answer, and I swallowed hard before answering.

'A little over six weeks. We met on the ship the first day,' I replied, feeling a pang of guilt. Despite being so different, Hamish was just as lovely as Aaron, and I realised my heart truly belonged to him.

'I'm hopin' ya give me at least that long before ya discard me.' He reached for my hand and held it, sending warm tingles down my spine.

Feeling quite overwhelmed and uncertain of myself since this riveting young man and I had been forced together, I discreetly pulled away. I didn't even know this unusual boy—I was in love with Hamish—but he had lit a spark in me I couldn't extinguish. I could feel it flickering inside me, waiting to burst into full flames, which was the last thing I wanted.

'We will just have to wait and see what comes of it over the next fortnight.' I swallowed hard, feeling utterly and completely confused.

Aaron rose to his feet, then stared into my eyes for a moment, his handsome face unreadable as he pulled me to my feet. He held my hand in his as we strolled side by side to the stables to ready his horse, chatting about Australia and how delightful the weather, even in the colder seasons. I ensured I remained a safe distance away as he led the intimidating beast out of the enormous stable doors, its saddle and bridle already securely in place. He strode over and gave me a polite kiss on the cheek, mounted quickly, and rode away at great speed. I stood and watched his powerful form melding gracefully with the horse as he galloped down the driveway, the sound of the beast's hooves thundering on the ground reaching my ears even after he had gone from my sight. I remained where I was for a time, gazing out over the property towards the empty gatekeeper's lodge, mesmerised by the lush paddocks that seemed to go on forever, long after he had disappeared.

I had not been back inside for long, sitting at the kitchen table with my head in my hands and a million things running through my mind, when there was another distant knock at the front door. I could hear Polly running to get it, no doubt hoping and praying to all the saints it would be Angus. The antsy girl had been impatiently waiting for him since we'd arrived this morning, and I had come close to skelpin' her. I was more than pleased to have found some solitude in the kitchen while everyone was settling in and becoming familiar with the house while exploring the magnificent property.

I could hear shrieking from the entrance and assumed the Makenzie boys had arrived. I sighed deeply, feeling wretched, guilt settling on me like a black cloud. Hamish came rushing into the kitchen, clearly looking for me. When he saw me, he picked me up from my chair and swung me around, kissing me. My euphoria at being in his arms once more slowly turned to dread; I realised I would have to find the right time and the right words to tell him about Aaron.

Harry had sent word for some of the farmworker's wives to prepare the cottage for Hamish and Angus to stay the night. Bessie was taking the matter very seriously indeed, ensuring the boys would both get to bed at a reasonable hour and the door to the main house was securely locked until the morning.

'So, now we're here, tell me. When are you goin' to marry me?' Angus asked as he sat at the table with Polly on his lap. She clung to him tightly, her arms around his neck. They both looked ecstatic to be together, causing my misery to deepen.

'I would marry you tomorrow, but Abi says we must do it properly and have an engagement party, then a church wedding,' Polly replied, appearing pained. I rolled my eyes before snapping at them.

'Oh, come on, you two, it's only a few weeks.' Their love for each other was annoying me right now when I knew the awful news I had to tell Hamish. I was nervous about how he would react, leaving my hands trembling and my heart beating so fast I expected it to explode at any moment. 'Hamish, can we go for a walk?' He gave me a slow, sweet smile. I slipped my arms around his neck, but avoided his gaze.

'Aye, of course. I can't think of anythin' I would enjoy more. This property is magnificent, Abigail. You told me you had a house, not a grand estate. I'm genuinely thrilled such a beautiful woman owns a home just as lovely,' he replied, then kissed me gently on the lips.

We strolled across the immaculate lawn and down to the stables, hand in hand, before coming to a halt at a fence bordering a small paddock. Hamish leaned on the wooden railing, watching the horses, the birds in the distance filling the silence with their songs, all different and unfamiliar, but equally beautiful.

'There is something I must tell you, and I cannot find the words. I don't know where to begin...' My voice broke, and I felt choked up, afraid if I continued I would cry, and I was determined not to.

'Shh, dinnae fash, lass. Just tell me.' His eyes flickered with concern as he thoughtfully led me over to a newly built seat. We sat down on the bench, and he slipped his large arm around my shoulders and squeezed me tight, a feeling of dread settling on me as I sensed everything was about to change despite my yearning for it to stay the same.

'I saw my solicitor today, as you know, and he told me some things I didn't like, and you are going to hate one condition I am supposed to meet.' I could not hold back my tears a moment longer. I buried my head in his chest and silently cried. He stroked my hair and made comforting noises as I struggled to find the words I needed to say as my body shook. 'Here it is, Hamish, and I'm sorry for it. Mr McPhee told me, according to my great-aunt's Will, I am betrothed to a man from Geelong—and have been for the past fifteen-years—and I must let him court me.' Hamish stopped stroking my back and pulled me upright so he could look at me.

'Naw. You must be mistaken, Abigail. No one would make you do that, especially now you have me. You dinnae even have parents to force you into such a match.' He stared deeply into my eyes, confirming the truth of what I had just told him. 'You're naw goin' to do it, are you?' His face flushed as I looked away.

'This solicitor advised me in no uncertain terms I must give him a chance, and I don't have any recourse but to go along with it for now to meet the terms of the Will. Hamish, I'm so confused. I've been promised to someone all my life, and I didn't know about it until today. How am I expected to process what any of this means when no one will give me any time to think? I'm so sorry and completely understand if you throw me over for someone else.' I lowered my head and sobbed, my heart aching as he grunted angrily.

'How can you say that to me? You've obviously been waitin' for me to find someone else ever since I told you of my past with women—an' I've tried every day since I met you to prove meself, but I can see you still doubt me.' He moved away from me then withdrew his arm, turning to stare silently across the paddock. I pushed myself up next to him and held his hand, feeling terrible for him—and myself. After a long pause, he spoke, his voice subdued.

'So, when does this man start courtin' you? Tell me honestly—do I have anythin' to be worried about?'

'He visited me today, stayed for lunch, and then left. Nothing happened, I promise,' I replied truthfully, returning his stare.

'You dinnae answer my question. Do I have anythin' to be worried about?' he asked again, softer this time. I didn't want to lie because I liked Aaron, and I had to at least give him a chance despite feeling like a traitor. If I didn't, I would lose everything. I now carried a burden I had not expected and felt the heavy weight of responsibility to support those who now relied on me for their livelihood.

'I don't know, Hamish. Mr McPhee ordered me to treat you both the same and see who I am in love with at the end,' I answered as honestly as I could, trying not to hurt him further, but I could see he was badly damaged.

'Christ, Abigail. I now have to court you alongside another man an' fight for you when I already had you? We were makin' plans together, for God's sake. He cannae just walk in here, an' you welcome him in an' accommodate him as if I mean nought to you. What the hell do you expect me to do?' he shouted angrily and jerked away. I exhaled slowly, closing my eyes for a moment.

'Hamish, you don't have to do anything you don't want to do. Even though you don't understand it, and I barely do either, I'm stuck with trying to figure it all out.' I stood and, without looking back, hurried towards the house.

Polly was still sitting on Angus' lap when I returned, telling him everything we had been doing since we saw him last on the ship. Three days ago. I sighed deeply, wishing my own life was as uncomplicated, before sitting down next to them. Leo poured me a cup of creamy, sweet coffee before offering me a freshly baked scone.

'So, Angus, how was it to be reunited with your father?' I asked, trying to distract myself from my own problems.

'I have to say it was better on the ship,' he replied, shaking his head. 'My parents are already arguin', and we've only been here two days.

I can hardly stand it. I'm hopin' by the time Polly and I are wed at the kirk, they'll not be speakin', and we will have peace in the house again.'

It must have been serious, given Angus wasn't a person who concerned himself over trivial matters. He found life a big joke most of the time, laughing at the most inappropriate moments, always making me giggle. He and Polly planned to live with his parents after they married, as Mr Makenzie expected both his sons to work on the property with him from morning till night.

'Ah, yes—about you and Polly, after you get married,' I said. 'I have been thinking about it, and I want to offer you the cottage. It's far enough away from the main house to have privacy, but close enough we can see each other when we want to. You can eat at home, since there's a modern kitchen there, or take your meals here with us, so you don't have to cook. It has always been Polly's and my dream to live next to each other when we married.'

I looked across at Polly, tears in her eyes as she sniffed, choked up with emotion. I knew she didn't want to be far away from me, and if she had to move, she would miss our daily contact just as much as I would. Nevertheless, I believed this might be the solution for her—and Angus, too, considering he didn't want to live with his parents.

'Is it all right if we have a look inside and talk in private before we decide?' Angus asked, serious for once.

'Of course. Go,' I replied happily. Polly skipped out of the kitchen with Angus in hot pursuit just as Hamish came in and sat down at the table opposite me. He looked like he had been crying. I went around and sat beside him, taking his hand in mine.

'I love you, Abigail, and I will prove it to you,' he said, his voice barely audible. 'It's against my better judgement, but I will fight for you for that reason alone.' He clasped my hands between his and kissed them. I felt horrible about myself for putting him through this, but I had to be sure before I made up my mind, and I didn't want my decision to be influenced by money, despite my fear of starving and having no roof over my head. I wanted my choice to be driven only by love and who was best suited. Presently, I felt that it was Hamish. The only problem was when I thought about Aaron, I could not deny my attraction to him. The fact they were both surrounded by a beautiful golden aura made things even more complicated. Hamish gathered me in his arms, stroking my face before kissing me, and then pulling me onto his lap. 'Are you goin' to let me sneak into your bedchamber tonight?' We had only spent that one night in bed together, and it had been difficult not to take things further than we intended.

'I feel we probably went too far last time, and I don't want to have sexual relations before I get married,' I replied, stroking his hair back from his face. He was wearing it loose, and it hung down around his shoulders, reminding me of a black lion.

'I promise you the same as before. I will not take off any of my clothin', and I will nae touch you in places I shouldn't. Come on, Abigail. I only want to hold you and kiss you and have you close to me.' I could see he needed this—I needed it, too, to reconnect with him and get Aaron out of my mind.

'All right, but you promise?' I asked, and he nodded. Against my better judgement, I agreed. 'After dinner, say you feel tired and must go to bed. I will walk you out, and you can sneak up the stairs into my bedchamber and wait for me. I won't be far behind you, but you must tell Angus, so he doesn't come looking for you.' He kissed me gently on the lips and smiled in noticeable relief.

'Angus will figure it out. But that's only one reason I love you—your devious mind,' he whispered, and I kissed him back.

We relaxed in the sitting room, my stomach ready to burst after the decadent dinner Leo had proudly served us. Bessie appeared unusually tired, while little Mary was full of energy, nervously pacing the room, before sitting to continue the scarf she was knitting for me.

'Bessie, are you feeling well?' I asked, concerned for her. She did not look bonny to me at all.

'A bit of a chill, Mistress, nothing more. I think I will retire if you don't mind?' she replied, coughing into her handkerchief.

'Of course. Goodnight, my dear Bessie, and please stay in bed tomorrow morning. I can prepare myself for the day without assistance.' I squeezed her hand as she walked past me, accompanied by little Mary, who would have been uncomfortable if left alone with us. Bessie and Mary had agreed to join us in the sitting room tonight until the new staff arrived tomorrow and had decided they would spend their nights in the staff quarters with the new friends they were sure to make. I hated the fact Bessie felt unwell, but relief washed over me. I didn't have to lie about sneaking Hamish into my room.

Leo leaned back into the lounge, appearing content. He was such a good person, and I couldn't believe I was lucky enough to have him as my friend and private chef, as he liked to call himself. I had looked at all the food in the kitchen today, and I couldn't imagine what to make out of it or where to begin, but Leo had made luncheon and dinner with an ease I couldn't believe. And it was delicious. He had made dishes I had never tasted before, with herbs and spices I had never heard of or had the pleasure of eating. He carried in his bag ingredients from all over the world he had collected in his travels. They were his most prized possessions, along with his knives. It was these small but significant items he had refused to leave behind in London.

When Leo had advised me he was a renowned chef during our first meeting, I put it down to braggadocio, believing him more a cook, but he had surprised and delighted me today. I felt so proud of him. I wondered if he would ever find true love again and how difficult that would be here in this new, rugged land, where men were men and women had to behave like ladies or be damned.

'Leo, how is your new bedchamber?'

'It's wonderful, even though my townhouse in London was majestic.' He raised the cup of hot chocolate to his lips and took a slow sip. 'I will use the word cosy, which is far more polite than what I was going to say. They set each room up just like a tiny house, with new curtains, a comfy bed, and a lounge with a table and chairs to match—oh, sweetheart, I'm beside myself with joy it's mine. I strolled through the garden and picked so many flowers for my room; it's like a flower shop in Whitechapel now, only without the poor people begging for food and haranguing you for a penny. I stripped most of your rose bushes, but I hope you don't mind. It was wonderful to be back in the kitchen today after so long and to create again. I really am the best chef in the world, as you have all now witnessed. The angels above have blessed you with me, and you're very fortunate to have me. Yes, Abigail. Blessed. And fortunate.'

He sat back in the lounge, a self-satisfied look on his face. To be so passionate about a vocation almost made me jealous. I hadn't found mine yet, but I couldn't wait until I did, and once I discovered it, I would never let it go.

'I'm goin' to bed. Goodnight all.' Hamish gracefully rose to his feet, bidding everyone farewell before I accompanied him to the front entrance. Instead of going out the door to find his bed in the cottage, he slowly climbed the marble stairs to hide in my bedchamber. My stomach dropped at the thought of him holding me tonight.

I returned to the sitting room and sat down next to Leo, patting his leg affectionately. He grabbed me, threw me on the lounge and pinned me down, pretending he was going to spit on me. I giggled, pushing his chest, attempting to get him off me, when he paused, his face grave as he let go of me and sat up.

'Abigail, what are you going to do? Which one will you choose as they're fairly well matched?'

Angus and Polly lay on the other lounge, talking about their engagement party and impending wedding. Utterly absorbed in each other, they didn't overhear our quiet conversation.

'That's the thing, Leo. I don't know. As it stands right now, it's Hamish, but even then, I worry he will go back to his old ways with women. However, I must tell you, between us, this Aaron has me more than a little intrigued,' I whispered, and he smirked.

'And I can understand why. Aaron has the most attractive rear end I have ever seen, except for Hamish. If you were a man, they'd call you a womaniser. You already have half the men in the district wanting to bed you, and I feel you encourage them as you thrive on the attention, you fat tavern trollop. I think I will have to invent a word opposite to a womaniser. Let me think for a moment.' He furrowed his brow, appearing deep in thought. 'I have it. You are a maniniser of the worst kind.' His face lit up as he clapped his hands together at his own wit, and I screwed up my face.

'You think you're so funny—and you're not. You know I'm torn between them, but Aaron has stirred up feelings that frighten me a little.'

'Tell me why he intrigues you, yet terrifies you at the same time?' He appeared delighted as he shifted in his seat and reclined in his most comfortable gossiping position. I told him everything Aaron had said to me, how he made me feel, and what Hamish meant to me. He listened without interrupting, compassion in his eyes, and held my hand as I spoke my truth to him. I felt like I could tell Leo anything, and he would never judge me or try to convince me to do something I didn't want to do, and here he was again, listening sympathetically. 'I don't envy you, Abigail, but maybe try to look at it like this. You have one last chance before you commit to Hamish to see what else is out there. You have had little experience with men, and that worries me. I don't want to speak out of turn, which I know is unlike me, but I wonder if you haven't rushed into this with Hamish too soon and, whatever happens, you need to slow things down.' I knew he was right. I didn't want to be married and have children yet, although I enjoyed the romance with Hamish, who made me feel safe and loved, and he acted as though he cherished me. Aaron was another boatload of fish. He was handsome and charming in an outdoor, manly way, but what had taken me by surprise was how honest he was with his feelings. He didn't care if he looked silly or embarrassed himself, and I found that more attractive than anything physical Aaron or Hamish possessed.

I kissed Leo on the cheek goodnight, hugged Polly and Angus, then slowly made my way up the stairs to my bedchamber, wondering if this was a good idea now my situation had changed so dramatically in one day. Opening my bedchamber door felt strange, almost like I was doing something wrong now I had two suitors, and was giving one an unfair advantage. I hurried into the dressing room and changed into my nightgown, then went to get into bed with Hamish. As I climbed in, he grabbed me and pulled me close to him with such passion I was breathless by the time he let me go.

'What was that for?' I asked, gasping for breath.

'Because I love you, and I'm no goin' to lose you to this man. What's his name, by the way?' he asked, holding my body close to his.

'Don't make me tell you that, Hamish. I am hoping to God you both never meet.' I pulled away from him as he studied me thoughtfully.

'Have you gone mad, Abigail? Do you really think that is goin' to be possible? He is goin' to be here every day, so our paths will cross. I will be a perfect gentleman as long as he keeps his hands off you, which I'm not goin' to do right now.' He slipped his arms around me, pulling me close again before kissing me deeply.

Much later, as I lay in his arms, I fell asleep dreaming of two men arm wrestling, an enormous horse chasing me, and a giant, black snake with a thick forked tongue.

Chapter Five

HAMISH HAD QUIETLY RETURNED to the cottage as the rooster crowed, leaving me lying awake and alone, worrying about what the day would bring. Aaron had told me he would be back sometime today. Concerned Hamish would be upset by his presence and unable to control his temper had caused an ache in my stomach that would not go away. I hoped Hamish would be gone by the time Aaron arrived, but had a strong feeling he would wait around as long as it took for him to show himself and size up his competition.

I had never had two men competing for my attention before, and, despite what they said in the novels, it was not a pleasant experience. My nerves already frayed and feeling on edge, I didn't know how much longer I could stand it. I threw back the heavy quilt and rose to my feet, yawning loudly before I swiftly dressed, pulling on a house-dress that required no assistance. Bessie was ill, and I hoped she would stay in bed for the day. I made my way down to the kitchen to find Leo cheerfully preparing breakfast. I hugged him good morning before putting on a coat that hung on a peg at the back door, leaving him calling out behind me as I hurried down to the cottage.

Hamish was still in bed when I arrived, his soft snores filling the room. I slipped off my coat and slid into the bed beside him, placing my hand on his chest as he opened one eye suspiciously.

'Hamish, I want to be sure you won't be nasty to Aaron, as it's not his fault either. He is being pushed into this as much as I am.'

'Ah, so Aaron is his name? Does this Aaron not have a sweetheart he secretly wants to be with?' he grumbled, lifting his head from the pillow and glaring at me.

'Not that I'm aware of, but he may have. I'm just asking you not to be too hard on him, that's all.' Hamish took my face in his hands, kissed me gently, and then ran his fingers through my hair and down my back. I could stay like this forever, I thought, as his hands became more desperate to hold me and touch me, his lips demanding I respond to him. Finally, he pulled me on top of him, and I lay along his body, kissing him and holding him, until I drifted back into a deep slumber, knowing things would never be the same between us.

I saw Aaron as he rode up to the stables. Hamish was in the sitting room, having decided he and Angus would stay another night. I met Aaron coming up to the house and asked if he would like to walk with me.

'See, Abi. I knew ya would become accustomed to me, an' here ya are acclimatising already,' he teased as he smiled and winked cheekily. I couldn't help but smile back.

'I wanted to tell you that the other man courting me is here. His name is Hamish.'

'And that bothers ya? That we're both here at the same time?' he asked, appearing surprised.

'Well, yes, it does, actually.'

'Ahh, Abi, don't even think about it. I've a question for ya, though. Have ya allowed Hamish to kiss ya?' His impertinence startled me. My mind raced as I considered ignoring the question, but felt obligated given the situation.

'Yes, I have, but that is as far as it has gone,' I replied, knowing that was a barefaced lie.

'I wouldn't have expected anythin' different, Abi. The one thing I know about ya first an' foremost is you're a lady—an' a kiss doesn't count when you're married an' happy with me.' He laughed as he watched my face flush pink.

'You are so sure of yourself, Mr Cavanaugh. How do you know if I am only allowing your attention to free myself from any obligation I might have to you?'

'You know how I can tell? By the way ya look at me an' laugh when I talk to ya, an' the way ya held me hand yesterday. Just give it time, Abi, an' you'll come to see it as I do, but there's one thing we'll have to fix first.' I stared at him for a moment; however, his face gave nothing away. 'He has an unfair advantage. He can kiss ya, an' I cannot, so I think we should get it out of the way.' He gazed into my eyes, his twinkling brightly as I averted my gaze and moved away slightly. I took a deep breath before turning back to face him, forcing a weak smile.

'All right, let's get it out of the way,' I replied, expecting this to be a business-like exchange. Instead, he took me in his arms. I felt hot pins searing through my body to my belly, leaving me tingly and warm all over.

'Are ya ready?' he whispered, his face tender, and I nodded. He kissed me on the forehead first, then my eyes and nose, then gently all over my cheeks. I instinctively put my arms around his neck. He looked down at me for a moment, staring at me for a time before kissing me full on the mouth, slowly at first, then demanding more. If he had never had a sweetheart before, I didn't know where he learned to do this. I was doing everything in my power to remain sensible and keep my wits about me, despite how my body reacted to his touch.

'Get your hands off my fiancée,' I heard Hamish growl, startling me.

Aaron stopped immediately and straightened up; however, he didn't take his arms from around me as we turned to find Hamish standing behind us, his handsome face twisted in fury.

'G'day, mate. Ya reckon ya could've given us a bit of warnin' before creepin' up like a tarantula. From how I understand it, if Abi is any-one's fiancée, she's mine.' Aaron smiled across at him before stepping forward. He attempted to shake his rival's hand, but Hamish was having none of it.

'Excuse me, but shouldn't I have a say in this?' I snapped. 'I am no one's fiancée, and I may never be to either of you since I haven't even decided if I am going to get married at all.' I folded my arms across my chest and stared at them in defiance.

'How could you kiss this man behind my back, Abigail?' Hamish demanded to know.

'It wasn't behind your back. It just happened, Hamish, and I have hidden nothing from you,' I snapped again, stepping away.

'I will leave you two here and return inside. When you have finished, Abigail, I hope you will join me,' he growled. I nodded before he turned and walked away, Aaron staring after him in silence, a bemused look on his face.

'He chucks in the towel easily for such a big bloke. There's no way I'd walk away from ya by choice, no matter who was challengin' me.'

He pulled me in tightly against his body again and kissed me one more time. It would have helped me with my decision if one of them didn't have the golden glow. I knew they would both be important to me because of this alone, but I didn't know which one would end up being my husband or if I would even choose either of them.

'Now, Hamish an' me are on a level playin' field. How about ya invite me for dinner tomorrow night?' I looked up at him and smiled weakly. He certainly wasn't shy like I was in the company of strangers, and he was far much more confident than I in every way.

'All right, come tomorrow afternoon, and you can sleep in the cottage later if you like. I would enjoy your company.' We meandered through the garden towards the stables. 'Aren't you going to ask me when Hamish is leaving?' He raised his eyebrows, clearly surprised.

'Nah. Why would I? Ya don't have me ring on ya pretty little finger yet. I trust ya, Abi, an' he's not even in the race 'cause I know in the end I'll win out. I can't help but feel sorry for him.' It surprised me he placed no pressure on me, just stated the facts as he saw them—we were going to be together, and that was that. There was no other choice in his mind, and I could see he didn't doubt himself for a moment. I found his quiet confidence attractive, and the fact he didn't appear to be a jealous sort was more than a relief. He kissed me goodbye before mounting his horse, which Harry had readied for him. 'Don't forget—tomorrow we're startin' with the horses.' I inwardly cringed as I lifted my hand to wave him off. Aaron politely tipped his hat and cheerfully called out his farewells before galloping away.

Dread filled me at the thought of returning to the house to be confronted by the full force of Hamish's wrath, my feet refusing to move as I stood next to the small paddock by the stables. I leaned on the wooden fence, staring across at the horses. There was a heavy-set mare, a newborn foal beside her, which was so similar in appearance I could not look away. She was breathtakingly beautiful, her silky, black mane flowing down nearly three feet, her tail skimming the ground, the long feathers around her legs thick and glorious, her heavy, muscular frame gently grazing on the luscious pastures. I watched in wonderment as the foal suckled its mother's milk before reluctantly turning away to trudge back up to the house.

I entered the sitting room to find Hamish speaking quietly to Angus and Polly. His body tensed as I sat down beside him, clearly still angry with me. Polly continued talking about her wedding dress and those for her bridesmaids before I reminded her I'd written to Catherine. I had asked her to design and make the dresses, along with all our staff uniforms. I told her I was waiting for Catherine to reply but just knew she would agree, reassuring her she did not have to give it another moment of thought.

I turned to Hamish and asked him if we could talk in private. He stood silently, and I led him up to my bedchambers and into the small sitting area adjourning the elaborate room. We made ourselves comfortable on opposite lounges before I locked eyes with his, thinking him so handsome it took me a moment to catch my breath. I waited for my heart to slow, clasping my hands together to hide just how much they trembled.

'I don't think you should sleep in here anymore.' His head snapped up, wide-eyed with disbelief, before he grunted.

'You're teasing me, no? He kisses you, and out of nowhere, you tell me I cannae stay here anymore? What, are you suddenly in love with him now, too?' He did not even attempt to hide his rage, his sarcasm hitting me like a blow to my chest.

'No, Hamish, that's not what I'm trying to say.' Tears stung my eyes as I swallowed hard. 'How would you like it if I let him sleep in the same bed as me under the same circumstances?' I raised my eyebrows, glaring back at him.

'I will nae allow you to. I forbid it,' he roared, slamming his fist down on the coffee table and scattering the few possessions I had placed there.

'Hamish, please calm down. All I'm saying is I don't want to sleep in the same bed with you until after we marry. I'm finding it harder and harder to control myself, and you told me you are, too. You know how important it is to me that I'm a virgin on my wedding night, and you have respected that so far. I'm worried if we keep doing this, we're tempting fate, and one night we won't be able to stop ourselves.' He sat back, appearing defeated as tears welled in his eyes.

'I dinnae want to stop myself anymore, Abigail.' He raised his hand to his head and brushed his hair back before closing his eyes for a moment. 'I love you, and I'm goin' to make sure I have you at the end of this sorry business.' I went to him, and he slipped his arms around me, pulling me close. I cuddled into his chest while he played with my hair, and I thought about having children with black, curly hair, dark-brown eyes, and beautiful smiles.

I met Mr McPhee at the front entrance and welcomed him and his entourage of staff into the parlour, showing them through the ground floor as we went. I assumed the formal-looking man with the group was the butler by how he stood, bowing formally, when Mr McPhee introduced us. His name was Gregory Masters, and he had worked in several grand houses in England and Scotland. He was middle-aged with salt and pepper hair cut short and kept neat, tall and of a solid build, with gentle, kind eyes. A familiar glow surrounded him, no longer startling me as it once had. I looked forward to getting to know him better, as he would be in charge of all the household staff.

The head housekeeper, Miss Maisie Campbell, was a lovely woman in her mid-twenties, whose smile held a hint of mischief. I immediately felt she would be kind and fair to her charges, and all I wanted was a happy household. My greatest fear was letting people down. Now, here I was with all these employees I didn't want and had been planning to get rid of within weeks who were now relying on me for their livelihoods.

It pleasantly surprised me to find the new cook, Miss Jenny Pickering, was familiar to me. She had guided us at Flinders Street station to our train yesterday, but had then disappeared before we could thank her. Younger than I had expected for such a responsible position, she was said to be one of the best food preparers in Melbourne. She was tall and charismatic, and I already found her to be a kind soul thanks to our encounter at the train station. I liked the fact many of the new staff were not much older than me, as I had seen many cooks and their assistants, just like auld Mrs Murphy at the orphanage, who were at the point of retirement but continued to work, preparing the most tasteless food ever served to a human being. First, Mr McPhee introduced me to Mary and Liza, both here to take up their new positions as housemaids—then Erin and Sarah, who would work in the kitchen—while the very young scullery maid was a sweet girl with dark hair named Sally. However, all appeared shy and would not look me in the eye, despite me plastering the brightest smile I could muster across my face.

Mr McPhee introduced the footmen, Samuel and Jonathon, who also looked down at their feet when I attempted to speak with them. Bessie and little Mary introduced themselves to the new employees and kindly offered to show them to the staff quarters. They had been told before their arrival just how modern the house was, and it was clear how excited they felt; every single one, except for Mr Masters, hurrying off to see where they would be living.

'I thought we could ask Mr Masters here to explain to us the workings of a house like this, given his experience,' Mr McPhee said, watching the last of our new employees leave. I thought it a fine idea given I had absolutely no idea about running one myself.

'As you wish, sir. It would please me greatly,' Mr Masters replied, bowing slightly. I motioned him to a chair in the parlour, which he accepted, sitting down politely, his back as straight as a board, his body and manner stiff. He cleared his throat, nodding his head before he began his lesson on running a grand estate. 'It is a privilege to meet you, Mistress.' I nodded politely, urging him to continue. 'Let me explain the role of the servants and who they answer to. In this situation, we do not have a full staff, therefore I will skip some positions that are not yet filled.' He sat back in his chair and placed his hands together in a steeple as he furrowed his brow. 'The butler—myself, in this instance—is responsible for all servants within the mansion walls, and the proper running of the household falls on his shoulders. Whether that be a large dinner party, or dinner for two in private. There are many things no one else notices, an example being the organising of the monthly bills and groceries that require payment. The housekeeper oversees the maids' cleaning and organisation, with the housemaids responsible to her, as is the scullery maid, who also answers to the cook. I understand you have a cook who calls himself a chef, who is adamant he will only report and answer to you. I will leave that for you to resolve, Mistress, and will accept whatever decision you make. In the usual circumstances, he would be answerable to me.' I smothered a smile as he sighed deeply, utterly unaware of just what he would deal with should he insist and his hand forced. He sat back in his chair before continuing. 'The footmen report to me, or the housekeeper, for their daily instructions, of which I am certain will be quite taxing in a home of this size.'

I understood most of what he had just told me; however, I still wondered how to utilise so many and keep them occupied each day. I nodded again before requesting to meet with Jenny Pickering, the new butler rising to his feet and hurrying away to fetch her. They returned shortly after, Mr Masters deciding to join Mr McPhee by the window. I led a tentative Jenny to a settee, an extremely hard lounge you certainly couldn't relax on, before encouraging her to sit down. She glanced at me shyly before averting her gaze to the colourful carpet beneath our feet, shifting uncomfortably in her seat as she patiently waited to hear why she'd been summoned. I swallowed hard, discreetly running my tongue along my dry lips.

'Well, Miss Pickering—Jenny—the problem I have is I didn't know Mr McPhee was hiring a cook, and I have employed my own chef,' I began apologetically. Her pretty face fell in disappointment as she looked down at her hands, appearing quite distressed.

'Oh, I knew it. I knew this was too good to be true and I would lose my job. But I didn't think it would happen before I even started,' she replied, her voice barely audible, while tears streamed down her cheeks. I quickly passed her a clean handkerchief.

'Oh, no, wait. That's not what I'm saying. Please stop crying. You still have a job here, Jenny. How would you like to cook on the weekends and assist the chef in the kitchen throughout the week, choosing your days off, of course?' I felt dreadful. I had upset her so severely and so quickly, without thought. She stared back into my eyes, appearing relieved. She took several moments to contain her emotions, wiping her face before blowing her nose on the handkerchief.

'Of course, Mistress, I will be happy to do what pleases you, and I will work with your chef without complaint.' She wiped away her remaining tears, then loudly blew her nose again.

'Keep the hanky, Jenny. Please tell me more about yourself. I did not know yesterday when we met in passing you were on your way to our new home.' She settled back in her chair; her shoulders relaxed as she stared back at me.

'My parents immigrated from Scotland before I was born. They set up a small restaurant in Lonsdale Street in Melbourne.' She stopped for a moment, sipping some water from a crystal glass I had offered her. 'I grew up watching them cook, then helping until I was competent to create my own recipes. People came from far and wide to request my dishes, but I was dreadfully unhappy. I recently came across an advertisement for this job in The Sun newspaper, and I thought I would try my luck in a new town, with new people. Fortunately, I was successful in securing the position.'

'It doesn't bother you that your parents and siblings are so far away?' I asked, feeling a little concerned, given she was so young. She appeared as though she was not yet twenty; although I found her quite sensible and mature.

'It's not that far, Mistress. If I can have my two days off a week together, during the weekday, I can travel home for two nights.' I felt drawn to her and liked her immensely, sensing we could easily be friends in the future, which delighted me. I was meeting so many new people and had appreciated everyone I had met here so far—except, of course, for Mr McPhee.

'You have my consent, Jenny. I will ask Mr Masters to arrange your time off each week so you can return to your family.' I nodded as she prepared to leave. Her situation would work perfectly, giving Leo the weekends off to have fun with me and ample time to explore the property and go on wonderful adventures. I hadn't failed to notice every single house servant was unmarried, whereas many of the farmhands had wives and children living with them in the small village nearby.

'Thank you for speaking with me and being so agreeable,' I said as she stood to leave.

'Oh, no, thank you, Mistress. I am thrilled,' she replied, curtsying to me. I cringed inwardly; however, smiled and politely let her go without another word.

Leo and I were exploring the extensive grounds when we came across the vegetable garden. A man was standing over a shovel near a mound of soil, scratching his head thoughtfully. We opened the gate and walked inside.

'Hello, I'm Abigail, and this is Leonardo.' I shook his hand, no longer surprised to find yet another person on our property surrounded by the golden glow.

'Good afternoon to you, Mistress. My name is Sean. I'm the man that sent up the sacks of vegetables and fruit for you all on the day you arrived.' He grinned broadly, nodding his head at Leonardo, then me, before continuing his work.

'I would like to thank you for your kindness. It was very thoughtful, and we appreciate your gesture,' I told him sincerely, making my way over to the pumpkins that appeared to be growing wild around the border of the magnificent garden. He nodded politely before fixing his gaze on Leo.

'You must be the famous chef Leonardo, whom I have already heard a great deal about on the grapevine. Or passionfruit vine, as I like to say here.' He stopped again and threw back his head, chuckling loudly.

'You should know right now that any gossip you hear about me is likely to be true,' Leo replied, staring around in awe at the abundant crop of vegetables, some extremely large, appearing odd to me. Sean laughed harder, leaning on his shovel for support.

Sean had been the head gardener for the main house for twenty-years and had been the one to design and plant the garden all that time ago. He was a short, thin man with brown hair and blue eyes and a calm and friendly manner. His wife, Margaret, and their four children lived at Willow Grove with him. He advised us he had no one to help him in the garden when times were busy, but could call on the farmhands for help when desperate, taking them from their work. It stunned me he managed the considerable workload mostly alone and clearly did a magnificent job of it. Leonardo continued to gaze across the garden in delight, clapping his hands together excitedly.

'I haven't seen some of these ingredients since I was in Italy. I think I have died and gone to edible heaven, Abigail.' He smiled at me. There seemed to be an enormous variety of vegetables, some I had never seen or tasted in my life. Sean and Leo walked through the garden chatting while I sat on a carved wooden bench to wait. They spoke of everything, from the crispness of the carrots to the rosemary and oregano growing on the boundaries. Leo appeared content, more so than I had seen him since we met. He was doing what he loved with people he cared about, and that made me happy. Leo returned to my side with an armload of vegetables, looking pleased with himself.

'I am making peppers, eggplants, and tomatoes for dinner tonight.' My mouth watered. I had never eaten that before and did not know what it would taste like, yet whenever he spoke about food, I suddenly became ravenous no matter what it was. We hurried back to the house, laughing the entire way. I stepped through the back door and into the bustling kitchen, Leo following close behind. The staff immediately ceased their work, turned around, and stared silently at me.

'What's going on?'

'I'm sorry, Mistress, but when you walk into the room, all the servants stop what they're doing out of respect. You are not a person we get to see often; unless asked to attend to you upstairs,' Jenny replied politely, curtsying slightly.

'Well, please stop it. All of you.' A smile touched my lips as I stared back at her. 'You will see a lot of me, so get used to it. If you stop what you're doing every time I walk into a room, then nothing will get done.' They smiled back before resuming their work while Leo took his place at the deep trough and began washing all the vegetables he had harvested. 'All right, Leo, I will see you after dinner.' He winked as I discreetly waved to him before turning to leave them all in peace.

'Dinner was delicious, but I feel so strange not eating with Bessie and Mary,' I complained to Polly as she shovelled the last bite of her stuffed peppers into her mouth. Leo had filled the vegetables with a mixture of minced meat and rice, along with ingredients I was unfamiliar with; however, it tasted so good, I vowed I would eat everything stuffed from now on.

'I feel the same way,' she remarked, reaching over to Angus and stroking his curly hair. They had agreed to take the cottage and planned to move in after spending two weeks at The Delmont Hotel in Melbourne for their honeymoon. I doubted very much they would leave the hotel at all during their time there, the way they were behaving. I was secretly glad I would have Polly so close and she didn't have to live with Angus and his family. Things seemed to go from bad to worse in that household. Hamish had told us during dinner he had seen his father in town with a strange woman on his arm, and somehow poor Harriet had found out within hours. During a blazing confrontation, his mother had chastised his father for being indiscreet and selfish, and she now refused to talk to him. Polly would have hated it there and been extremely unhappy had they moved in with his family.

'Have you told your parents you will live here?' I asked as they stared into each other's eyes.

'I told Mother, and she thought it to be for the best, but no surprise Father is yet again unimpressed with me,' Angus replied, unable to take his eyes from Polly's.

'Excuse me, but there are other people here in the room. Can you at least look at us when we are talking to you?' I complained. They both turned and stared back at me, appearing confused.

'Sorry, Abi. We don't even realise we are doing it,' Polly apologised, while Angus just grinned at me. We ate in the kitchen; the dining room far too big for the four of us, although our presence had unsettled the staff. They had been expecting to serve us in the dining room; however, I had given them all the night off to settle in and become familiar with one another. Leo stood on the other side of the kitchen, finishing our dessert. He brought it over on a tray, singing a tune as he placed it on the table.

'Here is my Abigail's favourite dessert,' he said proudly, setting large dishes of crème brûlée down on the table, which I adored, and he knew it. I wondered what he wanted from me initially; however, the look of delight on his face when we all took that first bite and complimented him showed just how much he loved what he did. He took a dish for himself and sat down with us. 'So, Hamish. You've controlled yourself well, all considering,' Leo spouted, and I wanted to smack him there and then. Instead, I saw Hamish's face harden as he looked back at Leo.

'Considering what? That chancer who was here today? It dinnae bother me. A confident wee shite he is, struttin' around with that smirk on his face, but he'll be gone soon enough. Then Abigail and I'll have nothin' stoppin' us from bein' together.' Leo smirked wickedly, raising his brows.

'Well, you are more convinced than I am,' he teased. 'I met him today, and he is like a Greek God, only blonde and not carved in stone and living in a museum. Oh, yes, he could put his boots under my bed anytime. He has promised me a walk around the property. Quid pro quo, you may say, but it's more eum amo, in my opinion. Now you must think of what you can do for me so I favour your cause and see she ends up with you.'

I choked on my apple juice, which I had noticed was the best I had ever drunk. The gardeners had picked the apples today from the orchard, then Sean crushed them in the press, providing us with litres of juice so crisp and sweet I believed I could drink the lot on my own.

'Ah, so the precocious shite is bribin' you already, is he? I dinnae need to sling a carrot at you, Leo, as the threat of death will be enough. Your death. Abigail will make up her own mind, and I'm confident it will be me she ends up with.' He appeared unaffected, eating his dessert before taking a sip of ale. We chatted about the upcoming engagement party and how unhappy Mr Makenzie was about the wedding. In his eyes, Polly wasn't good enough for his family. He was aware she was an orphan, thanks to Jemima, who had overheard her talking to Angus about her childhood while still on board the ship.

'Oh, away with him an' boil his heid,' Hamish told Angus as Polly gasped at his profanity. 'Since he cannae keep himself to one woman, no one cares what he thinks of our future wives. I wish Mother could find some way of gettin' him out of her life.' The others nodded in agreement.

'Your father gets out and about, from what I've already heard on the passionfruit vine,' Leo remarked, making me giggle.

'What passionfruit vine?' Angus asked, his eyes twinkling in amusement. Leo shook his head in disbelief, widening his eyes.

'Don't you know? Now we have my servants here—and they are here to serve me as well, Abigail—I discovered many are locals and grew up in the district after I harangued them for all their personal information. They're the ones who know from the passionfruit vine who your father is—and all about his other women—or bits of fluff, as he calls them,' Leo informed us, making me smile. At least no one could ever say it was boring in this house. We all retreated to the sitting room, where the boys sipped whisky and Leo, Polly, and I poured more apple juice from a large jug we had brought with us.

'Has your father always been so mean to your mother?' Polly asked Angus, joining him on the lounge.

'Aye. From my earliest memory and no doubt before. You will never have to worry you'll ever be treated so poorly, my darlin' girl. I will love you until I take my last breath. I dinnae need to say it in front of a priest in the kirk because you are my heart, soul, and life, and that will never change. We will grow old together, my precious Polly, and raise a beautiful family.' I felt tears sting my eyes, the love he felt for her filling my heart with joy. Hamish took my hand in his, squeezing it tightly.

It thrilled him Angus had found love, as he genuinely liked Polly and got along well with her. I could see he would treat her like a younger sister, despite having no time for his own. I yawned, realising how fast time had passed as I glanced at the clock on the mantle. The last thing any of us wanted was to upset Bessie. No one wanted to be at the end of her sharp tongue. The boys quickly agreed to retreat to the cottage to sleep.

I walked down the hall beside Hamish towards the back door, holding his hand. Polly and Angus stepped out into the garden to share a private moment before we cruelly forced them to part for a heart-rending eight hours, causing me to bite my tongue. I looked up at Hamish, then kissed him goodnight.

'Thank you for understanding, Hamish.' He nodded as he gazed down at me in silence. 'I know how hard this is on you, and Leo was right. However, you controlled yourself well today. I will speak again with my solicitor in two weeks, and maybe there is some way I can get out of this, but until then, I must go along with it.' I knew I couldn't tell him all the details because if I ended up with Aaron, Hamish would always believe it was solely because of the money. Hamish took a deep breath, staring deeply into my eyes under the full moon, its glow illuminating his lovely face.

'Aye, Abigail. It is hard on me, but I also see it's difficult for you. I dinnae blame you for any of it. I blame that insane great-aunt of yours, who did everythin' arse backwards. None of it makes sense, but I know it's naw your fault, and I will nae let it come between us. I love you, Abigail, and I always will.' He tenderly kissed me, picking me up in his arms and holding me close to him, my legs dangling in the air.

He whispered in my ear until I relented and agreed he could sneak back into my room tonight, as long as he left by morning. I knew, despite still being sick, Bessie would attend to me. After some time, he placed me down on my feet and went to drag his brother away from Polly. I waited for her, and we made our way upstairs, both having kissed Leo goodnight. I hugged her before retreating into the beautiful room I couldn't believe was mine to find Bessie unpacking one of my trunks while she waited for me.

'How was your night? Did you all behave, given I wasn't there to watch those two louts?' she asked, and I giggled as I crossed the room to her side.

'Yes, Bessie, we behaved just fine. You would have been proud,' I replied, leaning forward as she helped me undress. It felt wonderful to slip naked into my nightgown and climb up into my new gigantic bed, snuggling under the heavy covers. 'Goodnight, Bessie. Pleasant dreams and, as I told you earlier, if you still don't feel well, please stay in bed. You never listen to me when you're sick, yet I must do everything you bloody well say. I've been telling you for two days now to stay there till you're recovered, but knock me down and bugger me sideways, you refuse to listen to a word.' She skelped me on the arm before making her way to the door, taking the kerosene lamp in her hand to guide her way. I had already learnt some Australian slang terms and curse words from the farmhands, who were unaware I was listening, thrilling me at all the unfamiliar words I was memorising.

'Goodnight, Mistress. I will see you first thing in the morning, don't you fret about that,' she replied, her jaw set firm. I snuggled deeper into my bed and relaxed. When I finally drifted off to sleep, I dreamed of a koala bear, a knife, and a deck of cards.

Hamish kissed me awake. He had snuck into my room and placed the lamp down on my bedside table without disturbing me, then carefully climbed in beside me. Bessie had gone to bed over an hour ago, still feeling extremely unwell, so I knew she wouldn't bother us tonight. However, I still wasn't confident I had made the right decision in allowing him to sleep beside me, given we were finding it difficult to remain in control and not go too far when alone.

He had always been a gentleman, despite wanting to make love to me. At times, he pressured me; however, once I said no, he always accepted it graciously until the next time.

'Hamish, do you hate me for what I'm doing?' I asked sleepily, opening my eyes slowly and gazing at him. He was such a beautiful man, and I knew his heart better than anyone. He didn't let people get too close; however, he was different when alone with me. He sat up in the bed and stared into my eyes, reaching across to stroke my cheek.

'I felt angry with you, but no, I dinnae blame you,' he said. 'As you explained, you've been betrothed to him your whole life, and I believe you will need some time to get out of it in one piece. So, to answer your question, no, I dinnae hate you. On the contrary, I love you, lass, and always will.'

He slid closer to me, and I could feel the warmth radiating from his body as he gathered me into his arms. I discovered he had taken off all his clothes except for his undergarments. I felt confused; we had an agreement, which he had just broken.

'What are you doing?' I exploded, attempting to break his hold and get out of the bed, but he held on to me, trying to calm me.

'Shh, hush now,' he murmured soothingly, hugging me tightly, my back against his chest. 'I promise you the same arrangement as before. I just wanted to feel closer to you on our last night together until we marry,' he told me gently, and I felt myself relax slightly.

'All right, I believe you, but let go of me.' I pushed him away, shivering, then pulled another blanket over us. As I lay under the quilt, trying to get warm again, I felt him gently caressing my cheek with his fingers. He moved over toward me.

'Abigail, let's enjoy this last night together. We will nae be alone again for who knows how long,' he complained. 'I respect your decision, but it's gettin' more and more difficult to control myself when we're in bed alone. I dinnae mean to upset you, but surely, you must understand why I'm jealous? I come lookin' for you to find you in a passionate embrace with a man who is a stranger to us all. How would you feel if it were me with another lass?' I could see his point. I understood his frustration and pain, feeling like the cruellest person who walked the face of the earth.

'No, I wouldn't like it.' I extinguished the lamp and gazed out the window at the bright moonlight beaming in and illuminating my room with a soft glow. The clear, dark sky, filled with millions of tiny stars that looked like brilliant diamonds glimmering against the black velvet sky.

'Come, get into my arms so I can talk to you.'

I slid towards him and snuggled into him like sugar melts in a simmering jam. He felt so solid in my arms, and I could feel his hard muscles that rippled every time he moved under my fingers. His body felt lovely as I touched his bare skin for the first time, running my hand over his chest and belly. I had never felt the naked body of a man before, and, despite it only being from his waist up, I found him delicious and could feel my own body tingling at his touch.

He pulled me up higher, kissing me deeply. I knew this was wrong, but it felt so difficult to stop doing something that felt so good, and I promised myself it would be the last time. I lay in his arms for what felt like an eternity, listening as he spoke of having a family together.

'I thought you didn't want a family? I mean, I know you have teased me about having children, but you said you would never have them yourself when I met you,' I said, gently kissing his earlobe.

He scoffed softly, 'I dinnae want to father even one bairn before we met, but that changed, and I do now, but only with you. Remember? Eight of them. Four boys and four girls. I just imagine what sturdy sons I would have and the beauty my daughters would inherit from their mother, and I want lots of them. We will marry and establish this property together. I will manage Willow Grove, and you can stay home and look after the children—with a Nanny to help you, of course. You can spend your days socialisin' with your friends, and in the evenin' when the children are in their beds, you can spend your time with me.'

I looked at him in disbelief. I still didn't know when I wanted children, and here he was planning my whole life out in front of me, right down to what I would do during the day and night. It smacked of the controlling attitude of others I'd had to put up with all my life.

'Can we talk about something else?' I pleaded with him, and he gave me a wry grin.

'Aye, Abigail. But I think it's time we made love.'

'What do you mean, make love? You said we would wait, and what if I were to become pregnant?' It shocked me he would even bring the subject up.

'It will nae matter, as we'll marry soon enough when you stop this nonsense with Aaron. Who would notice a few weeks' difference if it happened?' So, he had us married in a few weeks? Well, I was going to need a lot longer than that to make my decision.

'No, Hamish. I said no at the start, and I mean it now.' He took my hands in his and pinned me down to the bed with one arm.

'Well, if I say yes, what choice do you have?' He appeared amused, holding me down with one large hand while tickling me with the other, before rolling back on top of me. I struggled to get out from under him, but couldn't shift his weight. He had both my arms immobilised and my legs restrained by his own and I was helpless.

'Get off me, Hamish. This isn't funny.' I violently struggled against him, gasping to catch my breath.

'I dinnae think it's funny, either, with another man out to claim you. I'm taking this very seriously, believe me.' He obviously thought taking my virginity would ruin me for all others, and it would force me to marry him.

'Hamish, I'm asking you for the last time; get off me and stop this.' I tried to push him off again without success, becoming so frustrated I wanted to scream at him. But he was right—he could do anything to me now, and I couldn't prevent it. I was at his mercy. 'Hamish, please get up. I can't breathe. Let's save it for our wedding night as we promised. I don't want anyone to ruin that for us.' I could see he was struggling with the situation, and it hurt my heart I caused his pain.

'Do you promise?' His torment was clear, but I couldn't promise. He released me and moved to the other side of the bed, turning his back towards me. I turned to embrace him, but he moved further away. I lay in silence, waiting for him to face me again; however, he rigidly remained with his back to me over something I was sorry about, but could not change. I dove in and out of sleep, my body resting, while my mind raced through confused and fragmented dreams I couldn't recall each time I awakened throughout the long, long night, finding no peace or comfort wherever I turned.

Chapter Six

I OPENED MY EYES to find Hamish gone from my bed, the sky still dark. I threw back the quilt and rose to my feet, deciding to visit him at the cottage before breakfast. He and Angus were returning home this morning to allow us to continue preparations for the engagement party being held a week from this coming Saturday. However, I still felt guilty that I couldn't promise Hamish I would stay his, as he expected to be my escort at the party.

Soundlessly, I pulled on my house-dress, then tiptoed downstairs, sneaking through a side door. I could hear the staff crashing about in the kitchen, chatting away cheerily to each other, while none of them noticed me creeping past outside the kitchen windows. I had brought a woollen cloak with me and put it on as soon as I hit the frosty morning air.

I loved this time of the day before everyone had awakened, just before the sun broke through, ready to spread its warmth, glistening down over the paddocks and the sea, sparkles of light dancing on the tips of the water. I opened the door to the cottage and heard nothing, so made my way up to where Hamish was sleeping and quietly opened his door. He was sound asleep on his back, snoring softly, tucked up warmly under the covers. I took off my cloak and crawled in beside him.

'Hello, stranger.' He sleepily opened his eyes, then pulled me close, hugging me tightly to his chest. He appeared to be feeling better, and his mood had improved dramatically. 'I missed you when I left, thinkin' it would be the last time for a while we would be together, or maybe never now, who knows?' Oh, how I wished this would all just go away, and it could be like it was when we were on the ship. I knew he couldn't be right—we would always be together—despite our current situation. That was what I had wanted to say to him, but I couldn't get the words past my throat. I wished I could tell him the truth about everything. I could feel his melancholy, so I remained silent, resting my head on his shoulder as I listened to his breathing, descending into a deep sleep where I didn't have to explain myself to anyone.

We had eaten breakfast and seen Hamish and Angus out to the stables. The boys stood over by their horses, packing the last of their things in their saddlebags. I waited for Hamish to come to me, as I was not going near him while he stood beside that beast. He finished, then strode over to me, while Polly and Angus embraced as if they would never see each other again in this lifetime.

'Abigail, I will be here every day to make sure I dinnae lose you.' His voice was low as he bent down and kissed my cheek. 'I will respect your wishes and be polite to him, although it goes against everythin' I feel right now. I know you love me, and I might not show it much, but I love you too. Madly and passionately. I cannae see any other lass but you. I am blind to them and all their charms. Once we are through this, we can get on with our lives together and forget this ever happened.'

He slipped his arms around my waist, and I embraced him. He kissed me for the longest time, not wanting to let me go when I pulled away for air.

'So, I will see you tomorrow?' I stared up at him and smiled before embracing him for the last time.

'Aye, I will come for lunch.' He gracefully swung up his leg and mounted his horse, grinning down at me as I maintained a safe distance.

The Makenzie farm was only one over from ours, so there had been no need for them to stay overnight, other than Angus and Polly wanting to be with each other every minute of the day—and Hamish wishing to be in my bed every night. I looked up at him, so handsome and strong on top of his mount with his beautiful, brown eyes looking down at me and his black, curly hair tied back off his neck.

As I watched him, I wondered how I could risk losing him over this ridiculous betrothal. But that was what I was doing—risking my future happiness with Hamish over a handsome, peculiar, and oddly compelling stranger. As they headed down the driveway, we waved goodbye, with Polly swooning over Angus, and me feeling lost and confused.

Aaron knocked on the front door, and was soon greeted by Mr Masters, who took his butlering somewhat seriously from what I could see. He showed him into the parlour, then came to fetch me. I made my way there and found him relaxing on a beautifully carved walnut settee with green velvet upholstery that matched the colour of spring grass. He was flicking through the pages of an art book left on the table. His face lit up when he saw me, and his eyes twinkled.

'I'm sorry he put you in here.' I stood in the doorway, indicating for him to stand. 'Come with me to the sitting room, where we like to spend our time, and I will organise afternoon tea. Of course, it's all very formal with the butler and the staff, but Mr McPhee tells me I need this number of people at the very least to keep the main house going.' I sighed as he rose to his feet and crossed the room to my side. 'There was talk of hiring a land steward, house steward, first and second footman, along with the footmen we have, a head nurse, an undercook, a page of tea boy... whatever that is.' I stopped for breath as he chuckled loudly, following me through the wide hallway. 'We already have what they call a head groom in Harry, or often called a stablemaster, I have found out, and he needs a groom, and stableboys, while Sean is the head gardener but requires the help of a groundskeeper, gamekeeper and gatekeeper. I am certain I have forgotten several more positions, but I've no doubt Mr McPhee will remind me. I just have to trust him, even though I don't think he could lie straight in his bed.' Aaron continued to laugh as we rounded a corner, amused at my bluntness.

We stepped into the sitting room, and I let out a deep sigh, settling myself down on a lounge and making myself comfortable while catching my breath. Aaron sat next to me, a little closer than I wanted. He leaned over, took my hand in his, and raised it to his lips, kissing it gently, then my wrist. His lips lingered for a moment too long before he let go of my hand, unlike any gentleman would do. He kept my hand on his lap, intertwined with his, and smiled at me.

'So, how did Hamish treat ya after I took off yesterday?'

'He was fine. He admitted to being jealous,' I told him, feeling I was betraying Hamish's confidence by even discussing him with Aaron.

'The poor bloke has a lot to be jealous about. I'm gunna marry the woman he loves, an' there is nothin' he can do to stop it.' He grinned widely, his smile warm and genuine. He was so damned good looking, with beautifully tanned golden skin from the harsh Australian sun, his long sandy hair with golden streaks like silk, and the body of a Greek God. Mr Masters coughed before he entered, carrying refreshments. He placed them on the large coffee table in front of us. 'The service here is bonza. It's like livin' as royalty in a palace, no different from the fairy stories ya tell the nippers. Are ya the white witch or the wicked one?'

'Leo calls me the Wicked Witch of Willow Grove,' I replied, laughing with him.

We ate our freshly made cream puffs and drank our tea while chatting about his father's fishing boat. He described how he was up in the early hours of the morning, and then, when finished working on the boat, he would now come straight to the house to see me. His family had a small acreage near the ocean backing onto our property, where they raised cows, sheep, and chickens, but their main diet was seafood—not because they had to eat it, but because they all loved it. Mrs Cavanaugh liked to look after her husband and four sons and cook them all their favourite foods and clean up after them, as they were a rowdy bunch who ate like bears. Their house was modest, but it was of an adequate size and built with funds given to them by great-aunt Isabelle, and they had made a decent home of it with all the modern luxuries.

Each morning, Mr Cavanaugh would take his haul to the market and sell it, always bringing the best fish home for dinner to be cooked fresh. Aaron believed he had lived a blessed life so far, and I agreed with him. His parents still loved each other dearly, having met in Donegal, Ireland, when they were still children themselves, and, if he was to be believed, they still carried on with each other the same way. They married young and moved to Scotland to live with his grandmother, where they had met great-aunt Isabelle several years later, who he credited for changing their lives. Now, Aaron's two older brothers, Patrick and Aiden, and a younger brother, Luke, also worked alongside their father. They all had left school at fifteen to work in the fishing industry. That was what they enjoyed doing. It was what they were good at, and no one could see sense in doing something they didn't love.

'So, have ya decided if you're feelin' brave enough to go down to the horses?' he asked, reminding me of my promise. Shit. I had forgotten about that. He looked amused. 'Go an' put on ya plainest dress so ya can have ya first lesson today with me,' he suggested, his sparkling blue eyes scanning my figure as if I were already in a state of undress. I could feel my cheeks becoming hot, forcing me to hurry out of the room before the shade of red on my face was clear for him and the entire world to see.

We met at the stables, and I reluctantly followed him inside, where he led me over to a stall containing a stunning black filly with gentle eyes.

'Will she do ya? She's the calmest girl of 'em all, aren't ya, me sweet darlin'?' he whispered to her. He stroked her head, and she whinnied. He slid open the door to the stall, but I couldn't bring myself to go in. Aaron turned towards me and smiled, reaching out and taking my hand in his and pulling me forward, sending tingles through every part of my body. 'I give ya me solemn oath. I won't let her hurt ya,' he assured me, leading me in very slowly and quietly. He had a rope tied around her head and was stroking her neck, making soothing noises. He moved me to the front of him, encouraging me to reach out and stroke her, knowing he was right behind me should I need him. I raised my hand and touched her warm, wet nose. She chuffed at me while Aaron went to get a carrot, placing it in my hand when he returned moments later. 'Offer this from the flat of ya hand, an' she'll take it without bitin' ya.' I did as he said and could feel the filly's lips as she took it from me gently. When she had finished eating the treat, she nuzzled my belly, making me giggle. Aaron came up behind me and slipped his hands around my waist while I stroked her neck and played with her long, glimmering mane. 'How does it feel now?' he asked, leaning down and kissing the top of my head.

'I don't feel as anxious as I did, but I'm still a little scared. She is very gentle, isn't she?' He looked at me, clearly puzzled, before gazing back at her.

'Ya do know this black beauty is your horse, don't ya? When I came in here before, I asked Harry if he had a gentle horse spare for ya to get to know. He brought her out an' told me she's yours an' ya only have to learn to ride her now. Then he laughed, so I think he has some doubts about ya courage an' pluck.' Harry knew how frightened I was of horses and apparently didn't believe I would ever ride. He had told me you loved them, or you didn't. I could certainly agree with that. I moved forward to scratch her ears, finding she seemed to know what I wanted to do, lowering her head so I could reach.

'I don't know how we are going to get along,' I told her, 'but I will do my best to like you... what's her name?' I stopped, suddenly feeling silly talking to a creature that couldn't talk back. I raised my eyebrows at Aaron inquiringly.

'I forgot to ask.' His face broke into a mischievous grin, which made me smile. 'Maybe you can call her Galloping Girl—or even Bold Racer,' he said with a laugh, showing me a quick wit and he possessed a sense of humour.

'Hilarious.' I stroked her neck again, feeling more confident because of her apparent gentleness. 'I may call her Angel, but I want to be sure.'

'Yeah, nah. Angel suits her, just like her new owner,' he said sweetly, and I smiled.

We left the stall and waited for Harry near his workstation to find out more about her. Aaron sat down in a chair, and I climbed up on a high workbench to rest my weary backside. After chatting for a time, Aaron stood up and approached me. He pushed my legs apart and stood in between the folds of my dress, pulling me into a tight embrace.

'How are ya today, Abi? I haven't asked ya yet,' he enquired, his face inches from mine. I felt incredibly self-conscious and silently wished he wouldn't stand so close to me.

'I'm well,' I said, breathless, his upper body pressing against me. He made my heart race. Sitting up so high on the workbench, I could look directly into his eyes.

'Strewth, Abi. Your words ring empty. Tell me how ya are truthfully? I want ya to talk to me, to at least be willin' an' able to tell me the truth of all that's in your heart,' he said, forcing me to look away. I wondered if I could trust him. He had been nothing but sweet to me and, from what I believed, very honest. I told him how difficult I was finding things, that sorting out my feelings confused me, and I didn't know what to do. He gazed back at me with sympathy, then placed his arms back around my waist. He kissed me on the forehead and ran his fingers down my back slowly, as if memorising the feel and shape of me. 'Look at me, Abi,' he whispered, placing his finger under my chin and forcing me to look him in the eye. 'If this is all too much hard yakka for ya, an' ya wanna be with Hamish, I'll walk away. I'm bein' fair dinkum, Abigail. I don't want to see ya anxious an' hurt 'cause of somethin' I'm insistin' on. If ya tell me no an' give me the flick, ya will never hear of it again from me lips.'

I wished for the hundredth time today Aaron knew the truth about the enormous burden my aunt had placed on my shoulders. If I didn't marry him, we would all be out on the street with nowhere to go. If I married Hamish, I refused to rely on his money and didn't expect him to carry my friends and me financially should I end up penniless. Whichever way I turned, it seemed I would hurt someone.

The problem was, I liked Aaron. I didn't want to, but I could see myself easily falling in love with him if I let myself. He was definitely handsome, but I also found him gentle and kind, with a rougher exterior when other people were around, which didn't surprise me. I had already noticed the trait in Australian men. They were highly masculine and often larrikins, with a unique sense of humour I was still learning to appreciate. Australians spoke differently from the Scottish and Englishmen I learnt only recently. They used slang words I did not understand, like larrikin for a rowdy man, or chook when referring to chickens. They called each other mates and cobbers and slapped each other on the back, rarely shaking hands with their friends.

Though different, Aaron and Hamish were the same in so many ways. I could see myself loving either of them and being happy for the rest of my life. I hated feeling I was being drawn into a web from which I could not untangle myself. To compare them did not differ from comparing two peas in a pod. I got along well with both; I could happily sleep with either of them, and they both had the golden glow. The universe was not making my decision easy.

'No, Aaron, if I'm to be completely honest with you, I like you courting me, and I enjoy your company. So I am giving you the chance you asked me for.'

'Is it workin'?'

'Maybe a little,' I replied, putting my arms around his neck and kissing him passionately.

I heard Harry cough politely as Aaron gently pulled away from me. He smiled as he crossed the room, slapping Aaron on the back.

'How are ya, mate? I forgot to ask the name of Abi's horse,' he said, and Harry smiled again.

'No name at the moment. It's up to the Mistress—and I will keep calling you that despite the eye-rolling, young lady—to choose a name for her.'

I remained where I was on the workbench, Aaron standing between my legs, casually chatting away with Harry. I felt self-conscious and discreetly tried to push him back. Instead, he remained where he was, unmovable as a tree, and continued talking about the horses. Finally, after kissing me on the lips again, he helped me down to the floor and took my hand. We said our goodbyes and walked out the stable door.

'Well, Abi, ya can call her whatever ya like. I can only imagine what ya will choose,' he said as we walked toward the back garden.

'I'm going to think about it for a while. Harry told me horses can live well into their thirties. That is a long commitment.' It had astonished me to learn of their longevity and was reluctant to name anything until I knew I would remain here.

'Yeah, my oath they can. You'll have her a long time, an' ya must be happy with the name. You'll be shoutin' it a hundred times a day. I know how important these things are for women.' He chuckled loudly as we strolled side by side through the immaculate gardens.

'Oh, so you would be happy with just any name for your stallion, such as Daffodil, would you?' I challenged him, and he stopped, his eyes twinkling in amusement.

'Nah, I wouldn't.' He chuckled to himself. 'You've proved ya point. You're smart as a whip, I'll give ya that.' He laughed again before we sat down on a sunlounger together near the swimming pool.

'So, what are your brothers like?' I was curious and nosey all at once, but I didn't care. I leaned against him, relaxing while we talked.

'The spit of me. We all favour our Da, an' the only difference between us is I have a brain in me head, while the three of them don't.' I laughed as he told me of his relationship with his brothers, who were all still single and living at home with their parents. They were a happy family and always had been, with the boys having many friends they had grown up with still to this day. They might not have had university degrees, but all were intelligent and hardworking young men, with their parents' morals and values instilled in them. I could tell by the way he spoke about his family just how much he loved them and how close they all were. He had what I always wanted, what I would have given anything for—a loving family. In comparison, he and Hamish had lived very differently, with dramatically unique experiences in life.

Hamish had come from wealth and knew nothing other than a privileged lifestyle. Aaron was from a working-class background and worked alongside his father on the fishing boat for five-years now. Hamish's parents' marriage was a mess, and he had grown up feeling distant and rejected by them, while Aaron had a close and affectionate family that was still intact. Hamish had attended school and attained a university degree, graduating just before immigrating, while Aaron had left school at fifteen to help his father in the family business.

Hamish had never worked and did not need to, although there was an unspoken expectation he would help run his father's property now, along with Angus. Aaron had to work to earn a living, as he had no money of his own other than what he collected at the end of each week, depending on how good business had been. Since the age of fifteen, Hamish had been a ladies' man and had been with many women, while Aaron had never had a sweetheart.

All his life, Hamish had his every want and need catered to by servants, and thought he was better than everyone else, while Aaron had a warm and caring mother who was present. She attended to him and his brothers, refusing to keep servants herself like so many middle-class families were now doing. Despite his upbringing, Hamish had turned out to be a good man who was still learning and growing with each new experience he had, and I was proud of how open-minded he was becoming. The problem was, Aaron was also a good man whom I liked, and I had developed feelings towards him. It was all too confusing for me to think about, and I pushed it to the back of my mind.

'How do ya like ya new house?' I lay the back of my head on his chest while we enjoyed the sunshine, his hands resting on my stomach.

'It's not really a house, is it? I mean, look at it from here. It's enormous. I could have fifty bairns living here and still have plenty of room. And if they wanted to play hide-and-seek, I'd never find them.'

'I'd like ta have a few ankle biters of me own one day. I expect ya ta give me at least two, preferably four—if ya tiny belly could hold 'em. You're so small.' He gently stroked my stomach as if I were pregnant, making me smile.

'Everyone else can have them, and they are much shorter and smaller than me. I see tiny women with six children trailing along behind them, so if they can, I'm sure I will be able to.' I felt relaxed laying like this with him and talking of things we didn't know about each other, just like Hamish and I still did.

'I would punt me last shillin' on it. Once you're me wife, it'll take no time till you're in the puddin' club and carryin' me babies.' I snorted, bursting into giggles as I sat up.

'Aaron, you're so sure of yourself, aren't you? I've known you a couple of days, and already you think I will give you children. You ask little from a girl you barely know,' I teased, and he chuckled softly.

'Abi, I just know that's the way it will go, an' you will too. It won't take ya as long as ya think to fall in love with me 'cause you're destined to be with me,' he whispered, stroking my hair and arm, sending tingles down my spine. I closed my eyes and relaxed deeper in his arms, letting my body soak up the sunshine as we lay together in silence, dreaming our own dreams.

Polly had eaten with Leo, Bessie, and little Mary in the kitchen, kindly leaving Aaron and me alone in the large dining room. It seemed such a terrible waste having the butler there serving us; the two footmen assisting him. Aaron seemed to enjoy the formality, something he wasn't used to, but I was fed up to the eyeballs with it. I would cringe in embarrassment when thinking back to the six weeks I spent in London with people bowing and scraping to me, then all the rules on the ship we were forced to adhere to just to be accepted by those around us. The last place I wanted to be formal or follow rules was in my own home.

The staff were getting to know each other, and some cheeky per-sonalities were emerging. Maisie, the housekeeper, was already trying to catch Mr Master's eye, to no avail, and the footmen and the housemaids were in love with each other—but with different people. We had finished eating another delicious dinner with crème brûlée for dessert when Aaron stood, took my hand, and led me from the dining room to the sitting room. He sat down and pulled me towards him. As I landed on his lap, he stopped and pushed my hair back from my face, looking serious.

'I dreamed about ya all of last night, Abi,' he whispered, tickling my ear. 'Ya already know I'm the type of bloke who says what comes to mind. There are things I have to tell ya, an' if ya think me mad, so be it, but I would rather tell ya an' have ya close to me than lose the moment an' have the words never spoken.' I looked up to find him staring into my eyes. 'I don't think I have seen eyes of that colour in me life—as green as emeralds. But when ya get upset, they go a deep green like the ocean on a cloudy day. Did ya know that?' he asked, and I shook my head. 'I noticed yesterday when we were kissin' an' Hamish stepped up to have a go, ya eyes changed colour. I notice small things other people don't. Me Ma says I would've made a decent detective, but I'd rather shove me head in the thunderbox.' We lay down on the lounge, and I turned towards him, where he met me halfway and hugged me tightly. 'Whatever ya choose to do, Abi, it'll be the right thing for everyone,' he whispered in my ear as he stroked my hair, 'including me, which me Ma wouldn't be happy about me sayin', but it's true. Ya wouldn't love someone if ya didn't want 'em to be happy.'

'Are you saying you love me?' I asked, taken aback.

'Isn't it obvious? Yeah, I do, an' I know we haven't known each other very long, but I knew as soon as I laid eyes on ya that you were goin' to be me wife. I've never seen a more beautiful woman—an' soon after I came to know the heart ya have—an' it was then I knew I was finished an' ruined for all other lassies,' he replied, smiling sweetly at me. He kissed me gently at first, then with unrestrained passion, and held me close. 'When I'm around ya, I wanna behave like a gentleman. As soon as I touch ya, I can't stop meself an' all me good intentions go down the shitter.' I giggled at him, and he gently pinched my cheek.

'How can you love someone you've only known for a few days?'

'I can't answer that, Abi, 'cause I don't flamin' know, either.' He sat up, smoothing his clean moleskin pants with his large hand before continuing. 'I've never been in love before, so I don't know the way of it all. Me brother, Aiden, tells me ya know you're in love with a sheila when ya wanna spend all ya time with her—an' ya think about her when ya not with her—an' dream of havin' children with her one day. That's what's happenin' to me,' he said sweetly. 'Since I left here yesterday, I can't stop thinkin' about how comfortable it feels in ya arms when ya wrap them around me neck an' hug me close. There are so many things I wanna tell ya, an' I will tell ya, but over time, not now. The only thing I can promise is I will love ya till the sun no longer shines in the sky, an' I will protect ya with me life—if ya let yourself fall in love with me.'

While certainly feeling something—what that was exactly, I was uncertain. I didn't know him well enough to love him, despite his feelings for me; however, I felt a strong connection pulling me towards Aaron and the thought of being unable to stop it frightened me.

'I haven't dismissed you for several reasons.' My voice faltered as I summoned all my courage to continue. 'I must be honest and tell you I'm feeling things I'm not even sure of yet, things that are surprising to me. If this betrothal to you had not happened, Hamish and I would likely be planning our wedding, blissfully unaware things like this could even take place in our day and age. Given I have no kin and my controlling aunt died so long ago, this is the last thing I expected-. I know I am in love with Hamish, yet suddenly I'm having my feelings pulled in two different directions, confusing everything for me. If I love him so much, why do I have doubts since meeting you? And if it's only doubts, I keep telling myself I will get over them, but I don't feel I will. Then I have the problem of wanting to be around you, to talk, laugh and have fun with you. All of this makes me feel bad about myself. I'm cruel and heartless.' I covered my face with my hands in despair as tears stung my eyes and a lump lodged in my throat.

'Fair crack of the whip, Abi. That's just not true. You're a good person who's been shoved into a situation not of ya own makin', an' you are doin' the best ya can. Yeah, ya have feelin's for Hamish, but you're already developin' feelin's for me. Isn't that tellin' ya somethin'?' I stared at him blankly. 'Abi, what I mean is if you an' Hamish were so close an' so deeply in love, it wouldn't have mattered a toss who I was. I could never have broken you apart or caused doubt to creep into ya mind. Ya can't tell me he isn't havin' doubts about ya now we're courtin'.'

'I don't think he is having doubts, but he's worried he is going to lose me.'

'Ya aren't convincin' me he won't lose ya, or ya wouldn't be seein' me like this.' His words hit me no different than if he had punched me in the stomach, but he was right. If I weren't considering this, none of it would be happening. It was getting late. Aaron's eyes were heavy, and he'd yawned more than once. During dinner, I'd asked if he wanted to stay overnight, offering him the cottage. He'd accepted my invitation, citing exhaustion, telling me he would appreciate the extra sleep as he hadn't been getting enough.

'I will walk you to the back door, but then I'm off to find my own bed.' I stood, then held out my hand to help him up, smiling as he reached out and took it, pulling me back down into his lap.

'Let me kiss ya before I go.'

He took my face in his hands, softly placing his lips on mine, then gently explored my mouth with his tongue. I liked how he kissed me; it made me feel loved, safe and cared for, but it also made me feel guilty, deceptive, and chameleon-like. Finally, he let me up, and we walked through the deserted kitchen to the back door. Once there, he embraced me tightly, told me to get a good night's sleep, then he was gone, whistling a tune as he disappeared in the darkness.

I made my way upstairs to bed, preoccupied with Hamish and Aaron, Aaron and Hamish—and how much I cared for them both. As I drifted off to sleep, I dreamed of two newborn lambs, two small puppies, and two teddy bears.

Chapter Seven

AARON WAS ALREADY WAITING for me in the kitchen, sipping coffee at the table alone while the maids bustled around the room. I settled myself down beside him, then kissed him good morning. He smiled, taking my hand in his and caressing my fingers, suggesting we go on a picnic later in the day to the far end of the property. The thought of being out in the fresh air cheered me immediately, and I kissed him again, wrapping my arms around his muscular neck.

I found the way he treated me and how he always spoke to me was gentle and sweet, and I was becoming more attracted to him every day. He demanded nothing, nor pressured me to do anything other than marry him. I thought it admirable and sweet he had waited to meet me before having a sweetheart. He was so confident he would win me in the end, not a lot bothered him, and his cheerful, laid-back attitude was breaking down my defences.

After eating breakfast with Angus, Polly, and Leo in the kitchen, Aaron and I sat drinking coffee while Leo made up a basket full of delicious food for our lunch. He included half a caramel cheesecake and a roasted chicken, among other delightful things making my mouth water as I watched him prepare it all from across the kitchen.

Angus had arrived early this morning to spend the day with Polly—and I'd never seen her so thrilled. During breakfast, Aaron and Angus appeared to get along exceptionally well. Angus was not the type to judge anyone. Despite his twin's anger and resentment towards Aaron, Angus was waiting to see what he was like as a person before deciding either way.

Polly and Angus soon left us to go for a stroll around the property, telling Leo they would be back by lunchtime. They would spend hours talking about their upcoming nuptials and counting down the days. Aaron and I had been whispering about my dislike for Mr McPhee. He slipped his arm around my shoulders and kissed my temple just as Leo returned to the table with the large basket. He sat down and looked at us suspiciously, narrowing his gaze.

'So, what do you dirty birds plan to get up to today? Obviously, you won't be here for lunch, so where will you be? You know the conditions of you coming here, Aaron; I couldn't have been clearer. To date, you haven't taken me for one romantic stroll around the property, so I'm unsure if I will let sugar lips out in your company today. Also, here's another little tip I'll give you for free. I don't like secrets. They drive me insane, like a chicken running around with its head cut off... or chook, as you lot say here. You must keep me updated on all you talk about and do. You seem to forget who her best friend is. Moi.' Aaron chuckled as Leo pulled a face at him.

'Leonardo, I doubt ya would ever let me forget who Abi's best friend is, an' I've no doubt you'll be a big, fat pain in me arse for many years to come. I can only give it a crack an' manage ya as best I can. An' with all the humour I can muster.'

Leo giggled. 'Oh, I wish I was a pain in your arse, Aaron. And I am interested to know more about that crack you are giving away to some lucky person.' I cringed, the urge to stand up and twist his ear overwhelming me, but Aaron didn't flinch.

'You're as cunnin' as a dunny rat twistin' me words like that.' Aaron chuckled to himself. 'I didn't wanna tell ya to ya face, an' was hopin' Abi would do it for me,' he teased before leaning back in his chair, his eyes sparkling in amusement. 'I'm sorry, but I'm in love with someone else. I know you're a pain in many people's backsides, but it's not me place to give ya an attitude adjustment for sayin' it in front of the ladies here. No doubt that'll come from Bessie.' He finished his coffee before asking if I was ready to leave. I emptied my cup, allowing him to pull me to my feet and into his arms right in front of Leo. He placed his lips on mine and kissed me while all the kitchen staff stopped to watch, and I heard someone sigh.

'Aren't you two meant to be off?' Leo snapped, pouring himself a fresh cup of coffee before flicking through the Geelong Advertiser.

'Yeah, we're goin' now. Thanks for brekkie, Leo, an' the basket. Ya blood's worth bottlin'.' Aaron thumped him on the back in thanks, much to Leo's delight. He looked as if he were about to jump up from his seat and kiss Aaron passionately.

'Yes, yes. We all know how brilliant I am. No need to skite about me, Aaron. Have fun, and do not let Abigail get you into trouble. She has a way of doing that,' he warned, wiggling his eyebrows wickedly.

We walked hand in hand out to the stables, and Aaron opened the heavy door for me. I stepped through, heading past the horse stalls to the extensive work area, with him following closely behind. I could feel his eyes on me, even though I couldn't see them. Harry turned around from writing in a logbook on the workbench and greeted us. Aaron thumped him on the back warmly and grinned.

'How are you, Harry?' I asked, unable to take my eyes from him. I had wondered, more times than I could count since arriving, why he had the golden glow, finding myself bewildered and my feelings conflicted. I liked him very much as a person and felt as though I knew him already; however, whatever our connection, it was unlike others I had experienced.

'I'm beaut, thanks, Mistress.' A shy smile touched his lips. 'I've the horse saddled for you. If you give me a second, I'll meet you outside with him.' I could not hide my confusion before he turned and hurried away. Aaron offered me his arm, guiding me back out of the large stable doors. Harry returned shortly after, leading an enormous gelding with flashing, intelligent eyes outside; the leather saddle and bridle gleaming, despite the overcast day. 'There we go. He'll get you where you wanna be without a drama.' Harry handed the reins to Aaron, grinning wide, before saying his goodbyes and returning to work, leaving me standing as far away from the shiny black monster as I could get.

'Do you mean I have to go up on that?'

'Well, ya aren't able to walk that far, an' we can't take a carriage where we're goin', so you've two choices. You can get on the front of the horse, an' I will sit behind ya, or ya can get on the back of the horse with me in front of ya. Which will it be?' he asked, chuckling to himself as I shook my head in disbelief.

'Well, I'm not doing that side-saddle nonsense.' Slowly backing away as I tried to compose myself, my voice failed me for a moment as I shook my head again. My backside hit the wall behind me, startling me. 'I have terrible balance even when my feet are on solid ground, and wouldn't last five seconds if I tried to sit like that. I'll have to ride like a man or not at all.'

'I wouldn't have expected anythin' different from ya, Abi. I can only imagine the scandals you'll cause in this district, but I'm not surprised ya want to do the opposite of what's expected of ya.'

'It's not that at all, Aaron. I am just practical. Who the hell can balance themselves in those strange-looking saddles? I looked at one yesterday, which I suspect belonged to great-aunt Isabelle. I am going to have problems staying on the horse anyway, so I might as well give myself the best chance.' Harry strolled past us, a bucket of grain in his hand, chuckling to himself.

'Lady Delmont rode astride like the blokes, and received a lot of negative attention for it, too, mind you. She was an aristocrat—holdin' an actual title—an' she had social standin' an' all, but never used it or spoke about it when she lived here in Australia. Very humble woman, she was. I kept the side saddles here for her friends who lived here, an' often rode with her. Some were proper ladies, too. An' some weren't.' He threw back his head and howled, his laughter still filling my ears even after he had disappeared from my sight. It sounded to me like my great-aunt was a very sensible woman, one I would have liked to have known.

'I'll lift ya an' then get on behind ya to hold ya there. It's all right, Abi. I promise ya once you're up there for a while, you'll forget all about ya fear.'

I approached the horse, ironically named Black Gypsy, and looked up at him. His back was taller than me and so broad, I didn't know how I was going to get my legs around him. Yet, I couldn't help but notice how beautiful these horses truly were, with their enormous build and gentle natures.

Aaron came from behind and lifted me without warning, and, although my body trembled, he had me on Black Gypsy's back in a split second. I held on for dear life, although the horse was happily munching on some hay and not moving at all. Finally, Aaron swung himself up behind me, took the reins in his hands, and securely slipped one arm around my waist.

'I promise it won't be that bad. But I suppose it depends how bad ya expect it to be,' he said, kicking the gelding into motion and out over the rolling green pastures, making me shriek in terror.

Despite not believing my fear would ease once I was on the beast, Aaron was right. I felt myself relax in his arms the farther we went, and I enjoyed what I saw around me. The property was enormous and, as we rode through the never-ending paddocks, I noticed different animals in each of them. There were small herds of sheep, cattle, and goats, along with the large number of horses that didn't seem to take any notice when we went past and disturbed their private sanctuaries.

I noticed a group of grazing kangaroos that hopped away as we drew closer to them. These marsupials fascinated me, reminding me of the day I had seen them for the first time at the London zoo. Aaron stopped the horse several times to point out a koala bear in a gum tree, with its baby on her back and platypuses in the wide river flowing through the property. Soon I could see the ocean, and I felt elated, tasting salt as I licked my dry lips.

Aaron pulled the horse up atop a cliff overlooking the bright blue sea, swung down, then lifted me off, placing me on my feet before tethering the horse. My backside was completely numb, my legs stiff and sore. It took me a moment to get the feeling back in one leg as I hobbled around, bent over like Sister Magda, who was at least ninety-five-years old and one of my favourites at the orphanage. Aaron took the picnic basket off the saddle and retrieved the blanket, when he looked across and smiled.

I was becoming more accustomed to his strange ways, but at the start, it had disturbed me—I could never understand why you would smile at someone for no reason, but Aaron seemed to have a gift for it. I had noticed anyone he smiled at couldn't help but smile back. To me, it showed Aaron was a good-hearted person, someone who cared about others and, whatever role he ultimately played in my life, I would be happy he was there. Aaron laid out the blanket on a flat, grassy area, and we sat while he unpacked the food.

'So, Aaron, if I were to marry you, tell me—what kind of husband would you be?' I looked out over the ocean, the enormous waves crashing onto the rocks lining the wild coast, many ships meeting their fate in the notorious Bass Strait triangle that separated Victoria from Tasmania. Aaron had told me between 1850 and 1890, 155 vessels were lost, along with hundreds of lives. I crossed myself and said a brief prayer before returning my attention to Aaron.

'I would try to be the husband you deserve, Abi. The husband who kisses ya good mornin' an' won't let ya get out of his bed—who must return home at lunchtime just to see ya. I'd use me body to protect ya an' give me life for ya if required. I'll always respect ya. I would only want to be with you, but then there is a side to me ya might not like,' he told me, a lump lodging in my throat as I waited to hear a dark confession similar to Hamish's. 'I don't like beans, so never make me eat 'em.' He grinned widely, chuckling to himself as I laughed aloud. He was a bit of a larrikin, but also had a sensible head on his shoulders. I had found a kindred spirit, someone who wanted to get the greatest enjoyment out of life, and knew how to have fun. While enjoying the beautiful food, we sat gazing out over the ocean, Aaron pouring me a lemon barley water while taking a small bottle of ale for himself Leo had kindly packed. 'How do you feel about me?' He leaned over and moved my hair from my face with his finger, then touched me on the mouth for a moment.

'All right, I will answer you. Confused. That is the only word I can think of to describe what's going on in my head and my heart.'

'Confused is better than bein' dead set on Hamish, an' that's good enough for me right now.' He took my hand in his, reclining back on the blanket and pulling me down beside him. 'Do ya know the first time I saw ya, I couldn't believe ya were *the* Abigail?' He closed his eyes, inhaling the sea breeze before continuing. 'My Abi. It took all me strength not to react to ya when we were sittin' in the solicitor's office. I found ya to be exquisite an' couldn't believe me luck. When ya gave a gobful to that wacker representin' ya, becomin' so enraged you unleashed all those filthy words, it was then I knew I had found the mother of me children. Once I got to know ya heart, I couldn't help but fall in love with ya an' want ya for meself.' He raised my hand to his lips and kissed it gently. 'This isn't how I expected it to turn out, either. I was raised to honour the arrangement made between our kinfolk, an' I did 'cause I'm a man of me word, but I often worried I might not find ya attractive or like ya as a person when I met ya. I always knew I would try to make it work, but deep down inside me, I felt we wouldn't go through with it if we didn't get along, leavin' us both to get on with our lives. That's possibly why I didn't think too much about it over the years, always knowin' if I didn't like ya, I wouldn't have to marry ya. Now here I am, desperately wantin' somethin' I never thought I would.' I raised my hand and gently caressed his cheek. I was now feeling just as comfortable with Aaron as I was with Hamish, and I had only known Aaron for a few days. He had a way about him that made people instantly relax in his presence, drawing people like magnets to him, meaning to or not. He had drawn me to him with his quiet confidence, kindness, calmness, and unconscious ability to make me feel safe.

I lay still, gazing up at the clouds, while he stroked my hair and told me the names of our future children. He made me laugh and want to hit him simultaneously, behaving no differently than Hamish. When we had packed up, I hung back from Black Gypsy while he attached everything to the saddle. He turned and grabbed me by my waist, then threw me in one swing on top of the horse, taking my breath away. Again, it seemed so high, and I clung tightly to the saddle. I felt him swing up behind me and take control of the horse, closing my eyes as he kicked him forward into a gallop, my screams rising above the roar of the waves crashing along the shore far below.

We rounded the bend in the gravel road, Aaron pulling the horse up short when he noticed Bessie and Polly standing on the back steps, both motioning for me to hurry. They appeared strained, and I wondered if they had another argument, given they both appeared so unhappy. Polly ran through the manicured gardens, slowing halfway to catch her breath.

'Hamish has been here, and he's angry,' she called out as Aaron kicked the horse forward to meet her. 'He arrived not long after you left and waited most of the day and only left in a temper a short time ago. I've never seen him blind-mad before, Abi, and I'm worried he'll hurt someone. He has a look in his eye even Angus has never seen before.'

I cringed, knowing how upset he must be to behave in that way, especially in front of them. It had slipped my mind I invited him for lunch today and then went off with Aaron, and soon I would suffer the consequence of my forgetfulness.

'Oh, for God's sake, calm down. Let me get off this horse first,' I called back, irritated I rarely got any peace from anyone. Aaron landed on his feet before helping me down, and it again took me a moment to straighten up and stand properly. 'Don't worry about Hamish; he is just being silly right now, but he will come back later today. We have already had a long talk, and things were fine between us the last time we were together.' I knew his temper well enough, and thoroughly understood why he was so upset, and I planned to apologise.

'Do ya need me to stay longer, Abi?' Aaron asked kindly, beating his hat on a fencepost before placing it back on his head.

'Abi? You call her Abi?' Polly demanded, placing her hands on her hips, a dangerous glint in her eyes as she stared up at him.

'Yeah, I do. Remind me how that would have anythin' to do with you?' Although a smile touched his lips, it did not reach his eyes.

'Only I can call her Abi. It's been a thing between us for years, so I would like it if you stopped calling her that now,' Polly snapped, her cheeks flushed while her silky black hair hung loose down her back. We stopped in front of the stables, Aaron's horse saddled and tethered to a post. Harry strolled over and greeted us, taking the enormous Martarino before walking the sweaty beast back inside to its stall to be groomed.

'Ya may not like it, Polly, but it's not gunna stop. Ya don't have a monopoly on what I can call people,' he advised her, his voice calm. He took the reins of his horse and gracefully swung up, finding his seat immediately. He leaned down, touching my cheek as I gazed up at him. 'If ya need me, send word. We're not far away. I'll see ya tomorrow, Abi,' he said pointedly, pulling me up into a passionate kiss in front of Polly and Bessie. I heard a loud gasp; however, he didn't seem to notice or care they were staring at us, their eyes wide. He let me slide back to the ground and abruptly rode off down the driveway at a gallop. Polly marched over to my side, her blue eyes reminding me of a glacier.

'What are you doing to Hamish? So it's true what Angus told me? You plan to get rid of Hamish for this idiot? You're letting him kiss you and everything. I'm fair disgusted in you, Abi,' she yelled at me. With that, she turned on her heel and marched inside, stomping through the back door, leaving Bessie and me staring after her in silence. I knew Polly would take this situation as a personal affront and, because of Angus, would stand up for Hamish no matter what, but it hurt knowing she was unwilling to support me no matter what my choices.

Despite my developing feelings for Aaron, I knew I still loved Hamish; however, I was carrying an enormous burden that was taking all my energy. It was taking its toll on me through lack of sleep, nightmares, and constant worry. I would have to see what happened over the next two weeks with them, but I knew I would need longer to make my decision—and that was if I got married at all. I reluctantly returned to the house, Bessie walking silently beside me, stepping into the kitchen to find Leo and enquire what was being cooked in the kitchen, confident he would have something delicious to soothe and distract me.

'So, what are you going to do, pineapple face?' Leo asked as we sat together at the table, drinking coffee he had purchased when we were in Melbourne. I liked mine sweet and creamy while he took his black.

'I don't have a clue. That's why I asked you, but you're no help because you think they're both attractive, and that's all that matters to you. So superficial.' I smiled weakly, and he giggled.

'The fact is, they are. I have seen handsome men in my life, including myself; however, those two are stunning in their own ways. I wouldn't be able to choose between them, so I understand your dilemma. I've had many a man chasing after me and I've found it hard to decide, too.' He made me laugh at how over-confident he was and how oblivious he sounded when speaking so highly of himself. Sighing deeply, I waited for Hamish to return while Leo chatted about all the love affairs he had experienced in his short lifetime. 'I knew the men would be after you from the moment we met. Despite what I think of your looks and level of attractiveness, other men seem to go mad at the sight of you. It's because you are so small and dainty, yet tall with not a bad body—for a woman. Your breasts are impressive, and I'm surprised your little spine can hold you upright. I often expect you to topple forward with the weight of them. Then I just have to look at your enormous feet to understand that, without them to balance you, you would fall flat on your face. Do you think they are the reason you're so clumsy?' I rolled my eyes as I sipped my coffee, our scullery maid, Sally, snickering as she passed by.

'You are pulling my leg, aren't you? My breasts are not that big, and they do not add to my so-called clumsiness, thank you. You are often the reason I trip over or stumble because you throw me around like I'm your personal rag doll. How many times have you pushed me over? I cannot count anymore.' He giggled loudly, reached over, and squeezed one of my breasts with his hand.

'They feel so warm and comforting, like holding a bowl of bread and butter pudding in your hand when it's cooled enough to serve, but warm enough to melt the clotted cream. If I ever had the chance to have boobies, I would ask for mine to be exactly like yours. How do you sleep on your stomach, though? Surely they get in the way?' He studied my chest for a moment before slipping both hands into the top of my dress. He cupped my breasts in his palms before jiggling them up and down just as Hamish walked in. He paused at the door, narrowing his gaze. Leo did not notice him as he continued to fondle my breasts, while Sally stepped into the pantry, her giggles filling the kitchen. I raised my eyebrows at Leo, nodding towards the door before smirking at him. He glanced over his shoulder and jumped, immediately jerking his hands away and placing them back down on the table.

'Hello, Hamish. Are you in a better mood than the one I saw you in earlier when our Abigail abandoned us for that beautiful newcomer?' Hamish glared at him, stepping into the kitchen then making his way to my side before sitting down heavily, his body tense. Leo stood to make him a coffee, leaving us abruptly as he turned his attention to me.

'So, did you have a nice day?' He seemed calm enough, although his shoulders were tense and his anger palpable.

'Yes, I did, thank you. I'm so sorry I forgot you were coming today. Please know I do understand what I'm putting you through, and why you're angry and upset. You are completely justified and I wouldn't blame you if you threw me over for someone else, Hamish. I really wouldn't. If you did this to me, I would run the other way, too.' His face softened, and he took my hand in his.

'I can't do that, Abigail. It's too late now, and I can't turn back or switch off my feelin's like that. We came here expectin' we would be together, and then to find out you're betrothed to someone else is killin' me inside. I hate it, and I hate you spendin' time with him. I know I'm possessive and jealous when it comes to you, but I can't change that, either. Accept me and love me as I am, Abigail, as that won't ever change as long as you are beside me.' He sighed and paused, trying to find the right words. 'I'm not angry with you,' he continued. 'I'm furious about the situation and the position your great-aunt put you in. She must have been a cruel and crafty old woman to manipulate your life like this. I don't understand what she had to gain, and the more I think about it, the less sense it makes to me. Please don't think I'm upset with you.' He slipped his arm around my shoulders and kissed my forehead. Leo placed his coffee in front of him, bowing exaggeratedly before sitting back down. I saw Hamish smile at Leo's foolery, relieved he still had his sense of humour.

'So, Hamish, it's a two-horse race at the moment. I'm very good at predicting these things; however, it could go either way in your current situation. He is just as handsome as you; and charming, and he has a body I could bounce pennies off, especially his derriere. He's already bewitched by our little witch of Willow Grove here. He visits here more often than you. Every single day so far since they met. Why are you glaring at me, Abigail? I'm only telling the truth.' I shook my head in disbelief, wanting to smother him with the nearest pillow.

'Hamish knows the truth, and we don't need to hear your thoughts and opinions on the matter. I thought you said you were making me a fruit trifle for dessert tonight,' I said, attempting to distract him. He smacked his head and immediately stood up, frantically rushing away while muttering to himself.

'I take it he forgot to make the dessert?' Hamish grinned, pulling me into an embrace and kissing me.

'That's why I mentioned it. Otherwise, he would never have left us in peace.' He chuckled, and we sat talking quietly for a few minutes before I excused myself to go to my bedchamber to get ready for dinner. I had been on the back of a pungent horse for hours, and all I wanted was a bath.

Chapter Eight

'MY ADVICE IS TO see who you feel strongly about over the next month and get rid of the other one,' Bessie said, wrapping my wet hair in a towel. I had enjoyed a relaxing bath, the warm water easing my anxieties about Aaron and Hamish, at least for that short period. 'I can see they are in love with you; that's as plain as the nose on your face, but what I don't understand is how they are so different. One is as dark as the other is light, and they look like they would be a good match in a fight. One is serious, the other a court jester, but it's easy to see how much you mean to each of them. If it were me, I don't know what I would do. My head would spin.'

She teasingly pulled a long face, and I attempted to smile—failing miserably. I had poured my heart out to Bessie and told her everything, except for one minor detail—if I didn't marry Aaron, we would lose every single thing we had gained, except for the clothes on our backs—and even then, I was unsure they would let us leave with even that. A condition only myself and Mr McPhee were privy to, and I was still trying to absorb the shock of that alone.

'Have you had word from Danny yet?'

'No, not a whimper,' Bessie replied, her face strained.

'It's only been a few days, Bessie. There is nothing that will keep him away. Give him a week to get settled, wherever he is, and he will be in contact. I'm sure of it.' I sounded more confident than I felt. She brushed my hair, pulling it up on top of my head before securing my curls with a green ribbon. I stood, bent down and hugged her tightly, before straightening up and marching down to dinner, determined to do things my way.

Hamish met me at the bottom of the grand staircase. 'May I speak to you in private, Abigail?'

'Of course.'

He took my hand in his and led me down the wide hallway towards the sitting room, not uttering another word. I sat down in the lounge and waited while he made himself comfortable, staring back at me silently. He appeared unkempt, and I noticed the circles under his eyes, which I had failed to see earlier. I shifted uncomfortably in my seat, the awkward silence hanging heavily over me. I tried to look anywhere but at him, the guilt I carried regarding my association with Aaron becoming unbearable.

'Abigail, do you know what this is doing to me?' he asked softly. 'It's making me insane—literally mad. I can't eat or sleep, and I have no concentration. You need to say no to this betrothal now and get him out of your life—get him out of your life so we can go on with ours. I love you more than I have loved anyone, and I'm not goin' to lose you. I'm not.' His voice broke, and he stopped, placing his head in his hands. It was apparent he'd had more time to think since I went to ready myself for dinner and no doubt had gone to the stables and talked to Harry.

'Hamish, you need to throw me over for your own sake. What I'm doing to you is unforgivable, and I can't ask you to stay with me because of it. You are a good person and deserve better than me, someone who isn't driving you mad and leaving you waiting. I can't do this myself anymore,' I said, bursting into tears. He held me by both shoulders and gazed deeply into my eyes.

'All you have to do is marry me, and it's over.'

'I can't talk about this anymore, Hamish. It's making me physically ill. I'm giving you the chance to walk away from me and start again with someone else. It's your choice if you go, and I do think it would be the best thing for you if we break up. I can't stand this. I am torturing you.' I had no control over my life and was clearly ruining his.

'I refuse to break up with you, Abigail, but I'm askin' you don't see him again,' he pleaded, gazing across at me intently, his large, brown eyes melting my heart. Finally, I sighed, sick of it all.

'I don't want to talk about it, Hamish. Please, can we leave it alone? It's time for dinner now, anyway.' I struggled to my feet, dismissing him with a nod of my head. He rose and took my hand in his, leading me from the room. Our footsteps echoed through the silence as we made our way towards the kitchen, a hall-boy I had never seen before scurrying out of sight as we rounded a corner and continued down the wide hallway. I wanted desperately to say the things in my heart, but could not speak the words anymore, given the lump now lodged in my throat.

We stepped into the kitchen, finding Polly, Angus, and Leo waiting for us at the table. I had insisted Leo eat with us at night. He was my friend first and my chef by default. I had offered him a bedchamber upstairs, which he had gleefully accepted. He had advised me how he felt staying in the staff quarters, with its constant stream of people and noise, was hindering his creative talents and making him moody. I believed his claim to be a furphy, given he was as highly strung as a cat on a hot tin roof, and that was on his good days.

Polly would move to the cottage soon, and I would be alone in the house, but I would not feel lonely with Leo in residence. He was getting along exceptionally well with the cook, Miss Pickering. She would have all the ingredients he required chopped up and prepared, so he could walk in and whip up his masterful gastronomic creations immediately. It gave him a vast amount of time off to annoy me and get up to mischief, much to Bessie's chagrin. He rose and quickly brought the food to the table.

'How was everyone's day?' Polly asked, directing an icy stare in my direction as she sipped her French onion soup from an exquisitely crafted silver spoon.

'I had an interesting day today; I must admit,' Leo sang loudly, briefly rubbing his hands together in delight. 'Being in the kitchen constantly, I get to hear all the drama and debauchery that goes on here and in the district.' He widened his eyes, picking up a piece of toasted bread and setting it on his plate before continuing. 'So far, the housekeeper is in love with the butler, but he won't show her any attention. At the end of every working day, they sit together in his office, drink brandy in secret and talk. They seem to get along, but he treats her all official like he does to us.' He stopped to sip his soup, wiping the corner of his mouth with a linen napkin before placing his spoon down next to his bowl. 'Then we have the footmen, one who has already defiled a housemaid and broken her heart. Now, I don't know who did what to who, but we have a teary maid who cries hysterically every time a footman enters the room and a butler trying to stay one step ahead of the housekeeper as she tries to find herself alone in the same room as him.' Leo raised his eyebrows wickedly as he giggled. He endlessly amused my friends with his colourful way of saying whatever came into his head, but not Polly, who glared at him while Angus and Hamish laughed.

We talked throughout dinner, enjoying the fresh produce collected from our gardens; however, Polly would not speak to me directly. Angus was his usual friendly self, continuing to draw Hamish into the conversation with little success and ensuring he talked to me. After we had finished dessert, I excused Hamish and myself from the table. I knew well if I remained, Polly and I would argue.

'You and I need some time alone to talk,' I said, taking his hand as we stepped into the hallway, leading him through to the bottom of the staircase. 'Not about the situation, which we've talked to death, but about us. Come up to my bedchamber. No one will disturb us there.' He remained silent but dutifully followed me upstairs.

We lay on separate lounges in my room, the air between us thick. Finally, I struggled to my feet and made my way to his side, snuggling down next to him before placing my head on his chest. We lay silently together, engrossed in our own thoughts, before he wrapped his arms around me and played with my hair.

'I'm not giving up, Abigail, and I don't want you to, either. Promise me that, and I won't mention it again.'

'All right, I won't give up on you.' It was nice to be close to him and not have to speak of anything. I could feel how hurt he was, not by anything he said, but by how he avoided my gaze.

'Come on, Abigail. Let's get into bed for a while. I want to be close to you.' I gave him a quick kiss on the lips before gently pulling away and rising to my feet, smoothing my dress as I smiled down at him.

'Let's go back downstairs and join the others instead.' I offered him my hand as he nodded reluctantly and allowed me to help him to his feet, grimacing as he placed his hands on my shoulders and gazed into my eyes.

'I love you more than anything in this world. I will fight for you.' I sighed deeply, sick of hearing the same thing repeatedly when I felt incredibly stuck. Hand in hand, we walked downstairs to join the others.

Bessie stood near the fireplace in the sitting room with Polly, Angus, and Leo, chatting about her day. She still hadn't heard from Danny, but I could see she was no longer fretting as deeply as she had been this morning. She bid us farewell before returning to her duties, her new leather shoes echoing down the hallway as I glanced out the pane glass window. It was dark outside, the full moon hanging low amongst the twinkling stars that seemed far brighter than I remembered them to be in Scotland. Angus and Hamish stood, both pulling on their heavy coats before preparing to head home. I had not offered them a bed for the night at the cottage, mindful Hamish and I were drawn to each other like the tide to the shore, and he would be back sneaking into my bedchamber in the dead of night. Instead, I stood and hugged him, his hand going to my waist before he kissed the top of my head.

'Come tomorrow after five o'clock so we can spend time together,' I suggested, touching his cheek affectionately in farewell. His face darkened; however, he nodded his head and squeezed my hand in acknowledgement before turning and following Angus from the room. In my heart, I truly believed I would marry Hamish. We could build a small cottage somewhere, and he could run his grazing property as he had always planned. I would not be unhappy with the lack of staff and money if I had him beside me. Unfortunately, a seed of doubt had been sown in my mind, and was now blossoming into a plant being nurtured by a gardener named Aaron. I bid Leo and Polly goodnight, Leo calling back farewell while Polly remained silent. I grunted to myself as I hurried from the room and made my way up to my bedchamber. Bessie was waiting to brush my hair and help me change into my nightgown. I seated myself at my dressing table and gazed intently at her reflection in the ornate mirror as she stood behind me.

'Do you think you would marry Danny if he asked you, and would you leave me, Bessie?' I asked curiously, watching closely to see her reaction. Bessie was the only constant in my life among all my current confusion, and I would hate to lose her now. I looked up to her like an older sister and trusted her. She gave me an odd look before running the horsehair brush along my scalp.

'You don't have to worry about me going anywhere, so get that out of your mind. I saw you with the new man today, and it didn't look to me like you've known him for just a few days. Not by the way he lifted you onto that horse and kissed you right in front of Polly and me. I'll be honest and tell you the God's honest truth. What I saw shocked me and now, with Polly being so mad at you, I can't see we'll have any peace in the house while those two boys are around. Tell me what's got into you to even consider such a proposal, Mistress?' Both concern and disapproval dripped from her voice as I flinched.

'If I tell you something in secret, Bessie, will you promise to keep my confidence and tell no one?' My lower lip trembled as she set down the brush on the dressing table.

'Of course,' she replied, her brow furrowed.

'My great-aunt's Will stipulates I must marry Aaron or lose my inheritance, and I have only two weeks to decide.' Tears stung my eyes as I reached for a clean handkerchief.

'Jesus, Mary, and Joseph. That aunt of yours didn't ask for much, did she?' Bessie gasped. She shook her head in disbelief, then patted the back of my head, indicating I was ready for bed. She hugged me tightly as I quickly wiped tears from my eyes. 'I am so sorry, Mistress. It isn't fair that young should be tormented like this. Especially by circumstances you had no involvement in.' I saw tears of sympathy forming in her eyes before she said goodnight and quietly closed the door behind her.

Snuggling under the quilts, I felt a sense of relief at having told someone the truth. At least Bessie didn't hate me and, even though she couldn't help me, at least she now understood I was standing on the edge of a precipice.

My footsteps echoed on the polished wooden floor, the smell of cinnamon and honey wafting through the dimly lit hallway as the sun struggled to rise behind the dark clouds that seemed to have settled on us for the day. I had slept fitfully, despite several dreams that had left me feeling discombobulated. I tightened my brown shawl around my shoulders, grateful Bessie had convinced me to wear it downstairs. It was challenging to stay warm in such a large space, no matter how many fireplaces were lit by the poor hall boy, the son of Sean and Margaret I had found out only a few hours ago. Finally, I rounded a corner and continued towards the kitchen, finding Aaron and Danny deep in conversation just outside the back door.

'What are you two doing here so early, as if I couldn't guess about you, Danny?' I laughed while Danny took off his hat and stepped inside. I embraced him, and he grinned at me before I led them into the kitchen. I ushered them over to the enormous redwood table, inviting them to sit before pouring them a fresh cup of coffee from the silver pot. I glanced across to find Leo singing to himself as he prepared our breakfast, wiggling his backside in rhythm with the music in his head as he whipped the eggs.

'Abigail, I'm here for two reasons,' Danny began, his body relaxing back into the chair as he smiled at me. 'The first is to see me Bessie, but the second is to ask for work. I'm willin' to undertake any job that may be vacant. I'm a hard worker, Abigail, and prepared to do anythin' you ask.'

With his threadbare shirt and tattered coat, he appeared down on his luck and in need of a decent feed. I liked Danny immensely and would happily employ him; however, I didn't know if we had anything available. I hadn't had the time to go around and talk to the foreman, or the workers, to find out if we had enough farmhands.

'Can you give me some time to find out this morning, Danny, and I will tell you as soon as I know?' I really hoped there was something here for him to do, for Bessie's sake alone. He nodded his head, clearly relieved as he reached across and picked up his coffee cup, closing his eyes as he took a long sip. Leo pranced across to the table with a large tray, still singing to himself as he placed their breakfast down in front of them, the aroma of the bacon now stronger than the smell of the porridge he had placed before me. He smirked down at me before patting them both on the head as if they were his pets.

'How are my boys today?' He pulled out a chair, taking a seat between them while I remained silent, concentrating on finishing my sweet, creamy porridge that smelt like Christmas, the brown sugar he had added giving it a flavour I had never tasted. 'We've missed you, Danny, and although Bessie will pretend she didn't even notice your absence, I can tell you she has been a royal pain in our arses, and not in a good way. She has been stomping around here like a koala with a sore head, snapping my own head off every chance she gets. Now you have arrived, peace will be restored for all of us, and I won't have to strangle her in her sleep or poison her with arsenic.' I smothered a smile as I ladled scrambled eggs onto my toast, taking several pieces of crispy bacon before Leo slapped my hand away. 'As for you, Aaron, you're still not in yet. Abigail and I have an exclusive club, much like the Freemasons, and I don't think you'll pass the test to qualify. However, if you go over to the bench and pick up that fork I just dropped but do it slowly, I may consider allowing you a trial membership.'

I glanced across at Aaron, who chuckled as he ate his breakfast, ignoring the fact Leo continued to play with his shaggy blonde hair hanging loose to his shoulders. Danny didn't bat an eye as he tucked into his enormous breakfast. Having shared quarters with Leo on the ship, he was familiar with his flamboyance, and very little surprised him when it came to his friend. Leo had ensured he served a large helping of eggs and bacon to Danny, who appeared tired and hungry and needed some meat on his bones. Although grey and dreary, it was light outside as the drizzle ran down the pane glass window overlooking the back garden. I wondered if he had even slept the night before, given the black circles under his eyes. Leo hurried away to retrieve two jugs of orange juice and one of apple juice, then brought over a fresh pot of coffee, which I poured for everyone. I admired the feast set before us—the bread, toasted and spread with freshly churned butter from our cows, eggs taken straight from under the white hens that roamed the property during the day, smoked bacon hung outside in the smoke shed, mushrooms picked from our woodlands, and tomatoes and onions grown at Willow Grove. I felt blessed to be given this opportunity to live in such a magnificent place, something I never envisioned, no matter how wild my dreams had been for a better life.

'So, what took you so long to get here?' I teased, Danny's eyes lighting up as he drank a full glass of juice without taking a breath.

'Well, Mistress Abigail,' he teased back. 'I set out from Melbourne towards Geelong on the day we arrived. Took me two days to get here, hitchin' rides on any cart that'd take me. I stayed at a boardin' house in Malop Street with some others who've recently immigrated an' are tryin' to establish 'emselves here in beautiful Geelong.' Aaron nodded, grunting to himself as he finished the last of his toast. 'Been lookin' for work for the past four days. I wanted to secure employment before courtin' Bessie, but with no luck. I couldn't wait any longer to see her, so here I am. But I didn't expect to find her livin' in such grandeur, or consider there could be employment, allowin' me to stay on.'

'I'm giving Bessie the day off to spend it with you. Does she even know you're here?' He shook his head, his eyes twinkling as he finished the last of the coffee. 'I'll let you go find her. You're welcome to take horses from the stable and explore the property with her.' I smiled as the sun broke through the dark clouds, the autumn garden appearing to glow a soft gold as the light touched its branches and leaves, the gentle rain easing as the grey sky cleared.

'They should take their tucker with them an' eat out in the fresh air,' Aaron suggested, staring across the table and into my eyes. I averted my gaze, focussing on the kitchen maid, Mary, as she scrubbed down the vast benchtops and stoves with a bucket of hot water, a mixture of vinegar and wash soap cutting through the grease.

'Yes, good idea. I will get the cook to organise a basket if you like,' I offered, thinking Jenny would be glad to arrange this for Bessie, with whom she was becoming close friends.

'Thank you, Abigail. Although it is highly unexpected, it is much appreciated,' Danny replied politely, using his fingers to smooth down his hair after Leo had stepped away from the table. I tried to attract Jenny's attention; however, she stood with her back to me near the pantry, deep in discussion with Sally, who was so timid. Finally, Aaron reached over and took me by the arm.

'Do ya mind orderin' somethin' for us? I'm takin' ya somewhere special this mornin' if you'd like to go?' His face broke into a slow smile. I nodded, remaining silent as I rose to my feet, collecting the dirty dishes on the tray before picking it up, surprised at the weight of it. He stared after me, deep in thought, as I went to order the baskets.

Aaron led the magnificent creature through the stable doors, stopping only a few feet from me. Although I still felt nervous around horses, yesterday had gone a long way toward dispelling most of my fears. Aaron silently placed me on top of Black Gypsy and jumped up behind me before setting off through the lush back paddock. I relaxed into the horse's gait more and more as time went on. Not that I could ride one on my own yet, but this was good enough for now.

Aaron was chatty, acting as if I were the same as usual, although I knew he could sense something was different today. I found it hard being so close to him. I could feel his body heat behind me as he held me tight against him while guiding the stallion with his legs. Finally, we came around a bend to find a magnificent river running through the property. I now knew where the name Willow Grove came from, the willow trees lining the riverbank swaying gently in the soft autumn breeze, their tendrils draped into the water as the current rushed along. I had dreamed of these exact trees; however, I had never seen one before today.

Aaron lifted me from the horse, and I thanked him as he placed me down on my feet. I wondered if the pain in my legs would stop if I rode every day. I muttered to myself as I rubbed my backside gingerly before following him down to the river's edge, where he laid out a blanket. We sat together in silence, watching the crystal clear water run over the polished black rocks. Aaron took out a bottle of wine, uncorking the top with his teeth.

'So, are ya goin' to tell me what's wrong?'

'Why, everything is fine, Aaron.' I smiled brightly at him—too brightly—as he straightened his shoulders and threw his head back before howling with laughter.

'Ahh, they've gotten to ya, haven't they?' He moved closer, taking my hand in his, forcing me to look at him. 'They've made ya feel guilty about Hamish 'cause they all get along with him an' want ya to be with him, but it won't work, Abi. He's not the one for ya. You're too free-spirited for him, an' he'll bog ya down with his conservative shite an' upper-class bullshit. He won't make ya happy.'

He squeezed my hand, leaned back against a thick willow trunk, and played with my fingers. I watched him relaxing, seemingly without a care in the world—even as I was about to break up with him.

'I think we should end this betrothal right now, and you go your way, and I go mine.' It was not what I wanted, but I couldn't have both of them. When I was with Aaron, he captivated me and I barely thought of Hamish. It was the other way around when I was with

Hamish. I enjoyed being with them equally; however, I knew what I was doing was unfair to them both.

'Anythin' else ya would like?' A slow grin spread across his face again, and I shook my head. He grabbed me and pulled me onto his lap, gently placing his arms around me and gazing into my eyes. 'Now, listen to me carefully, Abigail. I know it must be hard with everyone except Leo angry at ya, an' I imagine they're placin' a great deal of pressure on ya now to end it with me. Ya must look inside yourself to find out who ya love, an' that's not gunna happen for ya in a few days. Ya need time with me before ya make ya final decision. I'm sorry it's upsettin' Hamish, but that's not my problem—I'm the one betrothed to ya. I don't like hurtin' anyone, but I'm not gunna go away or chuck it all in an' make it easy for him—not when I could lose someone as beautiful as you. If ya didn't want to be here with me, ya would have asked me to leave this mornin'.'

He kissed me forcefully, taking my breath away. I couldn't help but kiss him back, my fingers entwining in his hair. Damn it all to hell. My feelings continued to vary depending on who I was with, which made me hate myself even more. I realised there was no getting away from him since letting him under my skin. Any argument I had, he would come up with a counter-argument in favour of his case. He was certainly persistent, and I had to give him points for that.

We spent the morning swimming in our undergarments, and I admired his physique, especially when wet. Tall, with broad shoulders and a muscular build from working on his father's fishing boat, his skin tanned a golden brown, he moved with a laid-back swagger that must have drawn the ladies' eyes. His backside was firm and had the most thrilling shape. I joined him on the bank and laid down on the blanket in my corset with my flimsy shift underneath, the thin, white muslin dropping to my knees; however, it had become transparent the moment the water touched it. I hadn't expected to swim with the weather as unpredictable as it was, and the water was frigid. Still, I was grateful my undergarments were slightly thicker and protected most of my modesty. I caught him sneaking glances at me when he thought I wasn't looking, causing my face to flush. If Mr or Mrs Malcolm could see me now, they would have torn strips off me and locked me in my bedchamber for a month.

'The parts of ya body I can see are in fairly good nick.' he teased, chuckling to himself, skipping a rock across the water several times before it disappeared, sinking abruptly to the riverbed six feet below. 'Ya have the longest legs I have ever seen—an' I've seen none up this close. You're the first an' now I've had a taste, I can't stop lookin'.' I felt even more self-conscious and tried to cover myself with my dress. My face felt like it was burning. 'You've no need to be embarrassed, Abi. You're a beautiful woman, even if ya don't realise it yet. Makes ya even more attractive. You're oblivious to what effect ya have on people. You're covered well enough an' not showin' anythin' ya shouldn't, but I can't help wonderin' what ya look like without these uncomfortable-lookin' garments on.' I tried to hit him on the arm as he swiftly blocked me, grabbed my wrist, and pulled me towards him into an embrace. He kissed me passionately, and I couldn't help but kiss him back. I had promised myself I would set him straight today and stop seeing him, but here I was, lying half-naked with him in my undergarments and kissing him as if I would never stop. Of course, if Bessie ever found out, she would smack me on the backside; however, Aaron had reassured me many people swam naked in secluded areas on their properties, so I was respectable in comparison. 'Once we're married, I'll take ya for ya first nuddy swim in the river,' he promised. We lay on the blanket staring up at the clear sky, my head on his shoulder, while the midday sun was warm on my skin. 'Just so we're straight—I haven't let ya throw me over. Ya just need a bit more time before ya realise ya can't possibly be with anyone else but me.' He chuckled, turning his handsome face to kiss me.

We sat on the riverbank for a while longer, having dressed and packed up our picnic luncheon. Aaron spoke of what he wanted to do with his life as I listened intently, attempting to skim a rock over the babbling river without success. He was the only son who wanted to get away from the fishing business and follow his own path, although he had yet to choose that path. I admired his sound sense of purpose and agreed only he could make his life the best it could be. Honesty and integrity were among his strong character traits, which I identified with and admired.

I found him to be far too truthful sometimes, leaving me speechless, but his high moral standards were important to me. Not once had he touched me anywhere that was inappropriate. Instead, he used affection and communication to show he cared—touching my face as we talked, stroking my back as he told me stories of his childhood, playing with my hair while describing our future together. While we slowly made our way home, Aaron let me hold the reins. He wrapped his arms around me and held me tight, making me feel secure, a feeling I appreciated but could rarely maintain.

We arrived back at the stables, and I hurried away to find Harry. He was standing at his workbench; however, he heard me and turned around, his face breaking into a wide grin, the golden glow surrounding his body much brighter today.

'G'afternoon, Mistress. Are you gettin' comfortable with the horses?' I watched a stable boy, his copper-red hair falling over his eyes as he took Black Gypsy's reins from Aaron and led him to a stall. He moved quickly, unsaddling him within moments and brushing his gleaming black coat before offering him a large feed-bag containing grains and nutrients. In passing, Harry had advised me yesterday the mixture was from an ancient recipe from great-aunt Isabelle's family, who bred these horses in England for nearly two-hundred-years.

'Hmm, I wouldn't say I'm comfortable, but I am getting better. I might ride one by myself in ten-years or so.' Harry grinned across at me, continuing to write in his ledger as I moved to his side. I felt my mind again scrambling to remember where I knew him from, causing me to shake my head in confusion.

'What can I help you with?' He straightened up, placed down his quill before turning towards me and raising his eyebrows.

'I wanted to ask you, are there any positions available here at Willow Grove? It's for a friend of my ladies' maid. He is a nice man, and I imagine he would work very hard.' He listened quietly, furrowing his brow before focusing his attention on me.

'Does he know anything about horses? I could do with another groom.'

'Yes, he worked his own farm in Ireland, so I believe he would be good at most anything. I will tell him to speak to you. Thank you, Harry. I appreciate your kindness.' I reached across, taking his hand in mine before shaking it warmly. He appeared flustered for a moment and abruptly withdrew his hand. I had forgotten once again women did not shake hands, and embarrassment washed over me as I turned and hurried away. He called out, my shoes click-clacking on the cobbled floor as I rushed to push the stable door wide.

'Tell him he can start tomorrow. We meet at six in the mornin' in the stable yard. And there's a room available for him at Jim's place down in the village. He's got that terrace to himself so won't mind sharin'.' I nodded, then thanked him and waved goodbye, not looking back, before stepping outside the stables.

I found Aaron near the entrance, readying his horse for the ride home. I stood to one side, watching him put on the saddle, tighten it, and slip the bridle on like he had done it a thousand times before. He noticed me after a time and smiled.

'Come over here before I go.' He guided me to a bale of hay, easing me down onto it before sitting beside me. 'Ya want to be with Hamish, I can see it. An' maybe he is the right one for ya, but I know meself it's a furphy. I reckon ya need some time to consider ya future, an' I promise to be patient. I'll be here every day till ya make ya final decision, an' I give ya me solemn oath to rack off if it's not me.' He reached out his large hand, stroking my cheek with his forefinger.

'Thank you for being so understanding, Aaron.' He gently kissed me goodbye and told me to stay strong and again warned me not to let others force their opinions on me before cantering off into the late afternoon sun.

I arrived back at the house to find Hamish had sent word he would not come today. His father demanded he and Angus have dinner at home this evening to consult with him about family matters. I felt cold and tired; my body refused to return to its normal temperature after swimming for hours in icy water and lying around in wet clothes. I climbed the endless marble stairs to my bedchamber, quickly removed my dress before realising I required Bessie's help. I pulled on a thin rope that hung near my door, satisfied she would see and hear the bell. It fascinated me when we first arrived to find a system that alerted the staff when their help was required by anyone staying in the main house. The large board sat above the kitchen table, a bell fixed to a description of each room alerting them to attend when it chimed, so much easier than chasing people around. The door opened, and Bessie stepped inside, tutting at me and muttering to herself as she removed my corset, hurrying away to find an extra-thick nightgown for me to wear for my nap before dinner.

'Bessie, I found a job for Danny,' I called out as I waited for her to return from my dressing room. She squealed in excitement, my nightgown over her arm as she returned to my side, clapping her hands before embracing me. I told her the few details I knew—he started tomorrow and would share with a farmworker in the village, just over the hill from the main house. I supposed now he could court her properly, and I would have a swooning, starry-eyed maid on my hands until they finally wed; but seeing her so happy brought me great joy.

Not that Polly was any better. She still wasn't speaking to me over my treatment of Hamish, causing tears to sting my eyes each time I thought of her. We had never had a disagreement this serious before, and it hurt me deeply. I would never have turned on her in this way if she were in the same situation. Every time I looked at her, she broke my heart, and I could not understand why she wasn't being a friend to me, especially now when I needed her the most. I closed my eyes, willing sleep to come; my body becoming heavy as I allowed myself to drift off to a place where babies floated amongst the clouds, a celebration surrounded me above the stars, and a woman who looked like me sat on a hilltop watching everything in silence.

Chapter Nine

I GROANED, YAWNING AS I slowly opened my eyes to find Catherine jumping up and down on the feather mattress, calling out for me to wake. Feeling famished from missing dinner and sleeping through the entire night like the dead, my stomach growled loudly as I stretched and yawned again. I glanced across at the clock on the mantle, finding I had overslept. She had sent me no warning of when she would arrive, deciding to turn up on the morning train and surprise me. She stopped jumping and settled herself down beside me. I spent several minutes filling her in on what had occurred since we arrived, avoiding the subject of the conditions around my great-aunt's Will. She remained silent, nodding her head somewhat dismissively. I watched her smooth back her blonde hair, several strands having come loose.

'What, Catherine?'

'Oh, it must be so hard to be you, Abigail. I mean, really? Two handsome men are fighting over you, and you don't know what to do. Choose one, for God's sake, and put everyone, including yourself, out of their misery.' I scowled and turned away, feeling no one understood the seriousness of what was happening to me. She reached out and placed her hand on my shoulder, her tone softening. 'Why don't you just enjoy it and see if you are really in love with either of them? If you are, get married and live happily ever after; if not, go on with your life. You have so much time ahead of you to get married and settle down with the right person. You are still so young and, although it is not unusual for girls to marry at your age, especially in the lower classes, maybe you should enjoy being young while you can. The responsibilities of raising a family are enormous and can be a burden we never expected, nor are we always prepared.' I nodded at her sensible advice, although in my case, it did not quite apply to me. I had limited time to make a decision that would change my life in every way, from the man I married to where I lived. Depending on my choice, we could lose everything, all bar the clothes on our backs. I desperately wanted to take her into my confidence, but I knew I would risk the very thing I was trying so hard not to lose. I needed to make this decision for love alone. Aaron allowed me to be myself and follow my dreams, whereas Hamish made me feel loved and secure. If I could combine them both into one man, he would be perfect. 'William is still studying hard at university,' she continued, 'and he has met a young woman he likes very much, which I suspect is why his temperament has improved. Of course, he won't tell anyone anything about her, which doesn't surprise me, knowing him as I do.' She threw her legs over the side of the bed and struggled to her feet, helping me to mine. 'Beatrice is still not talking, but she is calm enough when Nanny is beside her. She still has a morbid fear of men and screams hysterically when strangers come to the house. She is being home-schooled now because of this and coming along well.'

Catherine had brought all the material for Polly's wedding dress with her in an enormous bag, leaving it on the foot of the bed. I touched the chiffons and silks and imagined how beautiful the gown would be on Polly's petite frame. Underneath the white silk was the fabric for my bridesmaid dress, a glorious, soft-violet colour—that was, if Polly still wanted me in her wedding party, what with the way she was behaving toward me now. Catherine followed me to my dressing room and in no time had me corseted and dressed in a pale blue gown that was far too fancy, my hair pulled back and secured at the nape of my neck.

We made our way downstairs for breakfast, my stomach rumbling, and found Polly in the kitchen. She and Catherine embraced, both over excited about the dress—one to be making it and the other to be wearing it. Leo sat down with us to eat the fluffy pancakes he had whipped up earlier, the sweet smell of sugar, apples, and cinnamon filling the room.

'So, possum ring,' Leo said, glancing sidelong at Polly. 'I see your sister from another mister is still behaving like a stout, colossal mount of ice standing in the way of our happiness. Do you want me to fix her? It'll cost you money, though, and not pennies but pounds. If I get caught hiding the body—and that's highly likely given the size and weight of her—I could swing for it.' I smothered a smile as Polly narrowed her gaze at him, her face slightly flushed.

'I am here in the room and can hear everything you say, Leo, despite you pretending I'm not and I can't. I'm not fat, nor do I resemble an iceberg, thank you. You can bloody well keep that sticky nose of yours out of my business or I'll make sure you're swinging from that yellow gum out the window,' she snapped, turning her attention back to her pancakes. He smirked at me before raising his hand, his palm open, as he held it in her face.

'Icebergs have no ears, and for today I have decided you are indeed a lump of ice, and a fatty at that. I'm not backing down either. Poor Angus. I can feel how frigid you are from here. Brr-brr-brr,' he teased, wrapping his arms around himself, his teeth chattering loudly as he shivered, mocking her.

Polly glared at him, then abruptly rose to her feet, slamming her cutlery on the table. I reached up and placed my hand on her arm before she could stomp away, quietly asking to speak to her in private. She nodded, and I followed her upstairs to her bedchamber. I sat down on the bed and tried to get comfortable, an awkward silence hanging over us. She wouldn't look at me, choosing to sit on the wing-backed chair near the fireplace. I told her of the impossible choice I was facing, and her expression softened before she stood and made her way to my side, taking my hand in hers.

'So, if you marry Hamish, you lose everything? This house, the hotels, the money—everything?' she asked incredulously, looking around at the luxurious furnishings in her room. I nodded.

'I only told you because it was tearing us apart,' I began, my voice faltering. 'I don't want any pressure from this moment to choose one or the other, and you must promise not to tell anyone. Aaron is unaware of any conditions in that bloody Will, except for the betrothal part, and I can't tell Hamish. If I reject him, he'll just think it's about the money and hate me. But I'm basing my choice on love alone, do you understand?'

She leaned down and embraced me, tears in her eyes. 'Oh, Abi. I'm so sorry I didn't trust you and realise there was more to it than your head being turned by another man.' She quickly sat down beside me on the bed, the quilt almost matching my dress. 'I don't envy you, although I have to say it—and once I do, I'll not bring it up again—Hamish is the one who loves you and will be there for you through everything. He has already proven how dedicated he is to you by staying around despite what you're putting him through.' I gazed out of her window, looking out over the tiled swimming pool, the water shimmering as the early morning sun warmed the chilly night air.

'I know, Polly, but you have to let me do this on my own without trying to decide for me.'

'All right, I will support you and whomever you choose, even though I want it to be Hamish. I am here for you, Abi.' For the longest time, we held each other, and I knew I had my friend—my sister—back.

As expected, I met with Mr Masters in his office. Once settled in my chair, he discussed the staff and how they had adjusted to their new roles over the last week. He advised me most had settled in well and were pulling their weight while completing their tasks early or on time; therefore, he believed he was running a very efficient household. However, there was some concern about the housemaids having their bedchambers next to each other. They were prone to jealous fights over a footman, although this seemed to have calmed down in recent days.

Given I had provided consent, the pub down by the workers' homes was again under construction. Depending on how that went, I suggested we build a small general store beside it to save everyone travelling into Geelong for necessities. I also considered building a large dining hall for the workers as they took their meals in the staff quarters, and it was becoming extremely crowded.

Having these facilities in their small village would create a sense of community and somewhere to unwind and socialise after a hard day's work. Mr Masters believed it to be a good idea and said several farm workers' wives may be interested in running the shop—at least those who did not have children and had spare time during the day. Also, given Jenny Pickering was such an excellent cook and could prepare food for large groups of people without breaking a sweat, she would be the perfect choice to run the dining hall as head cook, leaving Leo to concentrate on the main house.

Danny, from all accounts, enjoyed working in the stables and had told me himself how pleased he was with his accommodation. Bessie was more than pleased he was pleased, leaving me pleased she was pleased. She wandered around in a daydream with a smile on her lips, always making me smile at how joyful she'd become. Since Danny's arrival, she rarely harangued me about anything regarding my behaviour. It delighted me she was blissful. Meeting a man was not something that had been in her plans when she set sail all those months ago. I had explained to her this morning that Catherine would stay as my guest for an indefinite time, as I needed help to organise Polly's wedding breakfast. She had nodded silently and floated out of the room.

Mr Masters and I had discussed the preparations for the engagement party and the wedding. Polly and Angus planned to marry in the Catholic Church in Geelong and hold the wedding breakfast in the ballroom of the main house here at Willow Grove. They expected around two hundred guests once his parents invited all their friends and people they wanted to impress. Angus and Polly couldn't have cared less if they married barefoot on the street—but they wanted to make sure everyone gave their blessing, and this meant pleasing the Makenzie family.

The engagement party was less than a week away, and the wedding two weeks after that, and we still had much to do. Leo was creating the menu for the eight-course meal the footmen would serve with the maids' help. I had never been to a large party before and thought I would find it interesting, but I found the entire process nerve-wracking. I had the additional worry that if something went wrong, it would be on my head.

Mr Masters had assured me everything was well in hand, although he disagreed with maids serving the meal, as that was the footmen's role; however, we didn't have enough staff if the women didn't help. I didn't give a damn if that was not the socially acceptable thing to do. We had to be practical. Why, I would even serve the food myself if need be, not caring what anyone thought about how I ran my house.

Mr Masters had made his feelings clear on the matter; however, I was not budging an inch. He believed I should listen to him and take his advice, given it was the first social function I would hold, a momentous event where I would meet my new neighbours, and he wanted me to make a decent first impression, bless his conservative black socks.

'I will meet with you tomorrow regarding the wedding breakfast. First, I must finalise the menu with that peculiar cook of yours. We do not have enough servants at Willow Grove, but I believe that will change as word spreads of the working conditions here. I expect those fortunate enough to secure a position under your employ to work hard. Including the cook.' He nodded before rising to his feet, his black pants and jacket immaculate, his crisp white shirt without a wrinkle, and his black cravat knotted neatly around his neck.

'Are you saying Leo doesn't work hard?' He shook his head, concern in his eyes as he stared down at me, the small log on the fireplace crackling as the flame touched the sap.

'Not at all, Mistress. I am aware he prepares your meals to the highest standard and is always on time. It's what he does before and after his working day, and the quiet time in between preparing those meals.' He raised his eyebrows before making his way to the door, turning back to stare at me for the longest time.

'I take it that whatever he is doing, you don't approve?'

'I do not believe anyone would approve of a grown man calling a child unfortunate looking; and in the presence of said child's mother.' He cleared his throat before continuing. 'Your cook advised Sean and Margaret their youngest boy resembles a leprechaun—an ugly one at that.' He shook his head, his cheeks flushing as he loosened his cravat, then discreetly wiped the sweat from his brow. 'The poor boy was present when your cook demanded they take him back to Ireland on the next ship before the kangaroos on the property ate him. As a result, the child now has a morbid fear of going outside.' He sighed deeply before bidding me farewell, loud laughter erupting from my lips the moment he closed the door behind him.

I closed my eyes, sinking deeper into my comfortable armchair as I continued to laugh. It was always a relief when my time with the butler was over. I detested meeting formally with any of the workers here, and then being expected to tell them what to do was uncomfortable for all involved. In fact, I found the entire situation extremely difficult. I believed everyone needed to do what made them happy, to follow a path only for them that brought joy and satisfaction of a life well lived. It could not possibly satisfy them having to tolerate someone like me ordering them about. Or having to bow and scrape to a fifteen-year-old who didn't have a clue in the world. I knew I would find no satisfaction in it myself, and doubted very much they did, either.

My worst nightmare had come to fruition. Hamish and Aaron arrived at my house that afternoon within half an hour of each other. I was in the sitting room drinking lemonade with Hamish, enthralled as I listened to the latest gossip about his father, when Aaron burst in unannounced. They shook hands without enthusiasm before Hamish made himself comfortable again in the lounge, coldly staring across at Aaron. He appeared upset; however, he did everything in his power to hide his emotions as Aaron leaned back in an upholstered chair, looking unperturbed. They talked of neutral topics for a time, the football and the profit earned from a sheep's back, appearing to agree on many issues. They seemed to get along on the surface—as long as I didn't move close to either of them.

'I hear you've been runnin' ya mouth around the district—tellin' any sod who'll give ya an ear—you an' Abi will wed in the summer. Do ya really believe that yourself, Hamish?' Aaron challenged him, a glint in his eye I did not recognise. I had not known him long enough to read his emotions; however, I was more than aware he spoke his mind, and I would not have to wait long.

'Aye, I do, Aaron. You don't frighten or intimidate me in the slightest. The difference between you and me is Abigail loves me.' Hamish straightened his broad shoulders before leaning forward and picking up his crystal glass, taking a large sip of his cordial. Leo would painstakingly pick only the most succulent balls of sourness from our orchard to make a thick lemon cordial while also using them to make the most divine lemon barley water. My great-aunt had planted the impressive orchard, mostly with her own hands from what Sean had told me, and it was one of my favourite places on the property. There were citruses I had never tasted before arriving at Willow Grove, with many of the fruit and nut trees I had wandered past being foreign to me; although their fruits were thoroughly enjoyed by all who lived here.

'Abi will realise soon enough she's no more in love with ya than she is with that vase on the mantelpiece. Trust me—it's empty an' hollow an' won't survive a little rough an' tumble.' Aaron forced a smile, his voice cold and void of emotion, while Hamish clenched his hands into fists beside him.

'Stop it, both of you! This situation is far too difficult to cope with for all of us. I'm putting an end to it. I don't want to see either of you anymore. Leave now, the both of you!' I stood in front of them, both silent, as I furiously pointed my finger at the door. Leo stumbled into the room, his eyes wide when he realised I was the source of the ruckus, immediately deciding to sit down to watch and listen, his panic subsiding as a look of fascination settled on him. They were both confusing and exhausting me, and I needed time to be on my own and think. I watched as Aaron rose to his feet, followed by Hamish as they silently glared at the other before stepping out into the hallway, nudging and pushing each other. They muttered insults as they moved down the long hallway towards the front door. I followed them out, Leo skipping along behind while clapping his hands, delighted in the shifting events and dramas of my life, giggling in delight as they shoved each other like eight-year-old street urchins. 'I'm sorry, but I can't do this anymore. Everyone here wants to be happy, and none of us are,' I shouted before yanking open the enormous front door. Neither had taken me seriously until this moment, and it was apparent the force of my anger surprised both men; however, neither uttered a word to me as they shoved each other out the front door. I left them on the front steps exchanging insults and slammed the door, muttering to myself as I made my way back to the kitchen that if I didn't see another man in my lifetime, it would be too soon. Leo did not count.

I felt exhausted both physically and mentally as I readied myself for bed, slipping into my nightgown. Sitting on the soft, feathered mattress, the corner of an envelope sticking out of my bag on the floor caught my eye. I immediately recalled the letter addressed to me Mr McPhee had handed over that first day in his office, sealed with a big blob of red wax. Bending down to look closer, I found the paper was old and of good quality. I sat back on the bed, breaking the seal and noting a strong odour seeping from the envelope, a mixture of vanilla and mint, a scent familiar but unrecognisable. Inside were two sheets of paper. One a letter, the other a drawing. I unfolded the letter first, my stomach in knots, then began to read.

Dear Abigail,

I hope this finds you settled in your new home, which has been years in the planning. I have included a document with this correspondence to show you where the underground cellar is located. They built the lower level years before they began construction on the main house. All my homes and that of my ancestors had this feature, and it is one that always made me feel secure and safe when I had no right to be.

I have left certain items for you down there to help you understand I want what's best for you, and have tried to nudge you in a direction where you will find security and safety, along with a life filled with joy and contentment. I know you could not possibly understand my motives; however, I only have your welfare and happiness at heart, and in this situation, I do know best.

My responsibility as your aunt was to ensure you were raised well, with morals and values instilled in you under circumstances that were not always easy. I hoped to build your character and prepare you for the wealth you are to inherit, confident dear Marigold would care for you. You would know her as Sister Mary Josephine, a lass I consider one of my own, my braw ruadh. I do hope you were indeed well loved by her, at the very least. That was at the forefront of my mind when I placed you there.

Willow Grove is dear to my heart, holding many wonderful memories I take with me. The property came into my hands soon after Geelong town was first invaded by the white fellas, as my dear Wathaurung friends would say. Although most of the extravagant buildings will have only sat on the soil of Willow Grove for two decades once you arrive and call the place home, my heart belonged to that land far earlier. I spent a great deal of time there in the three decades before you were born, only building most of the permanent structures in the latter years—but do not assume the land was empty. It would be arrogant. There was a thriving community of wanderers who called the place home, although I'm sure very little evidence remains of the humpies and lean-to's that once dotted that beautiful land. It's a special place for many people, and I pass it on to you with all my love and hope you find the happiness I experienced when I lived there. Be wise, my dear girl. Think of yourself and your future.

I know young Aaron will love you well, even though I only knew him as a four-year-old lad. I cannot tell you why, or even how I know this; however, please trust me. The Cavanaugh family are good people and will embrace you like no other. I imagine this is something you would crave, being here alone in Australia with everything being brand new. My dear friend Gavin Cavanaugh will treat you as his own daughter; that I know for certain. Choose well, Abigail. You will have an extraordinary life as my heir; however, an uncertain future if you walk away from all so generously left to you, most the reward from my own hard work and suffering.

I pray I have not been too hard on you, or my requests are more than you can bear: and as I write this, hope with all my heart as you get used to the idea, the more comfortable you will become with the life I wish for you.

Take care, my sweet girl, and enjoy each day—every moment of the glorious life you now live. Never forget to help those in need and live every minute as if it were your last.

'Life is mostly froth and bubble; Two things stand like stone; Kindness in another's trouble, courage in your own.'–Adam Lindsay Gordon (Australian poet, horseman, police officer and politician—and a very dear friend of mine).

Sincerely and with love,

Isabelle

Post-scriptum: The existence of the cellar has always been closely guarded, known as a fact by only a few outside of the men who built it. They signed contracts agreeing to disclose no information regarding their time at Willow Grove. I filed these documents with Mr McPhee for your records, who I hope is far more charming to you than he was me.

Post-scriptum-scriptum: You can trust Harry and Sean with your life; of this, I give you my word.

Overwhelmed with curiosity, I slipped on my soft woollen dressing gown, took the drawing and oil lamp in hand, and made my way down to what was now considered my office. Stepping inside, I placed the lamp on the solid oak desk and gazed up at the bookshelves filled with old tomes I was yet to read, then back down at the drawing on the crisp paper in my hand.

Slowly making my way over to the elaborate fireplace, I admired the well-worn leather armchair I assumed had belonged to my great-aunt placed comfortably in the room's corner. Bending down, I ran my fingers down the side of the brickwork until I found a small space with a tiny leaver inside. I fumbled several times before I felt something move and heard a click, and the fireplace swung away from the wall, exposing a door. My hands trembled slightly as I pushed the fireplace wall back further to find stairs leading down into darkness. Returning to the desk to collect the lamp, I held it high as I picked up the small broom the scullery maid used to collect the ashes from the hearth and brushed away years of cobwebs.

Extending my arm further to light the way, I stepped inside and found myself at the top of a wide staircase. Turning to close this secret door behind me, I began my descent, my heart racing as the shadows played tricks on me. The stairs, made from the same marble used throughout the mansion, direly needed a clean but were otherwise magnificent, reflecting the quality of the materials sourced to build this English castle on Australian soil. I stepped down into a wide hallway, observing the cellar to my right, as my great-aunt had apparently so humbly referred to it. Slowly moving forward, I gasped when I realised this hidden underground space extended the full width and length of the mansion above it; however, I had not a clue of its purpose, or what I would find.

I had only been aware up until now of the small cellar underneath the staff quarters, easily accessed through a door in the kitchen with wooden stairs leading down to the large room below; the walls lined with wood without a scrap of marble to be seen. The kitchen staff used the cellar to store preserves, root vegetables, and wine. In contrast, this underground space was not a cellar at all; the walls were perfectly plastered and painted white, while expensive rugs covered the floors. I found boxes and furniture covered in sheets piled up to the ceiling in many of the rooms I entered, while others held only a handful of items.

Continuing down the hallway, I stopped several times to look in rooms that held furniture from another time. I wandered through the rooms, fascinated by many of the items stored here, before stopping in front of a door with a key in the lock. Reaching out, I unlocked it, then turned the doorknob, stepping inside what appeared to be a vault. I held my lamp high, my eyes widening as I gasped in disbelief. My legs gave way and, without a thought for my clean dressing gown, I flopped onto the dusty floor, unable to breathe.

Once I calmed myself and looked closer, I realised there were hundreds of tightly bound bundles of money, from one-pound to ten-pound notes, stacked neatly on top of each other. Were these the proceeds of a robbery? I had heard of dangerous men called bushrangers that roamed the Australian countryside, stealing anything of value from innocent people, occasionally striking it lucky and intercepting carriages carrying tens of thousands of pounds of gold. I could not make sense of it, nor could I understand why anyone would keep this amount of money outside of a bank, leaving me convinced this was indeed the proceeds of some terrible crime. Wondering if someone unrelated to my aunt had squatted here undetected, given the house had been empty until recently, I held my lamp higher and studied the room again more thoroughly. I considered summoning the others to show them what I had found, but soon decided to keep this to myself for a day or two.

Calmer, I stepped back into the hallway, pulling the door closed behind me, then locked it with a trembling hand before tucking the key away safely in the pocket of my dressing gown. I explored many other rooms, realising a small village could easily live under the house and the residents above would be none the wiser. Stumbling across a stack of old leather-bound diaries that had belonged to an Izzy Howard, Isabelle Delmont, and Lady Isabelle Howard, I assumed my aunt was the author of all three; however, there were many, many more. Several belonged to a woman named Janet, a couple more to another called Katie, and dozens penned by an Abigail Sinclair among them. Someone had carefully packed away many more personal items, the boxes now covered in a thick layer of dust. I made a mental note to go through those diaries; however, I didn't have the time or inclination to sit down and read my aunt's private thoughts—or those of her friends whose journals and personal records and documents had somehow found their way into her safekeeping. I wondered, though, if it was really her who had placed everything down here, as there had been no mention of the money. Considering she seemed to control me from the grave and clearly wanted me to marry Aaron, providing me with a way out of this mess made little sense. None of it made sense.

I made my way up the stairs, closed the fireplace, and went back to bed, thinking hard about what I had discovered. That vault was built for a reason—one my aunt seemed to have no desire to share with me. Finding it could solve my problem, and I wouldn't have to marry anyone if I so chose. No one else knew the money was in there, to my knowledge, and there was nothing preventing me from taking a little with me to start again away from Willow Grove and those dictating the direction of my future. I hadn't counted it, but there had to be thousands upon thousands of pounds sitting in that room, and I felt at peace for the first time for as long as I could remember. Now, I could do what was best for me and everyone else. I drifted off to sleep within minutes, dreaming of a small cottage, a warm fireplace, and a place called Van Diemen's Land.

Over the next two days, Hamish and Aaron both called at Willow Grove, attempting to visit and talk with me; however, I refused to see either of them, and Mr Masters had politely turned them away. Instead, I concentrated on organising Angus and Polly's engagement party. Catherine had fitted us both and was making the dresses. Polly's gown was turning into a beautiful creation before my eyes. I wished I had her talent; I could not imagine designing a simple cushion cover, let alone an elaborate dress.

Catherine chatted away about several of her wealthy new clients and how, at first, they came to her because she charged a third of what her father demanded. Now they came as a preference. Determined to open her dress shop in two-years, when she had built up a solid and loyal clientele. I was proud. Unfortunately, Catherine did not meet many eligible men other than those her parents attempted to marry her off to, with no success to date.

'I might move down to Geelong and open my shop here when I'm ready.' Catherine smiled self consciously, watching for my reaction as she hemmed the skirt of my dress. The fireplace crackled and glowed in the parlour as it warmed the large room, a room we had very little use for other than when we did not wish to be disturbed.

'If you were nearby, it would be the best thing that could ever happen,' I replied, excitement welling up in me. She was such a sweet girl and so very special to me. She showed her kindness by doing thoughtful and extraordinary things for people, much like making Polly's wedding dress. Not quite finished, Catherine worked on it day and night since her arrival, and Polly looked more beautiful each time she tried on her gown.

'Well, that's enough for now,' Catherine mumbled, several pins held between her lips. Polly was fidgeting, and although Catherine had tried to be cheerful and entertaining, her boredom was obvious.

She impatiently waited for Angus to arrive, and had driven us mad, asking for the time when only moments had passed. Expected at the church in Geelong to meet with the priest, and time was ticking away. We helped each other dress, all the while talking and laughing about the things that could go wrong on their special day.

'Are we ready to leave?' Polly asked, appearing panicked. We stood outside the grand entrance waiting for Harry to bring the carriage around. We planned to attend our first mass in town, and had carefully dressed in our Sunday best, as Dana liked to call our fanciest gowns. I had given the staff the day off to come with us if they so chose, but many attended churches of different denominations nearby.

'Would we be standing here like a shag on a rock if we weren't?' Leo teased her as the carriage stopped beside him. He opened the door and jumped up, Polly and Catherine climbing in behind him with Harry's assistance. I rolled my eyes as Bessie and I followed, seating myself next to the large, open window. The carriage was not new; however, it was in pristine condition, requiring four horses harnessed tightly to move it. Spacious and far more comfortable compared to many I had seen, the purple velvet seats matched the curtains and carpeting on the floor, the dark, shiny wood trim complementing the majestic black horses that pulled it along. I stared out across the paddocks as the others chatted between themselves, closing my eyes as the rocking of the carriage calmed my frayed nerves, allowing me to drift off into a troubled sleep where demons and angels terrorised my dreams.

I stepped inside the imposing bluestone church, anointing myself with holy water, before taking my seat in a long pew with the others. Gazing around at the sacred décor, I let out a deep breath I hadn't realised I was holding, as I so often did. The interior reminded me of the chapel at the orphanage, although this was far grander. I found Mass comforting; it made me feel closer to Sister Josephine, even though an ocean separated us. She still thought of me and prayed for me every day, of that I was certain, although it would be weeks before I expected to receive word from her. Finding time only yesterday, I mailed the letters I had penned on the ship, along with others I had written since, given we had only been in our new home less than two weeks and I had been so busy. I noticed several members of the congregation glancing at us, then whispering between themselves, some covering their mouths with their hands, attempting to be discreet, but failing miserably.

'Do you think the roof will fall in? Bessie and Polly are in here, and we know how they're Lucifer's imps in human form,' Leo whispered, a maleficent smirk of his own touching his lips.

'Don't make me laugh in church. Sister would say it's blasphemous.' I smothered a smile as Bessie's head spun towards us. Her gaze narrowed, and she shook her head in irritation before reaching over and delivering a stinging slap to my hand. She swiftly repeated the same on Leo's leg before reaching up and pinching him hard on the face, rocking his head side to side several times. He gasped under his breath as fear filled his eyes, Bessie pinching him one last time for good measure before letting him go and turning back to face the priest, demurely clasping her hands in her lap as though nothing had happened.

'Ow. Did you just see what your revolting hatchet maid just did to me, Abigail?' Leo whispered loudly, his hand gently touching the purple mark on his face. 'Bloody Sunday Christian. She does not even have the decency to be that, assaulting me on a religious holiday and right in front of a priest—who is like a wizard, by the way, and has the power to strike her down where she sits. You can only do that if you have a direct connection to God, which we unfortunately do not have, or I would do it myself. Bessie definitely has it, but she belongs to the other side. You know? Burning flames and brimstones?' I remained silent, attempting to concentrate on the priest as he led the congregation through the Lord's Prayer. 'I'm not like the other men in her life. I will smack her hard across the face with my famous slap if she touches me again. She won't know what hit her. Keep the violent hag away from me, or I will chase her from this church and tackle her to the ground like they do in that game called football here in Australia. I do not understand the rules—and I have seen nothing like it before—but I do so admire the boys' uniforms. Just know I could easily jump on Bessie full-force like that without a drop of guilt and knock her flat on her back.'

I could barely contain the laughter that threatened to erupt, placing my hand over my mouth until Bessie turned her attention back to us. We immediately shut up and stopped looking at each other, both fearful of her wrath.

Once Mass was over, I greeted the priest, Father Sebastian Mc-Cleary, at the door and introduced myself and the others to him. He seemed like a decent man who seemed genuinely pleased to meet us, his grey hair cut short, while his blue eyes sparkled. He chatted to Polly and Angus for several long minutes before he realised other parishioners wanted his attention.

'Have you met Mr George Bradley and his wife, Regina? They live near your own property and only married a month ago.' Father McCleary turned to introduce us to a young couple, along with several other parishioners who hurried away without even a goodbye. I smiled at Mr and Mrs Bradley before shaking hands with them both, ashamed some in this wonderful community we had so recently joined considered the natives, as so many referred to the original inhabitants of this country, less than themselves—and appeared even more horrified a white woman had married one.

I caught movement out of the corner of my eye over by the carriage. Harry sat unmoving on the box seat in front, reading the paper while waiting for us, while Hamish covertly opened the carriage door and quickly climbed inside, closing the door behind him as fast as he had opened it. I wanted to spend time with Catherine and Polly and not think about him or Aaron. That was the problem; thoughts of both of them constantly filled my mind, and I knew I had to stop. We had only been in Geelong for such a short time, and I had several important matters that required my attention. Now I was becoming accustomed to the role they had forced me to play at Willow Grove, I felt some responsibility to those who lived there. I sighed as we approached the carriage, noting Hamish's horse tethered securely to the back.

'Hamish is inside,' I advised them quietly.

'How in hell did that silverback sneak into such a small carriage?' Leo called out loudly, stopping beside the carriage and waiting for Harry to climb down and open the door. 'I like his determination, though. He's stoic. In my book, that's another point for Hamish.'

'I told you that your points don't count. The way I'm feeling, I would rather marry you than either of them,' I snapped, my face becoming hot. Leo clapped his hands, jumping up and down on the spot as I began climbing into the carriage. He reached out and placed his hands on my buttocks, shoving me forward. I stretched out my arms, preventing myself from landing on my face at Hamish's feet, while quickly regaining my balance before taking a seat opposite him.

'What are you doing here, Hamish?' I tried to make myself comfortable while the others filed in behind me and found their seats.

'You won't see me, so I followed you. I need to talk to you, Abigail.' I looked away, staring out of the window at the passing properties while remaining silent for the rest of the journey, contemplating my response. Now I had found that money, I was free to marry him if I wanted, but something was holding me back. I knew some of that was because of Aaron, but some of it was not. They were both obviously going to continue trying to see me—regardless of whether I liked it or consented. I would have to manage until I knew what I wanted—or if I wanted to be with either of them at all.

I silently climbed the stairs that led to my bedchamber to change into something more comfortable than my church dress, finding Hamish waiting at my door. I hurried past him, ignoring his presence as I stepped inside before he followed me in, closing the door behind him.

'Abigail, please don't shut me out. I just need to be close to you. I will do anything you want me to if you'd just let me see you again.' I sat down heavily on the lilac quilt, sighing as I placed my head in my hands. He appeared sad and distressed, black shadows under his eyes that were not there before.

'Let's go downstairs and talk for a bit before you go. I have a lot to do with Polly and Catherine, so I'm fairly busy today.'

'No, Abigail. I want to talk here and now,' he roared, causing me to jump. I looked across at him standing by the window, startled he would use that tone with me; however, I felt more defeated with each passing day, and nothing would surprise me given the situation affecting us all. I did not want to talk, nor was I in the mood to be yelled at. All I wanted was for him to leave, but I was well aware ignoring the situation was far from helpful.

'I will let you see me three times a week, and we can start again from there, Hamish, but no more demands or arguing. I can't stand it anymore.' I rose to my feet, waiting to get past him. He finally let me by and followed me to the sitting room, finding my friend engaged in lively conversation while they waited for lunch. We joined them, and soon after, as I chatted with Leo, Aaron walked into the room, strode directly up to me, and pulled me into a passionate kiss that lifted me off the floor. The room went quiet, an awkward silence filling the room until he finally released me.

'I needed to see ya. Can we talk privately?' Aaron didn't seem to care who was there, and ignored everyone but me. I could feel Hamish's black stare on the back of my head as I left the room to see what he wanted. We stood in the empty hallway for a moment before I gestured impatiently for him to follow me to avoid well-meaning interruptions. 'How are ya, Abi?' I stepped into the kitchen, interrupting the maids, who smiled across at us as we sat down. Aaron picked up the ceramic pitcher that sat in the centre of the large wooden table, beautifully crafted from red gum sourced from Willow Grove. The padded leather chairs, intricately carved with native vines, sculptured down the smooth legs and on the corners of the table, the artist and creator who had made this glorious piece of furniture unknown and long gone, from what I assumed. He poured us both a glass of lemon barley water, his eyes sparkling as he passed it to me.

'I'm well, thank you. Quite tired of feeling upset and anxious most of the time, though.' My voice faltered, a lump lodging in my throat as tears stung my eyes. I picked up the tall glass, gazing across to the far window above the trough that overlooked the back garden. Those with years of experience in service back home who now worked here had cheerfully and repeatedly told me this house was unusual. Compared to similar grand estates where the kitchens were below ground, and the staff kept out of sight—here it was the central part of the home—the backdoor adjacent for all and sundry to come and go. I enjoyed the bustle and busyness of the warm and cheery room, always finding someone willing to spend time in idle gossip while enjoying a warm beverage now the weather was cooling.

'I needed to see with me own eyes you're in good spirits an' takin' care of yourself... an' tell ya, I missed me Abi. I was plannin' to lay down me swag at ya door if ya hadn't let me in today.' He smiled, his shaggy blonde hair framing his handsome face. I lifted my glass to my lips before continuing. He was far too pretty when that smile lit up his face.

'I didn't let either of you in today. You both just charged in here of your own volition, and without permission.'

Advising him he could call on me three times a week and which days suited before standing to show him out—he refused to move until Hamish agreed to leave. I grunted loudly before fetching Hamish from the sitting room, telling him in no uncertain terms it was time to return from where he came—adding I was sick of them both as I closed the front door behind them. I glanced out of the pane glass window beside the door to see they were talking, Aaron's hand on Hamish's broad shoulder. Their heads were close, both refusing to budge from the cobbled driveway that wound its way into a circular courtyard at the entrance to the grand building and into the stables. I couldn't quite hear what passed between them, but they stood nose to nose for the longest time, speaking low, before they separated and went to retrieve their respective horses. I sighed in relief as I watched them ride away in opposite directions.

That night as I lay in my bed, I dreamed of white roses, Charlotte, and twin lambs standing next to a waterfall.

Chapter Ten

I RECEIVED A WARM letter from Amelia Johnson informing me of her address in Geelong, where she lived with her husband and son, advising she would dearly love to reunite with me. I responded immediately, writing to invite her and her husband to Polly's engagement party. Today Aaron would visit, and I was still lying in bed, unable to determine how I felt about it.

Catherine had finished Polly's splendid wedding gown—it truly was a masterpiece, with a tight-fitting bodice, lace sleeves, and a full skirt of silk sprinkled with crystals. She was to return to Melbourne today on the afternoon train, and I was more than sorry to part, even for the short term, my mind racing as I planned my next visit to Melbourne. Bessie entered the room carrying a tray, efficiently kicking the door shut behind her with her foot before making her way to my side. She placed the tray on my lap before looking down at me, her hands on her hips.

'It is getting late. Leo became concerned when you didn't come down for breakfast, so he sent it up. He's worried about you. Unusual, I know, since he only cares about himself.' She bustled about, searching through my wardrobe for an appropriate dress for the overcast day while I moved my attention to what was before me. Leo had outdone himself this morning; his cheese-and-onion omelette on buttered toast, with a side of succulent field mushrooms, was delicious. I devoured the lot while Bessie chose my clothing for the day. Once finished, I quickly rose and sat at my dressing table in my nightgown. Bessie placed my dress on the bed before approaching me from behind, picking up a hairbrush. 'Now, don't you go getting all sad and confused because of them two wild boys. Even I don't know which one I like more.' Her musical laughter filled the silent room. I couldn't help but smile at her.

Just as she finished dressing me, there was a knock on my door. Maisie, our head maid and housekeeper, popped her head in the door and informed us cheerfully Aaron was waiting downstairs for me. Bessie glanced at me sympathetically, then tucked and pinned a loose strand of hair away from my face before dashing off to find Danny. I sighed and made my way down to the sitting room.

Aaron sat by the fireplace in a chair, drinking a glass of apple juice while chatting comfortably with Mr Masters about the best grains to use for beer fermentation. His face lit up when he saw me, standing immediately to greet me while Mr Masters remained at the door.

'Good mornin', Abi. I hope ya don't mind, but I arranged for us to visit with me family today. They're eager to meet ya. How would ya feel about joinin' 'em for lunch?' He grinned, raising my hand to his lips and kissing it politely before making himself comfortable back on the leather wingback chair. I sat down opposite him and smiled, pleased to see him and be back in his company.

'I'm sure I would enjoy that very much.' He nodded, glancing out of the window at the storm clouds approaching. I smoothed the skirt of my dress, grateful Bessie had forced me to wear several more petticoats and a warm tunic underneath, my thick, winter coat hanging on the peg at the backdoor along with everyone else's. It would not hurt to get to know my neighbours, even if I didn't end up marrying Aaron. I was curious about his family, especially his father. I had only met him for the briefest moment at Mr McPhee's office, but it was too short an encounter for me to form an opinion.

Mr Masters bid us farewell, and I nodded politely and promised to visit his office later in the day to meet with him. Aaron stood and enveloped me in a warm embrace, whispering in my ear he had dreamt of me last night and letting loose a thousand butterflies in my stomach that only appeared when he was nearby.

We rode through the front gates of Aaron's modest but more than comfortable, two-story home that stood behind the loveliest garden, a large oak tree standing strong and tall in the front yard. Two dogs ran up to us, barking for attention.

'Narla, Ben, that's enough. Shut ya snouts,' Aaron shouted before falling to the ground to play with them. 'Narla's a Great Dane,' he added proudly, rolling in the dirt with them. I could not believe the size of the dog—she was as big as a small pony. She possessed grey fur with a bluish tint and black spots covering her body. 'Ben's a mongrel, the poor sod.' I nodded as I slipped down from the enormous horse, assuming he had several breeds in him. He was completely black, with a pointy nose and a lovely disposition. There were several magpies under the large tree, all dancing around each other and fighting over a mound of fish heads, their loud squawking piercing my eardrums.

A woman appeared at the front door and smiled fondly at Aaron, now down on the grass, rolling around with the dogs. Petite, with sandy, blonde hair and an open, affable expression that framed the same blue eyes I recognised as Aaron's, she felt familiar, and easily recognised as his kin.

'Welcome, Abigail. I'm so pleased to meet you after all this time.' Her melodious voice reached us from where she remained by the door, and I smiled shyly across at her. 'Aaron, do stand up please, boy. You wouldn't want Abigail to think you were raised out the Nulla Nulla by the natives, would you?' She rolled her eyes before turning her attention back to me as we climbed the front stairs. 'I am Edith Cavanaugh, Aaron's mother. Let's go inside for a cool drink while we wait for the others to arrive.' Aaron lightly kissed his mother on the forehead, and we followed her inside to a warm and welcoming sitting room.

'Ma, Abi knows I have manners, an' you'll be pleased to know I behave meself when I'm at Willow Grove. Even try an' talk proper in front of the staff to make ya proud,' he teased. He grinned down at his mother, who shook her head in amusement, the faint golden glow around her becoming brighter.

The house was by no means extravagant compared to the middle-class homes scattered through the district of Geelong, many of them selectors on acreages, but it was far larger than most. I found his home warm, homely, and comfortable—just like his family. Mrs Cavanaugh took charge of all the household chores, taking the best care of all her boys, as she liked to call them. The family made their living by selling their catch at the market each day after taking the boat out in the early hours of the morning. It was a long day for Mr Cavanaugh, who rose at two o'clock each morning and fished until seven before bringing the boat back to shore and spending his day at the market. All four boys would assist him on the boat, then would take turns helping him at the market. I now understood why Aaron had so much time on his hands during the day.

'How do you like your new home, Abigail?' Edith asked, patting her hand on the empty seat of a brightly tapestried settee near the fireplace. Aaron made himself comfortable next to me as I waited for his mother to sit opposite.

'It's been a bit of a whirlwind, Mrs Cavanaugh, but I'm settling in quite nicely.' I smiled across at her, noticing how kind her eyes were and just how fine-boned her beautiful features were.

'Oh, please call me Edith.' She leaned forward and lowered her voice to a whisper. 'We don't need to be so formal; it sounds so—unfriendly. I have heard of your unfortunate circumstances growing up, which pains my heart.'

I cringed at the thought people knew I grew up in an orphanage, despising the pitiful looks it drew from many I hardly knew or wished to be acquainted with. Only recently had Bessie made me aware that many in the district of Geelong were curious about the new residents at Willow Grove, and a number of rumours about us had already spread among the locals. According to some, we were bohemians starting a commune, and to others, Polly and I were heiresses sent here from England to find advantageous matches. I hoped it was not common knowledge I had come from an orphanage, as I could not leave behind the shame it caused me, despite my circumstances changing significantly over the last few months.

The workers employed by my aunt at Willow Grove long ago had been overly curious about me leading up to our arrival. Since meeting us, they had been guessing how we lived and where we came from, as I had not shared a great deal of my private life with anyone other than my close friends. Of course, they discussed their assumptions and observations with their friends from other properties; therefore, the rumours had begun.

Aaron reached across and casually placed my hand in his. I felt my cheeks become warm and discreetly tried to pull away, with no success. Edith appeared pleased as she quickly rose to her feet before politely excusing herself to fetch the refreshments. Aaron used the opportunity to pull me onto his lap.

'Kiss me,' he challenged. 'I'm always kissin' ya. Now I want you to kiss me.' I assumed his mother would not be back for at least a few more minutes. I leaned in, took his face in my hands, and kissed him. He slipped his hands around my back and held me close to him. He kissed me back passionately, and I felt myself become lost in him. After some time, he gently pulled away and caressed my face. 'There's a lot I want to tell ya, but not till after you agree to marry me. If I tell ya too much too soon, ya might run away from me,' he teased. I looked at him inquisitively as I gently pulled away, smoothing my hair down while trying to catch my breath.

'Why, what are you hiding?' I asked suspiciously, feeling my stomach flip at the thought of him holding something back from me.

'Don't start whingin' before ya even have the ring. It's nothin' bad.' He chuckled to himself, kissing me quickly and letting me up just as Edith brought in a tray loaded with cakes and tea.

I liked Mrs Cavanaugh—she was the type of mother I used to dream of having for myself. We sat in companionable silence, eating the fluffy sponge cake filled with freshly whipped cream and strawberry jam. She settled herself back down opposite us and shared gossip in hushed tones she had heard in town this morning about a scandal involving a young local woman and her now-disgraced family.

'Why is it always the girls and their families who are shamed? It seems the man is equally responsible for putting his penis where he did,' I said adamantly, feeling infuriated for the young girl.

Edith choked on her tea, and Aaron burst into a fit of laughter, quickly handing her a napkin. Realising I had made another faux pas, I felt my face warm again. I wanted to hear another opinion on the matter, though. Edith composed herself, then turned her gaze to Aaron, her lovely face stern.

'There's no need to laugh at the poor child; she's still learning what is and isn't appropriate to say in polite company. That, my sweet girl, was not. However, you do raise an interesting point. I believe the shame should be shared, and that is the last we will speak of it.'

She moved the conversation along, describing what one should expect from life in Australia. I gratefully listened, but Aaron soon grew impatient. In the middle of our conversation, he interrupted her.

'Ma, we're goin' for a walk along the beach an' will be back before lunch.' Then, taking my hand, he pulled me to my feet and dragged me out the door. I looked over my shoulder to find Edith waving goodbye, her eyes twinkling with amusement. We walked down to the sand, hand in hand, and stood in silence, watching the waves sweep onto the shore.

'So, how does your mother know about my background?' I yelled over the roar of the ocean, the wind deafening.

It appeared a great number of people already knew a great deal about me, or at least assumed they did. I had not been in Geelong long, but I seemed to be the current topic of interest at every dinner party. Aaron looked down at me sympathetically, then slipped his arm around my shoulders.

'Ma hasn't mentioned anythin' to me, but with your solicitor not bein' the best keeper of secrets it's possible he spoke of ya to me father,' he said darkly, sitting down on the sand and pulling me onto his lap. 'I know little of ya history, Abi, an' I'm not goin' to ask,' he continued. 'From what I've heard around town, ya go from bein' a woman of royal blood to a gypsy who stole all this from a passin' traveller. I don't care where ya came from or who they say ya are. I love the Abigail I see in front of me, so none of that shite matters. You'll tell me if ya ever want to, an' I'll be there to listen.' He unpinned my hair, allowing it to whip around me for a moment as he laughed, before smoothing it down with his fingers then expertly winding it back up neatly and ensuring it was out of my eyes.

We rose, took our shoes off, and strolled along the sand, talking and laughing. While enjoying the feel of the warm sand shifting under my weight and filling the crevices between my toes, I realised how much I liked this man. I felt so relaxed in his company. We stood side by side, his arm around my waist and mine around his. I wondered if my ease in his presence was because of the golden glow. I had only ever had Hamish court me before, and although he too was surrounded by the golden aura I loved so much, there was no point in comparing the two. They were opposite in every way. Still, I had almost the same reaction to them, both physically and emotionally. They were decent, loving men; both intelligent and strong of character, although handsome in different ways. The closer I became to Aaron, the more I understood how difficult my choice had become. Finally, we headed back to the house. Aaron advised me his father and brothers should have arrived home by now before he stopped walking and pulled me back into his arms.

'Abi, don't be nervous. I can already see it on ya face. Here—stop an' look at me. Me family will love ya just as ya are. There's no need to be shy. I promise.' He kissed me tenderly on the lips.

'All right, I'll try.' I gazed out at the waves crashing against the shore and swallowed several times to dislodge the lump in my throat. 'I just find it difficult when I meet new people. They seem to judge me, often blatantly looking me up and down without speaking to me, which makes me feel self-conscious and uncomfortable.'

'You're a hard woman to take ya eyes from. 'Cause ya don't even realise how lovely ya are makes ya even more attractive.' His eyes twinkled as he took me by the hand and we mounted the steps to his home.

Within moments of stepping inside the front door, Mr Cavanaugh greeted us warmly, then introduced me to Patrick, Aiden, and Luke. They were big, sturdy boys with golden skin and healthy appetites, just like Aaron. Mr Cavanaugh was a slightly older version of his sons, only being in his early forties. Aaron's parents were an attractive couple, full of energy and vitality; it was clear just how much they adored their adult sons and each other.

The four boys had been born a year apart. Patrick the eldest, with Aiden arriving twelve-months later, then Aaron and Luke followed. They were all single, and except for Aaron, not one of them was courting. I could see how close their bond by their interaction, teasing each other affectionately as we followed them down the small hallway.

They were already seated comfortably around their large kitchen table when we stepped into the room moments later, hand in hand. Aaron's brothers hooted and cheered at us, momentarily taking me back to a time when I was young, and we would pass by the village boys each Sunday as we walked to Mass. I felt myself blushing yet again at the thought of how those tyrants would embarrass me, calling out for everyone to hear no one wanted to be friends with an orphan, laughing as they sucked on sweeties and played without a care in the world. Aaron laughed at them and offered me a seat, telling them to quiet down before sitting down heavily on the chair beside me, then protectively taking my hand in his under the table.

'I'm tellin' ya now; I don't believe this is the Abigail you're betrothed to,' Aiden called across the table, his blue eyes twinkling as he picked up his glass filled with cold ale. 'No one gets that lucky—especially not a cheeky bastard like you. She's supposed to be short, fat, an' ugly with no teeth, remember?' Aaron chuckled to himself, taking a piece of dark, roasted lamb from the platter in the centre of the table and placing it on his blue and white china plate while Mr Cavanaugh shook his head in amusement.

'I will tell ya why me boys are actin' like louts, Abigail,' Gavin Cavanaugh explained, taking a large spoon and serving himself a healthy amount of roasted potato and pumpkin. 'Ever since they were bairns, Patrick put it in their minds you would be a very unattractive woman with an unattractive personality to match. I always knew that would not be the case, particularly if you favoured your great-aunt, who was a magnificent lookin' woman with a generous and lovin' heart. Luckily for my son, I was right.'

Patrick smiled across at me before placing his large hand on his heart.

'Well, I was tryin' to prevent gettin' anyone's hopes up too high.' They erupted in loud laughter as I ate, discovering Mrs Cavanaugh was an excellent cook. Besides the three roasted lamb legs and vegetables, a feast under any circumstance—and one I learnt was appreciated by many Australian families every Sunday—the table overflowed with seafood of all kinds. Much of it unfamiliar to me. Mrs Cavanaugh cooked several varieties of fish and squid in oil, creating a crispy crust. Large prawns, boiled with their heads still attached, sat in an oversized ceramic bowl staring at me accusingly, while she served other strange-looking sea creatures raw, some straight from their shell. Fresh salads accompanied the delicious buffet, followed by a rich chocolate cake for dessert. It did not surprise me in the slightest the men in this family were large eaters, and the food disappeared at a rapid pace. I appreciated they constantly talked between mouthfuls as they ate, and did not seem to care about etiquette or proper social graces. They all possessed lovely manners; however, there was nothing formal about being in this house at all, a feeling I so wished to replicate in my own home, immediately putting me at ease in their company.

'So, we finally get to meet the sheila our idiot brother is moonin' over,' Luke teased, lightly punching Aaron on the arm. They both grinned as I inwardly cringed.

'Miss Abigail, why would a beautiful lady like yourself be interested in a mug like his?' Aiden enquired, his bright blue eyes sparkling mischievously.

'Well, from where I'm sitting, the four of you all appear to have mugs not unlike your father's,' I remarked, a shy smile touching my lips as Aaron threw back his head and howled.

Mr and Mrs Cavanaugh burst into loud laughter at the somewhat confused expressions on their sons' faces. They were a lively, unpretentious group of people, and humorous banter continued to flow around the busy table as we enjoyed the beautiful luncheon Mrs Cavanaugh had put so much time and effort into making. When we had eaten our fill, everyone stood up to help clear the dishes. Amid the warm glow of red wine and heady laughter, I remembered how, as a child, I had dreamed of being part of a loving family such as this. Soon, everyone went their separate ways, and Aaron and I found ourselves alone in the kitchen. I was feeling relaxed, warm, and sluggish due to three large glasses of wine.

'Come, Abi, let me show ya around the house,' he whispered in my ear, sending tingles throughout my body at the warmth of his breath.

He whisked me through the bottom floor, showing me several rooms in which his parents entertained. They were much more formal than the rooms we had been relaxing in, and I could see they were not in use every day. The rooms in the house were spacious and elegantly decorated, and not inexpensively, I noted as I gazed around the elaborate dining room. I wondered just how much money my great-aunt had provided for them to build such a magnificent house. Although grander than the average home in the district, each room was cosy and comfortable.

Edith Cavanaugh possessed an eye for detail, with each room decorated in a different colour to suit its purpose. I could see that apart from the kitchen, the sitting room was where they spent the most time. It held four large lounges, all facing each other, set near an enormous fireplace that took up half the wall. In addition, there was a table with six chairs where they gathered to play cards at night, and large wooden buffets on each side of the room. They'd covered the windows in heavy drapes with delicate lace curtains covering the glass.

He led me upstairs by the hand and showed me the six bedchambers, along with the washroom. After the tour, he pulled me into the last bedchamber and closed the door behind us.

'This is me room,' he said softly, drawing me towards him.

The more time I spent with him, the more attractive he became. He clearly stated his views, no matter how they may be received, while not imposing them on others. He did not like arguments and didn't go out of his way to cause any; however, if he believed in something, he wouldn't back down. Only one reason he and Polly had not seen eye to eye when they met. It was unfortunate they did not get along, but I reassured myself the situation would resolve itself once they were better acquainted.

He slipped his enormous arms around my waist and gently kissed my eyes, then my cheeks, and then my mouth. After some time, I pulled away and led him out of the bedchamber just as Luke stepped into the hallway. I did not feel comfortable being alone with him in his room while his entire family was aware and wondering what we were doing in there. Upon seeing us exit, Luke brushed past us silently, then awkwardly scuttled off to his room.

'Why don't we rejoin your parents and talk to them before we leave?' I suggested, firmly steering us back to the living room downstairs.

'Do we have to? They got what they wanted an' met ya. Isn't that enough? I don't wanna share ya even with me own family,' he complained as I slapped him on the arm, making him laugh.

We spent the rest of the afternoon sitting lazily on the back veranda with his brothers while discussing the fishing business and local gossip. I had not made the acquaintance of the people they spoke of and would not know them from a bar of soap. It was disconcerting to listen to them talking about these people, who seemed to know a great deal about me. They assured me, come hell or high water, the curious locals of Geelong and surrounding districts would eventually make sure I received the pleasure of meeting them, which made me giggle.

'Yes, there has been a great deal of curiosity about you and your sister. I understand her engagement celebrations are taking place tomorrow?' Edith inquired politely while smiling affectionately at her sons' then me. Pity crossed her eyes for only a moment, and I wondered again just what she knew about me.

'Yes, and they are to be married a fortnight from then,' I confirmed, going over the plans for the upcoming party in my mind.

I would accompany Hamish, and I looked forward to it more than I had realised. He was always fun to be around, and a strong connection lay between us. I was excited for Angus and Polly—they were finally so close to starting their life together. Catherine had, as a surprise, made a unique dress for Polly to wear at the engagement party, which only I had seen.

Aaron's brothers stood one by one and excused themselves to run personal errands or visit friends. They had all been very kind and welcoming to me and were sincere when bidding me farewell, stating it had been their pleasure to meet me. While Mrs Cavanaugh served tea and scones and chatted endlessly about Geelong and the surrounding districts—and the people who lived there—for what seemed like hours, we remained outside enjoying the afternoon sunshine.

'I hope you'll return to visit again, Abigail. We've enjoyed your company. You're a delightful girl, an' very much like Lady Isabelle. Even your speech favours her, which is disconcertin' given you're native to Scotland. I have to say, she was one of me favourite people in the world. She proved just how special she was, given we knew her for only a moment in time, an' we still talk of her nearly two decades on. Your aunt became family, just as you now are, an' we hope you'll treat our home as your own,' Gavin Cavanaugh said warmly.

'I, too, have enjoyed your company and hospitality and appreciate your kind offer very much to visit again. You are welcome in my home too, so please call anytime. You are also very welcome to attend the engagement party,' I replied with equal warmth.

I knew he was counting on Aaron and me to wed in the not so distant future, as was his mother, who appeared fond of me already. I wondered if there was a clause in his contract that stipulated he would have to return the money and property my great-aunt had given him if the marriage did not go ahead. His face gave nothing away as we exchanged our goodbyes in front of the house, then cantered out through the elegant gates for home.

After leaving Aaron's horse with Harry, we made our way to the sitting room. No one seemed to be around, and the house was un-usually quiet, although I heard faint noises coming from the kitchen.

'I like your family, and your mother is an excellent cook,' I re-marked, reclining in a lounge to get a little rest. I felt tired from our long day of socialising and closed my eyes for only a moment. Aaron looked over at me from the opposite lounge and grinned.

'I think they liked ya back. Me brothers aren't used to bein' in female company, but they appeared at ease around ya. They couldn't believe how beautiful ya are. Before they left, they pulled me aside an' said ya were a lovely person, too, an' that I am one lucky bastard.'

He stood, then crossed the room in two strides to my side, laying down beside me. I nestled in his powerful arms, almost falling asleep, while he whispered things only for my ears.

'So, is it true Leo picked ya up an' hung ya over the balcony rail of the ship, threatenin' to drop ya into the drink 'cause ya tripped him up?' Aaron asked, grinning as I stood outside to see him off for the night.

It was getting late, and I couldn't wait to get out of my clothes and into my nightgown. I wrapped my arms around his neck, his lips so close to mine I could almost taste them.

'Partly,' I replied wearily. 'He dangled me over the side of the ship, but I didn't trip the lying wee imp. He stumbled over the leg of a chair and then blamed me. The next thing I knew, he had me by both feet in mid-air and was threatening to drop me into the water. At that point, Bessie was kind enough to intervene.' Our eyes met, and we burst into peals of laughter.

'From what I've seen, you're as mad as cut snakes when you're together.' He chuckled again before kissing me goodbye, then swung his muscular frame up onto his horse. I waved as he trotted down beside the house and toward the back paddock to cut across to his home at the very corner of Willow Grove. I took a deep breath, made my way inside, and closed the front door behind me.

Chapter Eleven

I AWOKE WITH A start; my mind flooded with the long list of tasks to be finished before the guests arrived for the party tonight. I struggled out of bed just as Bessie entered the room to wake me.

'Good. I see you're up early for the big day,' she called out cheerfully as I looked up at her, bleary-eyed. She threw open the heavy drapes, moving from window to window until the early morning light flooded the large room.

'Yes, it appears so,' I replied with a yawn. 'But I think I'll need some coffee to wake me up.' Bessie had disappeared, the sound of her rummaging through my wardrobe filling the room. I suspected she could not hear me, but tried again. 'Just a house-dress for the day, Bessie. I don't know yet what I'll wear tonight,' I called as I went to my dressing table and sat down, brushing my hair until it shone, then pinned it up on top of my head so it was out of the way. After Bessie helped me into the russet dress she'd taken so long to choose, we made our way downstairs side by side; my dear friend chirping of how happy she was with Danny and how much she loved living in Australia.

Polly sat at the kitchen table waiting for us, nibbling nervously on the corner of a piece of dry toast.

'I can't believe it's today, Abi. In two more weeks, I'll be Mrs Makenzie.' Her face shone as I smiled, then bent down to kiss her cheek, taking a deep breath as cinnamon and burnt sugar filled the room.

Hamish and Angus sat opposite her, enormous bowls of porridge in front of them while fighting over the largest slice of bacon, each trying to spear it with their forks before the other one got it. Angus' hand remained on Polly's as he sparred and laughed with his brother. There was plenty of food and no reason for it other than their competitiveness. I couldn't help but smile while Polly giggled at them.

'And how are you feeling, Angus?' I enquired, smiling across at Jenny, who was dutifully gutting a dozen large snapper for lunch. The Cavanaugh family had kindly delivered several crates of seafood in the early hours of the morning on their way to Geelong market. His face lit up as he stared across at Polly, not taking his eyes from her for a moment, while addressing me.

'Abigail, today will be the second happiest of my life. The first will be in a fortnight when I wed my best friend. One I'll never forget, an' always treasure.'

'And you, Hamish?' I asked, sliding onto the seat next to him. He glanced across at me and smiled, causing my heart to beat faster, letting loose a thousand butterflies in my stomach.

'I've missed you, an' I know you'll be plenty busy today, but I was hopin' you might spare me a moment later?' He leaned across the table and pecked me on the cheek before straightening up and returning his attention to the food in front of him.

'I'll do my best, I promise. I have missed you, too.' I grabbed myself a piece of toast just as Leo strolled over to join us.

He looked so happy while watching those at the table devour the fruits of his labour so enthusiastically, and it made me content to see him glow. Despite his idiosyncrasies, I had grown even fonder of him, but Hamish had not. It was unfortunate there remained a rigidity between them, resulting from Hamish's vigorous support of the class system and belief it was appropriate for distance between employer and employee. I hoped he would soften over time and see it wasn't wrong or harmful to treat those in your employ well, or befriend them.

If it ever came to a choice between another friend and Leo, without doubt I would choose my friendship with him because of the deep connection between us. Unable to envision a time when I would not want him in my life, I did not understand why I felt this strongly for someone I had known only a matter of months, but there it was. I felt I had known him my entire life. He had no one else in this world and had finally found a home with us here on this magnificent property, finding a sense of peace, just as I had.

'And how are you, sugar lips? Come on, lay one on me.' Leo sat down heavily beside me and turned his cheek towards me. I obliged, much to Angus and Polly's amusement—and Hamish's chagrin. 'So, how does it feel, Hamish?' Hamish arched his black brows silently, narrowing his gaze. 'You know what I'm referring to, so don't play with me. How's your oversized ego and inflated opinion of yourself holding up now such a virile—and powerfully built, handsome blonde stallion—wants your woman to ride him?" Hamish continued to glare at him, but said not a word, his fists curled up into fists. 'Did you know she met his family yesterday? It's looking serious to me from where I'm sitting on my kitchen stool, you poor neglected brumby. I've done my best to distract him from her, but he'll have none of it—and I'm trying to spy on them as you asked me to, but they will not give me the chance. Will I be forced to return the five pounds you paid me to destroy him? If so, I must warn you now, I spent it on chocolate. Trying to retrieve it from the thunderbox may be difficult, and highly unpleasant.' A wicked smirk touched Leo's lips as Hamish flushed, his face soon a mottled purple, while Angus threw back his head and roared with laughter. Hamish remained silent, suddenly fascinated by the food on his plate.

'Really? You would stoop so low as to employ Leo as your spy? Seriously, Hamish, I thought you were more intelligent than that. He's just tattled on you to me not even twenty-four hours into your arrangement.' I attempted to smother a smile, and failing miserably, burst into fits of giggles. After some time, I pulled myself together and ate my breakfast while everyone chatted and laughed. Leo poured me a creamy, sweet coffee, and I stood, taking it with me. I kissed Hamish, who appeared sheepish, and made my way to the butler's office, calling out farewell to all in the kitchen, the busiest room in the house often filled with twenty or more souls at a time.

I met with Mr Masters often to discuss the running of the house, since it was all so new to me. I preferred holding our discussions in his less intimidating quarters rather than in my grand office, given it was much more relaxed. He was my saviour and was so generously guiding and mentoring me, although I would make my own decisions in the end. I knocked on the door, stepping inside when he called out for me to enter. I greeted him warmly before he motioned to sit down on a comfortable wing-backed leather chair opposite him.

'I would like to arrange a pay raise for every single soul who works here at Willow Grove of one pound per week.' Mr Master's raised his eyebrows and leaned back in his chair before gazing across at me. 'To thank them for their hard work and loyalty,' I added, my face flushed. The longer I stayed here and witnessed the long hours and back-breaking, often menial, repetitive and mind-numbingly boring tasks they carried out day in and day out, I appreciated them more—and my own situation even far more than that.

'Pardon me, Mistress, but that is extremely kind and exceptionally generous. Most of them do not even earn one pound a week. They will all be extremely pleased and grateful.' A hint of a smile touched his lips, a memory of something long ago crossing his face. 'I was fortunate in the early years of my career to secure a position under a great man—but his mother was far greater. A force to be reckoned with is probably the most accurate description I could give you. She insisted on the same with her servants and instilled this in her son long before he came of age and stepped up into his father's shoes. She was a very close friend of your great-aunt I have only recently discovered. I met Lady Delmont many times in the months leading up to her death, then comforted the dear Dowager for years after her loss. And it was a substantial loss.' I nodded slightly, a lump in my throat while his eyes glistened. 'She never got over it. They were closer than sisters, both blessed with benevolent hearts, but with minds considered far too open, and spirits far too wild to tame. I believe you are very much like them.'

Nodding again, I reached out to pick up a glass of water on the desk in front of me he had so kindly poured on my arrival. Lifting it to my lips, I took a deep drink, while an awkward silence hung over the cosy office. I had only recently found out most in service here had very little left for themselves by the time they sent a portion of their wages to their families. I was also well aware it was only for the grace of great-aunt Isabelle I, too, wasn't living as a servant, scrubbing pots and pans until my hands were raw and bleeding.

'Mr Masters, if you don't mind me asking, have you ever been in love?' He sat back on the comfortable leather chair behind his shiny, wooden desk, an odd look in his eye, almost sadness, mixed with regret.

'Yes, but only once. I was young and thought I had all the time in the world to establish myself first. However, I was wrong, and missed my chance. She married someone else. I have been by myself since, but I am quite content. Perhaps happier than most married couples, if you don't mind me saying?' He nodded, and I could not help but laugh as I returned his gaze.

'No, of course not, but may I also speak plainly with you?' I felt like a meddler, but he nodded his assent, appearing uncomfortable. 'I have been hesitant to interfere; however, the issue is now affecting the running of the house.' Again, he nodded, remaining silent as I continued. 'Maisie is desperately in love with you and does everything she can to draw your attention. It seems it is obvious to everyone here but you. I understand her feelings may be unrequited, but if there is the slightest chance you may feel the same way, please talk to her. The only reason I even raised the matter with you is her work is now suffering. In her recent attempts to impress you, I've heard there have been several breakages. She cannot concentrate and she's been bumping into things and knocking them over. I'm more concerned she will cause herself an injury or fall down the hundreds of stairs around the place.' Mr Masters flushed slightly, averting his gaze while shifting in his seat. He stared out the floor to ceiling window over the stable yard where Harry was busy trimming a stallion's hoof. I felt immediate regret for even broaching the subject with him.

'Enough please, Mistress,' he mumbled, turning back and picking up a small glass of water, avoiding my gaze. I changed the subject, and we spoke of other matters. He told me everything was on schedule. The house had already been cleaned from corner to corner, and they had opened several wings that held the guest rooms for those planning to stay overnight, and I had heard there were many. This would be the first time we had a full house, or anyone slept in the new beds, exciting me no end. I so looked forward to seeing all our friends again, most from Melbourne and too far away to visit for morning tea, unless you planned to stay overnight. Catherine and her family would attend the event, and I wondered for the hundredth time how I would get along with her mother and father, given we'd never met. From her accounts, they had been absent parents and had left the care of their children to Nanny their whole lives, which did not impress me. I hoped they were nicer than I was expecting them to be. 'Will that be all, Mistress?' Mr Masters asked, his tone formal, his voice loud enough to bring me back to the present.

'Oh, yes. Thank you, Mr Masters. And I do apologise again for putting you in such an uncomfortable position,' I replied just as formally, then stood to leave.

He nodded silently in my direction as I straightened my dress. I left him to his thoughts and hurried off to find Hamish, stepping out the backdoor to see him in the distance in deep conversation with Harry out by the stables. I had met with Harry earlier in the week to familiarise myself with the property and learn how they managed the farm and the day-to-day workings of it. From what I understood, he was in charge of the stables, along with the demanding breeding programs for the Martarinos. The farmhands', along with the stable-hands' and grooms, all answered to him. Even I recognised this was far too much for one man and suggested finding another manager for the farmhands. He agreed only after I advised him of my intention to hire more people to assist him.

The single grooms slept in the loft above the stables, while married couples and families lived in the terraces, of which we had many vacant. The farmhands, if single, could share a home with other workers, an arrangement that seemed satisfactory. Without hesitation or doubt, I offered the new farm foreman position to Angus, and he accepted without hesitation or doubt, and with much enthusiasm. He had his own money, left to him by his grandfather; however, Angus was well aware he would soon be obligated to support Polly to the same standard she had become accustomed to—and he wanted her to have everything. Relieved they could live at Willow Grove, he didn't have to concern himself with commuting to work for his father, whom he wasn't fond of, anyway. To have Angus work alongside Harry also gave me a sense of peace, given I already knew and trusted him like a brother.

Hurrying through the garden to find the stable-yard empty, I continued on, assuming they had gone inside. I stepped through the door into the warm stables, the smell of hay and manure tickling my nose. I could hear them before they could see me, my ears pricking up as I made my way towards the workroom in the centre of the building. Hamish stood near the tack-room, talking to Harry in the stall opposite.

'I'll be moving here in the next few months. Once I'm settled, I'll sit down with you properly, an' we'll sort it.'

'Hello, you wanted to spend some time with me?' I called out as I approached them, a bright smile on my face. He grinned at the sight of me, while I shook my head in disbelief at the cheek of him wanting to take over my property before we even married—if we ever married. However, I felt reluctant to raise the issue, especially in front of Harry and the workers.

'Aye, I believe I do.' I went to his side, stood on tiptoe, and placed my arms around his neck. He picked me up by the waist and kissed me deeply. 'It's good to see you, precious girl, and to have you to myself.' He placed me back down on my feet and took my hand in his. We said goodbye to Harry, then headed for the back garden, where we made ourselves comfortable on a chaise lounge under the wide verandah. We sat back, relaxing in the glorious Australian weather, the winter soon turning to spring. 'I can't bear it any longer, an' cannae bite my tongue, even though I dinnae want to ruin the day. Have you ended things with him yet?' I hesitated, feeling sick to my stomach, but could not form the words he wanted to hear. 'How long do I have to wait, Abigail?' he demanded to know, visibly upset. A wave of guilt crashed over me, and I answered him as honestly as I could.

'I'm not sure, Hamish. Perhaps a few more weeks. I have to satisfy that reptilian solicitor and prove somehow I made a genuine attempt.' He sat beside me, silent and unmoving, then lowered his head before running a hand through his thick, black curls.

'Aye. I know we agreed not to speak of it, but I cannae help feelin' jealous an' frustrated, an' dinnae know what to dae anymore. All I dae know for certain is I love you, lass, with every part of my bein'.' I placed my arms around him but remained silent, knowing anything I said was likely to make it worse. After some time, he took my hand and clasped it in his, the sun reflecting off his strong, handsome face. I wanted more than anything to tell him I would renege on the arranged marriage, take the hidden money, and marry him. The problem was, only yesterday I felt ready to share my life with Aaron and his adorable family. It was an impossible decision and would have been so much easier had I found the money the day of my arrival—since then, my feelings towards both men had become complex and even more complicated. Being pulled in two different directions, I could not stop it any more than I could stop my heart beating, nor could I choose between them.

Bessie had chosen a bronze evening gown for me. The corset was far too tight, leaving me barely able to breathe. It made my waist appear even smaller than it was, its enormous skirt held out by a crinoline made of whalebone I usually avoided at all costs. I found my simpler dresses only required several thick petticoats underneath and were far more comfortable. The gown's bodice, finely embroidered with tiny beads, framed my breasts in a "simultaneously acceptable and appealing manner" Polly had advised me when I had complained yesterday. I'd refused to wear it after the first time Bessie forced me into what we referred to as "the cage" while in London. Given the occasion, I had relented and agreed to suffer in silence only for the party and Polly's sake. I admired Bessie's work in the mirror, applying a small amount of perfume from a crystal bottle behind my ears and in between my breasts, before dabbing some on my wrists, the alluring scent of vanilla and musk tickling my nose.

'You look beautiful, Mistress. Your aunt would be proud if she saw you now,' she remarked, straightening up beside me while she looked me up and down. 'In the short time I've known you, you have matured. You're turning into a strong young woman. Promise me you'll enjoy yourself and not think about Aaron while you're with Hamish, and the other way around.' She rolled her eyes as I laughed aloud. 'It's the only thing I can think of to stop you going mad from it all.' I turned and embraced her before kissing her on the cheek.

'Thank you, Bessie. I will take your advice and just enjoy every minute,' I promised her. She squeezed my hand before I hurried away to join the party.

'You look wonderful, Abigail,' Hamish exclaimed. I reached the bottom of the grand marble staircase, and he took my hand in his.

'As do you.'

He did indeed look most handsome in his perfectly fitted, very expensive tailcoat and matching pants, his new bowler hat atop his head, his hair neatly secured at the nape of his neck. He offered me his arm, which I took, and he escorted me into the ballroom to meet Polly and Angus, discovering Mr and Mrs Makenzie and Jemima had already arrived. Polly greeted the first of her guests, and I took a glass of wine from Jonathon's tray as he passed by and tried to relax, while Hamish wandered over to his parents and their friends. Noticing me standing alone, Catherine—only just stepping into the elaborate ballroom moments before—guided her family towards me, her smile bright.

'This is my father, and my mother, Mr and Mrs Montague. Mother, Father.' She paused for a moment, sweeping her hand in my direction. 'I would like you to meet my dear friend, Miss Abigail Delmont.'

'We're thrilled to make your acquaintance, Abigail. Just thrilled. We have heard so much about you, and we are more than pleased Catherine has finally made a friend. She is such an awkward girl,' Mrs Montague said, her voice low while winking at me in confidence—despite Catherine standing next to her, appearing embarrassed as she averted her gaze.

I imagined Catherine was the spitting image of her mother's younger self. Mrs Montague was pleasant, while maintaining a degree of polite aloofness, a trait I recognised I should try to emulate if I was ever to become the lady everyone expected me to be. We talked for a time before I excused myself to welcome the other guests. I wandered around the room, greeting and speaking to each of them, while introducing myself to people I had not met before, and greeting those familiar to me. I had made a promise to myself I would not be self-conscious or shy tonight and would make my best effort to mix with people I did not know. Of course, the wine helped. After what felt like hours of mundane and insignificant conversation, I sat down beside William, a glass of whisky in his hand.

'How is your law course progressing, William?' I asked, letting out a deep sigh and kicking off my shoes under my dress.

'Hello, Abigail. It's going very well, thank you.' He forced a smile as he took a sip of his drink. 'And I wanted to tell you—I do apologise for behaving the way I did when we last spoke. You were right. I unfairly judged you. You have been a good friend to Catherine and myself and Beatrice when we were in London. Please reach out if there is anything you ever need. You know, I think we will make pretty good mates, as the Aussies say,' he teased and nudged me with an elbow. We both laughed. I was surprised by this turnaround in his personality and not entirely convinced of it, but I felt relieved and touched by what he had said.

'Bygones, William. It's all in the past now, mate.' I leaned over and briefly shook his hand, a broad grin spreading across his handsome face. Amelia stepped through the grand doorway, her husband beside her. She stopped abruptly and scanned the room, appearing anxious. When she saw me, she hurried over and embraced me tightly.

'What a magnificent home you have, Abigail. It's much grander than you portrayed. The way you spoke on the ship, I was expecting to find a one room humpy,' she gushed, her hand on my arm as she turned back to her husband. 'And you remember George?' I nodded at the small man beside her, who still reminded me of a tiny blackbird.

'Of course.' I smiled insincerely, and he nodded but said nothing. He looked just as disinterested as I felt, and I could see disliked talking nonsense as much as I did. Amelia glanced at me apologetically as I guided them to their table. People were arriving in swarms now. After spotting Dana and the girls, I greeted them and took them to where Amelia and George sat at a large, round table. Soon after, Tamara and Elizabeth arrived with their intended husbands, whom I had never met before. After they had all been seated, Hamish and I sat down to join our friends.

To my satisfaction, there was much laughter and merry chatter. Before too long, though, I noticed Hamish was drinking rather heavily. He turned to Charlotte, seated on his other side, and started flirting with her. Charlotte had been attracted to Hamish since meeting him on the ship and was now infatuated with him. I had never been jealous or spoken of it, as she had done everything in her power to hide it out of respect for me. Knowing we were courting, she had never flirted with him once; however, I could see she was finding it hard to resist his attention and charms. I was becoming exceedingly uncomfortable as Hamish's interest in Charlotte grew, and his devotion to me seemed to wane entirely. I tried to ignore them, but their flirtations soon became apparent to everyone at the table. Hamish had by now polished off half a decanter of whisky and was starting on the other half. He was becoming obnoxious and loud, much to my embarrassment. I did not know how to react, having never seen him like this before.

'So, Charlotte. If you love a man and want to be with him, is it right to play games and toy with his feelings? I don't think that's right, do you?' he slurred, pouring himself another glass of straight whisky and lifting it to his lips. Charlotte was looking increasingly uncomfortable with his sudden and obvious attention and increasing agitation towards me. Dana caught my eye and raised her eyebrows inquiringly. I shook my head slightly, indicating I had no clue what was happening.

'Don't Polly and Angus look happy?' I nervously exclaimed, not knowing what else to say.

'Oh, yes, they do,' Tamara remarked exuberantly, elegantly picking up the crystal flute filled with champagne and taking a long drink. Her fiancé was Mr Brian Wagner, a descendant of the owner of Cobb and Co. I had heard on the passionfruit vine he refused to work in the family business, recently purchasing a shoe factory in Footscray by the banks of Saltwater River. Of medium build, with dark hair and a thick moustache, he seemed charming enough, but I was curious why they didn't appear to have much affection for each other. Sadly, I noticed they had not touched the entire night and avoided each other's gaze, appearing quite awkward together.

'So, Abigail, how are you settling into your new home?' Dana asked, ignoring Hamish's behaviour as he continued to whisper to her daughter.

'I'm still trying to familiarise myself with the property, but everyone has been very supportive. There hasn't been a person who lives and works here who has not welcomed us, and they have helped me settle in comfortably. It was quite a shock to be brought here and told this was ours,' I replied, smiling weakly. Nearly everyone at the table looked at me with sympathy as Hamish flirted with Charlotte, sliding his arm around her chair. He finished the whisky decanter without assistance, and a footman placed another on the table just out of his reach.

'Aye, all this is yers, Abigail.' He spread his arms wide, emphasising his point. 'But are you happy? Naw, o' course not. A house isn't enough, is it? You also need people to manipulate. Does everybody know you have another suitor you're enjoying, an' all because of some silly promise made fifteen-years ago by an insane Aunt of yers?' He turned back to Charlotte and continued to flirt outrageously with her. As much as it stung, he had a point, and I knew it. Most at the table had averted their eyes, none knowing how to behave after Hamish's outburst. Embarrassed, I thought it best to remove myself, no longer prepared to be Hamish's catalyst. I stood and excused myself from the table, then hurried across the room, asking Polly to join me in the parlour as I passed her. She followed me without question, and as soon as I closed the door behind us and we had some privacy, I pulled her down onto the window seat, clasping her hands in mine.

'Polly, he's drunk already. I don't know what to do.' I burst into tears as I tried to swallow the lump lodged in my throat, my hand clutching my chest, a futile attempt to soothe the pain that pierced my heart. I tried to pull myself together, wiping my face with a linen handkerchief embroidered with yellow bumblebees. She took me in her arms, embracing me tightly.

'Yes, I noticed. Isn't he awful? You're not to blame, but he has been under a great deal of stress from this ordeal with you and Aaron,' she murmured, stroking my back, her voice full of sympathy.

'I gave him the option to leave me, but he chose not to, saying he'd wait. And now, I don't know what to do.' I raised my hands in helpless despair.

'That's because he loves you, Abi. I can't help you choose, but for everyone's sake, I suggest you make haste in your decision.'

I nodded, wiping my face again before sniffing loudly, realising how selfish it was of me to dampen Polly's evening. I looked at her fondly and sniffed again. She was radiant and so happy. I warmly embraced my darling sister before straightening my dress and checking my reflection in the ornate gilded mirror that hung over the fireplace, quickly wiping away several streaks of charcoal from my eyes that had run down my cheeks. We walked hand in hand back to the ballroom in silence, where Angus waited patiently. I left her to return to the dinner table, where Hamish had become even more inebriated.

'You know she has someone else in love with her, along with her peasant fisherman? It's that cook who likes to call himself a chef. He spends hours with her every day, an' he splits his time between bein' a servant, an' bein' one of us. It's the most humiliatin' situation I've ever witnessed,' Hamish slurred, his body rocking precariously on the chair.

'Please don't speak ill of Leo, Hamish. He has done you no wrong.' Anger rose in me, my face flushed pink. Tired of his antics, I scanned the room for his parents. Mr Makenzie stood along the far side of the wall with another gentleman, deep in conversation with a dark-haired woman. I rose to my feet yet again, then hurried across the room, politely nodding to several guests as I passed, my stomach in knots. 'Mr Makenzie, I hope you are enjoying the evening?'

'Aye, it's been bearable enough.' Feeling self-conscious, I motioned to speak with him in private, his companion staring at my breasts. The woman excused herself, then spun away and began a conversation with a young man standing alone by the hearth, who hadn't taken his eyes from her. Mr Makenzie stepped away from his companions and strolled over to where I stood near the door.

'I'm afraid Hamish is drunk. Would you assist him up to one of the guest rooms so he can rest, please, Mr Makenzie?' I hoped he would be of some help, although I believed him to be useless in every other way going by what his sons had told me.

'Aye, our Hamish dinnae fare well when it comes tae the whisky; although, havin' met ye has made him even more difficult tae deal with.' His gaze dropped to my breasts where it remained. 'Given the ordeal yer presently puttin' him through, I cannae blame my son for lookin' elsewhere for affection. I hope ye come tae yer senses, Abigail, an' marry my boy, for 'tis a wise match that'll benefit both parties. He has the name o' Makenzie—an' that can only benefit a bastard with no name tryin' to establish herself among the rich an' powerful here in our new home—while ye have the funds tae enable him tae become an important an' respected man in the district.'

'Will you help me or not? I don't have time to waste playing your games, Mr Makenzie,' I snapped before turning my back on him and preparing to leave. He sighed deeply before deciding to follow me, loudly greeting his many friends as he crossed the crowded room. On seeing his father approach, Hamish pulled himself unsteadily to his feet, losing his balance before falling head first onto the table. Bottles and glasses crashed to the floor, spilling their contents on those not quick enough to move from their seat, screams filling the room as the legs underneath the table snapped from his weight. Mr Masters hurried over to extinguish the candles that threatened to catch the tablecloth, now laying stained and crumpled on the floor. A hush fell over the ballroom before a hum of whispers permeated the room. Mr Makenzie pulled Hamish to his feet, and I placed myself under his arm for support, trying to ignore the gossip I was sure to hear tomorrow morning in the kitchen. The staff rushed over to restore the table while Mr Makenzie and I walked him up the stairs, stumbling as we went. Finally, we entered a guest room and laid him on the large four-poster bed, removing his shoes. I took a blanket from the cupboard and placed it over him, not surprised he had fallen almost immediately into a deep sleep. I leaned down and kissed his brow before stroking his face with my fingers, feeling guilty for leaving him dressed in an uncomfortable suit. Mr Makenzie quickly dismissed us both and departed without a word. I sat down on the bed beside him, stroking his brow, movement catching my eye in the hall. I looked up to see Charlotte standing in the doorway.

'Hi, Abigail. I just came to see if I could help. Is he all right?' Her red hair shone in its chignon while her blue gown enhanced her eyes, taking me back to the first day we had met, and I had admired her beauty.

'He will be perfectly fine once he sleeps it off,' I reassured her, glancing one last time at Hamish before making my way to her side. I closed the door behind us, and she took my hand in hers, kissing me on the cheek. We made our way back downstairs, chatting about the parties she had recently attended in Melbourne, and she told me of her plans to move to Geelong.

'The thought of having you and Victoria as neighbours delights me.'

'I'm sorry for what he said to you, Abigail. I don't know what's going on or who this other man is, but you didn't deserve to be shamed like that.' We stopped at the entrance to the ballroom, and she kissed my cheek before I embraced her then made my way over to Dana.

'I haven't thanked you for accommodating us at the Delmont. We have decided to relocate to Geelong. What a delightful town I find it to be, too, Abigail. I wanted you to be the first to know we will be neighbours.'

'You've met a man, then? Nothing I said seemed to convince you, so why else would you be moving down here?' I realised, looking across at her suspiciously. Her eyes twinkled as she stared back at me.

'Yes, I have indeed. His name is Martin Spicks, and I've taken him to my bed. To help matters, he is a wealthy tavern owner with four establishments in and around Geelong. I promise to take you to all of them. Only because he is the owner and adores me, he lets me into the public bar, where respectable women may never tread. It's all so wonderful, Abigail. We will have so much fun.' She flapped her hands in the air excitedly, causing me to smile as I hugged her before excusing myself.

I made my way over to Amelia to enquire how she was coping since arriving in Australia and being reunited with that unpleasant husband of hers. She insisted I see Matthew, who was growing so fast, and promised she would bring him for a visit next week.

We enjoyed each other's company, and the party lasted well into the early hours of the morning. Catherine and her family had left earlier and returned to Melbourne for another ball the following night, only a few who had chosen not to stay. We had said our goodnights, and I made sure the overnight guests had what they needed in their rooms before finally retiring to mine.

Soon after, Bessie knocked on my door. While helping me undress, she thanked me for inviting her and Danny to the party. I sat at my dressing table as she undid my hair, before brushing and plaiting it for bed.

'Is all well with you, Mistress?' She narrowed her gaze at my reflection in the guilt edged mirror. 'After the way Hamish behaved tonight, he's lucky I didn't smack him across the back of the head, the stupid boy. Drinking like that when already upset was only going to lead to trouble. He spat out some cruel things, and I want you to know it's not true what he said. He is only jealous and upset.' I sighed deeply, feeling sadness overwhelm me.

'Yes, he spoke harshly, but there was truth to his accusations. I am juggling two wonderful men, and eventually, I will break one of their hearts.' Bessie stared at me with some sympathy, securing the long plait with a strip of calico.

'But you know there's more to the story. No one else might, but Polly and I are very aware you're being blackmailed into choosing Aaron. I understand why you don't want to walk away from all you've inherited. Financial security is important to the likes of us orphans. You're in a terrible situation, and I do wish you would tell Aaron and Hamish of your predicament.'

'I can't, Bessie.' My brow creased, the candle on my dressing table flickering as I stared at my reflection, Bessie placing her hands on my shoulders. 'If I did that and I end up pursuing a relationship with Aaron, they will both think I did it for the money. If I end up with either of them, it will be for love and love alone. I do not want anyone to ever know of this condition in that bloody Will. I only recently realised what a controlling bitch great-aunt Isabelle was. She left me in that orphanage, where I had nothing, then dangles a golden carrot in front of me to manipulate me into a life I don't want, knowing I would have no other option. I am still in disbelief and shock. I do not understand what she could gain from this betrothal, especially when she's not even here to witness it. His father was just a nice man who sold seafood to her in Edinburgh.' She nodded silently, guiding me across the room, then helping me into bed before pulling the heavy quilt over me.

'I don't understand it any more than you do, sweetheart. Don't punish yourself. Try to get a good night's sleep and we will talk about it again in the morning,' she whispered before stroking my brow and bidding me goodnight. She left a small lamp burning, casting dark shadows across the room as I stared up at the velvet canopy that hung above.

I lay awake for what seemed like forever, tossing and turning, my mind racing; however, sleep would not come. I wondered if I should tell Hamish I was choosing him and be done with the whole thing. My heart was his—I would happily give up all my new riches to be with him. I knew I had to stop this and make my decision. I had gone over it all in my head a million times, and now it had finally sunk in—Hamish was the one I loved the most and who I wanted to spend my life with. He was the one I would marry.

I hurried out of bed, slipped on my silk dressing gown, and rushed through the endless hallways to the guest wing—the house dimly lit by lamps fixed high above on the walls, a keen eye kept on them by our hall boy, Conner, who hid at the sight of me. Turning the doorknob, I pushed it open slightly to find the lamp still burning on the sideboard, illuminating the room far too brightly for anyone to rest. I pushed it wide, then stepped inside, hurrying over to distinguish the wick before it disturbed his sleep. I reeled back in shock, gasping loudly, unable to take my eyes from Hamish, naked and in bed with Charlotte. She shrieked when she noticed me, and Hamish hastily pulled the covers over them. Dana heard the commotion from the next room and came running to the door to see her daughter trying to hide under the quilts, crying and ashamed.

'What the hell has happened?' she exclaimed, glaring at Charlotte, her eyes wide, while a look of horror crossed her beautiful face. Hamish had not uttered a word. He still appeared intoxicated as he stared at me, his face flushed while he stuttered and stammered, trying to find the words to explain away his behaviour.

'Dana, I'll leave Charlotte to you. Hamish, I want you gone by breakfast, and I hope to never see or speak to you again,' I spat before turning and bolting from the room, leaving Dana standing alone at the door, clearly infuriated as she ordered Charlotte from the bedchamber.

I staggered down the hallway toward my room. I had controlled my emotions from the sheer shock of seeing Charlotte and Hamish together, but with each step toward my door, my strength waned, and by the time I closed it behind me, tears rolled down my face.

He had betrayed me. And I was about to tell him I would marry him. My heart felt like he had ripped it from my chest and stomped on it without thought or care. He had made my final decision for me. As devastated as I felt, I gritted my teeth and told myself repeatedly I would eventually recover—I would just have to—even if it took years. Finally, exhausted after hours of sobbing, I fell into a deep sleep, dreams of stardust, a black tunnel, and a commune called Utopia filling my head.

Chapter Twelve

As I FELT THE first tug of consciousness pulling me up from the dark depths of sleep, I knew something was wrong, but at first, could not remember just what it was. Within moments, memories flooded my mind. Hamish. I felt like someone had punched me in the stomach and I couldn't catch my breath, no matter how hard I tried. But I couldn't think about it—it was too painful. I pushed the thought of him to the back of my mind, as I had so often done in the past when I did not want to think about something. I had guests to entertain and other essential tasks to carry out.

'Good morning, Mistress. It's a fine day outside today, and some of your guests are rising. Oh, my goodness, you look terrible. What have you done to yourself?' Bessie declared, eyeing me suspiciously. She bustled about the room, cheerfully organising my clothing, while I obediently threw my legs over the side of the bed and struggled to my feet, summoning all the strength I possessed to face the day. I did not want to talk about it. The fact was, I could not talk about it without breaking down.

'I didn't sleep well, that's all,' I explained abruptly, Bessie grunting as she nodded, although she continued to glance at me questioningly. I readied myself silently with her help before bidding her farewell and hurrying down to breakfast, finding everyone present and ready to eat. The sheer number of guests forced us to use the formal dining room, its elaborate table seating thirty people at the very least. The room was far too fancy for me; however, I had to admit it was truly beautiful. I adored its teal-coloured décor with silver trims and accents tastefully placed around the bright and cheerful room. I straightened up and crossed the room, smiling while greeting everyone as though nothing had happened last night. For them, it hadn't. I sat down heavily on the vacant seat next to Dana and made myself comfortable. Charlotte sat farther down at the end of the grand table, shamefaced and avoiding my gaze.

'How are you, Abigail?' Dana whispered as she leaned over discreetly, tucking a stray strand of hair behind my ear.

'Fragile, Dana. Extremely fragile,' I replied, and she squeezed my arm in sympathy.

We had full table service from the staff, a rarity in this house, with Mr Masters proudly going from person to person, allowing them to serve themselves from his tray, followed by the footmen, who were doing the same. I felt like I was at a fancy dinner party and should have put on my best gown rather than a house-dress. I turned to my dear friend and lowered my voice.

'Please know, Dana, I am not upset with Charlotte. It's Hamish who betrayed me, and I don't know I can ever forgive that. I love Charlotte, and I know she did not mean to hurt me on purpose. She is young, that's all.' As I served myself eggs from Mr Masters' tray, Dana gazed at me, then briefly at her daughter, before turning back to me.

'Charlotte bears half the burden and the guilt, Abigail.' Her cheeks flushed, her voice only a whisper as she placed her cutlery down on the edge of her plate. 'You are too sweet for your own good. You see only goodness in everyone and do not realise some people aim to hurt you deliberately in this life. As far as I am concerned, she is just as much to blame. I have told her many times that you should never take another woman's man. But, to bed him under your own roof; well, I must inform you, my dear friend, I feel deeply ashamed of her.' I respected Dana's opinion; however, in this case, I felt she was wrong. I had met bad people in my life who would harm you as quick as look at you, but Charlotte was not one of them.

'Don't be too hard on her, Dana. He has infatuated her ever since they met on the ship. She would have done anything for him. I will honestly be all right, I promise you.' I felt my words ring empty as I spoke them, but shook my head slightly in dismissal. Inside, I felt I was dying, but forced a smile for the benefit of my friends. I did not want this to come between Dana and Charlotte. They were as close as every mother and daughter should be—an experience I would never have. I picked at my crispy bacon and creamy eggs with little appetite, giving Dana some time to think about how she would deal with Charlotte when they departed Willow Grove later today. Amelia and George had left me a note advising they were pressed for time and forced to leave early to return home to care for little Mathew, but promised to stay in touch. Tamara and Elizabeth had already departed to catch the train for Melbourne, leaving before the cock crowed by carriage, so I had said my goodbyes to them the night before. Hamish was nowhere to be found; however, had left a message with Mr Masters advising he was sorry and would return later in the day to speak to me. I had instantly dismissed it and, much to his surprise, asked Mr Masters to ignore any further messages from him.

After breakfast, Dana, Charlotte, Victoria, and I strolled out to the wide verandah and made ourselves comfortable on the soft, cushioned chairs.

'Charlotte, I'm not upset with you about what happened. I hope we will remain the friends we have been since we met,' I whispered sincerely. Dana looked over sharply, shaking her head in disbelief. Charlotte's face flushed the same colour as the plump ripe beetroot grown in our garden, bursting into tears as she embraced me.

'I am so sorry, Abigail, and I pray you can forgive me. I've loved him since I met him, and I have tried to stop. When he told me you had another suitor, I thought that... I thought... Oh, I didn't think at all,' she wailed, and I hugged her back.

'It's all right now. As long as we have our friendship, that's what matters.' I passed her a clean handkerchief, which she accepted gratefully, wiping her face before loudly blowing her nose. Mr Masters stepped onto the verandah to announce Aaron had arrived, then turned to usher him out before hurrying away. I introduced him to everyone, then invited him to order breakfast, which he did, striding eagerly off to the kitchen. After he had disappeared from my sight, Dana grabbed me excitedly by the arm.

'Oh, my. He's divine, Abigail. They built him like a brick you-know-what. He makes me wish I was twenty-years younger, you lucky thing. Oh, I'm just so happy for you,' she sang, winking at me, and I felt myself blush.

She was so free in her thinking. I wished for the hundredth time she was my mother, as she always told me the truth regarding anything I asked. I explained about the betrothal and how Aaron and I were getting to know each other. Dana seemed pleased after what had occurred during the night and hugged me tightly. She was far too polite to chastise her daughter while a guest in my home, but I knew as soon as they returned to Melbourne, Charlotte would be in for some scathing criticism.

Aaron returned with his breakfast and sat down with us to eat. He chatted amiably with my friends, and it was apparent all present liked him and found him entertaining, laughing when he would tease them. I enjoyed my time with Dana and the girls, while watching on in amusement as Aaron worked his charms on them. He had a way of making those around him feel good, and I watched him closely now, thinking it an amazing gift he possessed.

Dana soon rose to her feet, advising they must depart no matter how reluctantly. I hugged them all, promising to visit as soon as they arrived in Geelong next week. Aaron and I waved them off, then made our way to the sitting room. Within moments of closing the door behind us, he stopped me, tilting my face up towards him to look me in the eye.

'I haven't been able to kiss ya good mornin', an' that's all I've wanted to do since I woke up.' I smiled as he drew me into his chest and kissed me deeply, then lifted me off my feet. He sat down on the lounge, settling me on his lap. 'Now, tell me what's happened. It's as clear as day you're upset.' He gently stroked my hair while I wondered if I should tell him the truth. I did trust him, and I certainly more than liked him. I started with what had happened earlier last night, and then what Hamish had done soon after. 'What a ratbag, doin' that to ya. Makes it easier for me now, but that's not the point. I'm so sorry you're hurt, Abi,' he said with such sincerity I started to cry. 'So, is it truly over with him?'

'Yes. I never want to see him again,' I replied through my tears.

'Good. The hold he had on ya is no longer, an' now ya can make up ya mind about me without Hamish doin' everythin' in his power to keep us apart. I'm sorry he did that to ya, I really am, but you've been pushin' me away an' keepin' ya distance because of it. You're the most breathtakin' woman I know. Isn't it better ya found out now rather than when ya had a couple of nippers with him, an' discover he has a mistress or two like his father?' I leaned back against his broad chest, and he slipped his arms around my waist. I cuddled against him, then told him of my childhood and what had happened since I'd turned fifteen, culminating in meeting him two weeks ago. 'Bloody hell, Abi. It's all true, then? Ya have no kin to speak of, not even Pollyanna?' I shook my head. He embraced me in a tight hug and stroked my face. 'So, that's what me parents meant about ya unfortunate start in life. Me family will adopt ya. Ya don't have to worry. Me Ma would love to have ya as her daughter; she's always wanted one but got stuck with us four mugs. I'm sad about what you've been through, Abi. I just wanna hold ya an' never let ya go. You'll find the family you're missin' with me. That I promise ya.' He gently kissed the tears from my face, then paused, a glint in his eye. 'I don't want ya to think I'm with ya for ya money. I've already agreed with Mr McPhee on the matter, an' told him I'll sign a document sayin' I've no entitlement to any of it,' he added, a mischievous smirk touching his lips. 'If you'd been unfortunate lookin', though, I wouldn't have signed it.' He grinned, and I grabbed his arm, pretending to shake him.

As we lay on the lounge facing each other, we talked for a long time. I still did not know if I would choose to marry him; however, Hamish's betrayal had taken an enormous burden from me. I no longer had to split myself in two, leaving me feeling anxious or guilty for spending time with one over the other. I liked Aaron, and now I could allow myself to get to know the type of man he really was.

Polly, Leo, Aaron, and I sat outside in the afternoon sunshine, silently gazing out over the back garden and its exquisite white rose bushes, when Angus walked around the side of the house and strode up to us.

'Abigail, Hamish is at the front door, an' he wants to talk to you.' He sounded apologetic, shifting from foot to foot while avoiding my gaze.

'Hamish can go fuck himself and shove his request right up his hairy Scotch clacker. I do not want to see him or talk to him. Tell him to get off my property, Angus,' I snapped before I could stop myself. Leo burst into a fit of giggles while Aaron chuckled loudly.

'Oh, I love it when she says those filthy words. I don't dare use them myself as her hatchet maid would strike me down where I stand,' Leo remarked before hastily looking around to make sure Bessie was not close by. I could feel the heat in my face as I looked at them, all laughing at me. If I saw Hamish right at this moment, I would punch the living shit out of him. I watched Angus grimace, clearly unhappy about the message he was now obligated to pass along to his twin. He nodded, then turned and strolled away, dutifully returning to Hamish to relay my words, no doubt steeling himself for his hot-headed brother's reaction.

'What's happened, Abi?' Polly asked, appearing worried. She glanced around at everyone else, who shrugged or shook their heads in confusion.

'Angus will tell you, I'm sure. I do not want to talk about it and have every intention of putting it behind me.' She arched her perfectly shaped eyebrows, surprised at my abruptness, but said no more. Recently, I'd noticed several characteristics I liked about Aaron, and he was right—I had always kept him at a distance—but now I was free of my obligation to Hamish. I could explore my feelings without guilt or pressure. Angus returned, his shoulders slumped, while his handsome face showed signs of strain. He motioned me aside, taking my arm and leading me down to a silver birch tree at the bottom of the garden to avoid being overheard.

'Hamish wanted me to pass a message on to you an' to make sure you listen. He says he's more than sorry for what he's done to you, an' if he could take it back, he would, but he was drunk, an' she seduced him.' He enunciated every word, concentrating hard to ensure each was relayed correctly.

'Horseshit. It's all excuses, Angus, and I don't accept his apology. I could kill the bastard with my own bare hands.' I screwed up my face, grunting as I raised my hands to his face and demonstrated exactly what I wanted to do to his bastard brother. 'He has only returned to his old ways, so what did I expect? I love you as my future brother-in-law, but I will tell you this only once, so heed me—I do not want to hear about Hamish, talk about Hamish, or for you to tell Hamish anything about me. Otherwise, we will end up having problems, and I don't want that with you.' He nodded in agreement, reaching out his massive arms and embracing me tightly.

'We will always be friends, Abigail, nae matter what my idjit brother does. He has gone now. I told him I thought it best to give you some time to calm down, if only to save himself from bein' struck down dead where he stands.' He led me back to the table before hurrying to Polly's side to kiss her. I sat down beside Aaron, happy to be in his presence, holding hands and chatting with the ones I loved most in the world. He interacted easily with all of them, apart from Polly, who had decided she did not like him at all. He slipped his arm around my shoulders, lowering his voice slightly as he gazed down at me.

'Do ya need me to come to the solicitor with ya tomorrow?'

'Actually, yes, Aaron, that would be splendid. I am certain he will want to talk to you, too,' I replied, squeezing his hand.

Polly rolled her eyes, then grunted loudly. I was well aware how he addressed me was the reason she held such disdain towards him. She had continued to tell him to stop calling me Abi, and he had bluntly refused—now they were engaged in a subtle war of tart comments, eye-rolling, and face-pulling—neither giving an inch. I ignored them both, finding it amusing they were behaving like bairns, while deciding once again to let them sort it out between themselves. Love would eventually grow—once they matured and stopped mimicking and making fun of each other.

I woke the following day feeling slightly unwell, my body shivering while my head ached. Bessie stood over me, her hands on the quilt to prevent me rising from my bed—although she knew full well I was obligated to meet with Mr McPhee, and she would make me late for my appointment at his office in Geelong.

'Mistress, you really ought to be in bed, or the chills will get you. If you stay there, I'll send word to Mr McPhee that you're ill, and he will see you another day. Please listen to me, sweetheart,' she cooed, her warm hands firmly massaging my aching neck as I lay in bed, shivering violently.

'No, I'm going. I promise as soon as I have concluded my business, I will let you do with me as you wish. I cannot let Mr McPhee down, even though he reminds me of that South American iguana I saw at the London Zoo.' She helped me to my feet, the blood rushing to my head and causing the room to tilt sidewards, her hand swiftly reaching and gripping my upper arm to steady me.

'You stubborn shite of a girl,' she muttered to herself before raising her voice. 'Mistress, it goes against all my instincts to let you go; however, you're a determined wee fiend, and I know you'll nag me until you have your way about it. You're to come straight back to bed, and I will make sure Leo has his special broth ready for you,' she scolded, guiding me into the washroom where she had prepared a basin full of warm, scented water to complete my morning toilette. Within only a few minutes, she had me washed and dressed in fresh undergarments, leading me by the hand back into the room where she swiftly dressed me in a plain skirt and shirt, then wrapped a thick woollen shawl around my shoulders before sitting me down at my dressing table. I could not stop sweating, allowing her to pin all my hair on top of my head to get it out of the way. Finally, she helped me to my feet, although she grumbled I was not wearing my finest when out in public. I left her in the room, muttering to herself as she tidied up, making my way slowly downstairs to meet Aaron, finding him at the bottom of the staircase.

'G'day, beautiful,' he called out, his face breaking into a wide grin before his expression changed to one of concern. 'What's wrong with ya? I take back that comment, too. Ya look like a sick chook.' His eyes twinkled in amusement as I tried to smile.

'I feel terrible.' I blew my nose into a clean handkerchief as I reached his side. He escorted me to the carriage waiting just outside the front entrance, then helped me in, calling out a cheery good morning to Harry. Sitting at the front with the leather reins in his calloused hands, he greeted us cheerfully before moving the horses forward into a trot.

'Come here, *mo anamchara*. Let me hold ya,' he said, attempting to pull me towards him.

'You'll catch it, Aaron.' I pulled away from him, then blew my nose again.

'I never get sick. People can be sick all around me, an' I never catch it. It's like I'm Jesus.' I couldn't help but giggle, thinking of what Sister Josephine would say about that. It's blasphemous would be one of those things, of that I was certain.

'What does *mo ann-am-kara* mean?' I asked, resting my head back down on the pillow. He moved closer, slipped his arm around my shoulders, then held my hand, showing me just how much he cared without a word.

'Tis a sayin' me father's said ta me Ma since I was a wee lad back in Ireland, but only ever in private.' I blew my nose again and cuddled into his shoulder, wishing sleep would find me again as he lowered his voice to a whisper. 'It means *my soulmate*.' He leaned down and kissed the tip of my nose, then started playing with my hair, calming and comforting me as I drifted off into a troubled sleep.

Aaron held the heavy oak door open, guiding me inside before allowing it to close behind us, his hand on my back to steady me. Mrs McPhee glanced up from her small desk, her grey hair pinned neatly to the back of her head. Her face broke into a warm smile as she greeted us.

'Look at the two of you. Such a handsome couple. I do hope you are getting along well.'

'Yeah, we are. Thank you for askin', Mrs McPhee,' Aaron replied politely. He led me over to a hard wooden chair that sat against the wall to wait our turn, sitting down beside me in the empty room. Mr McPhee soon came to the door and led us into his office. Aaron made himself comfortable in a leather chair, and I took the one next to him, not feeling as relaxed as he obviously did.

'How are you both? Are you getting along?' Mr McPhee focussed his attention on Aaron, ignoring me completely.

'I'm havin' a ripper of a time,' Aaron replied, grinning as he gave me a wink. Smiling back at him, I turned towards the little rodent, who appeared pleased with himself. I narrowed my gaze, his grey aura swirling around him like a storm cloud.

'I'm happy enough, but not for the reasons you may think. I need more time to decide.' I pursed my lips defiantly. He pushed himself back from his desk in frustration, while I returned his unblinking, reptilian stare.

'Miss Delmont, I gave you two weeks. That time has now ended. I cannot have you extending this on and on just because you feel unsure of yourself,' he snapped, folding his arms across his chest.

'Yes, but the problem is that two weeks is nothing when you are being forced to decide for a lifetime—and how dare you trivialise how I'm feeling? You told me we could discuss this if I wasn't ready, and I'm telling you I'm not.' My voice rose several octaves as I clenched my hands in my lap, conscious of the fact I was becoming angrier the longer I was around this irritating little man.

'I'm happy for Abi to take as long as she needs,' Aaron chimed in helpfully. Mr McPhee dismissed him with a wave of his hand, then fixed me with another stare.

'I have strict instructions to carry out all directions in that Will promptly,' he spat, waving his finger sternly in my direction. 'I only need your decision, not for you to marry right away. You have two-years to do that. What happens after you agree is up to you, and you can take that time to get to know each other better. I will give you another two weeks, but that is the extent of my patience. Even if I wanted to, I could not allow more time. All you have to decide. Yes, I will marry him—or no, I won't.' He sat back in his chair mimicking a whiny girl, his hands curled up into fists on the table, while Aaron shifted in his seat, remaining silent. I nodded wordlessly, my head aching as I pressed my fingers against my temple, averting my gaze, while staring at the log crackling in the fireplace.

At least now, I would have more time to spend with Aaron alone, without Hamish muddying the waters. I knew well enough that alone might bring me closer to a decision, but was also well aware it might not.

'All right, then. Thank you,' he said coldly, acknowledging my reluctant assent. 'I think you're unwell, Miss Delmont, so I will leave you to return to your home. I will see you after the two-week grace period is up. If you need anything, please send word.' He stood up, shook Aaron's hand before nodding coldly at me, then dismissed us by turning his back and gazing up at the crowded bookshelf.

I slept like the dead the entire journey home, my dreams tormented with fever. When I stood to get out of the carriage, I became giddy and Aaron had no other option but to take me in his arms and carry me up to my bedchamber, Bessie running along behind us. Aaron carefully placed me down on the bed, advising Bessie he would return once she dressed me in my nightgown and I was tucked up warmly underneath my quilt. Bessie tutted around me, complaining loudly about how I should have listened to her, and now she would be forced to call for the doctor and sit up with me all night.

Several heavy quilts covered me when Aaron returned. He lay on top of the bed next to me, wiping my face with a cold cloth and making me sip water, unaware of how it hurt my throat every time I swallowed. He stayed with me into the night until Bessie returned to sit with me—my dreams filled with fire, lava, and enormous rocks—and Aaron beside me, holding my hand.

Chapter Thirteen

I SPENT THE NEXT week bedridden, delirious with fever, while being fed soup and water—when they could get the fluid past my lips. Aaron visited every morning and stayed with me into the evening, wiping my face and neck with cool, wet flannels while caring for me. Bessie stayed with me at night, meeting all my needs. The doctor called in to examine me every day, advising them all they could do was wait while attempting to reduce my fever. Aaron wouldn't leave my side, especially during the days when I was talking nonsense and didn't know where I was.

The fever broke on the eighth day, and Aaron and Bessie finally relaxed, knowing I would recover. I opened my eyes to find him sitting fully clothed in the centre of my bed with his shoes off.

'Welcome back to the land of the livin'.' His handsome face broke into a broad grin as I smiled back sleepily. I felt much improved, but was weak and sore. Bessie had bathed me every night, trying to break the fever, while washing my hair with the shampoo I'd brought with me from London, the smell of honeysuckle and lavender still strong. She had changed my linen every day, slipping a clean, soft nightgown over my head before settling me into bed again. I struggled to sit up as Aaron plumped my pillows so I could lean back on them, then arranged the two beside me for himself. I smothered a smile at the cheek of him, assuming I still wanted him in my room now my faculties had been restored. 'Did ya know someone stole the Ceremonial Mace from Parliament House in Melbourne?' he asked, reading to me from the Geelong Advertiser just like a husband would, and I shook my head. He turned and stared at me. 'Yeah, me neither, so we're even.' He chuckled to himself, then kissed my now uncontaminated mouth. I noticed for the first time he had such luscious lips. I was seeing a lot of things with fresh eyes, it seemed.

It touched my heart. He hadn't left my side other than to sleep and had spent his days caring for me, expecting nothing in return. It certainly made me feel closer to him, and I had to face the fact he had now seen me at my worst and hadn't run away. Bessie came bustling in with a tray, bellowing my name before kicking the door shut behind her. I smiled lovingly as she placed the tray down on my lap, then handed Aaron a fresh mug of coffee.

'Now, this was sent up with the strictest of instructions that only the Mistress is to eat what's on the tray,' Bessie advised him, rolling her eyes in irritation. 'Leo's exact words were that you eat like a sea monster for such a pretty man, and will soon have a backside as large as an iceberg—as if he's seen the likes of such a thing with his own two eyes.' Aaron immediately snatched some bacon and a piece of toast from my tray and folded it into a sandwich, making Bessie giggle. I started to eat my omelette, filled with mushrooms and a very sharp cheese, before quickening my pace should he finish before me and want more. I drank my apple juice, then a smaller glass containing a ruby red liquid unfamiliar to me.

'What's this one?' I asked as Bessie sat down on a chair at the foot of my bed.

'Cranberry juice, Leo tells me. The berries are growing here in the garden, and no one knew what to do with them before Leo discovered them.' She raised her eyebrows, clearly surprised Leo could be helpful in any way for anything at all. I took another sip, finding the sharp, fresh taste addictive, and drank the whole glass. My first attempt at solid food in over a week, and I enjoyed every bit, right down to the juices. Bessie beamed at Aaron, telling me how impressed she was with him, how he took care of me, raving on and on about how lucky I was. I relaxed back onto the pillows, Aaron still beside me.

'I missed talkin' to ya when ya were sick, Abi. I hated seein' ya like that.' I turned to him and smiled, staring into his eyes, blue as the ocean.

'Thank you for being there for me. It means a lot.' I reached up and moved his hair away from his brow. He slid his hand up my back to my neck, pulled me towards him and kissed me passionately. His touch set my body on fire, just as Hamish had once done. Thinking of Hamish caused me to pull away, breathless, and settle back on my pillows. He stared at me, appearing amused.

'Do ya want me to read to ya?' he asked, abruptly rising to his feet before I could answer, his sudden movement almost causing me to bounce out and onto the floor.

'Yes, I would love that, Aaron. Thank you,' I replied, closing my eyes. Bessie had taken the newspaper from Aaron and was deeply immersed in an article. He went to find a book, soon returning with Thomas Hardy's Far from the Madding Crowd. After he'd read for a while about Bathsheba Everdene, a young woman who owned a big farm just like me, I stopped him and asked if he wanted to see a trick.

'Yeah. I love magic tricks.' I took the heavy book from him and ran my finger down the page within seconds, closing the book and reciting the entire text, word for word, back to him. He appeared fascinated, staring at me as if I were a freak in one of the many travelling circuses people liked to visit. He demanded I repeat this chicanery, as he called it, over and over with different pages until I tired of it. We fell back on the bed laughing as he continued to try to catch me out, failing every time. I lay cuddled up next to him, feeling everything was right with the world—and I could not wait to read the rest of that book myself. We were quiet for a time before he gently touched my face. 'I need to tell ya Hamish came every day to visit with ya, an' he left a hundred messages with Mr Masters. He stormed past that very patient butler of yours an' up the stairs, makin' his way to ya bedchamber before I could grab him an' chuck him out. I hope you're not angry.' I looked at him for a moment, considering if I was.

'No, I'm not. He's the last person I want to think about or speak of.'

He squeezed my hand and pulled me over onto his chest. We lay chatting in bed for most of the day and only stopped to eat. I was feeling much better by evening when it was time for Aaron to leave.

'You're still as weak as a kitten, but since the fever broke, you look much better. I was worried for ya, Abi—worried I was goin' to lose ya. That's why I stayed. I couldn't leave ya.' His eyes shimmered with tears he quickly brushed away. I kissed him on the mouth, silently thanking him for his love and care. He departed after a last kiss, just as Bessie came in to sit with me.

Within moments of settling ourselves down to gossip, we heard shouting drifting up through the open window—voices I recognised. I struggled out from under the heavy quilt and rose to my feet, slipping on my dressing gown, then hurried as quickly as I could down the stairs. Bessie was close behind me, calling out as she tried to catch up with me.

'You will catch your death, and with you just being out of your sickbed, too.'

I found Aaron and Hamish in front of the house. Aaron pushed Hamish to the ground, refusing to hit him as it was clear to all he had a skin full. Hamish kept trying to stand to hit Aaron; however, he would not let him get to his feet. Every time he was nearly vertical and tried to take a swing at him, Aaron would push him down onto the ground.

'Are ya finished?' Aaron asked him calmly.

'No, not until I get to talk to her,' Hamish roared, raising his large hand to his face and pushing several stray curls out of his eyes. He stumbled back, swaying precariously from side to side.

'Ya shouldn't be within a bull's roar of her in the state you're in, mate. Ya can speak with her here in front of Bessie an' me, but then ya have to piss off home. Is that all right with ya, Abi?' He turned to look at me and shrugged his shoulders. I thought if it would keep the peace and get him to leave, so be it.

'Yes, fine. Let's get it over with,' I replied coldly. I walked down the front steps as Hamish staggered toward me. 'I'm warning you, don't touch me, or I will rip your fucking ear off,' I snapped, pointing my finger threateningly at his face. He took a half step back in surprise, his eyes widening.

'Aye, I won't, I promise. Just hear me out. Let me speak, an' please don't interrupt me until the end. Promise?' he slurred, and I nodded despite feeling a mixture of disgust and anger. I stood with my arms folded, waiting for him to start. 'First, I'm sorry for what I did. I woke with her naked in my bed, an' she did things to me. I shut my eyes an' pretended it was you.' Tears threatened to spill down his cheeks as I crossed my arms and jutted out my chin.

'Well, it wasn't me, was it?' I snapped again, wanting to strike him as I stomped my foot on the ground. It took all my strength not to.

'Naw, it wasn't, an' I'll live to regret that night forever. Please forgive me an' let me prove myself to you. I cannae sleep or eat or think without you.' He stared up at me as if demanding sympathy, and I shook my head.

'Well, you can certainly still drink, you fat headed moron,' I spat, leaning down to point my finger in his face again. 'I'm sorry, Hamish, but you must listen carefully to me now. You are what they call at the taverns a funt, and I never want to set my eyes on you again in this lifetime. We are finished. Do you hear me? You need to stop coming here, as I will no longer entertain you privately.' He shook his head vigorously, unable to speak. 'Stop coming here! Jesus, Mary and fucking Joseph. I feel like I'm talking to a brick wall.'

I noticed Bessie cross herself, then look skyward, muttering under her breath. I did not have to worry about my soul or where it was going—Bessie had it all well in hand. Hamish broke down, tears streaming down his face. Aaron bent down and took him by the arm, gently pulling him to his feet before leading him away to his mount.

'I'll see him home, then return to me own. Don't be worryin' yourself about this. Go on an' get back to bed. You're weak, an' ya shouldn't even be up. Goodnight, Abi.' Aaron bent down and pulled Hamish to his feet before leading him over to his horse, then helping him up. I waved goodbye, feeling a pang of grief over the loss of Hamish, although impressed at how magnanimous Aaron was to escort him home after everything he had said and done.

I returned to my bed, and after some time, drifted off to sleep. I dreamed of two enormous kangaroos fighting in the bush, an empty cup and saucer sitting on a table, before finding myself stranded on top of a mountain, unable to get down.

Only one full day remained until Polly and Angus married, and, although I was gaining strength after my recent illness, I felt melancholy. I would have to see Hamish, as he would stand by Angus as his witness and best man, while I would be by Polly. Aaron would escort me to the wedding breakfast afterwards; however, he would attend the ceremony alone. For the sake of the bride and groom, he sensibly knew he must keep his distance from Hamish to prevent causing a scene. I was not looking forward to tomorrow at all.

Aaron and I had just returned from a ride through the hills, and it was invigorating. I had relaxed around horses—but only a little. Aaron patiently coaxed me to stand closer each day and encouraged me to stroke, feed, and brush them under his supervision. They were not as frightening as I had first thought. Of course, now owning my own horse had helped ease my fear—but only a little.

She was the most gorgeous creature I had ever seen, with the longest eyelashes, large doe-like eyes, and the glossiest black mane, shimmering in the light as if it were wet whenever she moved. As was all her breed, she too was a big, muscular girl—but far more petite than her brothers and sisters, while her kind disposition and sweet nature had helped me bond with her quickly. Harry had trained her to saddle for me, and she was the quietest horse I had ever seen. I named her Delightful Angel—affectionately known as Delly. Aaron had been riding her for me and teaching her little things Harry may have missed. Today she had done an excellent job yet again, carrying us proudly and without fault. If she continued to be so well-behaved, they told me I could try to ride her on my own in the next few days.

We dismounted, then brushed her down and put her away in her stall. Before I left, I fed her a carrot as a treat. We strolled back to the house hand in hand, then made our way up to my bedchamber to rest, both feeling tired. I soon dozed off in Aaron's arms, sleeping deeply for several hours. When I awoke, his hand rested gently on my cheek, a finger on my lips. He had been staring at me while I was asleep.

'Ya look so young when ya sleep,' he whispered, then leaned over and kissed my lips.

'Probably because I am,' I replied, kissing him back.

'Stop bein' a smartarse. Ya sound like ya mate who hangs around the kitchen.'

Once we stopped laughing, he reminded me he soon must leave to return to his own home. He knew I was busy with last-minute wedding preparations, and tomorrow would be a big day. I walked him out to the stables, and we said our goodbyes quickly, both of us having a lot to do and very little time to do it.

'So, how does it feel to eat your last dinner as a single woman?' I asked Polly, who was serving herself a slice of roast beef.

'It feels wonderful to know I will never eat alone again after today,' she said dreamily. I rolled my eyes, of which she took no notice. What were we, a kettle of fish? She hadn't eaten alone since I had found her, causing me to smother a smile. I assumed she felt if Angus wasn't with her, she was alone. Leo distracted me from my thoughts, sliding into a chair next to me.

'Come on, tell me what's wrong,' I said, picking up a crystal glass and sipping the aromatic red wine, a gift from Dana.

'I'm just trying to make sure in my mind I have all the preparations completed and nothing will go wrong.' He waved his hand dramatically in the air as I smothered a smile.

'Leo, you're worried about nothing. The engagement fare was magnificent, and the wedding breakfast will be, too,' I reassured him, nudging his ribs with my elbow. He was very hard on himself and his expectations were high, a standard he ensured he lived up to while expecting everyone around him to do the same.

We finished our meal, and I thanked the staff for their help, resulting in each of them bowing to me. I still didn't understand why things had to be so formal all the time. Maybe Aaron's laid-back attitude was rubbing off on me. He never talked down to any of the employees, whether they were house staff or farmhands. He treated everyone with respect and no different than if he'd been their friend for years, even calling them by their first names. I had not met a single person who didn't like him—well, except for Polly and Hamish—I disregarded them completely as I believed they had their own agendas.

We expected Dana to visit after dinner, although I wished she had eaten with us. Polly and I made our way to the sitting room, where we sat down and made ourselves comfortable. Dana had moved to Geelong with Charlotte and Victoria last week and settled into a house not too far away. She planned to visit to see how I was faring, and to catch me up on all the gossip. If anything worth knowing happened around Geelong, Dana knew about it.

Polly and I chatted about how far she had come and how she had never dreamed she would meet anyone like Angus. Leo had returned to the kitchen after dinner to continue his preparations with the other staff, who were all working into the wee hours, in order to be ready for tomorrow. Mr Masters showed Dana in, and she squealed when she saw me, running over and embracing me tightly. She sat down next to Polly and gave her a warm hug.

'How are you feeling, sweetie?' she asked, holding her hand.

'Oh, Dana, I am so excited I could burst.' Polly beamed at her, her skin glowing. 'But I must leave you two to talk. I have so many things I need to prepare for tomorrow.' She hugged me, then Dana, bidding us goodnight, appearing to float out of the room as we called out our farewells for the night.

'Well, at least she's happy, unlike you,' Dana remarked with a smile. She could see right through me, even when I was putting on a good front.

'Dana, I'm still so furious with him—and so hurt. I had decided to marry him, you know? I was on my way to his room that night to tell him when I found him with Charlotte.'

'He loves you deeply, Abigail,' Dana said. 'If you love him, you could forgive him and still marry. It's never too late. Charlotte told me what happened that night. She admitted she was the one who instigated it all. She believes she is in love with him, the silly girl. If she had eyes in her head, she would see he only ever looks at you with pure love.' She shook her head in disbelief.

'I wish I could, but every time I think of him now, all I see is him with Charlotte. The betrayal cuts me like a knife. However, the last two weeks with Aaron have convinced me there needs to be character behind the handsomeness, and I certainly feel something for him. Maybe my future lies with Aaron.'

'Ooh, I like the lies part. Tell me what it's like when Aaron kisses you? He is ruggedly handsome in that Australian outdoor way. I believe they call them larrikins. If he kissed me, I would just grab him and do things that have never been done to him before. But that's just me.' She gave a mischievous laugh, and I couldn't help but laugh with her. She was so refreshingly open with her thoughts.

'When he kisses me, I feel tingly all over and just want to crawl inside him. We often spend time together in my room during the day, and he holds me and says the loveliest things. He never tries to make me go farther than kissing, but the way he does that turns my body to fire, and the desire I have for him makes me want to combust.' I averted my gaze, suddenly feeling shy.

'That's a good start, and it's apparent you get along famously.' Her melodious laughter filled the comfortable room, the fire in the hearth crackling, its warmth penetrating deep into my bones. 'There are many successful marriages based on much less than that. From what I know of him and from all you have told me, he would take care of you and love you. The things he says to you melt my heart. But you must give a little back, too, you know? You cannot keep that wall up forever. He is doing everything he can to break it down, but you must help him, or he will give up. You can be hard work, sweetheart, and now could be the time to let the softer side—the side I know you have—come out.'

I regarded her thoughtfully. I always took her advice seriously. That unique, golden glow surrounding her and so many I loved connected us.

'I know you're right, Dana, but I'm finding it hard to let Hamish go forever. There is still a part of him I'm holding onto, and that's the side of himself he showed only to me and how special he made me feel.' I started to cry. She leaned over and took my hand.

'Abigail, you are a sweet girl, and despite how mature you are for your age and all you have been through in your brief life, you are still a girl. You have no experience in love, and to have two handsome, good men pursuing you would confuse the best of us. Ultimately, you must go where your heart leads you. It will be a hard decision to make, but I know you will make the right one. I have faith in you—all I want is for you to be happy.'

She slipped her arm around me and patted my back until the tears stopped and I caught my breath. In my heart, I knew she was right—I would have to let Hamish go and move on with my life—or forgive him, trust he would never repeat what he did and spend my life with him. I sniffed loudly, wiping my face with a clean handkerchief before deciding to change the subject.

'Tell me all about this new man, Dana. I want to hear everything about Mr Martin Spicks.' Her eyes twinkled as she thought of him.

'Oh, Abigail, he's divine, and the things he does to me make my body cry out for more.' She laughed so hard her body shook. 'He is fifty-years old, and I met him at a party in Melbourne. He owns four pubs, which I will take you to some time—and the wine I sent is from him. You received it, didn't you?' I nodded, thanking her profusely, asking her to tell him of our appreciation before indicating for her to continue. 'He lives in a grand house on the outskirts of Geelong. He isn't what you would call handsome by normal standards, but he is a beast in bed, is genuinely humorous, and treats me like a princess. More importantly, he is lovely to the girls. He tells me I am beautiful and the only woman in the world for him and says flattering words to me every day. He's asked me to marry him, and I've said yes.' I grabbed her, squealing as we jumped up and down on the soft lounge.

'Congratulations, Dana. When you set your mind on something, you get it. I will never forget the first day I met you on the ship, and you said you were coming here to find a rich husband. That's exactly what you did.' I laughed at her, and she giggled.

'All within four weeks.' She laughed harder before lowering her voice in the empty room. 'Martin was standing in the corner talking to one of the Chirnside brothers. I'm not sure if you've had the privilege of meeting *that* family yet. They're hideous, I must say.' She continued laughing, shaking her head, her eyes sparkling. 'Anyway, I digress. Martin couldn't stop staring, his eyes following me across the room, and I knew then I had his interest. He is tall and thin with dark hair and a lovely face, but he has severe burns down one side of his face and body and seemed self-conscious and shy about it." She smiled to herself, gazing into the glow of the embers, a new log catching on top. 'I chose my moment, approached him, and introduced myself. Although it took him a while to open up, we both got along like nobody's business, and I just knew he was perfect. By the end of the night, he asked if he could call on me. He visited me the next day at The Delmont, and we sat for hours talking. I had already decided he was the one for me and wanted him, so asked if he was willing to get the matter of going to bed out of the way. He happily obliged, and we have been together every day since. He rented me the house down the road from here until we're married to ensure I do not lose my reputation, but he comes and stays every night. The things we do for most of the night make me need to sleep some of the day away.' She winked at me, and I could feel myself blushing.

Dana had always been frank about enjoying sexual relations and liked to talk about it, right down to the finer details. She had taught me everything I knew. Although I had not practised it yet, I was confident I could, thanks to her. I had met no one like her in my life, and I loved everything about her. She knew how to be a lady but didn't always choose to be, and she was the strongest woman I knew.

'How is Charlotte coping after what happened at the engagement party?' I asked. 'No one else knows except us. All the other guests slept through it, and I'm sure no one will find out, nor will it ruin her reputation.'

Dana looked at me darkly. 'The way I feel right now is she deserves her reputation to be ruined. The silly girl sent word to Hamish last week when we arrived, advising we had moved to Geelong and provided our address. She's been waiting for him to call on her every day since; however, he hasn't shown his face. Instead, she has been moping around the house and snapping at everyone because she is so upset. Time will tell what will happen, I suppose.'

We finished the large cups of hot chocolate Leo had made especially for us. The drink was smooth, creamy, and full of velvety chocolate with lashings of sugar, leaving me wanting to curl up in a blanket and sleep. He walked into the room at that moment with his own cup of chocolate and bounced down next to me on the lounge, putting his slippered feet up on the coffee table.

'So, butterheads. What's the latest gossip in Abigail's life? Do you know? No? Neither of you has heard a word? Oh, for crying out loud, it's all around the district that our little Abigail is a bit of a whore,' he announced. My mouth dropped open in surprise as Dana gasped, appearing shocked as I turned to him and narrowed my gaze.

'And who might have spread that rumour among the workers, the very people who then take the gossip into town, given I don't really know anyone here yet?' I raised my eyebrows, while he smiled unassumingly back at me.

'Well, it could have been me, but how it ended up was not how I said it. I just told my servants in passing you were the jammiest bit of jam to have two handsome men in your bed, while most of the men in the district want to climb in there as well. Wanting very much to help you, I only suggested we wouldn't have to wait long to see a parade of men lined up through the hallways here, waiting their turn.' He widened his eyes innocently as rage bubbled up inside me. I reached up in indignation and grabbed his ear, twisting it hard while pulling his face close to mine as he screeched in pain.

'You and your injudicious mouth. How can you say shit like that about me? Now, look what's happened. Not even my neighbours will acknowledge me because of you, you wanker,' I spat, his face so close to mine I felt his breath as he tried to pull away from my steely grip, shaking him several times more by the ear. Dana started to laugh, his high-pitched screams a little higher as I twisted harder.

'All right. I give up. I'm sorry for opening my mouth again. Just let go of my ear. I don't know what injudicious means either,' he shrieked as I gave him one last twist for good measure, then released him. He held his ear, moaning like a five-year-old lass, then stood up and grabbed a fistful of my hair and yanked it hard. He ran out of the room before I could seek my revenge, while Dana howled with laughter, tears running down her face.

'Abigail, he is like no servant I have ever seen.' Her body shook as she laughed harder, unable to contain herself as I rubbed my scalp. 'They'd whip him if he behaved like this at any other grand home. You must pull him into line before he makes you a laughingstock in the district. He is so disrespectful of you; the way he says your derriere is enormous and your breasts sag is a disgrace is what it is. He really is impossible. He told me last time I was here when I asked how he was, he was as gay as a priest on a Sunday, whatever that means.' She wiped her eyes before continuing. 'Oh, Abigail. The situations you seem to get yourself into because of him. There will be no uncrossing that bridge in terms of your reputation.' She laughed again, then wiped the rest of her face with her handkerchief and calmed herself. Raising my hand, I rubbed my scalp again, trying to lessen the pain. I would find Leo tomorrow and fix him good, as I would have plenty of time to think about it overnight. I walked Dana out, hugged her at the door, waving goodbye as I watched her get into her carriage and trot down the long driveway into the darkness. She had given me a great deal to consider before my mind would rest.

I made my way upstairs to find Bessie waiting in my bedchamber.

'Did you have a pleasant night with Dana?' I let her undress me, slip a nightgown over my head and lead me to the dressing table, where I sat before the mirror, studying my face.

'Yes, it was lovely, thank you, Bessie.' I smiled weakly as she took a brush to my thick, wavy hair that grew like weeds.

'All I could hear every time I passed anywhere near you was laughter. That Dana really brightens you up, doesn't she?'

'Yes, she does that, all right. So, how was your day?'

'Well, I haven't told you my recent news, have I?' I shook my head, the glow from the lamp on the dressing table causing her eyes to sparkle. 'Danny joins me in the staff quarters to take his meals, and no longer eats with the farmhands or grooms. He kissed me goodnight last night for the first time.' Her eyes glazed over, and she glowed as she talked about him, sharing how nice he was to her and what a kind and lovely soul she found him to be.

'So, you will soon need those married accommodations then?' I teased, and she smiled at me.

'If so, it won't be for a very long time,' she said firmly, and I giggled.

After bidding Bessie goodnight, I sat down at the small dining table where I occasionally took my meals—the sitting room next to my bedchamber comfortable and warm—and wrote to Sister Josephine, a ritual I undertook every second night without fail, telling her all my news. I found it comforting to open my heart to her on the other side of the world, knowing whatever I wrote would stay with her. I told her about Aaron and Hamish, my fears and desires in life, how much I deeply missed her, and my belief one day we would reunite once again. In a previous letter, I had confided exactly what the conditions in my aunt's Will were, explaining my dilemma. She would not yet have received the first letter I had written on the ship, but I knew she would do the same and reply once they reached her. I was confident I would soon receive word every second day from her, even if her letters were all delivered at once. I planned to read them in order and keep them for the rest of my life.

I lay in bed thinking of tomorrow and all it would bring. Polly would finally marry her true love after what felt like an extraordinary amount of time. Was it not even a whole month since we'd arrived here? It would be the first time I would see Hamish since that night, and the thought of it made me feel ill. Although I had seen him only once since, he had been falling down drunk. We had not been alone since, and he hadn't had the opportunity to wear me down with his supposed remorse. Tomorrow, though, he would have me beside him most of the day, and Polly expected me to behave in front of all those people while providing me with no means of escape. I told myself I must remember how angry and humiliated I felt, steeling myself to hold on to that feeling when I was with him, or he would catch me up in his charms again.

I drifted off to sleep and dreamed of brides falling over, a seashell, and a man holding me in his arms as if he would never let me go.

Chapter Fourteen

MY EYES FLUTTERED OPEN, the sound of a kookaburra laughing in the distance waking me, his morning song filling the room, the dawn already breaking. I silently hoped it was a good omen and the sharp-beaked bastard was not making fun of my trepidations. I lay under the heavy quilt for quite some time, reflecting on my life, while contemplating just what I would do with it. Since moving here, I had rarely visited Geelong town itself, other than when Mr McPhee forced me to attend his office. I had been too busy on the property, getting used to how everything worked. I had only been there for brief visits—promising myself almost daily I would walk around the bustling shop fronts—but so far, had failed to do so.

The town centre was large and clean. Geelong sat on a hill beside a bay—a sight I thought beautiful every time I would pass in my carriage and look down on it. I didn't know many people as yet, so had recently decided to familiarise myself with the town and its inhabitants. I wanted to learn the names of streets, buildings, everything, just so I wouldn't appear uneducated and knew where to buy all that was required to run our property.

I had heard through Amelia there was a girls' orphanage, and I wanted to see if I could assist in some way, even volunteer my time during the week to help with the children. I couldn't sit around here anymore like the queen of the castle, ordering people around and trying to find productive ways to fill my day while everyone waited on me and catered to my every whim.

I thought of Aaron, as I did every time I awoke, and smiled to myself. We had become so close over the past two weeks since Hamish was no longer around. Sometimes I longed to feel Aaron's arms around me, to feel his heartbeat and deep, slow breathing, yet I was still finding myself unable to take that last step and love him completely.

However, I loved being with him and would have enjoyed having him with me day and night, but I had a wall up because of Hamish, as Dana had pointed out. The thought of seeing him today was giving me knots in my stomach. Of course, I wouldn't have to be alone with him until after the wedding when we were travelling back to the house for the reception, and Polly and Angus would be there, so maybe I was worrying over nothing. The truth was, I knew it wouldn't stop Hamish from speaking his mind no matter who was around, especially since he considered Polly and Angus his allies. Fortunately, Bessie came bouncing into the room, distracting my troubled mind.

'I take it Danny kissed you again last night?' I smiled, and she beamed back at me.

'Yes, he did, and it was marvellous. He took me for a walk in the garden—I hope you don't mind—and the moon was so bright. He grabbed me in his arms and kissed me properly, tongue and all. It was so romantic.' She giggled, and I burst into loud laughter.

Bessie had brought me a tray with breakfast, which I devoured far too quickly, still leaving me no time to go downstairs. She efficiently helped me into my bridesmaid's dress, acutely aware we had to leave soon after Polly dressed and they styled her raven hair. Impatient to leave and help Polly ready, I allowed Bessie to organise me without complaint. I studied my reflection in the large oval mirror in the corner—standing far taller than me—a forgotten relic from the old world left here by my aunt; I assumed. Impressed by the beautiful lilac gown, its lace sleeves and tight-fitting bodice stitched almost invisibly by Catherine's own talented hands. She had done such a magnificent job, and I had told her so hundreds of times already.

If I ever married, I would ask her to design my wedding dress. Polly's was a work of art. I could tell she would make a decent business of it when she finally went out on her own. I was looking forward to seeing Catherine again and her family at the wedding today. They planned to stay overnight this time, so I would have the chance to get to know her parents better. I also wanted to spend a little time with William. Since his hostility had abated, I was looking at him as a potential friend now, too.

I hurried down the hallway to Polly's room and knocked on the door. Little Mary—now assigned to Polly to work as her ladies' maid—was just removing the barely touched breakfast tray while talking sternly, her tiny finger waving in the air, her white cap on crooked. When she saw me, her shoulders slumped, and she gave a sigh of relief.

'She won't eat anythin', Mistress, an' I've tried everythin' to convince her, but she won't budge, the stubborn fiend,' she said despairingly. I took the tray from her, thanked her, and sat on the bed next to Polly. I looked at her smiling face and found it hard to be cross with her, especially today.

'I know you are excited, but if you don't eat at least half of everything on this tray, we are not going anywhere. You will walk into the church alone.' She glared at me but took the tray obediently, a scowl on her face as she ate. 'Come on, Polly, be happy. Today is the day you get your prince,' I teased, and her frown disappeared.

Her dress, hanging on a hook, was so voluminous it hid the door behind from sight. Catherine covered the silk sleeves and bodice in a beautiful white lace, the bodice hand stitched with crystal beading. The enormous skirt flared out from the tight-fitting waist, making it difficult to get anywhere near her. The veil—made of the same lace used for the dress—flowed over and away from the skirt. She looked beautiful in it and had tried it on for me dozens of times in the last week alone, but today was going to be special. Bessie ordered Polly to sit at the dressing table to apply face paint, then began undoing the small rags she had used last night to curl her hair. It had taken well, resulting in masses of curls in her ordinarily straight black hair. Bessie twisted, pulled, and pinned every strand into precise curls on top of her head, then pinned her headpiece in place on the crown of her head—a sparkling tiara I had bought for her in Melbourne. I had asked Catherine to pick it up and bring it down to me when she came for the engagement party, and I had given it to Polly just last night before she went to bed. She had cried when she opened the box and saw the glittering diamonds—promising to keep it forever to pass on to her daughters—God willing. Confiding the gift was the most meaningful and memorable she had ever received. She made me promise not to speak of it to Angus should it cause him to stop buying presents for her. We helped her into her dress, then stood back to take in her beauty. Angus would be beside himself with happiness when he saw her, although we knew he would feel the same way even if she turned up in rags.

Outside, Harry cheerfully helped Polly, then me, into the carriage. He smiled at us approvingly, then pushed our large skirts in behind us. We sat opposite each other as the carriage moved toward Geelong, everyone else following behind in convoy. I was so proud of how far Polly had come in such a short time, and it overwhelmed me with joy at her happiness. We talked the whole way, Polly showing no signs of nervousness at all. The journey passed quickly as we spoke of our lives at the orphanage and how so many wonderful things had happened since finding each other.

We soon arrived in Geelong to find Mr Makenzie waiting patiently outside the imposing bluestone church, Saint Mary's of the Angels, that sat on the hill overlooking the township of Geelong. He had offered to walk Polly down the aisle, given she had no parents, surprising us both very much given he was such a mean bastard most of the time and couldn't lie straight in bed.

Our spirits were high, our mood jovial as Harry helped us down from the carriage. We thanked him before making our way towards the imposing bluestone church, talking all the way while attending to Polly's large skirt and long veil. She was in great spirits and showed not a sign of nervousness as we stepped through the oversized doors. The music started, and I hurried through the entrance to the smaller doors that opened up into the church, feeling sick at the thought I would have to walk to Hamish and stand by his side. I noticed Amelia and George as I stepped inside, and she gave me a small wave. I gazed down the aisle toward the altar and saw Angus and Hamish waiting, both looking as nervous as cats on the roof of an ironbark hut as they watched me approach.

In the middle pews stood Dana with Martin, with Charlotte and Victoria standing beside them, while Tamara and Elizabeth, accompanied by their fiancés, sat a little farther along. As I approached the altar, I went to the left, then waited for Polly. I heard Angus gasp at the sight of her as she appeared at the entrance with Mr Makenzie, resplendent in his kilt and new jacket, his hair pulled back and secured in a ponytail at the back of his neck. She radiated pure love and was truly beautiful, reminding me of a princess I had seen long ago in a picture book. She marched up the aisle to the organ music with a determined stride and a smile that wouldn't leave her face, almost dragging Mr Makenzie along. When she joined Angus, she took his hand, and they moved to the altar, where Father McCleary began the ceremony. They never let go the entire time and did not take their eyes from each other for a moment.

I clapped when they were pronounced man and wife and had their first married kiss. Polly was now a Makenzie. She hadn't been a Delmont for very long. Tears of joy poured down my face for them. I could see them together forever and as happy as they were today when their days here were done.

The moment I had been dreading for two weeks had arrived—it was time for me to stand by Hamish and follow the glorious couple down the aisle to the waiting carriage. He came toward me and offered me his arm, which I took reluctantly. We began what I felt was an endless walk past guests, either smiling or dabbing tears from their faces, while the recessional music resonated in the church's nave.

'How are you, Abigail? I've missed you more than you know,' he whispered, smiling pleasantly while nodding at the guests as we slowly kept pace with the bride and groom.

'I am very well, thank you,' I replied coldly, looking straight ahead and concentrating hard not to trip over my dress with my enormous feet. The last thing I wanted was Hamish coming to my rescue in any shape or form. My arm barely touched his, yet he still sent shivers through me, an involuntary reaction that both annoyed and confused me.

'I'm glad to hear it,' he replied quietly, nodding hello to several family friends.

Dana caught my eye and winked. Poor Charlotte gazed at Hamish in wonder; however, he didn't acknowledge her existence at all as we passed them and continued along. She could not hide the hurt and embarrassment he had silently inflicted, upsetting me greatly as I fought the urge to twist his balls off where he stood. Once outside, we waited for the exiting crowd to congratulate the couple, Hamish leaving my side for a moment to greet a friend. At long last, we made our way towards the carriage. Hamish helped me up behind the newlyweds and then turned to speak with his parents, leaving me alone with them. I settled myself opposite the pair, their bodies entwined as they whispered to each other—embracing and kissing with so much love, I thought I would cry.

'Congratulations to you both.' I leaned forward as far as my dress would allow and kissed them on the cheek, Polly first, then my new brother-in-law. 'You are going to have the happiest of lives together, of that I am certain.' They smiled at me briefly before turning back to stare into each other's eyes. I could see they were going to be absolutely no help to me in my current situation. They were completely absorbed in each other, and I doubted they had even heard what I had just said.

Within moments, Hamish climbed into the carriage and closed the door behind him. He sat next to me, taking up most of the seat so I couldn't help but be near him. I had trouble keeping my breathing regular, my heart racing so fast, I thought it would burst.

'I need to talk to you, Abigail, and I don't care who overhears me,' Hamish pleaded even before the carriage moved. As I suspected, Angus and Polly were too busy kissing and whispering to notice anything said between us, and couldn't help me even if they did.

'Hamish, I don't believe there is anything you can say to me, or anyone else, to change my mind.' I stared out the window, ignoring him as we passed a haberdashery store that piqued my interest. I moved as far away from him as possible until I was pressed against the wall of the carriage.

'I regret what happened more than you'll ever know. I know it's no excuse, but I was drunk, an' I was worried I was losin' you.' He reached across and tried to take my hand in his, but I angrily shook him off.

'So, you fuck another woman? Yes, that's the way to a girl's heart, Hamish,' I replied icily. He ran his hand through his curly black hair, making a right mess of it, tears welling in his eyes.

'Abigail, I love you more than I've ever loved anyone.' His voice was deep and low, filled with emotion as I tried to ignore him. 'I want to spend the rest of my life with you. I made a terrible mistake, I know. She came to my bed an' threw herself at me. I dinnae want to do anythin' with her, but she was naked an' touchin' me. Half asleep, it reminded me of how I feel when I'm with you—so I pretended she was you. I know it was wrong, an' I'm the sorriest for it. But I want to try an' make it up to you, if you'll only give me the chance. I dinnae want you thinkin' it was me returnin' to my old ways, that's all. You're forever in my heart, Abigail—the only one who truly owns it. I dinnae want to move on to the next one, or anyone else at all. I adore you; you're the only person I want beside me. You have to believe me.' His voice broke, and he slumped in his seat, leaning away from me. I swallowed hard. I knew he was in pain and missing me—I was missing him, too—but I couldn't back down.

'I'm sorry, Hamish, but you betrayed me, and I don't think I can ever forgive that. What happens if we marry, you get drunk when we argue, and you jump into bed with another woman? How do you think I would feel then? I hope you will take care of Charlotte's heart. Like it or not, you have it now, and I would hate for you to hurt her.'

'I told you Charlotte was a mistake. I dinnae want to be with her. She follows me around like a sheep, an' I cannae get rid of her now. Can't you try? At least give me one more chance?' he begged, then placed his forefinger under my chin and moved my face toward him so he could look me in the eye.

My anger bubbled over. 'At least? At least give you a chance? I don't owe you anything, Hamish, after the way you treated my love for you. If I hadn't caught you, would you have told me what passed between you? Or would you have waited for me to be the last to know, not giving a fat rat's arse you turned me into a laughing stock around the district?'

'Aye, I wouldn't have told you, no.' There was deep sadness in his voice as he averted his gaze to the floor. 'I would have been too ashamed an' worried I'd lose you, but it seems I have anyway.' He said no more and turned to stare out the window. Watching Polly and Angus, entirely absorbed in each other as the carriage bumped along, I realised I was at an unpleasant fork in the road. I could choose to forgive and take him at his word, or I could let him go for good. Despite everything, I had already considered he had been drunk, and I was seeing Aaron—which I knew was upsetting him to no end—and he didn't know the ugly truth about my great-aunt's Will. Despite that, I couldn't get past the fact he had gone a step too far. I was so hurt and bitter I knew I couldn't let my wall down with him again. In some ways, I was glad it happened before I told him I would marry him. But, in others, I often questioned if things would have turned out the way they did if I had told him my decision earlier. I doubted very much I would ever truly know for certain, and I knew that would bother me until I took my last breath.

We returned to Willow Grove, and Angus and Polly went straight to the cottage to allow their guests time to arrive and spend some time together after being surrounded at the church by friends and family. I saw Aaron waiting for me near the front steps, and I made my way to him, smiling in relief. He lifted me off the ground in a warm embrace while Hamish glowered at him from a distance.

'How are ya, Abi? Ya looked so beautiful standin' in the church. If Miss Polly—or Mrs Makenzie I should be sayin'—wasn't the lovely bride she is, ya would have stolen the show,' he said and kissed me on the mouth. I wrapped my arms around his neck and kissed him back, not caring there were people around. 'Did Hamish give ya any stick?' He removed a curl from my face with his finger.

'Ha, he didn't give me any stick, as you so charmingly put it, but he was very emotional and wanted to talk. I really couldn't say anything he wanted to hear.' I smiled weakly at him, and he put his arm around my waist and smiled back.

'Good. The less talkin' between ya now, the better. I know how soft-hearted ya are, Abi. It shits me he's tryin' to talk his way back into ya life an' play on ya good nature.' The guests had started to arrive for the wedding breakfast, the staff bustling about, showing them to their tables in the ballroom. I saw Dana, Martin, and the girls, and we crossed the room to meet them. Dana embraced Aaron while accidentally letting her hand slip down to his backside, much to his amusement. She whispered to me later she would take it where she could find it, sending me into fits of giggles as she described Aaron's body in every detail. It was almost as if she had a magic gift to look at him and see him completely undressed. Polly had placed Amelia and George at the table with Dana's group; and Elizabeth, Tamara, and their future husbands with Aaron. Catherine sat at the next table with her family, along with Bessie and Danny, and another couple I was unfamiliar with. I said goodbye to Aaron, explaining I was obligated to sit at the head table with Polly and Angus, not to mention Hamish. I promised I would come and sit with him at the first opportunity.

'Don't ya be worryin' 'bout me, Abi girl,' he reassured me. 'I'm among friends, am I not? You go an' try to enjoy yourself an' know I'm here if ya need me.' He kissed me gently before letting me go and comfortably joined his group. I knew he would have spoken individually with every person at the table by the end of the night and would know more about them than I did. It made me feel at ease I didn't have to concern myself with his conduct or civility. I knew Aaron had a good time wherever he went, and the fact he didn't pressure me about Hamish or demand my full attention all the time took the burden off me. He made me happy, I realised, and the more time I spent with him, the more I found out how wonderful he really was. I wanted him in my life; however, I wouldn't allow anyone to push me into marriage before I was ready, and certainly not while I was still feeling so confused.

I found Hamish sitting at the bridal table and eyed the seating arrangement. He sat on one side of the elaborate chairs that stood side by side for the bride and groom, and I was on the other. Relieved I didn't have to sit next to him, I nervously took my seat, avoiding his stare.

'I saw how he kissed you out in front of the house,' he said, his voice low. 'He's in love with you—you know that? It's as plain as the nose on your face. Have you done the things with him you've done with me?'

'Not that it's any of your business, no, we haven't. He doesn't focus on that all the time, unlike someone else I know,' I spat, my face burning.

'Well, maybe he isn't as attracted to you as I am—or as in love with you, either—'cause I cannae help every time I'm near you, I want to take you to my bed an' keep you there forever, can I?' he asked, causing me to doubt Aaron for a moment.

I glared at him but chose not to respond. Angus and Polly finally arrived, walking hand in hand to the front of the room, then took their seats to the sounds of cheering and clapping. Polly looked radiant as she sat down next to me.

'Abi, we did it, and it was amazing, like nothing I have ever experienced before,' she whispered, and I could hear the sunshine in her voice.

I squeezed her hand under the table, thrilled for her and Angus. At least they now sat in between Hamish and me, and I no longer had to speak. He made me exhausted when I talked to him as he slowly chipped away at my defences. He already had me doubting myself again. For the past two weeks, I had been happy and content spending all my time with Aaron. I could scream—I was finding it all so frustrating.

The food was abundant and perfectly cooked and presented, course after course arriving at the table until even I could no longer fit in another morsel, feeling I would burst out of my corset. Finally, Leo entered the ballroom. Mr Makenzie introduced him to the guests, then complimented him on the wedding breakfast. Everybody cheered as he sat down at Catherine's table. I watched as he leaned back in his chair, his hand in the air waving madly as he enjoyed the guests' felicitations, then rose to my feet and made my way across the room. I had not spoken to the little shite since he yanked my hair last night. He looked at me warily as I slid into the seat beside him.

'What are you here to do, you violent little witch?' he hissed at me. 'You nearly pulled my ear off last night—thank you very much. I would have been deaf today if you had succeeded.' I merely smirked at him. 'What? Why are you smiling? You know I don't like people smiling for no reason. It means they are up to no good. What have you done?' he squealed, pointing his finger in my face. I relaxed back in my chair and made myself comfortable.

'Have you heard any more rumours lately?' I asked pleasantly. He eyed me suspiciously.

'No. Why? What's the rumour? Who is it about?' he probed desperately, unable to leave gossip where it belonged—in the privy.

'I heard a rumour today, and it's going all around the district as we speak,' I replied smugly. His eyes widened as he shook his head.

'Well, it's obviously not about you, considering how insane you go when it is,' he said primly. 'Last night was a prime example. You cannot cope when people spread scurrilous rumours about you.' I felt anger rise in me yet again.

'That's because you're the one who spreads the scurrilous rumours about me throughout the district, you shite,' I exploded. Our companions at the table collapsed into peals of laughter as they listened to us bicker. 'Anyway, I just wanted to leave you with this. Everyone now believes you are in love with a maid here and sneak into her bed each night.' He slowly turned, his eyes even wider, his face flushed pink.

'Abigail, how dare you? Now people are going to think I actually like the creatures. Do you know how many men will refuse to have anything to do with me now? The thought of it is making me feel quite ill. Oh, I'm never speaking to you again,' he snapped, his face now a mottled purple. I stood to leave, my job here now complete.

'Good. Maybe now you'll also never speak about me again, and I will have some peace around here,' I shot back, then hurried across the room without a backward glance, seating myself back next to Polly. Our friends laughed at whatever Leo was now threatening me with, but I was out of earshot and couldn't have cared less. Despite not spreading any rumours about him, I told Polly what I'd done, and she laughed hysterically. We reminisced about how we dreamed of a night like this when we were shivering in my bed at the orphanage.

Now the guests had eaten their fill, and the dishes had been cleared away, the quintet Polly hired played slow melodies at first, the pace soon increasing to encourage the guests to get up from their tables to dance. Aaron approached soon after, led me to the dance floor, and took me in his arms. I could feel Hamish's hateful stare but ignored him, entirely absorbed in Aaron's presence. I was here with Aaron, and I was going to enjoy myself at my only sister's wedding because I doubted she would ever have another.

After exhausting ourselves, we sat down at Catherine's table. Aaron had proved to be an excellent dancer, almost as good as Hamish, and I was having a great deal of fun with him. I looked across the table at Catherine's parents, who appeared to be having a good time, from what I could tell. They were extremely formal people, leaving me a little uncomfortable in their presence.

'How are you enjoying Australia, Mr and Mrs Montague?'

'Oh, my dear, we love it,' Mrs Montague replied, smiling politely. 'The weather is almost always perfect, and the gala events and parties held here must be seen to be believed. If you would like any introductions in the future, I would be happy to do so for you. We are hoping to have a coming-out ball for Catherine next year, and I do hope you will attend.'

'Of course. I wouldn't miss it for the world,' I replied, secretly knowing Catherine would refuse to take part in a coming-out of anything.

We continued to chat companionably—Aaron impressing Mr Montague no end with his wit, charm, and stories of fishing on the wild seas. Catherine and I whispered about the lack of opportunities for her to meet eligible men. Although she was not desperate to marry, she confided a relationship might be something she would enjoy after seeing Polly and Angus, Bessie and Danny, and Aaron and me together. Despite my concern regarding how they had reared their children, I found Catherine's parents lovely; despite being barely present in their lives. Her mother was a little uppity for my liking and quite cold, while her father was a quiet man who appeared reserved and was conservative in his views when he expressed them. It was clear to all they saw themselves as better than most; however, they were intelligent and polite and included everyone at the table in their conversations.

We moved on to the next table and sat with Amelia and George, while Dana and Martin were embroiled in a lively conversation with a friend of Mr Makenzie. Dana introduced him as Robert Chirnside, a pastoralist and owner of Carranballac Estate near Skipton. Aarron shook his hand while he nodded politely in my direction, the faint golden aura surrounding him no longer surprising me. Martin was exactly how Dana had described him, and clearly besotted by her, I liked him immediately. Although he was not the most outgoing person I had ever met, he could hold an intelligent conversation and appeared to be a sensible man. George was his usual irritating self, barely letting Amelia out of his sight and controlling the conversation.

'How is everything, Amelia? With George, I mean?' I whispered while he and Aaron were deep in discussion about the coach and dray business—soon moving on to the tanneries lining Saltwater River in Footscray.

'It's positively awful, Abigail. He is a mean little man, and he will have nought to do with Mathew. I thank God he's at work from the morning until night, but then he comes home. Once he's eaten his dinner, he wants me all to himself. He wants to do things to me I don't like. He hurts me, Abigail.' Tears welled in her eyes as she opened her heart to me.

'Oh Amelia, I'm so dreadfully sorry this is happening to you. Can't you leave him? Return to your parents? What a right royal prick.' I glanced up to ensure no one overheard us, kicking myself for opening my mouth yet again without thinking. It upset me greatly to hear a friend of mine was being treated in this fashion. I wanted to leap up and smack the bastard across the face right there at the table, but I restrained myself for her sake. She appeared alarmed by my suggestion—and slightly shocked at my cursing—tears welling in her eyes as she turned away from the table for a moment, staring across at the couples dancing together as the musicians continued to play.

'It would shame my family if I left the marriage, and they wouldn't have Mathew and me back in their home. They would cut me off, and I would have no one and a child to raise on my own.' I shook my head in disbelief, taking her hand in mine under the table. 'No, I am stuck with him. This is what my life will be until I die, knowing no love, nor a gentle touch, or a kind word. As my mother said, I am condemned because I took a lover before marriage.' She quickly wiped fresh tears away before George noticed.

'I'm sure that's not true, Amelia. Is there some way you can find your love and be with him?' I squeezed her hand discreetly, aware I was probably making it worse the more we spoke of it.

'No, my father ensured I will never see him again—not in this life or the next. One day he was there, and the following morning, he had disappeared. It left me at the mercy of George and my parents without my Tommy to protect me. I will never feel happiness or joy again, nor find comfort, security or peace, even within the walls of my own home. Tommy is lost to me now, and I must accept that and try to make the best of what I have for Mathew's sake.' She lowered her head, appearing so sad—so truly broken—I wanted to wrap my arms around her, but couldn't for fear of drawing attention.

'Amelia, you do have another option. You and Mathew are always welcome to come and stay here, or even live here, for as long as you like. There is always a place for you at Willow Grove while I'm here. How am I ever going to fill this house, anyway, even if I had twelve children?' I smiled and squeezed her hand again.

'Abigail, that is lovely of you. I might take you up on it when things become unbearable and stay as your guest for a night or two. You need to understand, I cannot leave him—not now or in the future—well, not permanently. I would disgrace my family and myself, and Mathew would grow up an outcast, whereas now he's the son of a wealthy businessman. I cannot give him a better future than that—not alone.' She looked at that moment like a trapped animal who couldn't escape its captor.

'You would never be alone, Amelia. Wouldn't it be better to raise Mathew with love and warmth with far less than in a wealthy house of lies and torment? Damn the rest to hell. Who gives a fat rat's arse what they think?' She raised her eyebrows, but remained silent. Nodding once, she turned away, sadly resigned to her fate as she stared again at the couples she believed had the one thing she would never have again. It hurt my heart she felt obligated to abide by her marriage vows to such a wicked little creature. She did not deserve to be abused by anyone, yet this man believed he had the right to do as he pleased with her body and her mind because there was a marriage certificate granting him some sort of ownership of her. She was my friend, and I cared about what happened to her and Mathew. I hoped whatever occurred in the future, she would use my home as her refuge—a place to come to when she felt scared or exhausted—a place where she may again find peace if only for a moment in time.

Chapter Fifteen

The staff had cleared away the last of the dirty dishes, and the guests continued to dance, the beautiful music filling the grand room. Polly and Angus held each other close as they swayed in the middle of the floor, not a sliver of light between them. Charlotte had left the table soon after Aaron and I arrived, hurrying off to find Hamish. She found him talking to friends, sat down beside him and leaned in close to whisper in his ear, her attempts to flirt completely ignored. I glanced over only once to find him looking at me, then glaring at Aaron, who ignored him. Hamish finally took Charlotte onto the dance floor, and at least one of them appeared to be having fun. I was happy to leave them to it and concentrate on the people at the table nearby.

Elizabeth and her fiancé, Mr Eric Benét, appeared to be genuinely in love. They were openly affectionate and liked each other, while Tamara appeared to be in love with love. Although accompanied by her fiancé, Mr Brian Wagner, he barely touched or acknowledged her. He did not appear to be an awful man, just disinterested. I wondered if he had another love and was also being forced into marriage, but unlike Tamara, hadn't fallen into a cloud of premarital oblivion. She boasted how Mr Montague himself was designing her gown, and how they would hold the wedding ceremony in the biggest church in Melbourne—continuing on about the wedding breakfast and how excited she was it would be held at The Delmont, the most exclusive hotel in all of Melbourne. I smiled to myself at her excitement, knowing full well this wedding would cost a pretty penny if The Delmont was involved in any shape or form. The last time I checked the price of the meals they served, I nearly dropped to the floor in a dead faint. Even a bowl of plain porridge cost more than a full sack of oats that would feed a family for a week. I had wanted to halve the prices at the very least, but management wanted to increase them even more and advised me to speak to Mr McPhee—who snarled a loud "No" at me, and made himself more than clear that would not happen, now or in the future. Eric Benét owned a construction company, already designing several grand buildings in and around Melbourne and Geelong. He could more than adequately support the lifestyle to which Elizabeth had become accustomed, and I could see already this would be a happy, comfortable marriage. I did not hold the same hope for Tamara.

The music had slowed, and the chandeliers above had been extinguished, the light in the room now dim, while the heavy velvet drapes were now drawn—the soft light casting a romantic glow across the ballroom. I gazed around at the hundreds of twinkling candles sitting on every available surface, feeling I was a character in a storybook read to me so long ago now by Sister. Aaron graciously rose to his feet and excused himself before taking my hand, then led me across the hardwood floor. Polly and Angus were still dancing, totally immersed in each other. I doubted they noticed anyone else was even there. He held me in his arms, then kissed the top of my head.

'How ya feelin', me Abi girl?' His voice was low and husky, his eyes twinkling as I took in how truly handsome he was—a mountain of a man—and the tallest in the room, bar Hamish. With his colossal frame and muscular build, someone had indeed built him like a brick shithouse, as the Australian's and now Dana would say. His face was exquisitely beautiful, his chiselled features carved by a master—his shaggy, sandy-blonde hair, hanging down to his shoulders, its white streaks bleached from the sun loose and billowing around him like a lion. He was the most handsome man I had ever met—next to Hamish—and I was finding it hard to keep my eyes and hands off him.

'I'm having a wonderful time,' I gushed, my feet following his unconsciously. Not wanting to change the mood of the day, I didn't tell him Hamish had broken down some of my resistance. Enjoying his arms around me, feeling his heartbeat in his throat against my cheek, I wanted nothing to ruin tonight for either of us. He swept me around the dance floor and then stood with me off to one side, guiding me slowly into place, then pulling me closer to him. I felt his erection pushing into my stomach as we continued to dance—now hidden in a dark corner away from the others—but not out of sight. I wondered if Hamish was wrong about Aaron not being attracted to me as much as he was. Maybe he was just more of a gentleman than Hamish, I thought to myself. Aaron kissed me on the neck, startling me from my own thoughts while sending tingles throughout my body.

'Never in me life did I think I'd be sayin' it so soon, but I do. I can't help it. I love ya, Abi girl.' I impulsively kissed him on his mouth, not caring who saw. It was rare I would show any kind of affection publicly, and it felt good to be the one initiating it. He kissed me back passionately. We no longer danced, and several guests smiled at us from where they sat at their tables looking on, while others whispered—except for Hamish, who appeared furious—although he sat beside Charlotte and blatantly encouraged her to flirt and touch him in front of every man and his dog without care or thought for her reputation.

We returned to our seats, and Dana winked, causing my cheeks to burn. It was clear she liked Aaron, and she had been quite vocal about the fact she felt he was good for me. She was no longer too keen on Hamish even being around her own daughter, and did not bite her tongue regarding the matter in public or private.

'Christ on a bike, Abigail. That was quite a show,' she whispered as I sat down next to her, trying to catch my breath.

'I didn't mean to do that, but I couldn't help myself. It's the things he says to me that make me want to just jump on him and climb him like a tree.' I laughed wickedly, and she laughed louder.

'Well, that's the best kind of relationship you can have, lovely girl. You can feel the passion vibrating around the room, making us all rather envious,' she whispered, giggling as my cheeks became even hotter. 'Just you wait until you bed him. It will be wonderful after the first time, especially if you do all the things I told you. But, remember—the secret is not to do them all at once,' she continued, and I tried to smother a smile.

I had memorised everything she had told me, but when I was with Aaron, I got the feeling we would somehow work it out between us if the need ever arose. Hamish approached our table, guiding Charlotte towards us, their voices low. They appeared to be in the middle of a disagreement, although by the time they arrived, they had ceased their bickering. Hamish pulled out a chair, then lowered himself onto the empty seat beside an extremely uncomfortable Charlotte, who I assumed was only there at his insistence. He was drinking whisky again today, and I cringed inside at what might transpire. He slipped his arm around Charlotte's shoulders, and I again hoped he wasn't playing with her heart. So many from the district present here tonight would be happy to spread the news they were courting. If word got out they were sleeping together, and she was discarded, her reputation would be ruined. I loved Charlotte—and liked her, too—and felt terribly sad she was so infatuated with him, and frustrated she could not see what he was doing. It upset me she was fighting with her mother about it all. I wished it would all just stop, and we could go back to how we were on the ship.

'So, Abigail, when are you gettin' married? Are you next?' Hamish glared at me, his tone bitter. I glared back, but chose not to answer. Aaron eyed him thoughtfully, he too choosing to remain silent on the matter. For now. 'Ah, she's naw talkin' to me again. Abigail used to talk to me a great deal about her plans. She mentioned many times she wanted to be with me forever. If this is forever, she'll have a different man every three-months,' he trumpeted. Everyone at our table—and the two on either side of us—appeared embarrassed, some looking away while shifting silently in their seats. Aaron fixed him with a hard stare.

'Mate, maybe ya need to ease off the whisky. Ya don't wanna be causin' any disruptions at ya own brother's weddin' now, do ya? I'm sure Abi is happy to lend an ear to ya another time when ya not so preoccupied with Miss Charlotte. What do ya reckon?' He smiled at them, his manner calm and friendly, and Charlotte smiled back shyly.

'Aye, you're right—Miss Charlotte. Isn't she beautiful?' Hamish asked our dining companions, his eyes not leaving my face for a moment. Several of my friends trying to appease him answered him in the affirmative, and he nodded before turning back to Charlotte, his eyes glazed, his speech slurred. Aaron took the whisky decanter, poured himself a large glass, then discreetly called for the footman to take it away. It was nearing dinnertime—or teatime, as the Australians called it, calling luncheon dinner—and most of the guests had not departed. Mr Masters came to me, his face grave, before bowing politely.

'I do apologise for the interruption, Mistress. May I speak with you in private, please?' I nodded, then rose to my feet, following him out and into the hallway. 'Dinner is ready. It is not as extravagant as the wedding breakfast, but Chef Leo realised earlier in the day many of the guests would likely remain and expect an invitation. He prepared a substantial meal. Would you like it served now?'

'Yes, thank you, Mr Masters. That would be wonderful,' I replied, surprised at how organised Leo was—given how scattered his brain. 'The food is like nothing I've ever tasted.' I felt my face flush as he politely stood before me, waiting for my direction. 'Do you mind thanking Leo for me since I cannot do it myself at the moment?' He nodded before turning and hurrying back to the kitchen, leaving me staring after him and wondering if I would ever feel comfortable in these new shoes I'd been forced to fill—shoes worn by a late great-aunt I never knew. Now long dead in the ground—this woman seemed to want control over every aspect of my life from the grave—and I still couldn't figure out why, finding no rhyme or reason in any of it.

Polly and Angus moved away from their enormous cake just as I sat back in my chair, my stomach about to burst after the lavish dinner we had only just finished. Leo had filled the layers with custard, whipped cream and strawberry jam, and it tasted amazing. I had already consumed two pieces, much to Aaron's amusement, even as he took his third slice. Mr Makenzie had escorted Hamish to their carriage to sleep off the large quantity of alcohol he had consumed in such a brief time. His father had seen what was happening, promptly came over, and hurried Hamish outside before he could ruin his brother's wedding. Hamish never argued with his father or brother when he was drinking, but anyone else was fair game. He was a nasty drunk, especially with how he now felt towards me, and I felt relieved he had gone. I still loved Hamish, though. He was a magnificent person without alcohol, but with it, he was malicious, doing and saying stupid things he later regretted.

Aaron asked me to dance again, escorting me back to where the musicians placed at the front of the room, elevated by a small platform. He gathered me in his arms, kissing the top of my head while pulling me close.

'I missed ya.' I looked up at him in surprise, unsure of what he meant.

'What do you mean? I'm here.'

''I mean, I missed holdin' ya. I look across the table at that face, an' I can't take me eyes from ya. You're the most beautiful woman in the room, an' ya have now ruined me for all others.' His eyes twinkled as I playfully punched him on the arm, and he pulled me in closer. 'It's been a bonzer day. Hamish was as full as a boot but didn't muck up as I expected. Did he give ya a hard time?'

'A little, but it's not worth mentioning,' I replied, squeezing him tight and enjoying his presence. Most of the guests gradually left as the festivities wound down until just a handful of us remained. The Makenzie family had departed with Hamish, which took the burden from me, and I could relax again. We all sat around the large table together, talking and laughing about the day.

William and Catherine had stayed, but their parents had retired to their guest room for the night, while Tamara and Elizabeth had departed with their fiancés—leaving Polly and Angus deep in discussion with Dana and Martin—while Amelia and George sat together but avoided speaking. Catherine smiled at me across the table where I sat between William and Aaron, who held my hand discreetly against his thigh, stroking my fingers between his own as he listened to William speak of university life.

'How are you, Abigail? You look happy, I must say,' William remarked, turning to me. I smiled as I studied his handsome face.

'I am happy, William, when I think about it. And how are you getting along—truthfully?' I asked, interested in what he might reveal.

'Well, I'm studying hard, and that takes up most of my time,' he replied, his voice low, 'but if you keep it to yourself, I will tell you I am seeing a young lady I like very much. Her name is Sarah, and she is studying to be a nurse.' I touched his shoulder in congratulations.

'Ah, so she is not part of the aristocracy?' I teased, unable to hide my amusement. He pulled a face at me but laughed in good humour.

'I'm just as surprised as you, but the difference between other elitists and me is I know I'm a snob.' He laughed to himself, and I joined in.

'So, what's she like?'

'She is small and pretty, with dark hair and a beautiful personality. She wants to help people; that's why she wants to be a nurse. I think I am serious about her, but I have four-years of study before I'm able to offer her a life,' he said regretfully, then smiled weakly at me.

'There is no rush, William. You don't need the damned pressure.' It continued to surprise me how everyone around me expected me to behave like an adult, despite my tender age and inexperience. Many married even younger—and some my age were already mothers—but I also knew many of them were forced into these marriages because of poverty. Children years younger than me were sold into service, living away from family and friends while they sent their wages home to their parents to ensure their survival. There, but for the grace of God go I remunerated in my head, bringing Sister Josephine to mind.

'I know that, Abigail, but I care for her so much I want to have everything with her right now. I think she likes me as much as I like her.'

'I'm glad to hear it, William, and I hope it all works out for you. I would love to meet her when you are ready—and don't worry—I won't tell Catherine,' I promised. He smiled at me, then patted my hand in thanks.

Polly and Angus looked blissful, and it surprised me they were still with us and not at the cottage together. I supposed they were savouring the moment and enjoying the last hours of their wedding day. When they finally bid us farewell to retreat to their new home, we embraced them and wished them goodnight. As my friends went off to find their own beds, I told Aaron I also planned to retire, saying goodnight to everyone before he walked me to my room. Much to my surprise, he followed me inside.

'Ya know how beautiful ya look? Ya always look lovely to me, but today ya took my breath away, an' that of half the guests. I had a ripper of a day with ya, an' if I could have one wish, it's that every day for the rest of me life would be like today—except for the Hamish part.' He pulled me to him and kissed me just as Bessie stepped into the room, tut-tutting as she hurried to my side.

'Be gone with you, Aaron, and if there is any tiptoeing into some-one else's bedchamber tonight, I will find out about it and come down on the both of you like a ton of bricks,' she threatened, shooing him out the door as he called out his farewells to me, his laughter receding as he made his way down the hallway. She helped me out of my cumbersome dress, which had weighed me down so heavily it forced me to sit down more often than I wanted. Relieved to be free of it, I poured myself into my nightgown and slid into bed. I continued replaying the day in my mind's eye, but my thoughts continued to return to Hamish and what he had said to me, no matter how hard I tried to block him out. Finally, I drifted off into a tormented sleep and dreamed of whisky, wedding cake, and a shovel.

I woke to find Bessie bustling around in my room, organising my clothes for the day. So many people had stayed overnight after the wedding reception and were expecting to be entertained.

'Come on, you. All your friends are up and waiting for you, lazy-bones,' she called out briskly. I groaned before struggling to my feet to dress, my throat dry and my head aching from far too much celebrating last night, then made my way downstairs to the dining room.

I sat at the head of the table as breakfast was being served. Leo was the type of chef who would not wait. If he told you to be at the table by a certain time and you weren't there, he would order the food be served without you, no matter what the excuse. I was becoming accustomed to his idiosyncrasies, and I rarely became upset with him. On the contrary, I was grateful he was so precise about everything.

'Did everyone sleep well?' I asked, looking around the oh-so-formal dining-room table. Amelia appeared as if she had not slept a wink, her face pale while dark shadows were obvious under her eyes.

'The beds are the most comfortable I have ever slept in,' Mrs Montague remarked, smiling brightly. We shared the different-flavoured omelettes, fried bacon, and eggs cooked in various ways, along with the platters of fruit and hot coffee. I sipped my coffee while everyone else chatted loudly when Aaron walked in. He came over, bent down, and kissed me full on the mouth before sitting down next to me and helping himself to the eggs and toast.

'You're here early,' I remarked, watching him fill his plate.

'For some unknown reason, I couldn't keep away. It must be the food ya have here. It keeps me comin' back day after day. If ya wanna get rid of me, ya will have to sack the cook,' he said, munching his way through two plates of food while still managing to chat with everyone.

'Amelia, I would enjoy some company. Would you be a friend and come and stay a few days with me during the week with Mathew? I'm sure George won't mind getting his own dinners for a few nights, will you?' I asked, turning to smile sweetly at George. His face remained congenial, but his eyes hardened. Amelia looked at him without expression, holding her breath as she waited silently for his reply.

'Of course. It would be good for Amelia and Mathew to stay with you for a brief time. With the number of servants you have here, she cannot avoid resting while they look after the child, and, no doubt, she will return home refreshed and ready to return to resume her duties and care for me once again.' He narrowed his gaze at her while she lowered her head and stared unblinking at the table. I wanted to throw a plate edge-wise at his puny head and decapitate the little bastard right at the breakfast table, but maintained my self-control, knowing overreacting would only cause more rumours. Aaron caught my eye—having noted what had just occurred and the look on my face—and grinned, his eyes sparkling in amusement. Soon he was deep in conversation with Martin, who offered to show him his pubs and buy him a drink in each one. I enjoyed the banter regarding who had made the biggest fool of themselves after having had a wee bit too much to drink during the reception.

I recalled Dana doing an Irish jig all by herself on the dance floor, having cleared everyone from it while in the middle of a waltz. Then there was Martin, who was dancing with a coat stand at one point—and Victoria, wearing the flowers from the centrepiece in her hair while she danced alone, holding onto her makeshift floral hat. Then, of course, there was Aaron, making sure all the elderly ladies had a dance and kissing their hands in farewell, charming them all—along with Tamara's amorous advances towards her fiancé—who was having none of it. They were all the best people I knew, and I felt honoured to be friends with all of them and to have them in my life.

Amelia was the one I was worried about now. I believed she was in terrible trouble. If George did not injure her body, he would cripple her mind and crush her spirit. A sad truth I believed was already taking place. I looked forward to having her to myself for a few days and getting to the bottom of it without him around. I disliked the man more each time our paths crossed, and I didn't like feeling that way about anyone. He rubbed me the wrong way in everything he did and said, and the effect he had on Amelia was distressing to watch. I shook my head, clearing my head of evil thoughts before turning to Catherine to thank her for the beautiful dress she had created for me.

'You are more than welcome, Abigail. It was a pleasure,' she said, smiling while she ate.

'Must you catch the train this morning with your family? Can't you stay a few days more?'

'If I could, believe me, my dear friend, I would. You don't seem to understand I would dearly love to accept your invitation, but I have so many gowns that need finishing this week. I promise I will open up my schedule in the next month and come and stay for a full week if my workload allows,' she replied, and I nodded my agreement.

Dana and Martin had shared a room last night, much to Mrs Montague's disgust on hearing they were not married. Dana had asked me if it would be all right, and I had unhesitatingly given my consent. As far as I was concerned, what people did behind closed doors was their business—as long as they were happy and no one got hurt. We retreated to the back garden, and as the morning wore on, their guests and mine started saying their goodbyes as luncheon drew near. Soon Aaron and I stood at the grand entrance of the house, seeing off the last guest. We had spent a lovely time together—Leo sending out what he called the hair of the dog—which in reality wasn't a dog hair at all but tomato juice with some other added ingredients that actually made me feel better after far too much red wine. Soon my body felt heavy and warm, as if I were drunk, finding out soon after I was drunk. The tomato juice had strong alcohol in it, Leo teasing me loudly and shouting how I was a brainless fool for not knowing it lessened the after-effects of too much grog. I had to admit everything was happier, funnier, brighter, and lovelier after drinking several glasses of the stuff. Still inebriated as I waved goodbye to everyone, Aaron held me up while I slurred and called out how much I loved them all, promising to be friends forever. They hugged and kissed me goodbye, appearing amused as they made their way home in their lovely carriages. Harry and the grooms had been scurrying around like lunatics, trying to have all the horses and carriages ready for the large number of guests who stayed overnight. I was unfamiliar with most of them, as they were the Makenzie family's friends. After the last had departed, Aaron carried me up the stairs and into my bedchamber, placing me down gently on the bed.

'It's time to rest ya head, me girl. Ya poor thing, not knowin' when to say no to a glass of tomato juice,' he said with a smirk. I collapsed into hysterical laughter, my body shaking the bed.

'Who would ever think to put alcohol in tomato juice? I had seven of them over that time, and no one told me. Didn't you think I was having a few too many?'

'Yeah, I did, but I believed ya to be a sophisticated woman who knew what she was doin'. Ya were as happy as a dog with two tails scullin' the devil's poison an' they didn't even touch the sides. Impressive for a sheila.' He joined in the laughter and flopped down next to me on the bed. We lay together, holding hands and talking for the longest time, until he pulled me close against him and kissed me. The way he ran his tongue softly around the inside of my mouth, exploring and then demanding I give myself to him, sent tingles all over my body. He held me so tight it felt like he would never let me go. I still missed Hamish dreadfully but thoroughly enjoyed every minute I spent with Aaron, especially after the way he had cared for me when I was ill. He had so much in his favour, yet I could not get Hamish out of my heart or my head.

Polly and Angus had left for Melbourne on the same train as Catherine and her family to spend two honeymoon weeks in The Delmont Hotel's master suite. I had Leo cook them a special breakfast to eat in the cottage, which they told us they enjoyed very much when they joined us mid-morning. I enjoyed having everyone here and the hustle and bustle of the people I loved being present around me. It felt lonely already with Polly and Angus gone, and if Leo ever moved on, I would be by myself in this great big house. Tomorrow, Aaron and I were meeting Mr McPhee in the morning to give him my decision. The two-week time limit had again run out.

'I need to be certain I am in love with you before we go ahead, and I have some things to think through.' He stared up at the ceiling, a slow grin spreading across his face.

'I'll support whatever ya choose; ya know that. Ya feel it, or ya don't, an' I'm happy to wait till ya do. I want ya to marry me for love, nothin' else.'

'Thank you for being so understanding, Aaron. I just need to be sure.' He abruptly took me in his arms again and whispered in my ear, sending tingles through every fibre of my being.

As I sat in front of my dressing table, Bessie brushed and plaited my hair for bed.

'Mary won't have much to do with Polly gone,' I remarked, feeling unwell. Although Aaron had put me to bed for a couple of hours and I had slept, I woke still feeling tipsy. He ate dinner with me in the kitchen and had just left for home.

'She will join back in with the housemaids, and I'm sure within the week, your house will shine from top to bottom,' Bessie replied as she laughed. Little Mary was a phenomenon in herself. I could sack all the other maids and just have her, and my house would be just as spotless. She adored Polly, and I would employ her solely as Polly's maid in the cottage as soon as they returned. Of course, Polly would have to live on Angus' wages now as he refused to accept any money he did not work for, but I did not see why I couldn't spoil her with a maid like little Mary, especially when the babies came along.

Tomorrow I would make it crystal clear to Mr McPhee he would not bully me into anything, and I needed more time before making any commitment to anyone. So much had happened so quickly. My life had turned into something so unexpected, full of people I loved, although we had all only known each other for just a few months. For the first time in my life, I felt like I finally had a family with people who cared about me—not because they had to, but because they loved me as much as I adored each one of them. Aware some around me thought me naïve, believing several of my new acquaintances had only befriended me because of the inheritance, but they had not a clue it could all be taken from me at any moment. I only knew I now had an obligation to ensure those here with me had a roof over their head and a comfortable life. There was always the room filled with money under the house, but it would feel like stealing if I took it to start a new life. I felt like I had the weight of the world on my shoulders with no one to help me carry it, despite them all wanting to help. And I couldn't get Hamish out of my heart or mind.

The only family I ever had comprised Polly and Sister Josephine, who I missed dreadfully and would often cry for when I felt melancholy or confused. She was the only mother I had ever known, and I needed her here with me now to advise me and help untangle my thoughts. She would have known what I should do, but I felt so alone without her here beside me, so unsure.

I was deeply fond of Aaron and thoroughly enjoyed the time I spent with him, but I still had feelings for Hamish, despite him breaking my heart. I knew he had struggled when he found himself suddenly competing for my attention, triggering his betrayal; however, I was uncertain I could ever bring myself to forgive him or trust him. I also knew he was a good person deep down—most of his actions and his golden glow confirmed it. But, so far, I couldn't get past his senseless mistake.

Thank goodness I still had my darling Bessie. She was not only my maid but my dear friend and confidante. I knew it did not matter what I told her, she would never judge me and would support me, whatever decisions I made. However, I was not ready to open up fully to anyone about what I felt for Hamish and Aaron—even my trusted ladies' maid and friend. Bessie helped me undress and slip my nightgown quickly over my head so I could climb into bed. She gently covered me with the quilts and kissed my forehead.

'Now, you sleep well, Mistress, and don't fret about tomorrow. Everything will turn out just fine. I have no doubts about that.' She quietly bid me goodnight and shuffled out of the room, closing the door behind her.

I curled up in my warm, comfortable bed, wishing I had someone who could tell me what I should do. Instead, my head was saying one thing, my heart, another. I felt completely torn in half and lost. I did not know where my life would take me, along with the fact I had the constant pressure of having to deal with my new status as an employer, friend, and landowner. All I knew was significant changes were coming that hinged on the hard decisions I had to make, and it was not something I looked forward to.

As usual, though, I pushed everything to the back of my mind. I finally drifted off into a fitful sleep, waking often and remembering in sharp detail images from each of my dreams—a butcher's knife glinting in the flickering light of a burning candle, two boats, and a golden calf.

Chapter Sixteen

A SHAFT OF SUNLIGHT angling through the cut-glass vase on my windowsill hit me in the eyes, waking me. It reminded me of the unused wine glasses atop the cabinet in the parlour back at the orphanage, an image of Sister Josephine flashing before my eyes for a moment and causing me to smile. As I stretched my body and burrowed deeper under the covers, I heard someone enter the silent room. I turned to gaze across at the door, finding Bessie carrying a carved wooden tray and beaming back at me.

'I thought there was no point in you going down for breakfast and eating all alone.' She kicked the door closed and hurried to my side. 'Leo is busy this morning, so I brought this up for you.' She placed the tray on the bed and took a seat. I sat up and eagerly began to eat. Leo had made me toast with thinly sliced smoked ham spread thickly with a chutney of tomatoes, onions, and capsicums. He had also made my favourite—pancakes with maple syrup imported from Canada. In the short time we had been in Geelong, Leo had quickly made contacts who could supply him with unique products he could not buy in the shops here or we couldn't grow at Willow Grove. He told me he was forced to pay dearly for these ingredients, but he believed I could afford him to have the best, given I was a wealthy woman. Whenever I complained about how much was being spent on the kitchen just to stock the pantry alone, he threatened to quit. He demanded the best of everything and would not compromise.

'I've noticed you're letting Aaron get closer to you over the past few days. After the way Hamish has behaved, it's a good thing, draping himself all over that Charlotte for everyone to see. How do you feel about it all, Mistress?' I stopped munching on my toast and remembered to swallow before opening my mouth.

'I haven't reached a conclusion yet about any of it. I hadn't been thinking about Hamish much in the past two weeks. Then he talked to me on Polly's wedding day, and those few words sent me into self-doubt again. I don't know what I'm doing, but I do know I'm enjoying being with Aaron more and more.'

'Thank the Almighty for that, I say,' Bessie replied. 'You couldn't find a better man than that boy. The way he looked after you when you were sick, I never would have believed a boy that young had it in him. He rode home late every night and was straight back by daylight every single day, even though Leo offered him a bed. He didn't want anyone to say anything to blacken your reputation. You have a good one there who will take care of you and love you; you need to forget about Hamish.' She paused for a moment, then made herself comfortable at the foot of the bed. 'What's holding you back from Aaron? It can't be Hamish after him hopping in bed with Charlotte.' I remained silent before finishing the remains of my breakfast.

'I do not know how to put it into words, but, yes, Hamish is still playing very much on my mind. I don't know how to stop it.' She fixed me with a dark stare before abruptly rising to her feet.

'You need to put that boy out of your mind for your own sake; and everyone else's sake, too. It's not fair to either of them, carrying a flame for them both. That's my opinion on the matter.' She stood over me and crossed her arms. I couldn't tell her I had been about to tell Hamish I would marry him on that fateful night and was still recovering from the shock of what I had discovered. I threw off the heavy quilt and hurried out of bed, allowing Bessie to fuss and dress me for my meeting with Mr McPhee. She remained stone cold silent. I knew I was upsetting her by not deciding, but I needed more time, and she wouldn't understand. As far as she was concerned, I had met the best man I would ever meet, and my decision should be easy. All she wanted was for me to make a good match and find a happy union, and she believed Aaron was the one who would take care of me. I felt like I had a mother pushing me into marriage before I was ready. She pinned my hair up and secured my hat to the top of my head, transforming me into the lady she expected me to be.

I made my way downstairs and found Aaron sitting in the kitchen with the staff, eating breakfast and chatting with everyone. He caught sight of me, and his handsome face lit up, his blue eyes sparkling.

'Ah, you've discovered me secret hidin' place where I come to find the answers to the world's problems among these wise people.' He bowed as he swept his arm wide to include eight of my household staff. They were all laughing at him and smiling at each other as they got on with their chores.

'All right, funny man, we have to leave soon, so finish your breakfast so we can go.' I leaned down and pecked his porridge-tasting lips. He liked his porridge the way I did, sweet and creamy, and I could taste the sugar lingering on my lips as we walked to the carriage. Once on our way, I tried to relax but couldn't due to the thought of having to deal with that sour-faced lawyer.

'Now, can I have a repeat of that?' Aaron tapped his finger on his lips. I smiled and leaned over, kissing him again, this time lingering a while. When I pulled away, he slipped his arm around my shoulders. 'Much better. I like your kisses best when we're alone.' We sat side-by-side holding hands as the carriage rocked comfortably, talking of the upcoming meeting with Mr McPhee and our thoughts on the matter. 'What can the wily rat do to ya if ya ask for more time? Tie ya to a bullant nest? Feed ya to the sharks off me Da's fishin' boat in Bass Strait?' I gazed out of the window at the farms that seemed to roll on forever.

'I don't know. We will have to wait and see, won't we?' I replied calmly, clasping my shaking hands in my lap while my stomach lurched, dread overwhelming me as we drew nearer to Geelong town and a meeting I feared more than if I were walking to the gallows.

Mrs McPhee advised me her husband wanted to see us separately today, with me being first on the list. I left Aaron in the waiting room, happily chatting away to Mrs McPhee, and made my way to his office. I knocked on the heavy wooden door and entered. He was already sitting behind his desk and did not stand. I waited awkwardly near his desk, waiting for him to invite me to sit.

'Please make yourself comfortable, Miss Delmont. Now, have you come to your decision?' he asked sharply before I was even seated. I straightened in the chair and cast my eyes critically over the rude little man.

'No, I need more time.' His eyes widened as he threw his quill down on the desk, then threw his hands up in the air in frustration. 'I'm sorry, but this is a big decision—probably the biggest of my life—and I need to be sure I'm in love when I make it.' He narrowed his gaze before throwing himself back in his chair and grunting.

'I'm sorry, too, Miss Delmont, as your time has run out. I need your decision now, or I am sending a letter to the next benefactor of the Will to advise them they have inherited everything. You will have a week to move yourself and your friends out,' he snapped, staring at me without emotion over his spectacles. I froze; the shock of his words hit me in the chest as I gasped aloud. My mind raced. I could not believe this man was so inflexible. I would lose everything today, and we would have nowhere to go. He sat rigidly in his chair, treating me as if we had never met. 'I told you at our last meeting all I need today is your decision. You don't have to get married immediately. That's up to you, as long as it's within two-years. If you renege on the engagement, though, you will still lose all you have inherited, every last penny.' I couldn't breathe and was unable to move, not knowing what to say. I liked Aaron, and I felt I could fall in love with him, but I wasn't sure, and I needed more time. Unfortunately, it seemed this little arse hair would not give me any other option than to agree. I stared back at him, not breaking his gaze.

'This is so unfair. You are a sadistic bastard taking great pleasure in marrying me off to someone I'm not in love with,' I spat, then stamped my foot hard on the floor to emphasise my point. He flinched, appearing startled.

'I assure you that sentiment is untrue. Please do not shoot the messenger, young lady. I am only following the instructions of the Will, as I am paid to do. The decision is yours; you have the free will to choose. No one is forcing you, and no one has anything to gain whether you go through with this marriage or not. Well, except you and the relatives of Lady Delmont, who are named as the next beneficiaries. I imagine it will thrill them to hear you so stupidly walked away,' he remarked, disgust written all over his face as he shook his head.

I sat in silence for several long minutes, staring at my hands, which would not stop shaking. There was that money hidden underneath the house. It would give me a normal life, but it wouldn't support wages for anyone after I had purchased my own property, and I was still unsure of Hamish even if I did steal the money.

I didn't trust him. It would take a lot for me to reconcile with him—and that was if I could ever forgive his actions—actions that had hurt me deeply. But it was too much to lose everything for someone like me who had grown up with nothing. I looked across at Mr McPhee bitterly, and then finally sighed in defeat.

'Fine, then. Have it your way. Do I sign some sort of contract or wedding licence now? How do you plan for this coercive business arrangement to go?' I asked, my voice shaking with rage.

'Your word is good enough for me at this time. I will be checking with you to ensure the engagement is genuine.' He gave me a wooden smile and looked at his watch. 'Now, I need to see Aaron and complete our business for the day. I ask that you return at a later date once I draw the contracts up. Now you have agreed to the terms of the Will, I may tell you of the exact nature of the properties and land you now own. I will be free to advise you of the conditions of your trust fund and an estimate of your yearly income from businesses and bank interest.' He was trying unsuccessfully to sound kind, and I didn't believe him for a moment.

'Fine,' I snapped again, stood and marched out of the room, slamming the door behind me. I stomped down the hallway to the waiting room, where several people looked at me in amusement. I went to Aaron, who was grinning broadly. 'It's your turn,' I said tersely and slumped in the chair next to his. He stood to go, then took my hand in his.

'Whatever's wrong, it'll work itself out. Nothin' lasts forever—the good or the bad.' He squeezed my hand before turning and strolling towards the hallway to meet Mr McPhee.

The elaborate carriage moved away from the bustling town, the farms stretching for miles coming into view. We had not spoken a word since leaving Mr McPhee's office; both lost in our own thoughts. I turned to Aaron and studied him intently.

'I suppose we should talk about it,' I remarked, but he shook his head.

'Can we kick that can down the road for a while? I'd rather have a yarn about mathematics?' he apologised, gently taking my hand in his. Mr McPhee had told him of the content of our meeting, but he did not seem to want to discuss it either. I relaxed back into him, reminding myself it was not his fault Mr McPhee wouldn't give me more time, and he was being pushed into this as much as I was, despite him thinking he was in love with me.

We stayed in comfortable silence the entire way home and then went up to my bedchamber to be alone for a while. Bessie knew we came here to talk or lie down during the day, but she also knew what we did was innocent. She would walk in and out throughout the day, seemingly not noticing us lying on my bed and talking. I placed my head on his chest, not knowing what to say to him. He moved my hair back from my face, then pulled me towards him, gently running his finger over my lips before undoing my hair, pin by pin, until it fell down my back. He kissed me slowly, his tongue exploring my mouth and setting my body on fire. We lay there until lunch, not speaking but communicating subtly with a touch here or a knowing look there.

'I'm goin' home after lunch. I need to help me father with a job on the farm.' He smiled, and I shyly smiled back.

'Of course, Aaron. I appreciate you taking the time to come with me to see that horrible little man.' It would be nice to have some time for myself to think things through. I knew he wanted some alone time himself. He didn't want to stay and talk about it. I guessed that meant I wasn't the only one with doubts. We made our way to the kitchen and spoke of neutral things over lunch, and soon after, I walked him out to the stables to see him off, bidding him farewell before watching him canter off into the distant paddocks.

He behaved no differently from every other day and treated me with his usual warmth and kindness, only avoiding what was fore-most on both our minds—we were now engaged.

Melancholy had settled on me, and without Polly here to talk to, I slipped on my nightgown and took to my bed. All I wanted was silence, and I certainly didn't plan to get up again today. Bessie had changed my linen, which was clean and crisp when I slid beneath the covers. I lay perfectly still, staring up at the ceiling, while thinking today should have been the happiest day of my life. But here I was in bed, alone, my thoughts tormenting me.

I drifted into a dreamless sleep, only to be awakened by Bessie bringing my dinner on a tray. I sat up in bed and ate mechanically while she talked about her day, then advised Leo would visit with me after dinner as he was concerned. Once finished, I was in no mood to talk to anyone and tuned Bessie out. She busied herself tidying the room and didn't ask me to get out of bed to plait my hair. I hadn't brushed it, but she bit her tongue and let me be, sensing my mood.

Leo knocked on my door fifteen-minutess later, hurrying to my side before making himself comfortable next to me.

'You could talk to me if you like; I am a good friend, you know?' He wiggled his eyebrows.

'You, a good friend? Who in the world throws a grown woman into the air and then forgets to catch her? You left me helpless, lying there on that kitchen floor. You were lucky Bessie only skelped you across the head. She thought you broke my back—and she had every intention of breaking yours.' I remembered how much I wanted to kill him, and grimaced for a moment.

'Oh, that wasn't even my fault, so keep your hatchet maid away from me before I report you both to the coppers for assault. I get blamed when it's you who hurts yourself at least ten times a day. If you hadn't screamed like a banshee when I tossed you up, I wouldn't have been distracted and forgotten to catch you. I picked you up off the floor and helped you to bed afterwards, didn't I? See? I'm a fabulous friend.' I rolled my eyes and gave up in defeat. 'I know something has happened, and I don't know what it is, but you don't have to tell me unless you want to.' His voice was calm and low before he clapped his hands frantically, then climbed up on the bed, jumping up and down. 'That should mean a lot, given you know how I enjoy a bit of gossip. We can talk about other things, though. Like how I have a secret boyfriend,' he squealed, making me laugh.

Aaron was forever chastising him for throwing me around like a rag doll, which would often bruise me, sometimes seriously. He only stood a few inches taller than me but was double my size in width and weight. Despite our constant bickering, he was a staunch friend. We talked about everything down to the last detail and would make each other laugh constantly. He was my sunshine, my confidant, becoming so in such a short amount of time it surprised me. I loved him dearly, although my close friends, particularly Polly, were unimpressed with his behaviour and what they thought I let him get away with. He was careful around people he didn't know, and when in public; however, here at Willow Grove, he was making it his home, too, and it was the one place he could indeed be himself. I knew some workers here were uncomfortable with his effeminate manner, but he made no advances unless they wished the same. I had heard a groom comment recently in passing on the matter. He believed Leo was just an eccentric European with little common sense, and I had to agree with that last part. He was intelligent, but without a drop of common sense in him.

'So, tell me the most important bit? Who is it?' I asked, staring at his radiant face. I loved it when he was happy like this; it lifted my own heart, feeling downtrodden and confused.

'Now, that'd be telling, but it's someone from here,' he replied, kissing my nose.

'All right, then. I won't make you say, but promise you will if it becomes serious?' I tried to smother a smile, knowing he wouldn't be able to help himself.

'Of course, my precious butterface. I wouldn't leave you out. How dare me?' He laughed, hugging me tightly while smoothing my hair, muttering to himself at the mess I was in and what a fright I was to look upon.

'Maybe I should just marry you. I love you just as much as I could love any husband.' His eyes widened in horror as he pushed me away.

'Me, marry you? Even if I were a hetero, as you say, you would be the last woman I would hitch my wagon to, honey. You'd be far too much work—what with the foot-stomping and the chin pointing—not to mention the hands-on-the-hip thingy.' He shook his head, his hand unconsciously going to his head. 'The ear twisting is the deciding factor, though. No. And I'll say it again. No. I refuse your proposal of marriage, and don't even try to trick me into it in the future,' he shrilled in indignation. I smiled as I closed my heavy eyes and drifted back into a deep sleep, leaving him to his gossip with himself.

Bessie stood by the bed in her nightgown, still half-asleep, the lantern held up high above her head.

'Mistress, you need to wake up,' she called, yawning widely. I tried to open my eyes and focus on what she was saying, but felt as if my head was submerged in water. The room was bright, the full moon shining through the windows, the night clear and silent other than the occasional sound of the native nocturnal animals that fascinated me so very much. I glanced across at the clock on the mantle and felt panic rise inside me, knowing she would only disturb me if it were necessary. 'Mr Aaron is here, and he needs you to get up and get dressed. He wants to take you somewhere, but he won't tell me any more than that,' she whispered loudly, yawning again as Leo groaned and rolled over.

'Where does he need to take me at this hour of the night?' I looked across at Leo, who had gone straight back to sleep only moments after Bessie had awakened us.

'He won't say, other than to put on something warm and meet him in the stables.' I loosened Leo's grip on me. He turned over again and continued to snore softly when I got out of bed.

'This better be important,' I whispered hoarsely as I crossed the room, feeling chilled and out of sorts. Bessie sat me down in the dressing room and raised an eyebrow.

'Everything is important to boys of this age, Mistress,' she said, stroking my face. 'Who knows what the cheeky man is up to now? He's so besotted; it wouldn't surprise me if he has a priest waiting at the stables ready to perform the ceremony. Still, it's sweet to see such a man as him go weak at the knees at the sight of his love. Take some advice from someone who knows; you won't find a better man than Aaron, but you need to give him something of yourself. You're an affectionate girl and sweet, but you haven't given your heart to him, and you keep him at arm's length. Let him in, my darling girl—once you do, he will never give your heart back to you. I'm certain he will cherish you with every fibre of his being.'

Bessie helped me dress warmly before kissing me on the cheek. I smiled before grabbing my thick, woollen cloak with a hood trimmed in mink, leaving her and making my way silently out to the stables. Aaron met me just outside the door, looking bright-eyed and cheerful.

'Now I'm not tryin' to pull a swifty on ya, so trust me.' He picked me up by the waist and placed me on top of Delightful, who, in her usual, sweet manner, whinnied when I spoke to her. I leaned forward and stroked her neck as he swung up behind me. He walked her towards the back of the house and then kicked her on towards the ocean. After only a matter of weeks, I could easily sit a horse now with him behind me and didn't have to grip the saddle for dear life, as I had done in the beginning. I was becoming used to moving my body with the horse as she cantered through the night towards the coast, every star in the sky like diamonds on black velvet, the moonlight even brighter than it had been in my bedchamber.

The night was pleasant, and we enjoyed being close to each other again. I hated how we had left it between us this morning and hadn't talked about the consequences of our meeting with Mr McPhee. I realised he was probably as anxious as me and couldn't sleep, deciding now was the time we needed to talk. He was such a strange and unique boy, so completely unpredictable. But it was his spontaneity that played a part in drawing me to him.

I relaxed the further away from the house we travelled—feeling a sense of freedom, as I always did when I was on Delly with Aaron. He had me take the reins while he wrapped his arms around me, holding me close and kissing me on my neck. Once we arrived at the ocean, crashing furiously against the shore, a distant storm brewing out to sea, he lifted me down and then tethered Delly.

We held hands and stood at the top of the cliff, gazing out over Bass Strait, the moon full and bright. I looked up to find him staring at me, an odd look on his face. It wasn't nervousness, but he certainly wasn't at ease in my company, and something had changed. I knew he had raced into this too fast, deciding he loved me before really getting to know me. He had become something more to me than what I had ever expected when I met him, and I knew if he backed out of the engagement now, it would hurt me. I hadn't realised I cared so deeply for him until the very moment I might lose him. He stood tall, clasping my hands in his while he stared into my eyes.

'I love ya, Abi. My Abi. Me heart. I've met no one as beautiful inside an' out. I wanna spend the rest of me life with ya. Not 'cause I must or any promises made by others, but 'cause I want to. Me greatest desire is to have a family with ya an' be alongside ya every day for the rest of me life. It's me mission to make ya happy every day of ya life an' ensure ya never regret for a moment ya choice to be with me.' He dropped to one knee, not letting go of my hands. 'Abi, would ya do me the honour an' the privilege of bein' me wife an' best friend till the day I'm no longer on this earth? Will ya marry me?' He waited silently for my response, an uncertain expression on his face. He looked so vulnerable and sweet, I felt my heart flutter.

I stared back into his eyes, so honest and trusting, and something shifted inside. The wall I had been maintaining so persistently crumbled away. I knew if I married him, it would be for love—not because some legal document forced me to do so. He had gently chipped away at the shell surrounding my heart and had waited patiently and calmly for me to love him back. I looked down into his earnest blue eyes, the colour of the ocean on a sunny day, and felt tears prick my own.

'Yes, I will marry you—and I do love you, Aaron. It's just taken me a while to realise it.' I pulled him up into my arms. He smiled, then suddenly appeared perplexed.

'Ahh shit. I forgot somethin'.' He dug around in his pants pocket with one hand while he kept the other on my shoulder. His face relaxed as he found the object he had been searching for. 'I need to do this again.' He appeared sheepish as he dropped to his knee again and grinned broadly up at me. I saw a velvet-covered box in his hand. 'Will ya marry me, Abi?' he repeated and opened the box to expose the most brilliant diamond I had ever seen. It looked extremely old. Set in a band of yellow gold, the enormous round stone surrounded by smaller diamonds cut in the same fashion glinting in the moonlight.

"Yes," I screamed into the wind. He jumped to his feet, then lifted me from mine, kissing me so passionately he took my breath away. He put me down, then slipped the ring on my finger, which fit perfectly, and kissed me again.

'You've made me the happiest bloke alive, Abi. We're goin' to have a magical life together. Full o' surprises.' He let his hand slip down from my waist to my backside and gave a squeeze, making me laugh.

'Where did you get this? It's the most beautiful ring I've ever seen in my life.' I held my left hand up in the moonlight and admired the priceless gem. 'I saw some of the most exquisite jewellery when I was in London and even bought myself these earrings.' I pointed at my earlobe before continuing. 'These cost me a small fortune, so I cannot imagine what this is worth, Aaron. I'm worried about wearing it. I would never forgive myself if I lost it.' I stared in awe at the sparkling heirloom on my finger. He held out my hand so he, too, could admire the stone.

'Yeah, it's beautiful, alright. It was given to me Da by ya great-aunt Isabelle before she died—an' not long before we moved here—intended for me future wife. This ring was always meant for you. I know nothin' of the history of it, other than it came from the Delmont family.' I couldn't help but wonder how my great-aunt could be so certain I would accept him she was prepared to leave a precious diamond to a five-year-old boy for his possible future bride. I didn't understand at all what she sought to achieve by manipulating my life in the way she had. The fact it was turning into something extraordinary was beside the point. Aaron wrapped his arms around me while I burrowed my face into his chest as the wind whipped around us. He ran his hands down my loose hair, blowing all around me. 'Ya hair is so beautiful. Never cut it.' He twirled several strands around his fingers as he held me close, gazing into my eyes. 'I give ya me solemn promise I'll pash ya like this every single mornin'.' He pulled me towards him, kissing me passionately.

'And I will pash you back exactly the same way.' I reached up and touched his face gently with my fingers before placing my arms around his neck and letting myself melt into him.

Chapter Seventeen

I T WAS DAYLIGHT WHEN Bessie hurried into my bedchamber, flinging open the heavy drapes to let the sunshine pour in, then noticed Aaron sleeping in his clothes on the bed next to me. 'And what do you think you're doing in here at this time of the morning?' she asked sharply, hands on her hips while tapping her foot on the ground impatiently, waiting for his response. Aaron smiled sleepily at her, then whispered of the events of the night. Bessie screamed, jolting me out of a deep sleep to find her and Aaron hugging each other and jumping up and down in excitement in the lounge area. Bessie rushed over to the bed. 'Show me the ring, Mistress. I must see it to believe it.' She laughed loudly, hurting my ears. I stuck my hand out from under the quilt and placed a pillow over my head, hoping I could get more sleep and leave these two fools to themselves. 'Oh, my goodness, it's beautiful. It suits your hand so well, but is it heavy? It looks so big.' Bessie's eyes were wide, tears shimmering, her voice hoarse. 'Congratulations, Mistress. I hope you will be very happy in your new life together. In fact, I know you will, as I feel as though I've hand-picked Aaron to be your husband.' She seemed proud of herself as I stared up at her blankly, feeling confused. As far as I knew, she had nothing to do with me meeting Aaron, but I remembered how she had encouraged me to take him seriously after the first week of our arrival. She wrestled the pillow from me and kissed me on the cheek. I gazed back at her affectionately before taking her hand in mine.

'Thanks, Bessie. Your blessing means more to me than you know, and I'm sure it does to Aaron too—yours will be the face he wakes up to every morning once we marry.' I laughed—now Aaron appeared confused for a moment before his face broke into a wide grin.

'And what a lovely face 'tis to have the pleasure of seein' each time I open me eyes.' He bowed to Bessie, who giggled and softly smacked him on the head. I told Bessie I would lie in and asked if we could have breakfast trays brought to us later when Leo was ready. She agreed, then appeared to float out of the room as if she were walking on a cloud, leaving us alone. Aaron slipped under the heavy quilt, fully clothed, something he had never done before, always choosing to sleep on top of the bedding, with me underneath. He pulled me close to him. I felt naked in my nightgown compared to when I lay with him while dressed. He ran his hand down to my waist against the silk of my nightgown, then slowly up my back, pausing at the back of my neck, holding me still while turning my face towards his. He leaned down and kissed me with more passion than I had ever felt before. 'I promised ya I would kiss you like that each day, an' I don't break me word.' I sighed with happiness and kissed him again. 'I want to marry ya tomorrow, Abi. No party, just a simple ceremony with you an' me.' He gazed down at me, his face serious. 'I know it's not fair to make ya miss havin' the weddin' of ya dreams 'cause of me own impatience—so I'll wait—but please don't make me wait too long.' I stroked the back of his neck while he spoke, sending waves of warmth pulsating through my body. He lay on his back with one arm around my shoulder, the other behind his head, appearing thoughtful.

'When do you want to get married?' I enquired, kissing him softly on the mouth.

'As soon as ya pull ya finger out,' he teased. 'Plannin' weddin's an' piss ups wasn't somethin' me headmistress taught when I was writin' me letters on me slate an' dreamin' of bein' a drover.' I turned and gazed out the window at the grey sky, the leaves from the gum tree in the centre of the garden fluttering in the wind. I had agreed to marry him, so there was no point in delaying the inevitable. Despite my rejecting the Catholic belief system, I knew it would be important to Sister Josephine I marry in the church and raise my children in the faith. Aaron was also Catholic, making it all far easier—we would have no conflict regarding their religious upbringing. I intended to expose any children we were blessed with to the teachings of many religions once they were older, and then they could choose for themselves.

'Well, I've only recently had some experience on the matter. It took a month to organise Polly's wedding. I would need at least that. Maybe I could do it in that amount of time if I really tried. I would have Polly, Leo, and Dana to help me, and there is Catherine, too.' He nodded thoughtfully, his eyes lighting up.

'So, the priest could wed us within the month?'

'I can't see why not—if that's what we've decided.' I nuzzled my face into his shoulder and kissed his neck gently, then placed butterfly kisses up his neck and all over his face, which made him smile.

'We have,' he whispered, holding me as if he would never let go.

We sat up in bed companionably, eating our delicious breakfast. Bessie had informed Leo of the engagement, and he had sent up a special selection of sweet, creamy porridge, eggs on toast with sliced baked ham covered in a creamy sauce, along with fluffy pancakes with pure maple syrup from Canada. He had even placed a white rose from our garden in a vase on the tray for me. His thoughtfulness touched me. I watched Aaron enjoy his meal with his usual enthusiasm. Having him move in here soon would undoubtedly keep the staff busier than they were after only looking after me. However, I knew they would enjoy his company; I could often find him in the kitchen with them all sitting around laughing and joking.

'So, what do you plan to do after we marry? Are you still going to work on the boat with your father?' I enquired between mouthfuls. He chewed slowly for a time before answering.

'Strewth, I haven't given it much thought. To be honest, I didn't expect ya to accept me proposal so soon. I thought ya may need me here?' He appeared self-conscious as I leaned over and kissed his lips.

'Yes, but does your father need you more?' He shook his head adamantly.

'Nah, he told me he's well covered with me brothers an' some local lads should I ever wanna go an' share me talents somewhere else. He knew a year past I was sick of the fishin' business, leavin' me free as a snapper in the sea to do whatever ya need me to do.'

'Well, as my husband, you own half of everything. I suppose you could take over talking to the foremen, Angus and Harry. You could be the problem solver when issues come up between them and their workers and fix anything that arises before it gets out of hand, the way some things tend to do. Then, as an owner, they would keep you advised regarding the management of the farm. But only if you want to.' I smiled shyly, feeling I was dumping an enormous workload on him, but his face broke into a wide grin.

'Yeah, I'm willin'. Harry an' Angus are from good stock, an' I get along with all the blokes who work here. What about the accounts for the property? Who's the king cockie?'

'Mr Masters keeps a very efficient book for the house, but has been forced to take on the extra responsibility, calculating the profit and loss each month regarding the farm. It then all goes to Mr McPhee, who pays all the outstanding bills, taxes, and wages, then banks any leftover money.' That was my understanding of the current situation, as Mr McPhee had explained in vague terms.

'I'm willin' to keep the books an' accounts in order if ya want me to? I've always shown some talent for numbers,' Aaron offered graciously. 'Then I'll know exactly what needs orderin' an' how the breedin' program is progressin'. I'm impressed by the sheer number of fillies an' colts ya have here sold before they're even born. I've been wanderin' 'round like a lost jumbuck for a while now, an' helpin' ya here may bring me back to the flock.' He smiled at me and winked before continuing, 'I'm willin' to do anythin' that has ya involved in it—especially if I get to have a perv at that fine bum ya drag along behind ya.' He made me laugh, and I loved that. Now I had let down my wall, I felt far closer to him. I ran my hand from his shoulder to his large arm, placing my hand in his. He squeezed gently. 'Since agreein' to wed me, you're very affectionate,' he remarked, looking into my eyes and making my heart melt. 'It's a big change for ya.

Despite ya reserve, you've never been a frigid woman, an' you've been nothin' but sweet an' kind to me. Ya see—no one ever taught ya to be affectionate 'cause ya received so little of it as a child. Ya didn't have parents like me, who acted as role models for how a marriage should be.' He leaned over and kissed some sauce from the side of my lips. I loved how thoughtful he was, always trying to find out the deeper meaning behind things. His mind was sharp, and I found him to be highly intelligent.

'Well, now I don't have any reason to hold back. Hamish is gone from my life, and I now accept that I love you and want to spend my life with you. Now I don't have to be worried about hurting you or getting hurt, so I can relax and be myself.' I lifted a forkful of pancake to my lips, my mouth watering as the smell of buttermilk and syrup wafted up to my nose. After one bite, I reminded myself I would eat maple syrup on everything, becoming addicted since my first taste only weeks ago.

'I ask ya to tell me true. Is Hamish really gone from ya life?' he asked, his voice strained, interrupting my thoughts about what they would serve for lunch. His trepidation surprised me, given I had accepted his proposal.

'Well, he is, in a romantic sense—that's dead and buried—but because of Angus and Polly, he will always be in my life in some capacity. I am obligated to at least try to get along with him for their sake. Once some time passes, I'm sure we can be friends.'

'Then, it looks like I'll have to make a new mate, too, if he's still goin' to be a part of ya life. So long as he never touches ya, he an' I won't have anythin' between us that'll cause me to beat the livin' daylights out of him.' We sat back in bed and drank our creamy, hot chocolate, something Leo had included as a special treat. 'I'll be like a cat on a corrugated iron roof on a forty degree day till our weddin' night.' I saw the glint in his eye as he looked down at my breasts, decently covered in a thin nightgown; however, the material was so fine you could see their shape and outline.

'So, you do desire me then?' I wondered if I really wanted to know the truth as I pulled the covers up over myself.

'More than anythin', Abi. Ya don't know how difficult 'tis for me to be next to ya without touchin' ya where I shouldn't. Why would ya question that?'

'It's only something Hamish said to me on the day of Polly's wedding.' He raised his eyebrows, questioning precisely what I meant, then took his tray and set it on the table before climbing back in beside me. 'He said because you have always been a gentleman to me and we haven't gone further than kissing, it means he desires me more and is more in love and passionate about me than you are.' My voice shook as I remembered how that had made me feel. Aaron gazed at me sympathetically, then reached over and took my hand. He studied my face with such trust and love, setting loose a hundred butterflies in my stomach.

'How far have ya gone with Hamish? Have ya made love to him?' he asked gently. I felt him squeeze my hand tighter, not appearing to notice.

'Oh, no. Nowhere near that far. Not even close to half that far.' He nodded, appearing relieved—but still wanting to know exactly what we had done. I told him the truth. All of it. He was silent for a moment, staring out over the back garden.

'Well, there's no harm done, is there? But it sounds to me he was tryin' to push ya into it.'

'Yes, he was, but that was only after I met you. Before that, he behaved like a normal person. He is even quite lovely when you get to know him. One thing I will say for Hamish is he has many negative traits, but his heart is made of solid gold just like his mother's, whom he favours. You did not get to meet him before, but you really would have liked him then. I hope now he will move on with his life and return to the man I know he is. Once we were at Willow Grove for a week, I stopped letting him into my bed, as we would have gone too far. They put you in a terrible position, set up against each other from the start, and it became like a competition.' I felt sad as I thought of Hamish. Others did not know him the way I did or how kind and caring he was deep down. He had only ever shown that side to me by his own admission. Aaron was quiet for a moment.

'Don't lend ya pretty lug to him. He's spinnin' ya a yarn. If I'd had me own way, I would have bedded ya the day I met ya, but I know it's important for ya to make love for the first time with ya husband—that's why I keep control of meself. There are times where I think I'll lose me mind an' I have to use all me strength not to grab ya and throw ya on the bed before havin' me way with ya. The thing is, what ya think, feel an' want is at the forefront of me mind an' I wanna make everythin' come true for ya.' He took my empty tray, put it beside his on the table, and brought back large glasses of freshly squeezed orange juice for both of us. 'One of the perks marryin' ya is the service here,' he said with a chuckle. 'At home, we never even had a housekeeper like so many do these days, leavin' me Ma doin' everythin' for us. She demanded we help around the house, even though our Da has always loudly declared keepin' the inside of the home is women's' work. I know how to cook an' clean as well as the next girl.'

Giggling at his very Australian sense of humour, I admired how his parents had raised their boys, ensuring they turned into hard-working, generous men who would make any woman a wonderful husband. I knew the main thing he looked forward to, apart from having sexual relations, was the food served here. He could eat whenever he liked, and, as a fellow food connoisseur, I completely understood his excitement. I lay against his chest and entwined my fingers in his as he brought them up to his lips.

'You've made me the happiest man alive, an' I'll do me best to make ya life easier an' more enjoyable than it would if I wasn't in it. Even if ya had've rejected me, I still would've chased ya like a fatty chases cake.' I laughed aloud, aware just how far he would go to chase a freshly baked cake himself. 'When are ya goin' to tell Hamish? I don't wanna interfere, but after everythin' that's passed between ya, don't ya think he should hear it straight from ya lips, rather than read about it in the newspaper—or it reaches his lug through a stranger?'

'Oh, shit. I hadn't even thought of that. Tit, bum, piss, bullocks.' He chuckled and brushed my hair off my face with his fingers. Damn it to hell. I had not even thought of Hamish in that way since Aaron had asked me to marry him, and now I was going to have to see him. Worse, it was to tell him I was getting married. To Aaron. All within the month. I hoped he would control his temper—I couldn't stand it if he fought with me again. All I wanted was peace between us, given he was not likely to go away anytime soon because of Angus—and the fact that, to the best of my knowledge, he was courting Charlotte. 'Do you mind taking me to the Makenzie farm today? Only so I can speak directly with Hamish before we officially announce anything?'

'Of course I'll come with ya if ya want me to,' he replied. 'I'd be reluctant to let ya go an' see him alone. I know he will have one last crack an' try an' talk ya out of it. By the way, as ya beloved chef likes to say, I believe ya ready to learn to ride Delly by yourself. Then ya can have the freedom to go where ya choose, when ya choose, instead of havin' to rely on Harry harnessin' the horses an' transportin' ya to where ya need to go.' I wondered if I could ever ride her by myself, no matter how many lessons I endured. But I trusted Aaron, and if anyone could teach me, it was him. I loved her deeply now and spent time every day sitting in her stall, feeding her carrots and talking to her. She would nuzzle me and let me stroke and brush her. If I was sitting, she always had her head in my lap, wanting a scratch. I wanted more than anything to ride her on my own and have the freedom Aaron promised it would give me. It was because of Aaron, Harry had given her to me in the first place, and they both had a hand in training her. I never wanted a horse of my own, but I was grateful to him for this gift I never expected. To ride around Willow Grove and explore the unknown nooks and crannies excited me no end, and I was determined to take my lessons seriously.

'When are we going to tell your parents, Aaron?'

I felt self-conscious, wondering what his family would think, having only met me once. Although we had gotten along famously, I did not know what they thought of me. I wondered how his parents would greet the news we were moving so fast, not to mention his brothers, with whom he was close. They would lose him, not only from the family home, but from the family business. They would probably think I was pregnant, I thought to myself with a grimace. He watched me intently as hundreds of thoughts flitted through my mind.

'I only have to look at ya to know what ya thinkin'. Ya have a glass face an' everythin' shows in ya eyes, Abi. We can tell me oldies an' the boys after ya have spoken to Hamish,' he said, kissing me. I ran my tongue over his top lip; his mouth so delicious I could kiss him all day.

'Yes, that would be good. How do you think your family will react?' I felt nervous in my stomach. I questioned if they covertly disapproved of me because I didn't behave the way others of my 'station' behaved, as my friends and workers constantly reminded me. I wasn't a wild animal who didn't know basic manners; however, I felt uncomfortable and self-conscious mingling with those considered part of high society. I didn't understand what they expected of me. No one told you as an adult—the Nanny was supposed to teach you in childhood how to behave as a lady should.

I hadn't received that training, other than private instructions from Dana, Richard, Hamish, and Harriet Makenzie, who was still a dear friend. She had tried to remain neutral, making it clear we were friends first, and whatever happened between Hamish and me was between us and would not affect our friendship. She was hoping we would reunite; however, today, she would find out the truth, which I knew would shatter her.

'They'll be as happy as pigs in mud,' Aaron reassured me. 'Me Ma will be rubbin' her hands together in glee at the prospect of future grandchildren. They always wanted a girl but were never fortunate to be blessed with one, so they'll look at you as the daughter they never had. They're fond of ya, Abi, an' me Da has been bangin' on somethin' chronic about ya an' askin' when ya comin' back to visit.' I felt relieved they would be happy—if Aaron was correct—and he nearly always was. I took a deep breath and relaxed.

Bessie returned, and I went into the dressing room with her. Within a quarter of an hour, I was sitting at the dressing table about to have my hair done. Aaron, who had been watching closely, interrupted Bessie's chatter.

'Could ya please leave her hair down, Bessie? I love when it's flowin' down around her waist,' he pleaded. Bessie eyed him warningly, grunting several times to herself.

'Don't be putting thoughts in her mind, you lout. She has enough obtuse ideas of her own,' she retorted crossly. 'The Mistress has to wear it up as all ladies do, and that's that. She's not leaving the house with it down—I'm telling you that now, Mr Aaron.'

'I like it up, too, Bessie, an' ya do a wonderful job with her hair every day. It's only I like to run me fingers through it an' play with the lovely strands,' he said, a wide grin spreading across his face.

'Humph. Well, you can keep your big mits to yourself or do that in your private time in the future—not during the day when the Mistress is expected to look presentable around people—thank you very much, boyo.' He tried a different tactic, and I smiled to myself at his dogged persistence.

'How is Danny gettin' along, Bessie?' I saw her expression soften and her eyes mist over.

'Oh, he is wonderful, Mr Aaron. I will remember you to him. He likes you very much,' she told him, but continued putting up my hair.

'That's very kind, Bessie. I'd very much appreciate it.' He winked discreetly at me while admitting defeat over my hair for today. I knew this would be an ongoing battle between them and smothered a smile.

I sat in front of Aaron as we rode to the neighbouring farm owned by the Makenzie family. Nervous about the prospect of seeing Hamish and telling him the news, my hands trembled slightly. I had made my choice, and I didn't know how he would react, now there would be no chance of us getting back together. I gazed out over the rolling paddocks as we drew nearer to their mansion.

'What's wrong, Abi?' Aaron leaned forward and kissed me on the cheek.

'How do you know anything is wrong?' It surprised me he asked, given he could not see my eyes to read them as he so confidently believed he could.

'Ya entire body tenses up when you're thinkin' about somethin' bad. That's how I know.' His fingers caressed my waist unconsciously as he spoke. He would touch me sometimes without realising he was doing it, taking my hand or stroking some part of my body gently as we talked. I loved how he was so affectionate. It was helping me overcome intimacy issues related to my childhood of never having enough, other than what Sister Josephine had given to me freely with her whole heart. Now it was time for me as an adult to learn how to be affectionate to the man I loved.

'I'm just nervous about telling Hamish, that's all. I don't know how he will react.' He tightened his arms around me and kissed the side of my neck softly.

'Ya only have to say what ya need to an' get out of there. If he does his block, I'll be right there beside ya, ready to step in at any time,' he reassured me. I leaned my head back against his broad chest and let the horse's rhythm relax me. We were nearly there, and I was not looking forward to this at all.

Delly carried us down the long driveway of their enormous property. Their mansion soon came into view, and Aaron pulled her up in front of the grand entrance, where he quickly slid down, landing solidly on his feet. I dismounted for the first time without help, staggering back into Aaron, who caught me before I could fall. I climbed the steps and knocked on the door. A maid answered and arched her eyebrows inquiringly, I assumed, due to the early hour.

'May I speak to Hamish, please? Would you tell him Abigail is here to see him?' She nodded and led us to the library, my nerves overwhelming me. Aaron stood by a window looking out over the property, obviously impressed. As I sat and waited, I pressed my skirt down, smoothing out the crinkles after riding Delly. I hated side-saddles and rode astride as the men did, much to everyone's horror. Hamish walked in and smiled when he caught sight of me, spreading his arms wide to embrace me. When he noticed Aaron standing by the window, he stopped dead, his arms slowly dropping to his side. My heart was in my throat, and my stomach flipped wildly. Hamish appeared confused as his gaze flitted from me to Aaron and back again.

'What's this about, Abigail?' He took the seat opposite me, lowering his enormous frame onto the large settee. I laid my shaking hands on my lap and looked straight into his face as I tried to form the words.

'Hamish, I've come to tell you I'm going to marry Aaron. I wanted you to hear it from me. You deserve that much.' The blood drained from his face as he stared at me, clenching his jaw. He glanced toward the window as Aaron came and sat beside me, then turned back, an odd look on his face as though he was in some sort of physical pain. He stood and shook Aaron's hand stiffly, then nodded formally in my direction.

'Congratulations.' He forced a smile; however, I noted his fists clenched at his side and the tenseness of his body. I leaned back in the chair, readying myself to leave. 'I couldn't be happier for you both. This is difficult to admit, but I was at a point where I wanted to break up with you, but didn't know how without hurtin' you, Abigail. I warned you my limit with a woman was about two-months—at the longest, three. The thing is, I've wanted to bed Charlotte since I met her, an' now I have the opportunity, I'm not interested in seein' you romantically. I haven't been for a while but didn't know how to escape from you. You see, you're a tease. You'll do certain things an' not others in bed, an' I like to be with women who know what they want an' go out to get it. That's not you. I'm sorry if I hurt your feelings, but I have to be honest.'

The coldness in his tone made me feel like he had just punched me in the stomach. He had been using me for all this time when he truly hadn't cared about me at all. Tears pricked my eyes, my face flushing at my naivety. I had genuinely believed he cared deeply for me, and couldn't understand how I could be so wrong about someone I thought I knew. I sat unmoving, not knowing what to say, an uncomfortable silence now hanging over the room. Aaron placed his arm around my shoulders protectively while Hamish fixed him with a stare.

'How does it feel to be marryin' damaged goods, Aaron? I had her first, an' now you're stuck with her after I've discarded her. I warned her I was like this, an' she still let me get close to her an' do things—things you'll never know. You will always wonder when you touch her if I touched her there before you, or made her feel like that first. I wouldn't want to marry someone like that. You can find a dozen just like her down the local tavern.' I gazed at him in silence, feeling deep hurt and regret I had ever met him. My clenched hands trembled, my heart raced, and I tried to catch my breath. Aaron took both my hands in his large one to steady them and looked back at Hamish calmly.

'Mate, I know what's passed between ya, an' I don't give a toss about any of it. It's me she's marryin', an' me who'll get to make love to her for the first time on our weddin' night. I'm not threatened by ya, an' never have been. What we do have to sort out in the future is a way for us all to get along for ya brother an' Polly's sake.' He tightened his grip around my shoulders, while continuing to hold my hands so Hamish wouldn't see how upset I was. I had kept the tears at bay, but knew I was close to breaking down. Hamish glared at Aaron for a moment, his face softening into something more pleasant as he rose to his feet.

'Aye, I'll try, but make sure you keep your fiancée off me since I'm with Charlotte now,' he warned, glancing at me in disgust as I lowered my head.

'Yeah, mate. I'll keep a rope tied around her neck when she's around ya, an' I'll make bloody sure I give it a sharp tug should she look in ya direction.' Aaron stood and pulled me to my feet, his face giving nothing away. My legs felt like jelly, but I was determined to walk from there under my own strength if it was the last thing I did.

'See that you do, Aaron,' Hamish replied, putting his arm around his shoulder and walking him out the door. I lagged a little behind so I could calm myself. Outside, they shook hands before Aaron untethered Delly, lifted me onto her back, then swung himself up behind me. Hamish politely bid us farewell, then closed the front door abruptly behind him. Aaron kicked Delly into a canter, and we hurried away from the Makenzie estate.

'Ya know, he didn't mean the filthy shite he was spewin' about ya? He's just coverin' his feelin's an' savin' face. He knows what he's lost.' He gripped me around the waist, my back against his chest.

'No.' I shook my head adamantly, an attempt to clear my muddled thoughts. 'It's true what he said about using girls for a few months at a time and throwing them over when he meets someone new. He told me he did that, but made me believe he had changed. He fooled me. When a man tells you something about himself, believe him and never expect to change him.' I burst into tears, feeling humiliated. I had allowed him to become so close to me, and now he was just plain foul and mean-spirited. Aaron seemed surprised by my reaction.

'He was lyin' an' is nothin' but a bullshit artist, Abi. Can't ya tell?'

'No, not really, Aaron,' I replied through my tears. 'I take people at their word, just like I expect them to do with me. If someone lies to me, it's on their conscience, not mine.' He looked at me adoringly as I turned my head and smiled at him weakly.

'You're so innocent—so beautifully innocent. I love that about ya,' he whispered, pulling me into a kiss.

When we arrived at Aaron's home, we were greeted loudly by his family the moment we stepped into the sitting room, including his brothers, Patrick, Aiden, and Luke. His parents were enjoying a cup of tea, and Edith Cavanaugh rushed off to get a fresh pot while we made ourselves comfortable. The brothers were boisterous and teased each other mercilessly, which made me giggle. They resembled each other closely—all tall, powerfully built men with golden skin—I assumed as a result of spending so much time out in the harsh sunlight.

'So, Miss Abigail, this is ya second visit to our home. Not one of us sittin' here believes the good Lord above is still lettin' our drongo of a brother hang around such a lovely lady as yourself. We've had to wonder if ya are indeed as intelligent or sane as we first thought,' Aiden remarked cheekily, making the others chuckle. I didn't know what to say. I wasn't accustomed to his family as yet, so just smiled. They were so outgoing, leaving me slightly overwhelmed in their company. I was a little shy until I came to know people, and these boys had picked it up a mile away, gently including me in their teasing. They were never nasty, all possessing a cheeky sense of humour, and I couldn't help but giggle as I listened to the things they were saying while Gavin, their father, looked on proudly. When his mother returned and placed our tea in front of us, Aaron nervously cleared his throat. I never once had seen this man uncertain of himself, and for some reason, it amused me greatly. He appeared to not know what to say for the first time since I had met him.

'I have somethin' important to tell ya all, so pay attention. Shut ya cake-hole, Luke—an' bloody well listen,' Aaron called out over the noise. His parents waited expectantly, while his brothers, finally lowering their voices and falling silent, could not quite sit still. Aaron looked around at them, his face serious, and I could see they were expecting bad news. He placed his arm around me protectively. 'I asked Abigail to marry me last night, an' she accepted. We're to be married in a month.' An enormous grin spread across his face while a pandemonium of congratulations erupted, with hugs and lots of handshaking and backslapping going on. Patrick lifted me off my feet and embraced me, then passed me to Aiden, who did the same. Aiden handed me to Luke, who hugged me warmly before finally putting me down. I could see these boys were going to throw me around, just like Leo did. I was confident the way they easily passed me from brother to brother to congratulate and welcome me into the family was a sign of things to come, and I smiled to myself. Edith came to me, her eyes shining as she embraced me tightly.

'I finally have a daughter after praying every morning and night since I was first married. I am so happy for you both. Thank goodness you behaved yourself, Aaron, and didn't act like the little shite you are at home.' She burst into tears and was immediately comforted by her husband, who appeared overjoyed at the news and beamed at me while the others laughed at their mother. I again wondered what would have happened if Aaron and I had not fallen in love. Would they have required his father to return everything great-aunt Isabelle had given him? She had undoubtedly looked after this family and secured their future. The fact Gavin Cavanaugh had been provided with an expensive fishing boat so he could make his living showed me how intent my aunt had been to ensure Aaron and his siblings had a comfortable life growing up. No one understood why she had done this, not even Mr McPhee, who I loathed. Once everyone returned to their seats, Patrick turned to me and narrowed his gaze.

'Have ya joined the puddin' club, Abigail? Did he pop one in ya combustion stove? Is that why ya havin' a shotgun weddin'?' he bellowed, a smirk on his face. Edith leaned over and smacked Patrick hard across the ear, only making everyone laugh more as he held his aching head, laughing along with the others. We enjoyed our lunch, and the feast laid out before us, then settled in for the afternoon, laughing, talking and getting to know one another. Aaron's parents fussed over the engagement ring, telling me how terrified they'd been for years someone would steal the precious stone. They did not know its value, only that it was extremely old and had one of the largest diamonds they and their friends had ever seen. They expressed relief it was now safely on my finger, where they believed it belonged.

I enjoyed the company of every member of this family and thought them a wonderful, close group—I couldn't wait to be a part of it, to feel I belonged with a family who cared about me. Seeing the love they bestowed on their own boys, I was confident they would do the same for any children we were blessed with in the future. I thought how different a life our own children would have compared to mine and wiped away a tear that threatened to fall.

I held Delly's reins as Aaron kissed the side of my neck and murmured comical squibs in my ear that made me blush. Then, he took my earlobe between his lips, nibbling and sucking on it before nipping it, sending chills throughout my body. When he stopped, I asked him if he wanted to have children.

'With ya? Does a wombat shit in the scrub? Yeah, I wanna have as many nippers with ya as I can. I don't care if we have one or ten, but I've always had it in me mind I would have four. Boys or girls, it doesn't matter—I'll love 'em the same. I can't wait to hold a tiny me an' you in me arms an' give him or her all the love ya never had.' He spoke softly as he held me tightly around my waist, the black and white magpies calling out to each other in the gumtree towering above us. I stroked his thigh as I pondered my future. It meant a great deal to me he acknowledged my childhood as he did and was well aware it still caused me great pain.

I was now really looking forward to marrying him and being his wife. When he proposed, it was as if someone had removed a veil from my eyes, and I saw him clearly for the first time. The wall I had kept around me for protection crumbled and was now rubble at my feet, my heart vulnerable, with nothing to prevent it from being torn out. I truly admired the way Aaron had behaved in my solicitor's office.

The way he had avoided the subject after meeting with Mr McPhee, not wanting our marriage to be a business-like arrangement, then planning his proposal based on love alone, had drawn me closer to him. That meeting had convinced me I was choosing the right path to share with the man I loved. I was enjoying getting to know him better each day. He would often surprise me at how open he was. Nothing ever seemed to bother him; he just went with the mood, getting along with everyone who crossed his path.

Aaron pulled Delly up in front of the stables and dismounted, assisting me down safely to my feet. I helped him remove Delly's tack, then brushed her until her coat glimmered in the autumn sunshine. She was big and muscular, yet so placid and sweet. After placing her in her stall, we made our way to the sitting room, where we found Leo relaxing while sipping a small mug of coffee. He looked up from his newspaper and smiled.

'How are you two lovebirds? Congratulations, by the way. I think you're insane, Aaron, to take on such a feisty, volatile woman whom, I must say, is quite unbalanced in more ways than one—if you catch my meaning.' He raised his finger to his temple and moved it slowly around in a circle while pulling a face that made him appear slightly insane. Aaron grabbed me as we made ourselves comfortable opposite him and pulled me onto his lap. I placed my bare feet up on the lounge and exhaled.

'I'm up for it, Leo. It's the two of ya together that has me worried.' Aaron chuckled as Leo burst into giggles, then smiled and flirted with Aaron, much to my amusement.

'I have made a celebratory engagement dinner for you tonight, and I hope you like it. It's your favourite dessert in those oversized glasses—crème brûlée,' he said proudly, winking at us. I looked at him lovingly. He was so thoughtful at times, yet at others was a complete shithead. I smiled and thanked him. It was my absolute favourite dessert in the entire world. The way he served it in a gigantic glass that held ten times the usual and polite amount was the perfect size for me. 'Tell me, when is the big day? Am I going to be a chief bridesmaid?'

'I haven't decided on anything like that yet. Certainly, you cannot be a bridesmaid. The men in Australia—and anywhere in the world, really—would string you up on the nearest gumtree. But, maybe in another lifetime, things will be different. Hopefully, their belief systems will change as we move forward into modern times.' He nodded thoughtfully and squeezed my hand.

He was my best friend, and, of course, I wanted him up there standing next to me; however, there were some things even I knew were not possible. Aaron filled Leo in on all the details he knew so far, and they chatted away for what seemed like forever. I snuggled into Aaron's shoulder, listening but not commenting, as they talked and laughed. I was so happy they got along so well—the two men I loved.

Bessie brushed my hair gently, talking of her day, when Aaron knocked on the door, then stepped inside. She touched the back of my head and nodded, seemingly satisfied, then bent down and kissed my cheek before leaving to find her own bed, quietly closing the door behind her. Since we had announced our engagement this morning, she had relaxed her rules about Aaron and me being alone in my bedchamber. I crossed the room in my nightgown, and although it had no sleeves, it was perfectly respectable. I pulled back the covers and climbed in as he stood beside the bed, staring down at me.

'Are you staying for the night?' I asked, smiling at him. He shifted from foot to foot, appearing uncomfortable.

'I want to, but no. I have to be strong for only another four weeks. Every time I stay here, it gets harder an' harder for me to keep me hands off ya. Then there's ya reputation, Abi. I don't want people sayin' untruths' about ya. I'll make sure you're a virgin on our weddin' night—that I promise ya.' He lay down on top of the covers and gathered me in his arms. He was so sweet and understanding. He knew it meant a great deal to me, as I had always promised Sister Josephine I would save myself for marriage. I had never broken a promise to her in my life, and had no intention of doing so now. 'I'm only goin' ta hold ya till you're asleep. Then I'll leave, knowin' you're in dreamland till I see ya again when ya wake. I'll be here before the sun rises.'

'Yes—probably in the kitchen.' I laughed as he drew me closer and kissed me on the mouth for the longest time, stroking my face with his fingers, although enormous, soft and gentle.

'I've already told you some of the things I plan to do to you when we're married. There are more, I'm sure, but I've a month to think 'em up.' A slow grin spread across his face as I giggled.

I kissed him goodnight, then turned and put my back against him so he could cuddle me to sleep. I lay unmoving, thinking about how lucky I was—I just couldn't see it until now. Finally, I drifted off into a deep sleep and dreamed of crème brûlée, an enormous diamond, and finding a small wombat wrapped in a blanket, all safe and secure.

Chapter Eighteen

'MISTRESS, YOU NEED TO get up—it's urgent,' I heard as Bessie gently shook me awake. She looked agitated as she hurried me out of bed. I stumbled across the room to look for a dress. She stopped me and held up my dressing gown. 'You don't have time to dress; just put this on.' Something in her tone made my stomach flip. The fact she was going to let me go downstairs in my dressing gown was enough to send me into a panic. Something was obviously very wrong. She would usually smack me on the bottom if she caught me in the kitchen dressed this way.

It was daylight, but early—far too early for someone to call on me at this hour. I followed Bessie to the kitchen and, to my surprise, found Amelia sitting at the table, wrapped in a blanket and holding a cup of hot chocolate. Leo had a comforting arm draped around her shoulder.

Her face was black and blue. There were superficial cuts near her eye and on her nose and lips, and she was shaking and crying on Leo's shoulder while he tried to soothe her, to no avail. Erin held Mathew, rocking the bairn in her arms as the kitchen staff huddled around him, cooing and speaking in soothing tones. Amelia stood up as I hurried to her, sobbing loudly, then fell forward into my arms. I waited for her to calm before uttering a word, aware I often made the situation worse by offering my unsolicited opinion. Holding her until she stopped weeping, I gently eased her back onto her seat, where Leo placed his arm around her again—the sweet, darling man. I sat down opposite and looked her in the eye.

'He did this, didn't he?' The anger in my voice made a statement of it rather than a question. Tears poured down her face. Her lip trembled, and her body shook with fear.

'Yes, he did, Abigail. I cannot stand it anymore. I'm sorry, but I had nowhere else to go, and I had to get away... ' She looked at me, her eyes so full of sadness and misery as her voice trailed off to a whisper.

He had beaten her last night for not cooking potatoes with his meal—their supply had run out, and, with Mathew being so unsettled, she could not go out to buy more. Leading her into their bedchamber, he flailed her with his fists, a belt, anything he could get his hands on until she lay unconscious and bleeding on the bed. He left her there while he went to eat his dinner—minus potatoes—while she cleaned herself up and fed Mathew before putting him to bed.

She had returned to her room and pretended to be asleep when he came to bed later in the evening, lying sleepless while not daring to move or even breathe, should he awaken. The moment she heard the front door click shut behind him when he left for work, she'd gathered some things for herself and Mathew and headed straight for Willow Grove.

I asked Bessie to get her settled in one of the guest bedchambers, give her a warm bath, and put her to bed with a tray of breakfast while I arranged for a doctor to come. I planned to talk to her privately once she had been attended to by Bessie. I also assigned little Mary to be Mathew's Nanny while he was here, who appeared overjoyed by the news given her fondness for infants. I asked that Mathew be placed in another guest bedchamber not too close to his mother's, as I wanted Amelia to rest. All the staff were upset by what had happened to Amelia, and rightly so. I stayed in the kitchen and chatted to them while I sipped a cup of hot chocolate with Leo. Finally, I could not contain myself.

'I want to kill that wee bastard,' I fumed. 'Strike him down dead where he stands with a bloody stock-whip. How dare he inflict such pain on her? That piece of shit!' Leo rolled his eyes at me as some of the kitchen staff gasped.

'Now, Abigail. First of all, I know you're as cross as a frog in a sock, but haven't ya learnt ya cannot kill a bullant with those whips. Ya should know that better than anyone given the number of times you've tried to do the exact same thing to me, my sweet little butter-face. Promise me if he comes here, you'll not go twistin' off his lug. You're an intelligent girl, and we love ya despite the fact ya have a few loose Roo's in ya top paddock, but sometimes you're as thick as a brick.' I rolled my eyes before reaching across and grabbing his ear.

'Now I have your lug, you bloody well listen to me. Stop copying the Australians and trying to talk like them as I've had a gutful. And stop calling me butterface—Aaron has told me what it means.' I let go of his ear, his loud shrieking causing unwanted attention from the staff still working in the kitchen. He sat back in his chair, his left hand pressed to the side of his head before realising—although I had every intention of injuring him—I hadn't had the time.

'Fine. I'll stop but only because you are as mad as a cut snake.'

'I warned you.'

'Oh, fine. Where was I after you so rudely interrupted me?'

'I was talking about Amelia,' I growled through clenched teeth.

'Ahh, yes. Well, I was trying to remind you she is George's wife and to keep your sticky beak out of it. He can do what he likes once he legally owns her through that insidious institution they call marriage. Remember that,' Leo warned me darkly as I stared at him in disbelief. 'You don't want to get yourself involved in other people's marriages. He has the power to sign her into an asylum if he so chooses. For no reason at all other than teaching her a lesson, let me remind you. Tread lightly—despite your fat arse and fatter mouth. Be her friend, but stay out of it. I am asking you extra nicely. When you have a typical Abigail reaction to situations and want to lose your head, try to do the opposite of what you want or intend to do. Go against how you usually respond, and that should be the correct reaction,' he teased. I pinched his arm, making him giggle.

'Oh, very funny, Leo.' I could not help smiling at him, albeit weak-ly.

I was wondering what to do when Aaron casually walked in, kissed the top of my head, and sat down for a cup of coffee. Leo immediately told him what had happened to Amelia. He appeared disgusted and shook his head.

'A real bloke would never raise his hand to a woman, no matter what the circumstance—an' she has the little one to look after, too. At least she's safe here among friends,' he remarked, smiling at me sympathetically. He helped himself to the breakfast Leo continued to place on the table before him, a look of pure delight spreading across his handsome face.

'I was informed the other day yet again I'm not permitted to see the dark recesses of the kitchen. It's not considered proper.' I munched on a piece of toast and flicked through The Geelong Advertiser. Aaron glanced at me and snorted in amusement as Leo sat back down at the table and rolled his eyes.

'And since when did ya care what was proper, Abi?' Aaron asked as Leo sniggered loudly.

'She wouldn't know proper if it bit her on her big bum. She has known for the longest time it has never been acceptable for her to eat in the kitchen, but she chooses to ignore it,' Leo commented, then sipped some coffee and flicked through a magazine with all the latest fashions from Paris. I pulled a face at him and continued to eat while Jonathon sat down next to me to have his breakfast. I smiled at him, and he returned the favour. The kitchen was warm and bustling all the time, and you could always find someone to have a chat with or a beverage, and I liked it like this. Aaron was right. I did not care what was proper, and it seemed neither did my great-aunt, who had ensured the kitchen was the heart of the grand building and not hidden away underground next to the cellar, as nearly all of them were in houses such as this. Here I was sitting at the kitchen table in my dressing gown with a footman sitting next to me, not even noticing since they already thought me odd.

It was starting to feel like family here, and I was fairly certain every-one was happy. They had all received their first four-pound-a-month bonus at the start of the week, and I had never seen so many satisfied people walking around under one roof. However, given most of them did not receive nearly close to a pound a week in their wages, the word was starting to spread that we paid more than double the weekly wage. I had already had three inquiries for employment this week, men who were hard working with families to support who I was sadly forced to turn away.

'Are ya goin' to be in ya nightgown all day, Abi?' Aaron enquired as Leo sniggered again.

'If you are lucky, yes, I will be.' I poked my tongue out at him, stood up to leave and, after saying my goodbyes to everyone, found Aaron following closely behind by the time I reached the stairs. Within moments of stepping into my bedchamber, he jumped onto what he now called his side of the bed. I started to look for the dress Bessie had put out last night but could not find it while he comfortably watched my every move.

'Hey, Abi. Come back to bed for a little while. It'll be some time before Amelia is ready to see ya. The quack will take a while to arrive since someone has to ride over there to get him.' He patted the space beside him. He could see how upset I was by what had happened to Amelia, so I relented and slipped back into bed. Besides, it was still early, and I was not generally up for another hour or so. He was under the covers, too, and quickly found me and pulled me to him. 'Ya body feels different under me hands without ya clothes on. Much better. I plan to have ya naked every minute of the day after we're married,' he said smugly. He ran his hand over my nightgown, feeling my ribs one by one and then slowly up my back.

'Hmmm, you really want me walking about Willow Grove in my birthday suit?'

'Or the nuddy—either or—an' only in here,' he chuckled. 'Good mornin', mo anamchara.' He kissed me deeply, then held me tight for a long time. So far, he was true to his solemn promise he would kiss me passionately each day, which made me smile.

We talked as I lay in his arms until Bessie came in to help me dress. I retreated to the dressing room with her, and she picked out a bronze house-dress that was comfortable and suited my colouring. She advised me in hushed tones Amelia was ready to see me, describing how damaged her naked body looked when she was in her bath. Once Bessie was satisfied with my appearance, she followed me out, Aaron calling out his best wishes for Amelia as I waved to him and promised not to be too long.

'Bessie, could you please ask Mr Masters to summon me when the doctor visits this morning? First, I want to make sure Amelia has no broken bones, and she has not sustained a concussion.' Bessie nodded as she followed me down the hall, leaving Aaron in bed.

'Oh, Mistress, if you could only see her bruised and battered body. It's despicable,' Bessie said just before I knocked on the door. When I entered, I found Amelia sitting up in bed, looking slightly better than she had before she had been bathed and fed. I sat down next to her and took her hands in mine.

'How are you, Amelia? I want the truth,' I said, noting her bruised and swollen face. It looked as if she had been kicked by a large, angry horse many times over. She stared at the floor as if she did not know where to begin, and I encouraged her to take her time. She squeezed my hands and gave me an agonised look.

'I had to leave. George said he planned to sign me into an asylum. He claims I am insane because I am always crying and cannot stop. I do not know what to do anymore, Abigail.' She started to cry, and I held her in my arms.

'No one will be taking you anywhere or signing you into an asylum.' Although I spoke with authority, I knew full well I had none at all and was relatively powerless in such a patriarchal society where men ruled and women had no voice. 'You don't have to do anything yet because you have already done it. You have left the brute, and you and Mathew are here and both safe. That's the most important thing. No one can hurt you at Willow Grove. That is all you need to think about right now. Sleeping, eating, and resting are your priorities. So I will not hear any more about it. Mathew has Mary as his full-time Nanny for now. He is perfectly happy and healthy, and she dotes on him. Mary will bring him to you whenever you want to see him, but you must take the time to rest and recover.'

She nodded, appearing relieved as she let out a deep breath and allowed her shoulders to slump. I helped her lay back on the pillows, and within minutes, she was fast asleep. I gently let go of her hands and covered her up, leaving her to the bliss of unconsciousness.

While Amelia slept, Aaron and I went to speak with the priest at St. Mary's of the Angels in Yarra Street, Geelong, where we had decided to be married. We stepped out of the carriage, and I gazed up in awe at the imposing building. It sat atop the hill where the township of Geelong had been settled in March 1836 by three squatters, David Fisher, James Strachan and George Russell, and was first declared a town in its own right the October of 1838. With its almost fort-like towers on each side of the entrance and the solid, blue stones of which it was constructed, it certainly was an impressive building. From what I could see, it was by far the tallest building in Geelong, and it was beautiful.

Angus and Polly had been married here; however, today, it looked completely different and new because I would soon be saying my own vows here. When we walked inside, I automatically dipped my hand in the holy water and crossed myself, as did Aaron. We sat in the front pew together and waited for the priest. The church's interior was truly spectacular, with colossal stained-glass windows and ornate gold cups and plates placed near the tabernacle. Soon a slender man wearing an ecclesiastical robe came towards us, smiling brightly. I knew Father Sebastian McCleary, the former priest, had been assigned to another parish, but I did not expect his replacement to be so young.

'Weel, a guid afternoon tae ye both,' he said, welcoming us warmly. 'I'm Father Micah Donnelly. Ye must be Aaron, an' ye must be Abigail. Come wit me, please.' He led us to a small office out the back of the church. It was cluttered, forcing me to discreetly move a pile of papers from a chair to sit down. You could not see the desk surface at all; it was filled with mounds of papers and books. I had always imagined priests were obligated to be organised, given they were responsible for leading their flock to God; however, this one needed a secretary like Miss Delaware. He leaned back in his chair behind his unholy looking desk and studied us closely. I felt as if I had been transported back to Sister Monica's office, waiting to be punished for some terrible misstep or misbehaviour. 'I understand ye 'ave decided tae get married?' He smiled at us. He appeared to be a pleasant man with an air of authority accented by his black robes and his Bible by his side. He asked us about our relationship, had we been acting morally, and if we were committed to raising any children we may be blessed with in the Catholic faith. When he was satisfied with our answers, he seemed to relax. 'I will be able tae conduct the service in just under four weeks from now. Ye wull need tae start comin' tae Mass each week, though. I believe it's important ye start as ye mean tae finish,' he said kindly and looked up from his desk at us both. He had lovely eyes and brown hair and was very young for a priest, I thought again. Typically, they were old with grey hair and bad tempers—the ones I had met, anyway. We agreed we would attend on Sunday and stood to leave. Father Donnelly escorted us out to our carriage and waved us goodbye. I was relieved we had at least arranged for the church service to be conducted. On our way home, Aaron reached over and touched my cheek.

'I'm shootin' through early today. I have to see a man about a dog.' He took my hand and put it to his lips, appearing deep in thought as I gazed out of the window, feeling truly happy.

The first thing I did when we arrived home was check on Amelia. The doctor had examined her, reporting that, although she had sustained no long-term damage, her body needed bed rest for at least a week due to sprains and torn muscles, along with her contusions and abrasions. She was sleeping when I opened her door, so I softly closed it and went searching for Aaron. I found him in my bedchamber again. It was getting harder to keep him out of there.

'And what are you doing here? I thought you had a dog to find.'

'I still have a bit of time on me hands.' He stretched out on the bed, his feet hanging over the end. 'This room is all you, an' the place I feel closest to ya. I love spendin' time with ya here when I can, me sweet Abi?' he said so tenderly I could only smile. I knew we would spend a lot more time here once we were married, and I was looking forward to that. He grabbed me and threw me onto the bed, making me giggle, and then jumped on top of me. He was so heavy I couldn't breathe.

'Get off me, you big brute.' I laughed and tried to push him away. He lifted himself up and placed his weight on his arms, but he had me pinned to the bed. I could feel his erection against my leg as he kissed me demandingly. He suddenly stopped and rolled off me onto his back, breathing heavily, until he finally caught his breath. He lay with his hands behind his head and stared at the ceiling.

'Have I done something wrong?' He took my hand in his and placed it on his chest, and I could feel his heart pounding fast and hard.

'Nah, *mo anamchara*, ya haven't done anythin'. It's me. I'm actin' like a selfish prick. I can't stop meself from wantin' to be with ya. Now I know we're gettin' married, I'm findin' it harder an' harder to control meself from takin' things too far.' I didn't know what to say. It was true I was finding it difficult, too, wanting him to be with me all the time now, but we would just have to be strong and wait as we had promised. He quickly sat up and looked at me apologetically. 'I have to shoot through. I'll come back in the mornin' an' wake ya up,' he promised, kissing me goodbye. I felt disappointed he was gone so suddenly, but it gave me more time to spend with my suffering friend. I made my way back to Amelia's room and found she was awake, lying motionless in the enormous bed and staring at the ceiling. When I got into bed with her and took her in my arms, she sobbed as if she would never stop. We lay there until dinner, not saying a word and trying to find some comfort in a world full of turmoil. Neither of us understood how one person could intentionally harm another as George had done, the situation making no sense to me at all, and I knew it never would.

Bessie brought our dinner in on trays. We sat up and ate, chatting while we enjoyed the food and drink. Amelia seemed in much better spirits, even though she looked like a steam engine had hit her. I returned to my room to change and then re-joined Amelia to stay the night to comfort her if she experienced nightmares.

We lay side by side in the comfortable bed chatting about Australia—even laughing at times—until Leo came in and climbed into bed on the other side of Amelia. We all lay together in the dark, with Leo telling us stories of when he worked in the kitchens of London—causing us to laugh until our sides hurt—especially when we heard about a man named Mr Fudknuckle. Then, slowly, one by one, we drifted off. I dreamed of two kangaroos boxing, spilled blood on a white floor, and a tall man with white hair.

Aaron startled me with a kiss and held me until I was completely awake. I had returned to my bed in the early hours because of Leo's snoring and the fact he kept fondling my breasts. However, when I took Aaron's hand, something felt wrong. I lifted it to look closer and saw his knuckles were swollen and bruised.

'What on earth has happened to you?' I enquired curiously. He held his hands up and looked at them.

'Ah, it's nothin'. I was fixin' some machinery at home, an' I stripped me knuckles. Nothin' to fret about, me beautiful girl.' He smiled, placing both his hands over my hand on his chest. He had such enormous hands, double the size of mine. 'I'm goin' to Thacker's printers to collect the invitations we're havin' printed for the engagement an' weddin'. Is there anythin' else ya need in town while I'm there?'

'No, but thank you. We have everything we need. I plan to spend some time in the stables with Delly and the rest of the time taking care of Amelia. She has bruises and contusions to every part of her body. I'm surprised nothing was broken.'

'As long as she's improvin', that's all that matters.' He nodded thoughtfully before kissing me farewell. I got up to dress and go about my day, which passed quickly. That night, I fell into bed exhausted and dreamed of a silver spoon, a possum, and an aboriginal man with a spear.

Chapter Nineteen

AMELIA HAD BEEN OUR guest at Willow Grove for five days now, and I was enjoying her company. Her wounds were starting to heal—at least on the outside. She was now spending time resting outdoors in the fresh air on the sunbeds with Mathew, and joined us in the kitchen for all our meals. She did not want us to use the large dining room on her behalf and assured me she was just as happy eating in the kitchen as we were. Given her upbringing, this had completely surprised me. She was one of the true ladies of high society I had met and liked, and the more time I spent with her, the more I grew to love her.

We were sitting together outside in the sunshine when Mr Masters hesitantly approached. He stood rigidly beside Amelia, bowing slightly before addressing her.

'Mrs Johnson, there is a visitor who has called upon you. Mr George Johnson, I believe.' He looked uncomfortable. The staff all knew what had happened to her. She immediately looked frightened, and her hands started to tremble.

'Please ask Aaron to meet us in the parlour as quickly as you can, Mr Masters,' I requested, quickly rising to my feet.

'As you wish, Mistress,' he replied, then hurried away. Amelia was shaking and looked terrified.

'He cannot hurt you here with us around, I promise.' I waited until she calmed herself, then took her gently by the hand. I led her inside to the parlour, where Aaron was waiting. It was apparent he had been told George was here, and his face was like thunder. I had never seen this side of him before, which surprised me because of how unruffled he usually appeared. We all took our seats, with Amelia sitting on the other side of Aaron.

'Please bring him in, Mr Masters—and stay at the door while he is here if you don't mind?' I asked politely. He nodded stiffly and hurried off while we waited in silence. Soon we heard footsteps coming toward the door, and Mr Masters entered, presenting Mr George Johnson. No one stood up, and no one shook his hand as he hobbled into the room. I was surprised to see he had a broken arm strapped tightly to his chest and what looked like a broken nose, with significant bruising to his face. He leaned on a carved wooden cane and limped towards us. I asked him to sit down. He finally managed to take a seat on the opposite lounge as we waited to hear why he had called on us without warning.

'I've come to see my wife and apologise to her... and take her home.' He glanced nervously at Aaron, who held his gaze so intensely George averted his eyes.

'Well, George, you can see her, and you can apologise to her, but you are not taking her anywhere until she has recovered—and she chooses to go,' I said to him firmly. He gave me a startled look. He glared at me but did not respond. Instead, he turned to Amelia, ignoring Aaron and myself.

'I'm sorry for what I did to you. I should never have lost my temper like that, and I promise if you come home, I will never raise a hand to you again. I will allow you to stay here until you are well, but I want you and Mathew at home. Please, I am begging you, Amelia. I will never hurt you again. People are starting to gossip, and I will not have my good name or reputation ruined by your stubbornness.' His face was void of emotion, and his voice distant and cold. I viewed him with disdain, feeling dumbfounded—what a nothing of a man. An oxygen thief, I thought, as I watched him intently. Amelia looked at him for a moment and nodded.

'Who hurt you?' she asked coldly, raising her nose in contempt. His face started to flush, and his breathing became heavy.

'As if you don't know. You send your friends to beat me up as I'm leaving work in the night and leave me there for dead. It was lucky I was found and taken to the hospital. I hope you feel like you have evened the score,' he spat furiously while Amelia appeared puzzled.

'I don't know anything about who hurt you,' she told him, clearly surprised he would accuse her of causing him such horrific injuries. He glared at Aaron, and I suddenly recalled his swollen and bruised knuckles the day after Amelia had arrived, and everything fell into place. I looked at Aaron inquiringly, but he averted his gaze without saying a word.

'Well, what's done is done, George. We will see you back here in a week to enquire how Amelia is feeling, won't we?' I said, unable to hide the scowl on my face. No matter how hard I tried, I couldn't mask my feelings the way so many others could.

'Yes, of course,' he replied tersely.

He stood up to take his leave, giving Aaron a withering look and limped out of the room. Aaron clearly had sides to him I had not seen yet. He obviously would take matters into his own hands if the need arose, whether I liked it or not, and he hadn't felt the need to tell me about it. Actually, I felt quite proud of him, given I could not tolerate that little piece of pig-shit, and as far as I was concerned, he had gotten what he deserved.

With less than a week until the engagement party, I had more important things to focus on—one of those was getting Aaron alone for even just a few minutes. I had been so busy caring for Amelia he had been pushed to the side since she arrived. Leo came in to check everything was all right and the impromptu meeting with George had gone smoothly. He sat next to Amelia, trying to make her laugh and taking her hand in his. I saw the opportunity to leave and take Aaron with me.

When we stepped into the bedchamber, he grabbed me as soon as he had closed the door, kissing me passionately. Despite the fact he was here every day, he had been keeping himself busy learning the running of the farm and its people. We would snatch moments together whenever we could.

'Will you stay with me tonight, Aaron?' I slipped my arms around his neck as he stared deep into my eyes, preparing to return to our friends but wanting to stay alone forever.

'I will meet ya here after dinner, as ya call it, or tea, how all the normal people refer to it,' he replied before gently touching my cheek with the bruised knuckle of one finger, and I smiled.

I closed the door behind me and sighed deeply. It was later than I had planned, but we were delayed after dinner by Amelia and Leo wanting to play cards with us, and we were unable to refuse. I had started to undress when Aaron walked in. I quickly held my dress up to cover myself. He smirked at me, but did not avert his gaze.

'I've seen ya in ya undergarments before. Don't ya remember? When we went swimmin' in the river that time. It took all me strength not to ravish ya that day, let me give ya the drum,' he said, my mind going back to the day we had spent together when we first met. I sidestepped my way to the dressing room so he could only see the dress-covered front of me while he laughed. I finished undressing and slipped into my nightgown. When I returned, I found Aaron already in bed. As it was her birthday, I had given Bessie the night off to spend with Danny. If she had known Aaron was staying, she would have kicked him out on his backside by now.

Aaron and I had still managed to maintain control of ourselves and had taken it no farther than kissing. I was proud of us both. We gravitated towards each other until we were pressed up close, our body heat melting into one. He kissed me for a long time, then whispered goodnight to me as I cuddled into his shoulder and closed my eyes. As I drifted off to sleep, I dreamed of tiny men, a small graveyard and a steel rod.

I woke to the usual sounds of birds singing and the kookaburra laughing in the distance, but my room was oddly quiet. Usually, Bessie was bustling around noisily, or Aaron was lying on the bed waiting for me to wake up, but this morning there was no one. Given it was our engagement party today, I assumed they were letting me sleep. I could not believe it was finally here. There were now only two more weeks to go until I was Mrs Aaron Cavanaugh, and we could start our life together without any restrictions. I looked forward to seeing my friends today, although many guests were attending, I had never met. Aaron's parents had invited their friends to the party, and since they had been living here for more than fifteen-years now, that was a fair number of people.

Polly and Angus would be returning this morning on the first train, not knowing yet I was engaged, let alone holding the party today. I could not wait to see them. I had missed them so much. I heard the door open and opened my eyes to see Aaron strolling in.

'Good mornin', me beautiful fiancée,' he called out, then flopped down on his back next to me. I turned over on my side, facing him.

'Good morning, future husband,' I replied, leaning over and kissing him.

'Only a few hours till it begins. I can't wait to see how ya dress turned out.' Catherine had made my engagement dress with only one fitting and was bringing it down with her on the train this morning. I found it amusing how Aaron and Leo were both so fascinated with everything I wore. Yet, they were very different men with completely different reasons for showing such an interest. One liked to look at what was on me, while the other wanted to tear it off and wear it himself if he had the opportunity. I could hardly wait to see it myself and started to get butterflies in my stomach at the thought of today. At least from now on, we could be more openly affectionate around other people if we wanted to, which I was of two minds about, feeling so shy.

'Do you know all the guests who are coming?'

He laughed. 'Nah. They're me parent's friends. I grew up with several families with whom they're close, but as for the rest, I only know them by name. Don't worry yaself, I will be meetin' then all for the first time, too,' he reassured me, pulling me close and embracing me warmly.

'I wonder how the cake will taste. Leo has been such a nasty piece of work over the last two days while making it and won't let me near the kitchen,' I complained.

'Me, either,' he chuckled, making me smile. Bessie entered carrying our breakfast trays and placed them on the bed.

'Good morning to the both of you,' she sang cheerily. 'How are you feeling about today? It's the last step before you make the whole thing final. I am so happy for you both. Danny and I have been counting down the days for you.' She set about tidying the room while we ate.

Leo had prepared us another beautiful breakfast. He always prepared enormous servings, given he was well aware of just how much we both liked to eat. I appreciated how Leo cooked different foods from all parts of the world and rarely served me the same thing twice unless it was something I enjoyed, which he would then put on the regular menu. Bessie took our trays away while we drank our coffee.

'Come here, me lovely girl,' Aaron said, setting our cups aside and pulling me to him as soon as she stepped out of the room. He kissed me long and hard with the promise of more to come and held me in his arms. 'Only a fortnight left. We've made it halfway since we became officially engaged.' A wide grin spread across his face as he winked, making me giggle.

'Do you wonder what it's going to be like to make love, Aaron?' I rested my arm across his chest, and he placed one hand over mine.

'Only about twenty times a day,' he laughed. 'I imagine it's gunna be the most amazin' experience I've ever had. I mean, it must be good as it's every bloke's ultimate goal every day—an' at any time of the night—when offered. When ya think about it, it must be pretty remarkable. What about you?' He looked directly into my eyes.

'Yes, I think about it, but the main thing I worry about is it's going to hurt. Dana says it does the first time,' I told him with an air of expertise.

'Does she? What else has Dana told ya?' He smirked wickedly, his eyes twinkling.

'She has told me everything about how to make love and enjoy it myself, not just letting the pleasure be for the man, like so many do.

She warned me the first time would hurt, and I will bleed, but it gets better soon after. She told me how to pleasure you until you cannot help but moan and bite your lip and things to teach you to do to me. That's about it,' I said, running out of breath. He gave me an amused look.

'It seems I've been worryin' for nothin' neither of us would know what to do when the night comes, an' we'll both be sittin' here like stunned mullets. Ya seem to have it all in hand, thanks to Dana's tutoring.' He laughed loudly, teasing me.

'I don't feel like I do. Do not forget, I might know about these things, but I have never practised them. I imagine going by what she has told me, it does take some practice, so I do not think I will be good at it initially. I want you to be satisfied. I don't want you going to other women for sexual relations because you're unhappy with me.' Hamish's face came to mind as he stared at me thoughtfully.

'I'll never be unhappy with ya. It wouldn't matter how ya do things; I will be more than satisfied. I know that already. Don't let thoughts of me even lookin' at another lass touch ya mind, 'cause it's not real. Why would I when I already have perfection?' He made my heart leap sometimes with the things he would say.

'I'm not perfect, Aaron, and you will see that when we have our first argument.' He grinned broadly, glancing across at me affectionately before staring out the window.

'Ya think I don't know ya faults yet, or what ya see as faults? Ahh, but I do. You're stubborn an' determined, an' ya won't be told what to do. You have the dirtiest mouth I've ever heard on a woman. Ya rush into things without thinkin'—an' live to regret it—but you're also the kindest, most lovin', generous-in-every-way, gentlest, honest, an' thoughtful person I know, an' that's perfect enough for me.' I felt tears prick my eyes at how lovely he was to me and how highly he thought of me. I knew marrying him would be one of the best days of my life.

Catherine rushed into my bedchamber without knocking, her arms full as she carried my dress wrapped in brown paper and tied securely with twine.

'Hello, you two,' she called, bending down to kiss me first, then Aaron, who was genuinely happy to see her and made it obvious. 'Now, out you go, Mr Cavanaugh. I need to help the lady dress. You will see her soon enough downstairs, so off you go. Get into your formal clothes and start greeting your guests. You are the man of the day.' She grinned at him and shooed him off the bed. He kissed me again and got up to go, ruffling Catherine's hair as he walked past her, to which she playfully slapped him on the back.

Bessie soon arrived to help and hurried me over to the dressing table so they could do my hair and makeup before I dressed. Bessie began twisting my hair up then pinned it to the top of my head so it cascaded down the back of my neck, falling in big, loose curls, while Catherine worked on my makeup. By the time they finished, I was completely transformed. I hardly recognised myself in the mirror. Bessie pulled the dress from its bag and held it up.

It was the most brilliant green I had ever seen—almost between a blue and a green that stood out brilliantly against the brightness of the room. They helped me into it, and as they finished the final touches, Bessie gasped. The bodice was studded with silver beads and crystals, while the fabric clung tightly to my waist, then fell to the floor, showing off my shape. The sleeves were long and fitted and came to just below my shoulders, where they joined to the bodice, with the neckline low-cut and flattering.

'You look beautiful,' Bessie said with tears in her eyes, unable to look away. 'I feel like it's my own daughter who is getting engaged.' She wiped her face with a handkerchief. She had been highly emotional for two weeks now. Ever since she had found out we were to be married, she would break down and cry with happiness, driving me mad at times.

The three of us made our way downstairs and slowly walked out to the manicured lawn where the party was being held, chairs dotted around in groups for people to sit and chat. I stood at the top of the garden looking for Aaron, but he saw me first and was already making his way towards me. He was standing with a group of his friends and staring straight at me, oblivious to those around him. He held me close for a moment, slipping his arm around my waist.

'Strewth, Abi. Ya look even lovelier than usual. Make me wish we were at the church today,' he whispered and took my arm in his. As we walked toward our guests, everyone started to clap and cheer. Aaron went to find a footman to get me a cup of punch while I greeted his parents and brothers, of whom I was certain would cause some mischief by the end of the night. His parents proudly introduced us to their friends, many of whom we had not met before today, which ended up being the majority of the guests. I liked that their friends were all working class. They were nothing like the Makenzie's friends at Polly and Angus' engagement party and wedding.

The staff, dressed in their new uniforms and looking extremely smart and professional, were preparing to bring the trays of food around to the guests. Leo had told Catherine what designs he wanted for the kitchen and house staff, to which she had readily obliged, coming up with the most beautiful and professional uniforms I had ever seen. They wore fashionable dresses in teal with white aprons over the top and a small white cap for the maids, while the kitchen staff wore white jackets with long teal skirts for the women and trousers for the men. Catherine had made them three dresses each and five aprons and fitted out Mr Masters and the footmen in new pants, shirts, and tails in teal and white to match the girls' outfits. So much more cheerful than plain black and white, I felt.

I noticed Dana rushing towards me, weaving through the hundreds of people that filled the garden, her face drawn and a look of consternation evident for all to see.

'I'm so sorry, but I wanted to get to you first to speak with you and tell... ' Her voice trailed off as she saw me notice Charlotte standing with Hamish over by the olive tree. Aaron had not seen him yet, as he was too busy talking to Angus about how he planned to structure the farm and its workers.

'Don't worry about it, Dana. It will not ruin our day. But please keep him away from the bloody whisky, for God's sake,' I begged, squeezing her hand tightly.

'Of course. I will do everything in my power to make sure he behaves.' She nodded apologetically before hurrying away to watch over him as I looked across the garden at him again. He was staring back, not taking his eyes from me for even a moment. I turned away from him, back to Aaron and Polly, who came over from talking to Kate, one of our neighbours. She hugged me and squealed, jumping up and down, clearly excited to be home.

'Hamish is here,' I said to her quietly.

'I know, I just saw him. That was why I came to you.'

Polly gushed of how they had enjoyed the most wonderful honeymoon at The Delmont and barely left the room each day—choosing to spend most of their time in bed together—and thanked me for the gift.

'I want to assign little Mary to you as your ladies' maid—although she is happy to keep your house organised and spotless as well.' She shook her head, her smile wide.

'Thank you, dear sister, but I must decline.' I nodded as she went on to tell me how she wanted to do everything herself, from cooking to cleaning, as she did not want people in the house with her and Angus, invading their privacy at this early stage of her marriage.

'But you would have more time with Angus if you would allow me to help even a little.' She was silent for a time while I gazed out over the garden at the mature trees, some I believed hundreds of years old.

'Oh, all right. I'll agree to have our meals prepared by Leo in the main house for now, although we want to decide which meals we take in our cottage. If he offends me even once or tries to boss me in my own home, I'll rip his ear off next time myself.' She paused as I smiled to myself. 'I'll allow little Mary to come twice a week and clean the cottage from top to bottom, but that's it. Angus and I want our privacy.'

They appeared so happy together, and she glowed. Liza, the maid, brought over a tray with tiny lamb cutlets on it. They had covered the bone in paper to pick it up, so I took a small plate and placed two cutlets on the side. There was an explosion of flavours in my mouth as I bit into the first cutlet—the meat so tender it fell off the bone. It was delicious. I ate both and went off looking for more, leaving Polly to find Angus.

I approached the footman, Samuel, who had just stepped into the garden with a full tray and took a few more. As I turned around, I nearly bumped into Tamara and Brian. I embraced them warmly, and we chatted about how things were in Melbourne.

'You must come and stay as our guest, Abigail. Surely you can spare the time after we marry? I promise to take you to the best social events in the colony.' Smiling, I nodded and feigned excitement. 'We plan to have children immediately. Of course, I will be forced to stay home for a time to ensure my nannies raise them exactly how we want them raised.' I embraced her again before hurrying away to find my future husband.

Aaron, who introduced me to his friends from school. Steve, Edward, and John all seemed friendly and were larrikins like Aaron and his brothers, being cheeky as soon as they met me—but it was clear they were larrikins—no different from Aaron and his brothers.

The food the staff passed around was spectacular. Leo had truly outdone himself, preparing bite-sized pieces of every type of savoury food I could imagine. People stood or sat in groups, sprawled out across the extensive manicured gardens, happily eating off plates while chatting. I much preferred this to a formal sit-down meal.

From what I could see, the guests were enjoying it as well. Aaron took my hand, led me away from the party and around the side of the house, then kissed me passionately against the wall.

'Are ya enjoyin' yaself?' he asked, resting his cheek against mine.

'Yes, I am. Better than I thought, given there are so many strangers here. They really are very nice people.'

'They're friends of me parents, who are nice also,' he snorted through his laughter.

We returned to the party to mingle with our guests, finding Amelia eating and laughing with Elizabeth and Eric. Her bruises had faded enough now we could cover what remained with makeup, and her spirits had lifted immensely. I had reiterated many times over that she could live with us for as long as she liked. Thanking us for allowing her to stay and treating her so well, she had decided to return to George when she was confident he would not harm her again. Amelia believed Mathew needed his father, dismissing how her parents had used her as a pawn in a deal with the devil that should have nullified any agreement, in my opinion. I spotted Dana and moved to her side, sitting beside her and Martin, who nursed a glass of whisky while chatting with Aaron.

'So, are you still a virgin? I wouldn't be if I could have him rolling around in my bed,' she whispered, glancing wickedly at Aaron's derriere. I smiled at her and nodded. 'God, you're a good girl. I don't know how you do it. Maybe it's only once you have experienced such pleasures, you crave it all the time.'

I did not want to tell her how much I was craving it, even though I didn't know what it felt like to experience the pleasures she so unashamedly spoke of whenever given the opportunity. When I was with him, though, my insides would ache to be filled by him, and his touch would set off my nerve endings. It felt like I had an itch deep inside me that needed a good, hard scratch.

'How are you and Martin getting on?' I asked, changing the topic.

'It's still wonderful. Of course, his skills in the bedchamber are tippy-top, and I love spending time with him. It will be nice when we are married, but we are not having a party like this. It will be small and intimate with close friends only. But, of course, you and Aaron will be there.' She smiled and looked across at Martin, who smiled broadly back at her as if no one else was present. I liked him immensely and felt privileged to be invited to spend such an intimate moment with them.

'We wouldn't miss it,' I reassured her, meaning every word.

'As you can see, Hamish is courting Charlotte, the silly girl.' She shook her head bitterly, her bright orange hair immaculately coiffed. 'I only had to look at him today to see how in love with you he still is.' She stared across at him, talking quietly to Angus at the edge of the garden, the yellow gum standing tall above them.

'He has been more than honest about how he feels about me.' I told her of my last meeting with Hamish and the hurtful things he had said. She laughed aloud, causing people to stare at us.

'What a load of codswallop. Maybe he was a womaniser before he met you, but Hamish was certainly not like that when he was with you. You forget, I saw you together from the first day you met, and I only have to see him now to know he's using my daughter to make you jealous and manipulate you to reunite with him. He does not care about her at all. Look at them now. See how she is leaning in and touching him? He isn't even looking at her—not to mention how his body is leaning away. That in itself tells me I'm correct.' I glanced over and saw Dana was right. He did not appear happy or enamoured with Charlotte. His back was turned to her while speaking animatedly with his brother, who nodded his head sympathetically. When he noticed I was watching, he turned to Charlotte and kissed her, stunning the poor girl.

I glanced back at Dana and rolled my eyes. I hoped all this didn't hurt Charlotte, and I wasn't harming her without meaning to—if, indeed, he was using her to hurt me.

Mr Masters made his way to my side, advising it was time to cut the cake as he bowed deeply. Aaron and I moved towards the enormous, multi-tiered chocolate cake filled with thick caramel and chocolate cream that sat on a table, a wispy, white linen cloth underneath moving gently in the breeze. Aaron had hired Mathews Photographers from Moorabool Street in Geelong to take pictures of all our guests. The photographer took another of us, slicing the cake with one knife between our entwined fingers. We kissed when the knife touched the bottom of the cake board, and everyone clapped. Leo stood at the table and served slices to every guest and staff member several times over until there was only the large bottom cake left, which he took inside for us to eat later. He would eventually have to hide it. He was well aware I would eat it continuously for days until it was all gone.

As the afternoon wore on, many of the guests started to leave. It relieved me, as all I wanted was to sit down with my friends and spend time with them. I would have preferred to have held a small and intimate engagement party like Dana and Martin planned, but I didn't want to disappoint Aaron's parents. They had been looking forward to all this, and I wanted them to like me. Charlotte and Hamish had left at Dana's direction, and I was happy to see him go. At least he had stayed sober today.

I kissed Aaron's family goodbye, leaving only our close friends. We retired to the terrace near the swimming pool until the sun went down. Aaron started a fire in the centre of our circle as the day turned into a starlit night, a slight chill in the air. Leo came and sat next to me and Aaron, who had his arms wrapped around my waist as I lay back on him in the sun lounge.

'I seriously can't believe you are doing this, Aaron,' Leo said, his mouth twitching. 'You had the chance to have me and foolishly dismissed it. I hope you are aware you will never have that chance again. I don't go with married men.'

'Does that mean you'll stop flirtin' with me? If that's the case, I'm takin' Abi to the church an' marryin' her tomorrow,' he replied, chuckling good-naturedly to himself.

'No. Flirting is allowed; however, you aren't permitted to touch my special places anymore.' I burst out laughing, spitting my cup of tea down the front of my dress.

'Leo, I've never touched ya special places, an' I have no intention of ever doin' so. Are ya sure ya didn't dream it?' Leo looked up at the sky thoughtfully as he lay back in his sun lounge.

'Now that you say it, I believe I may have. Just the other night, I had this dream where...'

'Stop,' Aaron barked, putting his hand up in Leo's face. 'It's bad enough what we hear when you're awake—but to have to listen to what goes on in ya head at night, too—well, ya must be mad as a meat-axe to think we'd do it willingly. Yeah, nah, that's enough.' Leo and I giggled wickedly as Aaron shook his head.

We remained outside, enjoying each other's company until the early hours of the morning, continuing to eat and drink until we were full again. Finally, Aaron stood, took me by the hand, said goodnight to everyone, and walked me to my room. When he did not enter behind me, I turned back, raising my eyebrows questioningly.

'What's the matter?'

'I don't think I'm strong enough tonight. I can't sleep with ya, Abi—at least, not tonight,' he apologised.

'Aaron, that's fine.' Not wanting to make it worse, I gave him a quick kiss on the lips and said goodnight. I hurried across the room and into my dressing room to change, but when I returned soon after, I found him there. 'I thought you couldn't stay.' I gazed down at him lying on top of the covers on his side of the bed.

'Yeah, I couldn't not be here, either. I'll stay to see ya to sleep, then spend the night in one of the guest rooms,' he replied as I slipped under the covers.

He stayed on top of the quilt to ensure he didn't get close enough to my body for anything to happen, and I placed my head on his shoulder to go to sleep. Within moments, he embraced me and pressed his body against mine, although the thick covers made that almost impossible. He kissed me hard and demanded I respond to him—which I did—wrapping my arms around his neck and running my fingers through his hair. Suddenly, he moaned and shuddered, his kissing more zealous, as he held me tighter to him. I ran my hands up and down his back, trying to steady him until the worst of it was over. Finally, he slowed, kissing me gently and lovingly, touching my face softly with his finger.

'Did you know that would happen?' I asked, feeling shy all of a sudden. He looked back at me, his face filled with love.

'Yeah, I couldn't stop it. I warned ya I couldn't stay with ya. I knew I wouldn't behave like a gentleman—an' I'm sorry for it, Abi.' He kissed the top of my head, then pulled me close to him and gently kissed my face.

'That's all right. It didn't harm me. How did it make you feel?'

'It was nice holdin' ya in me arms when it happened—nothin' like when ya do it alone. I could sleep with ya next to me forever.' He yawned, then kissed me goodnight—this time meaning it—and got under the covers. 'Nothin' will happen now, I promise.' He laughed softly before gathering me back into his arms. I fell asleep dreaming of a chocolate cake, a quilt, and a one-eyed snake.

Chapter Twenty

I WOKE THE FOLLOWING morning wrapped in Aaron's arms, still in the same position I had fallen asleep. I must have slept like the dead, I thought, as I opened my eyes and looked up at him. He was wide-awake, staring up at the ceiling.

'Good mornin', *mo anamchara*. How did ya sleep?' he asked softly and brushed my hair away from my eyes with his fingers. I hadn't bothered to tie it up last night, so it was everywhere.

'I must have slept well. I feel refreshed and ready for the day. What about you?' I asked, running my fingers through my hair in a vain attempt to tame it.

'Like the dead. I don't remember wakin' once.' He attempted to smooth my hair a little more, then started to laugh. 'Ya hair is just about as wild as you are. Ya need to let Bessie plait it for ya at night so ya don't strangle yourself.' He continued to run his fingers gently through it, and I snorted with laughter.

'You're the one who is forever telling her to leave it down.' He gave me a broad grin.

'I'll have to learn how to plait it. Then ya can leave it down when I make love to ya an' tie it up afterwards,' he told me smugly. I raised an eyebrow, amused.

'Ah, well then—as long as you have it all worked out in your mind.' He pulled me towards him and kissed me, then lay there thoughtfully as I cuddled into his side and placed my arm across his chest.

'Me mates were shocked yesterday when they met ya. They have known about the betrothal since we were scallywags an' would tease me mercilessly ya would be a naggin' moll who would destroy me life. They were forever tryin' to get me to step out with girls we went to school with, sayin' it would be me only chance of ever bein' with anyone pretty—an' you would be short, fat, an' very, very ugly with not a tooth in ya head an' mangy hair. But, after seein' ya, they're all laughin' on the other sides of their faces,' he chuckled while I stared back at him in confusion.

'What does that mean?' I asked, hoping he wouldn't make fun of me.

'Let's just say they now have no reason to take the piss outta me ever again. In fact, I don't think I've been thumped on the back as hard in congratulations for anythin' before.'

He seemed to be friends with everyone in the district and knew almost everyone who lived, or had lived here, over the past fifteen-years. I had met some of his friends and noticed how they gave each other odd looks and smiled when talking to me; however, I had no clue why. I had noticed Aaron puffing up proudly like a male turkey in front of them, which had made me giggle as he showed me off.

I was glad the engagement party was over, and we only had the wedding to get through. Hating how people stared at me yesterday, I was now highly concerned how I would react when they focused on me as a bride. I wished we had planned for a small ceremony at home, but it was too late to back out now. He kissed me again just as Bessie walked in, mumbling to herself. I stared across at her in silence as she stomped around to get my clothes organised.

'An' a good mornin' to ya, Bessie. Isn't it a wonderful day? I've never seen the sun shine brighter,' Aaron called out cheerily as he sat up in bed and leaned back on the pillows.

'Wonderful? Oh, what a pile of horse-shite,' she snapped. 'It would be wonderful if I didn't have to worry about what you two are getting up to in here with just two weeks till the wedding. You could still ruin her reputation if word of this got out.' He smiled at her as I rose to my feet to ready myself for the day.

'Carn, Bessie. I give ya me word before ya God I won't touch her till we're married in the church,' he promised, and I saw her soften a little.

'Well, I suppose it is less than two weeks now, but you keep that promise, boyo. I mean it. Otherwise, you will be very sore on your wedding night in an area you take great pride in,' she warned, scurrying into my wardrobe then calling for me to follow her.

Aaron let out a deep sigh, resigned to the fact Bessie was now his boss, too, then folded his hands across his stomach and closed his eyes in defeat.

We held hands as we went down to meet the others for breakfast. Catherine's family had departed yesterday, leaving her here to stay for the week to help me prepare and complete my wedding dress.

'Ah, so you two finally graced us with your presence. We all know Aaron snuck into your bedchamber last night and got caught by Bessie this morning,' Leo called out, winking at us. I narrowed my gaze as Aaron and I took a seat across from him.

'Well, I know Bessie wouldn't have told you that as she thinks you are the worst gossip she has ever had the misfortune of meeting, so you must have been listening in on a private conversation,' I told him crossly. The others smirked.

'Hello. Of course, I was—otherwise, I would hear nothing around this place. They all believe me to be a terrible gossip because of that troll Bessie.' He widened his eyes and shook his head in disbelief that anyone could accuse him of such a thing. I rolled my eyes at him, and he giggled. 'So, do you still have your cherry?' he asked loudly. I choked on the mouthful of egg and toast I was just about to swallow, sending bits of chewed up food across the grand dining-room table. Aaron patted me on the back and chuckled. Did nothing bother this man? I gasped for breath before taking a drink of mango juice.

'Of course I do! Not that it's any of your concern. It doesn't affect you if I do or I don't, so stop announcing my private business to the world.'

Breakfast had started before we arrived due to Leo's strict time-keeping, and now the banter was flowing thick and fast as Aaron and I ate to catch up with the others. Mr Masters and the footmen came to serve us a second time, bringing my buttermilk pancakes while we listened to the others talk. I smothered them in maple syrup and listened to Dana, who had become quite boisterous, making me smile.

'Oh, we all know most men are selfish in bed. They have no consideration or care if their women enjoy the act or not—just jumping on and wiggling it around, pleasuring themselves—then the selfish sods roll off and go to sleep.' Amelia had turned bright red but kept silent and focused on her food as if her plain buttered toast was the most fascinating thing she had ever seen.

'With all respect, Dana. What a load o' scaffy,' Angus remarked. 'Most of us want to please our woman, but if she willnae show us how, of course we give up an' take care of only ourselves.' Dana sat straight as an arrow, as all ladies did, while she sipped her coffee, her gaze fixed on Angus while her eyes sparkled in amusement.

'That's wombat shite, Angus. It's just an excuse to be lazy as far as I'm concerned.' She picked up her cutlery and started to eat her pancake.

'But Angus isn't lazy in bed,' Polly sang out, missing the point entirely as she came to his defence. He smiled lovingly at her and took her hand in his.

'I'm not saying he is, Polly, but if you hadn't come to me on the ship and asked me all those questions, you wouldn't know anything about it,' Dana pointed out, winking affectionately at her. 'If Angus had jumped on you for less than a minute, you would think that's how it's meant to be. Now you know, of course, you wouldn't put up with it.' Polly nodded, understanding now. Leo smirked wickedly as he looked around the table.

'This would have to be the only house in the colony—this prison without walls, I remind you all—where there are ladies present, and this highly inappropriate topic is considered polite breakfast conversation. The problem is, it's the ladies discussing it.' Leo snorted loudly as those around me collapsed into loud laughter.

All except for poor Amelia. She looked as if she wanted the ground to open and swallow her. She appeared mortified they would discuss such topics in polite company; however, she stayed on at the table like nothing had happened, ignoring Leo's teasing. He loved living here and combining his work with his family life, and that's what he felt he finally had found here—family.

Aaron steered the conversation to something more neutral, and Amelia calmed down and returned to her usual colour. Aaron and I had to attend church this morning for Sunday Mass, as Father Donnelly had asked us to do, so we finished breakfast and sat outside with everyone until it was time to leave.

We said our goodbyes and left them there debating the morality of opening pubs on a Sunday. Less than two weeks to go now, and everything was underway. All our planning would be finalised by the end of the week, just in time for our wedding day. Catherine was still making suits for Aaron and his brothers' and bridesmaid dresses for Polly, Dana, and herself. I was so happy to have them standing beside me on my special day, as I knew I would be nervous with people paying me so much attention.

Tamara and Brian's engagement party was to be held next Saturday in Melbourne. We had decided to spend the weekend at The Delmont, as Aaron had never stayed in a large hotel before. I was looking forward to exploring the city's shops and parks. I had only spent a moment in Melbourne when we first arrived, and had since been too busy settling in at Willow Grove and dealing with Aaron and Hamish. After the wedding, I could relax and concentrate on learning to find my way unassisted around this place I now called home.

Aaron helped me down from the carriage, and I took his arm as we entered the bluestone church with its graceful arches. As I walked down the long aisle, the pure beauty of the architecture overwhelmed me. We found a pew and genuflected, then sat down and made ourselves as comfortable as we could on a hard, wooden bench. There were small, open carvings in the pew at the end of each seat. I ran my fingers along the inside of the smooth wood as I inhaled the frankincense threatening to choke me. Father Donnelly said Mass, and I followed along. I did not take communion. I had not been to confession since leaving the orphanage, so Aaron went alone, although he certainly had something to confess. As we left the church, we shook Father Donnelly's hand at the door.

'It was wonderful tae see ye here. Not long tae go now,' the priest said, smiling at us both. We nodded and moved along to let the people behind us greet him. We strolled back to the carriage hand in hand, feeling we had done our duty.

We stepped into the dining room just as our friends sat down to luncheon. It was feeling far less formal lately in this very formal room, despite the lavish surroundings. No one bothered to dress up for breakfast or luncheon anymore, and the more time we spent in the dining room, the more relaxed and at ease we became.

'How did it feel doing your duty, Abi?' Polly's face lit up, her musical laughter filling the room as she thought back to our childhood at the orphanage. We would often make references only understood by us or those who had experienced a similar upbringing.

'It made me feel guiltier than I already do,' I replied, laughing along with her.

'Do we have to keep goin' to church once we're married?' Aaron asked as we sat down to eat. I caught Polly rolling her eyes in his direction, but chose to ignore her.

'I don't really know. I suppose we do not have to do anything we don't want to do, Aaron. You're not the type to be forced into anything, anyway.'

'I s'pose we don't have to decide now. Who knows? I may come to like it—Abi.' He turned his head, glancing smugly at Polly for a moment, who, in turn, made a rude gesture at him with her finger. He threw his head back and chuckled loudly as Polly turned away in disgust.

Although Aaron was Catholic, his parents had never bothered attending church—except weddings, christenings, and funerals—so it was not something he was eager to commit to unless obligated. It didn't bother me if I went or not, so I would leave it to him to decide at a later time. We would have to go when we had children, though, as Aaron and Sister Josephine wanted them raised Catholic—and we had given our word to Father Donnelly.

We enjoyed our midday feast, the humorous banter and lively conversations invigorating my soul. I reluctantly stood as Dana and Martin took their leave, walking them to the front entrance. The others planned to spend the afternoon exploring the property on horseback so Angus could check on the progress of the work carried out by the farmhands. They had not gone out together for a ride since we arrived here—not wanting to leave me out—but today they knew Aaron was giving me my first real riding lesson, and they could freely go without guilt.

We met outside the stables, where Harry had five beautiful horses saddled and ready to ride. Aaron disappeared through the hefty stable door to retrieve Delly's saddle, bridle, and a long rope so he could guide her from a distance. Angus helped Polly mount her enormous steed, while Leo reluctantly assisted Amelia and Catherine before awkwardly climbing up onto his mount with Harry's help. Finally, they called out their farewells before trotting off for their day of exploring and adventure—while I made my way inside to Delightful's stall, where I brushed her down and waited for Aaron. Several minutes later, he joined me, stopping at the door and gazing over.

'I'm proud of ya facin' ya fear, Abi. You're as game as a pissant.'

'A pissant?'

'It just means ya brave.'

'Brave or stupid—it's often the same thing,' I muttered, and he smiled lovingly at me. He saddled Delly, then led her out to the stable yard while I followed behind at a distance.

'Or foolhardy,' he called out, chuckling to himself. 'I think we'll start in here till ya feel confident to ride in the paddock.' He stopped in the centre of the yard, turning to lift me onto her back. I settled myself in the saddle, placed my feet in the stirrups, and gathered the reins in my hands. It felt strange without him behind me, and I froze, not knowing what to do next.

Delly had not moved an inch since I mounted, and now we both stood as still as the statues lining the halls of Willow Grove in companionable silence, waiting for something to happen. Aaron secured the rope to her bridle, then moved over to a wooden fence made of posts. I felt panic rising inside me—and I fought to ignore it—despite the fact I was sitting on a wild beast in the middle of the stable yard with Aaron standing far, far away. He held the very long rope from such a great distance; it was likely to be ineffective should she decide to bolt.

'Take her over there, Abi,' he called out, pointing to the farthest corner, then leaning back on the fence to watch. I kicked her softly, and she jolted forward. Trying so hard to steer her, I grunted as we stopped in the corner—but a different corner in the opposite direction from where he had pointed. I reached down and patted her neck, waiting patiently as Delly remained where she was.

'I tried to make her go to the corner you directed me to go to, but she likes this corner,' I called back. He laughed loudly as he approached me and undid the rope.

'She's not gunna do anythin' stupid. Are ya, my sweet girl?' He gently stroked her face as she nuzzled into his chest. He strode away and sat on the fence to watch me—and boss me around. 'Take her to the corner again,' he ordered as I grimaced, muttering to myself. It was so easy for him—his arse had been in a saddle since he could walk. I fixed him with a hard stare before trying again—and this time we made it after a few stops and starts. I walked her around the yard, gaining some control, but not nearly as much as I had hoped.

I was enjoying the feel of her head in my hands through the reins, only having to move my hand slightly and finding she would turn her head in that direction. She would then go at the pace I wanted, depending on how hard I squeezed my legs. I was only walking her today; I did not know whether I could stay on her back if she trotted without Aaron behind to hold on to me.

'I think ya have done sufficiently well for today—if you've had enough. Tomorrow, I will get me horse, an' we can ride together in the paddocks,' he said as he lifted me down. The stiffness I had first experienced after riding had virtually disappeared now due to Aaron forcing me onto the back of a horse nearly every day since arriving at this beautiful property.

We walked back to the house, holding hands. As a wedding present for Aaron, I had asked Harry to choose the most magnificent stallion available, whom he had been breaking in for the past two weeks. I knew Aaron would love him. He was a bit too fiery for my liking; however, I was well aware Aaron liked his horses to be spirited. Delightful was far too placid for him. He had told me he preferred a bit of wildness in his horses—and his women. At least on the equestrian side, Goliath was the perfect fit. It excited me to gift him the horse, and I enjoyed giving presents as much as receiving them.

We walked through the empty hallways, finding we had the house to ourselves. I reached out to open the sitting-room door, planning to relax until our friends returned; however, Aaron came up behind me, picked me up, and threw me over his shoulder.

'What are you doing, you fool?' The blood rushed to my head as he held me upside down, climbing the stairs two by two while holding my legs in front of him as my body dangled down his back. I assumed he was going to my bedchamber, and within moments, he stepped inside and quietly closed the door behind us.

'Ya did well, me girl. I didn't think ya would be ready to ride in the paddock by tomorrow, but ya are,' he remarked, dropping me ungraciously onto the bed. I sat up, and he proceeded to take all the pins out of my hair until it fell loose around me. Finally, he lay down on his back, and I cuddled my body into his side. 'I'm sorry about last night, Abi.'

'Please, Aaron, we are almost married—and it was nothing. But, if I didn't know better, I would think attending Mass this morning has made you feel guiltier about everything, too.' I giggled, kissing him on the lips before he smiled and shook his head.

'It wasn't nothin' to me. It meant somethin'.' We talked in hushed tones of our future together and our dreams, the usually busy household now quiet. 'Dana has strong opinions when it comes to blokes, an' how they perform their duties, doesn't she?'

'I don't think she means to come across as rude or aggressive, Aaron. She has to be the most openly sexual person I have ever met, and I love her for it.'

'I don't know much about anythin', but even blind Freddy can see she has taken you girls under her wing—then led ya all astray.' He chuckled to himself as I smothered a smile and closed my eyes.

'You have no idea.'

We had only just finished dinner and retired to the sitting room when Mr Masters knocked on the open door, bowing slightly.

'There is a visitor here for Mrs Johnson. Mr Johnson, madam,' he said, bowing to Amelia. Amelia stood, and Aaron and I followed her into the hallway, leaving the others to continue talking excitedly about their day and how wonderful it had been riding the amazing creatures born on the property and the feeling of freedom the horses provided.

We entered the parlour and found George seated on the lounge, fidgeting nervously. He still used a cane, and his arm was still bound tightly in a sling—but his bruises had faded to a pale yellow now. He carried a bunch of red roses with him he handed to Amelia, who placed them on the table without a response or showing any emotion. They sat on opposite chairs. Amelia said nothing but gave him a distasteful look and waited for him to begin. Instead, he glared at Aaron before swallowing hard.

'I've missed you, Amelia. Are you ready to come home yet?' She gazed at him for the longest time—making him squirm in his chair and appear even more uncomfortable—a task I thought impossible.

'I want you to know something, George. I will no longer be your punching bag, or your slave, or have you in my bed ever again. If you force me or hurt me, I will make sure every single man in your employ finds out, and I will ruin you. Do you understand me, George?' she spat, her eyes glinting dangerously as she leaned forward, her face like thunder. He seemed surprised but nodded and sat back in his chair, speechless for the first time since we had met. 'I want separate bedchambers and a ladies' maid. She will also protect me from you by being my witness to your behaviour. You are never to come through my bedchamber door ever again. I will return after Abigail and Aaron's wedding when I have employed a maid and a Nanny as I deserve. We will have a full staff of servants now, and not just me as your slave. You have kept me isolated and away from other human beings and won't have them in that mammoth house, which is far too big for the three of us. I will no longer accept any of it.'

He looked at her darkly. 'It would be easier to get a new wife,' he mumbled.

'Well, get one then, George. Go out and get one. I don't care what you do,' she replied calmly and appeared to mean it. I attempted to hide my surprise at how strong she was, displaying no fear of him anymore; however, I failed miserably, unable to mask my expression.

'No, I don't want a new wife. I want you. Yes, I will agree to the arrangements until you can find it in yourself to forgive me, and we can resume our marital relationship,' he replied so quietly I could barely hear him. Aaron watched him closely. He had not uttered a word throughout the entire encounter.

George stood to leave and gave Amelia an awkward handshake. I tried to smother a smile, admiring how she had him where she wanted him. Uncertain what had changed in her, she had transformed from a passive, nervous woman into a roaring tiger. I was impressed and told her so after George had left. We returned to the sitting room, where our friends were still talking about their day.

'This property is so big. I cannot believe how it goes down to the ocean. To see it all on horseback was pure joy,' Catherine remarked, dreamy-eyed as she lay back on a lounge looking up at the ceiling.

'And the rivers passing through here are so peaceful,' Polly chimed in as she sat on Angus' lap, her arms around his neck.

'I'm impressed with the horses,' Angus added. 'Their gait is so smooth, your arse hardly moves when they gallop. I suppose that's 'cause they're so big an' heavy.'

After some time, Aaron and I excused ourselves and said goodnight, hugging them all.

'I'm not stayin' tonight,' he advised, smirking when we reached my bedchamber. 'I will see ya to sleep, but I have to go home to me own bed. Me family will be wonderin' where I've gone.'

We both knew his parents were well aware of where he was all the time, being more than happy about it. I slipped into bed next to him before wrapping the quilts around me, then moved towards him. He ran his hand up and down my bare arm, sending me to sleep dreaming of roses in the rubbish pile, a walking stick, and a stagnant pool with sea monsters lurking in the murky water below.

Chapter Twenty-One

I STEPPED OUTSIDE THE front entrance to check if Aaron had arrived at the stables. Harry stood in the distance; his head bent as he checked the horses were harnessed securely to the elegant, canoe-shaped carriage I had recently found out was referred to as a landau. My great-aunt had quite a collection of carriages; some imported from England long ago, while others had been purchased from Cobb & Co here in Australia. I gazed across at the shiny black exterior, the dark blue undercarriage showing not a speck of dirt, while a thick black line edged both sides in white featured on the large wheels. I was aware these practical, all-weather vehicles were a status symbol and the most comfortable of carriages—seating up to four inside with room for the driver and a groom on the box seat on top. Nevertheless, I silently wished he had chosen one of the plainer carriages, or even the small buggy, as I returned his wave before turning and climbing the stairs to the front door.

We were obligated to leave for Melbourne twenty-minutes ago, and I was more than aware we were likely to miss our train. I sighed as I bent down and picked some mint from a pot Leo was growing on the wide veranda. It seemed there were new pots of herbs added to his collection every day, and despite having a large kitchen garden at the back door, he found great pleasure in lining the wide veranda surrounding the mansion with them to fragrance the air. I straightened up and leaned against the bluestone wall, bruising the mint between my fingers and inhaling deeply as I stared out beyond the stables and over the lush paddocks where the horses grazed. Aaron was never late and was always where he said he would be at the agreed-upon time. Until today. Harry had already loaded our trunks in the back of the carriage, and he was supposed to be here hours ago. I worried something had happened; his tardiness was completely out of character. Harry turned, cocking his head to one side as a horse came thundering down the long driveway. I hurried down the stairs and towards the carriage, relieved he had finally arrived. Aaron pulled up his sweaty mount outside the stable door, then leapt down onto his feet. He left his horse in the capable hands of a young groom before running to the carriage, shouting out greetings to Harry, who climbed up onto his seat and prepared to leave.

'I'm sorry. I was delayed in town,' he panted, quickly pecking me on the forehead with his dry lips. He helped me into the carriage before we took off at great speed. After several minutes, he regained his composure. 'Only one more week, an' I don't have to leave again.' He had been returning home each night because he found it challenging to be close to me and didn't want history to repeat itself—or maybe worse. I was uncertain how we would be received this weekend. We would spend two nights in Melbourne in the same hotel room, and were not married. If word spread, my reputation would be ruined, despite the fact we did not intend to make love. It would force me to lie and say we had married just to avoid a scandal, which disturbed me greatly. But, as Aaron would often say, there wasn't a problem in the world that couldn't be fixed. I was finding I was less anxious being around him, as he never seemed to worry about anything.

We arrived at the Geelong station to find the train to Melbourne moments from departure. We boarded the first-class carriage to find no other passengers in our compartment. Aaron sat down next to the window facing forward, as it made him feel sick travelling backwards, and pulled me over beside him.

'If someone else gets on, you're next to me.' He smiled and pulled me into his chest in a warm embrace as he reclined in the seat. The train whistled long and loud, and within moments, I could feel it picking up speed as I held my fingers in my ears until the piercing shrill stopped. Aaron made himself at home, stretching out his legs onto the opposite seat. We gazed out of the window and watched the passing scenery in comfortable silence. The rhythmic rocking of the train lulled me into a deep sleep for most of the journey, half-waking occasionally when Aaron would kiss me.

We arrived at Flinders Street Station and exited the train into a bustling crowd. The Delmont carriage waited outside, only a few yards from the clocks, where many would meet up with friends for an outing in the lively town, even though it was less than a two-minute walk to the hotel. We stepped inside the elegant carriage, feeling ridiculous but remaining silent as Aaron thanked the driver, a small man with a homely face who appeared cheerful as he climbed back into his seat whistling a tune I didn't recognise. Within thirty seconds, we had arrived at the front of the grand hotel. The reception area was as beautiful as I remembered it from when we had stayed here upon our arrival in Australia. Staring around in wonderment, Aaron appeared overwhelmed. I thought back to when I had first entered The Delmont in London and how I had never seen an electric light or experienced running water.

We were shown to our room, different from the one we had stayed in what felt like years ago now. That suite contained three bedchambers and catered to a family. In contrast, this one was romantic, with a large bedchamber and a sitting room looking out over Melbourne and the Yarra River. The manager, Roger Kendrick, cheerily advised these were our private rooms, assuming Aaron was my husband, before explaining the elegant suite had been set aside for the owner and had not been used by anyone else. Only we had access to it in the future. He provided Aaron with the key before bowing slightly and politely excusing himself. I had kept my left hand hidden in my muff and was relieved I did not have to lie to such a lovely man.

Aaron moved to the window to admire the view while I made a mental note to visit one of the city's many parks and gardens I had recently read about in the Geelong Advertiser. I crossed the room and stood behind him, slipping my arms around his waist. I squeezed him tight and held my cheek against his back as he gazed down onto the busy street. It was not long to go now, and I felt nervous about the wedding night. Aaron turned abruptly and picked me up in his arms before striding across the room and dropping me onto the bed.

'Let's have dinner here tonight,' he suggested. 'And I think we should get into our night clothes now an' get into bed. I don't want to be around people at the moment. I'm exhausted from workin' all week an' just want to spend what's left of the day here with you.'

He walked over to his trunk, one I had given to him. I owned so many I had brought with me from England and had no further use for—unless I was to travel or move to a new place—and all he possessed was a canvas bag he carried when away from home overnight. He removed his shirt, and I averted my eyes. I jumped off the bed and hurried to the dressing room where my belongings had been placed. The adjoining water closet, wainscoted in marble tile and containing a full-sized bathtub and flushable toilet, was impressive. A large oval mirror sat above the handbasin, a luxury for those who lived outside the larger cities who still relied on chamber pots or commodes that required emptying, enduring the backbreaking task of heating and carting water, along with the absence of electricity.

Thoughts of what had happened the night Hamish had gotten into bed with me in his nightclothes filled my mind as I struggled to disrobe, silently thanking Bessie and appreciating her all the more while I squirmed and grunted until my dress fell around my feet. With only a week to go, I hoped we didn't ruin it now. Returning to the bedchamber in the thick nightgown that covered me from neck to ankle, I found him already tucked up in bed. I pulled back the covers and slipped in beside him, unsure what he had on. I moved towards him to find his warmth, put my arm around him, and placed my head on his shoulder. He had an undershirt on, which was a good start, but that was not why I worried. Finally, I couldn't stand not knowing, and I reached over and lifted the covers to see what he was wearing—and saw soft, long pants. I sighed in relief. He didn't want to ruin it any more than I did—he just wanted to sleep comfortably.

'I don't think it's fair you've been instructed in the art of face makin' an' I wasn't as fortunate,' he said, stroking my hair. 'I think ya need to become me private instructor. After all, there isn't much time left for me to learn.'

'Face making?'

'Makin' babies.'

'Oh, now I understand.' I giggled to myself as he nudged me with his elbow.

'Stop avoidin' me question. Ya have a way of doin' that.'

'Oh, Aaron, it's so personal, but you're right.' I felt my face become warm. 'I will explain to you what I can. If it's too embarrassing, I'm not telling.' I slowly repeated nearly everything Dana had told me. My face burned as I hurried to finish.

'Ya don't need to be embarrassed with me. I'm the one ya will be doin' it with, so we need to learn together. Is it true women can really have the same feelin' a man does, just by doin' that?'

'That's what Dana says, and I think she would know.' I giggled, remembering her graphic descriptions.

'What else? Tell me more,' he prodded, cuddling me while continuing to stroke my hair.

'Well, you don't just have to do it with the man on top pushing inside you. You can sit on top of him and ride him like you're on a horse, or you can kneel, and he can do it from behind you—like a dog,' I said, with a little more confidence. I would not tell him a woman could put a penis in her mouth and suck on it. Dana told me to keep that as a surprise for the honeymoon. She promised me I would thank her later for the advice.

He stared at me, appearing fascinated. 'What else?' he asked softly as he kissed my forehead.

'There were some other things, but it was more for girls, or it's too embarrassing to speak of.' I placed my palms on my cheeks to soothe them. He said nothing more and closed his eyes, a blissful smile touching his lips. 'What's wrong with you? I've never seen that look on your face before.'

'Nothin'. I'm just imaginin' ya doin' those things ya described, especially the one with ya sittin' on top of me in the nuddy.' He laughed loudly, and I playfully punched his arm. He straightened his body, adopting a formal pose as I giggled. 'Well, thank you, Miss Abigail Delmont, for your lesson on how to fornicate.' He nodded before closing his eyes again. 'Ya know, I'm glad ya told me, but I won't be able to stop thinkin' filthy thoughts now.' He placed his hand on my hip. 'This is where I'll have me hands when you're on top of me.' He slid his hand back up to my neck. 'Or somethin' like that,' he added, sounding a little uncertain.

There was a loud knock on the door, startling me. Aaron sprung out of bed and hurriedly slipped on his robe as he crossed the room to answer the door. It was the dinner we had ordered. I specifically asked for the famous Delmont dessert, a combination of custard and chocolate and cream with syrupy berry layers and softened biscuits broken and mixed through. I had been given the recipe at the London Delmont from the chef, Hannigan, then presented it to Leo when he started working for me. It had become Aaron's favourite, the dessert served in an oversized glass dish, just as I had requested. His eyes lit up at the sight of it. We ate our dinner in the sitting area and then climbed back into bed to eat dessert.

'Do ya know I've never stayed in a hotel room? Haven't needed to before now,' he said thoughtfully. 'I'm doin' a lot of firsts with ya, me dear Abi. I never realised this before, but your bedchamber at home is like a hotel room. Ya have ya hatchet maid, as Leo likes to call her, who is at ya beck an' call—comin' in an' out even before ya hear the bushman's clock till the moon is high in the sky—an' food bein' brought to ya whenever ya want it. Ya neighbours weren't far wrong to believe the Queen herself had up an' moved to Geelong,' he teased as I started to giggle. He was right—only I had never thought of it like that. Some days, my bedchamber was as busy as Flinders Street Station. 'Do ya think we could have more privacy, Abi? Ya know, like an agreed time for Bessie to start in the mornin', an' makin' sure no one disturbs us if we're in there durin' the day spendin' some quiet time together?' I nodded. I could see it could become a problem in the future as, like me, he wasn't used to having staff living and working in his private home.

'I only need Bessie in the mornings and evenings. We could ask her to come in at eight o'clock in the morning and not return until after six o'clock at night. Then, while we are having dinner or busy through the day, she could do her mending and organising and everything she likes to do, then again at bedtime to help me bathe and change for bed. How does that sound?'

'Beauty. It'll just be nice to have one room in the house for ourselves. But don't take it the wrong way. I enjoy havin' everyone around—includin' the staff—but the house is always overrun with people. All the time. It's difficult to get time alone. You're always busy doin' somethin' or are with someone demandin' ya attention. I'm happy ya spend time with other people, but I wanna make sure I'm also one of those people.' I smiled at him while we finished our dessert, hoping the busy lifestyle at Willow Grove did not negatively affect our marriage.

'I'm so full I could burst.' I burped loudly, forgetting to cover my mouth. He shook his head, an amused grin slowly spreading across his face.

'When ya eat like this now, I dread to think what the cost will be when you're eatin' for two. I still can't believe ya haven't got fatter since I've known ya. Me Ma eats like a bird to keep her figure. She says it's a woman's burden to carry for the sake of bein' attractive to her husband. I can see you've no fear there—ya don't seem to care if I like ya thin or fat.' He threw his head back and laughed loudly, and I laughed with him, knowing full well I ate every meal as if it were my last.

We lay together talking for what seemed like hours, and he had me in fits of giggles the entire time. The one thing he could always do was make me laugh. The moon was high in the sky now, the street-lights down below casting a soft glow across the room. My eyes were becoming heavy as I listened to his deep voice talk of memories from when he was a boy, occasionally answering when required. Finally, he noticed I was drifting off to sleep. He turned to me, pulled me close, and kissed me goodnight. I turned over—nestling my back into his chest while he tucked his legs under mine, spoon-like—slipping his arms around me and holding me in a tight embrace. As I drifted off to sleep while he nuzzled my hair, I dreamed of desserts, a dingo, and a dandelion.

The morning sun glared through the large window, the room silent bar the sound of Aaron snoring softly beside me. I remained still, enjoying the peace of not having to listen to people coming and going in my room as they went about their duties—a feeling reinforced after our discussion last night. I turned over in his arms and kissed him good morning. This time next week, we would be getting ready in our separate homes and preparing to walk down the aisle. When I looked up, I found him staring into my eyes; however, he remained silent, which I knew to be entirely out of character and very much unlike him. He had such beautiful blue eyes. I could stare into them forever. They relayed so much emotion—only I hadn't figured out all that was in there yet—or what it meant.

'I love ya, Abi, with all my heart,' he finally whispered.

'I love you back.' He touched my face, drawing his finger down to my lips and sliding it across from side to side. It made my lips tingle until he stopped and kissed me.

We made our way downstairs to the restaurant for breakfast; the waiter leading us to a table that sat in the corner overlooking Swanston Street. We had decided to eat there to see for ourselves the guests the hotel attracted. I pointed out on the menu recipes Leo cooked at home so Aaron could avoid them and try something different. While he studied the breakfast menu, I noticed how lovely the restaurant was.

Everything from the wallpaper to the floor coverings was of the finest quality—the rich, mahogany furniture intricately carved by a skilled craftsman—while luxurious fabrics used for the heavy drapes and upholstered chairs in beautiful tones of red and gold complimented the elegance of the room. They brought our breakfasts to us within moments of our orders being taken, impressing me greatly and leaving me wondering how that was even possible.

'There is something I would like to do while we're here,' I said. 'I would love to go to the botanical gardens with you. When I was in London, I had to spend most of my time locked up in the hotel or at Mr Malcolm's home under his supervision, but I got to go to a couple of gardens while I was free, which I enjoyed so very much.' He smiled and nodded, taking a large bite of his buttered toast.

'I'd enjoy that, too. At least ya free to explore this town at your leisure—an' you're tinny enough to get to do it with me.' We talked throughout breakfast, noting the disapproving glances from society's best, the cream of the social scene, the wealthy guests who seemed to be the only ones who could afford to stay here.

We finished our meal, enjoyed our coffees, and headed for reception, holding hands and ignoring the stares and whispers. Aaron tipped the waiter as we left—he knew I liked to reward anyone kind enough to offer their services to make my life easier. However, I had not forgotten I would most certainly be in their position if things had been different. Or worse.

We passed by the front desk, greeting the concierge as he held the door open for us before descending the stairs and stepping out onto busy Swanston Street. The street was bustling with people shopping, many hurrying along the pavement, some with purpose, while others ambled along, taking in the sights. Carriages rushed by, along with people in carts and on horseback. We strolled hand in hand, looking in the windows, until we stopped at a small shop front on Little Lonsdale Street. Aaron gazed up in silence at the sign above, A J Dawson- Diamonds, Timepieces and Novelties.

'You know, I forgot about the weddin' rings,' he remarked, trying not to grin.

'Hmmm. I didn't think of it, either. Let's go in and buy them, then.'

He took me by the hand and led me inside, the bell tinkering overhead. Mr Colin Dawson greeted us and asked if he could help. When we advised him of why we were there, he turned and disappeared behind a thick, blue curtain that led to the back of the shop. He muttered to himself as he rummaged around before returning to the counter and placing a tray down before us. Tall and with red hair, his face broke into an easy smile, and he seemed like a lovely man to me.

'May I please see your engagement ring, Miss? Only to ensure the wedding ring will match,' he asked politely. I raised my hand to show him, and he gasped before taking several steps back. 'That is the most exquisite ring I have ever seen—both the diamond and the setting. It's splendid. Where on earth did you get it?' He returned to the counter and took my hand in his, raising it up to his face before studying the ring under an eyeglass. 'I believe it's quite old. I would estimate from the late 17th century—and I must say—it is quite valuable. Only the wealthy bother with engagement rings, and even then, it's rarely set with a diamond.' He gently slipped it off my finger to look closer, smiling to himself.

'My great-aunt left it to my fiancé, who then presented it to me. I have no idea where it came from or its history,' I replied casually as I, too, admired the large rock he held in his hand.

'She must have liked you a great deal.' He turned to Aaron, who grinned broadly. 'I will have to make a special ring to go with this. I have nothing here that would remotely match anything like it,' he added, a troubled look on his face.

'It already has a band to go with it. I think it's an eternity ring rather than a weddin' ring,' Aaron advised him, much to my surprise. 'I would like one made to match the two others, so they all fit together. We're returnin' home tomorrow an' gettin' married next Saturday. Do ya think ya could have that an' me ring completed by then?' I was unaware my aunt had left him two rings and wondered why it wasn't suitable as a wedding band. Much to my embarrassment, I did not even know what an eternity ring was or its purpose.

Mr Dawson smiled. 'If I close my shop now and work all night, I will have it finished by tomorrow.' He appeared reluctant to go on, his face flushing. 'It will cost a pretty penny because of the quality of the gold I need to use, but you seem like a delightful couple, and I will help you. Come back tomorrow morning, and I will have them finished. By the look of your hands, Sir, I will have to make yours to fit as well. Your fingers are rather large. We don't get many men with hands your size requesting jewellery.' He chuckled to himself as he measured our fingers, then sketched a drawing of my engagement ring.

'Would you like us to pay now or leave a deposit?' I asked. I had brought along a decent amount of cash from under the house.

'Nah, I trust you. I can tell with people, you know?' he replied kindly, then smiled at us before disappearing once again behind the blue curtain.

After walking around the town for hours, we returned to the hotel, tired and ready for bed despite the sun beating down, still high in the sky. I knew shopping always made me feel that way, yet I still put myself through it. I planned to sneak a nap before leaving for the gardens because I wanted to enjoy every moment. As we entered our suite, Aaron placed the *DO NOT DISTURB* sign on the door and closed it firmly behind him. Aaron appeared weary, too, after exploring shop after shop. He removed his jacket before throwing himself on top of the quilt—while I slipped onto the bed beside him and snuggled into him—dozing off within minutes.

Aaron woke me, gently kissing my forehead and whispering it was time to leave. I yawned before struggling to my feet, retreating into my dressing room to tidy my hair. A maid was soon at the door with a picnic basket he had ordered, and fifteen-minutes later, we were walking down Birdwood Avenue towards the botanical gardens. I summoned all my strength to appear calm, stopping myself from jumping up and down with excitement just as my dear Leo would. I had read there were thirty-eight hectares of gardens containing thousands of varieties of trees, plants, and waterways—and I couldn't wait to see all of it.

We stepped through the iron gates, my eyes going wide as I gasped at its beauty. Aaron took my hand, and we strolled along the paths, stopping at times to look closely at a plant or tree we didn't recognise. Finally, we found a place to sit beside a lake where we could see Government House, an imposing building even viewed from a great distance. We reclined on the bank, enjoying our picnic while talking about our future together and the meaning of life—the waterfowl splashing and quacking nearby in their search for food.

'If I tell you something, Aaron, will you promise you won't think me mad?'

'I promise nothin' ya ever tell me will make me think ya mad—unless ya really do go mad—an' then I will have to protect ya from yourself an' employ a nurse to save Leo takin' ya to Ararat himself.' He smiled as he reached over and affectionately stroked my cheek. I swallowed hard several times.

'I see auras. It's more like a golden glow radiating from certain people. I see it around you—and Hamish has it too—as do many of my friends.' I paused for a moment and took a sip of ale as Aaron stared out over the lake, remaining silent. 'I don't know what it means or why I'm the only one who can see it. Some I love don't have it at all, like your brothers; however, your parents do, which confuses me no end.' He sat up and brushed the grass from his trousers.

'I can't say I understand it, either, but I believe ya.'

'Just like that—you believe me. What if I am actually mad? Is that how you go about protecting me from myself?'

'Well, Abi, I believe it. If ya say it's true, then to me it is. I've not known ya to lie to me yet. There may have been times when you didn't tell me certain things, but one thing I'm sure of is I trust ya completely.' He gazed at me with such sincerity I knew then I could keep nothing from him—whether it be a thought, a situation, or even the way I was feeling.

We spent the afternoon walking the immaculate gardens and admiring the native birds that lived there. Aaron jokingly suggested we employ the head gardener who maintained the magnificent grounds to make Willow Grove look the same.

We strolled down St Kilda Boulevard back to the hotel to get ready for the engagement party—departing shortly after for Stonington Mansion in Glenferrie Road, Malvern—the newly built home of Tamara's future in-laws. Lit up like a chandelier, the sun setting over Port Phillip Bay several suburbs away, the home was magnificent. Aaron helped me down from the carriage, careful not to spoil my bronze silk evening gown, and I smiled in appreciation.

'Ya look beautiful, Abi,' he whispered, kissing me on the ear, sending tingles through my entire body. A butler stood just inside the massive front door. He greeted us formally and took our coats before accompanying us to the grand ballroom and announcing us to the room. I felt awkward as the guests turned to stare and felt uncertain how to react. Aaron took my hand and led me towards a footman who held a tray of champagne glasses. He handed one to me before taking his own and scanning the room confidently. 'Just drink that an' ya won't feel so self-conscious. People look at ya 'cause you're stunnin', Abi—not to make fun of ya or judge ya.' He led me over to a loveseat, then sat next to me with his arm around my shoulders. People were indeed staring disapprovingly at us now, but not because of how I looked. I had only recently learnt you could not express affection publicly—even once married—a social rule I thought the most ridiculous I had ever heard. And they had forced me to learn them all.

Tamara approached, looking even lovelier than usual, and embraced us. It was as if she were floating on a cloud, appearing like an angel in her exquisite, apricot-coloured gown, so obviously a Montague creation. She sat down next to us and gestured for the footman to come and refresh our drinks.

'I'm so pleased you came. I worried you wouldn't attend at the last minute.' She took my hands in hers, her eyes shining. 'Oh, Abigail. Did you ever imagine we would both find such happiness here? You had me so worried on the ship. It gave Elizabeth nightmares—all the things you were saying about our future husbands and how dreadful they could be—but thankfully you were wrong in this case.'

Brian strode over to us, then bowed to me and shook Aaron's hand. Tamara looked at him lovingly as he sat down; however, he focused his attention on Aaron and me, ignoring her completely.

'I'm so pleased you could make it,' he said, an amiable smile touching his lips. 'You have always shown us great hospitality when we visited you, and I am honoured to do the same.'

Elizabeth called her sister away to speak with an important guest of their father's. Many of the guests present represented society's best—the best in business, in industry, in politics, in law—not to mention Tamara's future father-in-law, John Wagner, was a founding partner of Cobb & Co carriages. I certainly felt like I stood out like a sore thumb and wondered how Aaron was faring. Brian, however, sat back comfortably and relaxed the moment Tamara left us.

'So, are you excited about your upcoming nuptials?' I asked. He stared back at me, a hint of sadness in his eyes.

'It was the right decision to make, Abigail, but my parents are the ones who made the match. I respect them, so of course, I would never go against what they ask of me. I will do my duty, and be a good husband and treat Tamara well,' he replied flatly, and I felt my heart break for him. Finding him to be a nice man on the occasions I had spent time with him, I felt dreadful he was so obviously unhappy with his life. 'Well, it's your turn in a week,' he said brightly, clearly no longer wanting to discuss his private business. He and Aaron continued to talk as I curiously looked around the room. All dressed in their finest, I could see Mr Montague had been working extremely hard of late by the number of women who were wearing his unique creations. Guests stood together in groups or relaxed on chairs placed around the room, surrounding the walls, talking and mingling with one another. Tamara soon returned as I admired the beautifully decorated ballroom, lowering herself into the chair beside me and clasping my hand in hers.

'I adored your engagement party, so I did the same for mine—the food, the standing around, and everyone talking,' she told me, her eyes shining.

'Then I truly hope it is, Tamara.' She was so in love with love. Even when attending another woman's engagement party, she found it so romantic and perfect she wanted to recreate it for herself, the poor darling. I hoped with all my heart this marriage would work for her; however, I had an uneasy feeling ever since I first saw them together, with Brian virtually confirming my suspicions tonight.

Aaron and I resumed chatting after the engaged couple left us to mingle with the crowd when another guest approached us. He was in his thirties, handsome and charming. He introduced himself as George Maslow and explained he was a barrister with a thriving law firm—a friend of Tamara's father. I couldn't take in much of what he said, though. All I could see was a black aura radiating around his body as he stood before me—my vision fading to grey—before blackness engulfed me.

'Abi. Abi. Can ya hear me?' He slapped my cheek gently as I slowly regained consciousness and realised I was lying on the floor with my head in Aaron's lap. 'Ya fainted, *mo anamchara,* but you're all right now. I've got ya,' he murmured, stroking my head. A crowd of people stood around me, staring down in curiosity. I attempted to stand with Aaron's help, my head spinning as my legs gave way from under me. He sat me on a chair, and then someone brought me a cup of tea with lots of milk and sugar while he fussed over me.

'I'm perfectly all right, I promise you. Please, just take me back to the hotel.' I felt sick to my stomach, and I could not stop trembling. I looked around the ballroom to find George Maslow watching me from the other side of the room, still surrounded by that mysterious black aura. Just being near him had sucked every bit of energy from my body, and I felt weak and confused.

'I'll go an' arrange the carriage,' Aaron called over his shoulder as he hurried out the door, taking such long strides I would have to run to keep up with him. Tamara sat next to me, visibly upset. I apologised for ruining her night. When I saw tears welling in her eyes, I felt terrible and knew she would blame me forever.

'Oh, you have ruined nothing, Abigail. The night was ruined before it even began. No one is mixing as they did at your party, and no one seems to be having fun. All I've heard is people making snide remarks and saying nasty things about each other behind their backs. These people don't have a pleasant word to say about anyone,' she sniffed, and tears started to roll down her face.

It forced me to admit Tamara was right, but it wasn't her fault. Her father chose the people they expected her to socialise with. As the rumours went, her parents only allowed her to be friends with me because I was wealthy. They believed I would be a favourable social connection for her and Elizabeth once I started behaving like a lady and not beneath my station.

'There, there, Tamara. It's not as bad as all that. It's been a lovely evening, and we have enjoyed ourselves.' I continued to reassure her, even as I sat back, utterly exhausted, and closed my eyes while waiting for Aaron. The black aura I had seen differed from anything I had seen before—and the effect it had on me physically was like nothing I had ever experienced. I could hardly raise my arm and felt so weak—and very tired. Feeling I could sleep for a month, my mind was foggy and confused, and something prevented me from thinking clearly while that man was near.

As he continued to stare at me from across the room, I felt he was pulling something from inside me towards himself. He made no move to come and inquire about my welfare, and seemed perfectly normal—but I sensed the surrounding evil even from the other side of the room. He stood beside Mrs Mary Chirnside, a wealthy and powerful widow who owned most of Werribee since the death of her husband, Andrew, only months ago—and his brother, Thomas, three-years prior. They appeared quite familiar, which unsettled me for no apparent reason other than the grey aura surrounding Mary. How this man would affect me in the long run, I didn't know, and again became frustrated with myself for not understanding any of it. I wondered what the point was in seeing these auras if I couldn't discern what they meant or even the meaning of the three different colours I had seen so far.

Tamara looked extremely disappointed, even as I tried to reassure her again how much we had enjoyed ourselves—going on to say her engagement party was the loveliest I had attended.

'But you only just got here, and the next minute you're on the floor. How could you have enjoyed yourself?' she asked, eyeing me suspiciously. I held her hand and reassured her yet again the party was perfect, and I was certain everyone was having a lovely time, or they would have left by now. 'Yes, you're right. The house is full, and you should see all the gifts. It was worth having for that alone,' she whispered, and I laughed aloud. I could only imagine the expense involved, with everyone trying to outdo the others by giving the most elaborate gifts.

We had commissioned a sitting with a prominent Australian painter by the name of Lois Abrahams, who had agreed to paint their portrait to hang above their fireplace. It thrilled Tamara when I told her. This painter rarely did such work, and to have one of his pieces hanging in your home boosted you up the ladder of high society—the exact place she aspired to be. I always tried to give my friends what I knew they would love, not what interested me.

Tamara and Elizabeth were both proper ladies of high breeding, which showed in their every action and word. However, when they came to stay with me at Willow Grove, they relaxed and didn't have to worry about all that nonsense. Ours was an odd friendship, given we were like night and day, but you couldn't choose who you loved, and I loved them both dearly. Aaron returned and hurried to my side, his handsome face creased with concern.

'Come on, *mo anamchara*, let's get ya back to the hotel so I can put ya to bed. You're as white as a ghost.' He helped me up; however, my legs went from under me again. He quickly grabbed me by the shoulders and gently sat me back down on the chair. 'Abi, do ya need to go to the hospital? We're not that far from The Alfred.'

'No, Aaron, I just need to lie down. I will be fine once I can lie down.' Tamara held my hand before he leaned down and gathered me up in his arms to carry me out to the carriage.

'I'm sorry about all this, Miss Tamara—an' you too, mate.' They nodded silently as Brian pounded him on the back. 'We regret we have to leave in the middle of things, but as ya can see, Abi is under the weather. Have a ripper of a night, an' thank ya so much for invitin' us to celebrate with ya. We will see ya next week at our own weddin'.' He carried me out, the engaged couple accompanying us to the front door.

The other guests stopped their gossiping for a moment to observe the fuss I was causing and then resumed their conversations as if nothing had happened. Mr Maslow hadn't taken his eyes from me since the moment he'd seen me, nor had he spoken a word to me. It was odd. He didn't appear frightening or threatening. All he did was smile at me each time I looked over at him.

Aaron placed me in the carriage, then climbed in beside me. I waved to Tamara and Brian as we trotted off, then leaned back against the seat and closed my eyes. However, since leaving that ominous presence, I was already feeling a little better.

'What happened in there, Abi? Do ya remember?' I told him what I had seen around George Maslow and how that was the last thing I could remember. 'Ya were sittin' as still as a stone statue from the moment he approached us, an' then turned white as a sheet. Ya didn't speak, an' the next minute, I saw ya startin' to faint. I caught ya an' laid ya down on the floor.' He gripped my hand as I stared out at the passing shops on Malvern Road, silently willing the horses to go faster.

'Aaron, I have experienced nothing like that in my life. It had a real impact on my body, which I'm still feeling. It was as though he drained all the energy from me and disrupted my mind. I am only starting to think clearly now. I never want to experience that again. It's frightening and makes me physically ill.' I leaned back in my seat and closed my eyes. I felt his lips on mine. He ran his tongue along them gently, and then he sucked my bottom lip softly. I couldn't wait until I could touch him where and when I wanted without guilt. He put his arm around my waist and pulled me to him. I rested my head on his chest and listened to his strong heartbeat.

'It doesn't make sense to me, Abi. From what ya told me, ya mostly see gold, an' it's a good feelin', not one that makes ya reach for the smellin' salts.' He looked as confused as I felt. I sighed and closed my eyes again.

'I don't know what it means, either, but I do know it isn't good. Of that, I am certain.' He held me tighter and said nothing more.

I waited in the suite for the maid to arrive and help me undress while Aaron changed into his bedclothes in his dressing room. I couldn't stop thinking about George Maslow and his intrusion into my psyche. It made sense anyone I saw with the glow was important to me, but I had no idea what grey and black could mean. I knew black was evil beyond a doubt, and I needed to beware of it; however, grey had me confused.

Sister Monica, the Appleby's, Jemima and Mr McPhee were only some of the souls I had witnessed with grey auras. Although we weren't fond of each other, we had no plans to assault or kill the other at this point in time. Now a stranger, Mary Chirnside, possessed the same; however, I did not feel threatened by her at all. I had met evil men before, like Leroy and Robbie, but they didn't have the black aura, even though I had experienced their malign natures firsthand.

I knew I would drive myself insane thinking about it. Hopefully, I wouldn't have to if I didn't see that man again in the future.

The maid knocked and entered the suite, and I patiently stood still for her to help me undress in the sitting room. I felt much better once I was in a fresh nightgown. The polite little maid sat me down to brush my hair when Aaron entered the dressing room, lowering himself onto a chair to watch.

'Ye 'ave the most beautiful 'air, Mistress, if ye don't mind me sayin'. It's so long an' thick an' wavy—an' a colour I 'ave never seen afore. Of course, it's red, but it 'as flecks o' cinnamon an' gold in it—an' when ye look closely, it's naw one colour,' she said, running the silver brush through it for the two-hundredth time.

'Thank you, but I think my hair is finished now,' I said, smiling at her. She started to blush before gently placing the brush down on the dressing table, nodding her head as Aaron bid her goodnight and left her to her work.

'Oh, aye. I'm sorry, Mistress. I must 'ave been daydreamin'. I'll finish ye off now.' She bent forward and arranged my hair into one long plait, her nimble fingers moving swiftly.

Aaron was in bed when I returned to the room after letting the maid out and locking the door. I had left instructions we were not to be disturbed for any reason, and we would let someone know when we were ready for breakfast. Placing our order with the restaurant manager ahead of time, I wasn't feeling as weak as I had been when we arrived back at the hotel. Although I still felt strange, the haze around my mind was slowly lifting. Aaron gazed at me as I slipped off my dressing gown and climbed into bed beside him, thinking how no bed now was ever as comfortable as my own. I snuggled in and pulled the covers up. Aaron slid over and placed one arm across my stomach while pulling me close.

'At least Tamara looked happy,' he remarked, our faces only inches apart.

'So, you could see it, too? I'm glad it's not only me just being pessimistic. Brian looks dreadfully unhappy, doesn't he?' Aaron nodded, the moon softly illuminating the room.

'I've never seen a bloke about to be married lookin' more miserable. It's as though someone he loves has passed over the great divide. Do ya think she really can't see it, or chooses not to? I mean, if you an' I can, surely she must have noticed he doesn't touch her or look her in the eye—or even talk to her, now I think about it.'

'You do notice everything without others even being aware, don't you?' I gazed at the silhouette of his face, my heart filled with so much love for this man.

'It's a gift.' He laughed as he pulled me closer to him. 'I've been this way ever since I can remember. Me Da always said when gettin' to know people not to speak unless ya have somethin' worth sayin', an' focus on their reactions rather than only listenin' to their words. It's somethin' I've always remembered. I like to know what lurks deep down, not just what's on display for the world to see 'cause I find all God's creatures interestin'—even the two-legged variety. Everyone's so different. No two are alike. Don't ya find that fascinatin'?' I stared at him wide-eyed. That was precisely how I felt, wanting to meet as many people as I could.

'Oh, yes. I have wondered the same thing myself ever since I could remember.' I laughed quietly as he lifted his head and looked at me closely. 'Yes?' I asked, raising an eyebrow inquiringly.

'I'm just thinkin' about the fact this time next week, you an' I will be in bed naked. How long ya friends wanna stay at the party isn't me concern, an' they have me blessin' ta drink till the sun comes up. I'm not doin' what Polly an' Angus did an' waitin' for every sod ta leave when the food an' grog run dry. As soon as tea's finished, I'm takin' ya to bed.' I stared at his lovely face and those blue eyes that looked so deep into my soul.

'I won't disagree with you on that subject, my love.' He stared at me, appearing surprised before he sat up in bed to get a better look at me.

'Do ya know that's the first time you've called me that, or, anythin' endearin'?'

'I didn't realise I called you that now,' I replied, laughing again. He pulled me to his chest and kissed me for the longest time, whispering all the sweet things held close to his heart. I went to sleep dreaming of a tiger snake, a mansion just like Willow Grove, only different, and a dark monster chasing me through the dark hallways, leaving me nowhere to hide.

Chapter Twenty-Two

I AWOKE IN MY own bed at Willow Grove, realising immediately what day it was. I had been counting down for what seemed like forever, and there were only three more days left until I married the love of my life. Only three more days and I would become someone's wife, and possibly even a mother, one day. I turned over to find Aaron lying with his head on his outstretched arm, staring at me.

'What are you doing here so early, Aaron? Did you wet your bed?' He threw his head back and laughed as I yawned sleepily and gazed around my beautiful room—more of a suite with its gigantic fireplace and small sitting room. With its heavy velvet drapes surrounding the enormous, four-poster bed, the same drapes covering the windows while completely blocking out even a shimmer of light when closed. I loved how the large dressing rooms were hidden away. The adjourning washroom was luxurious and spacious, with an enormous bathtub that could be filled from the pipes leading out to the underground water tank. I was amazed how the large cauldron was always filled, the fire underneath the fixed structure always burning with embers. He smirked as he kissed me gently on the forehead.

'I was studyin' the outline of ya body under the covers, but then ya woke up an' I thought I should behave as a gentleman would, an' covered ya back up again.' I hit him on the arm playfully as he grabbed my wrist and pulled me into his arms. He wished me good morning with a long, passionate kiss and then held me in his usual gentle manner. He was like a colossal bear, and I loved being next to him.

'You deviant. Leo does the same thing to me when he sleeps in my bed. He is forever touching my breasts and feeling the outline of my body.'

'Yeah, but he doesn't look at ya the same way I do. Instead, he treats you like you're his own little doll to dress up an' do with as he pleases.'

'I've told him once I'm married, he can't play with my body the way he does.' Aaron shook his head in amusement as I sat up and propped up my pillows before leaning back into them.

'Ya think that's gunna stop him? He's hopeless, an' he'll blame me if ya stop him touchin' ya boobies as soon as we're married. Leave it alone for a while an' just put up with it so he doesn't make the connection.' He chuckled loudly before pulling me closer. 'Three more nights to go till there's no turnin' back, ya know? Ya can always back out now if ya have any doubts. Maybe I've rushed ya a little?' He stared deeply into my eyes, making me smile. I squeezed him tightly.

'I don't have one doubt in the world you will be the best husband I could ever find. You are my best friend and will be my lover for the rest of my life, so I don't feel rushed at all. I don't want to wait any longer than need be to start my life with you, Aaron.' I ran my finger down his cheek and along his jawline to his neck, where I caressed him. He kissed me deeply before letting me go.

'Me parents loved seein' ya yesterday,' he remarked. 'Ma told us she already feels like she has a daughter an' can't figure out what terrible sin she must have committed in a previous life to only deserve sons. She talks about ya endlessly to anyone who'll listen, skiting about how wonderful ya are.'

Aaron's mother was the loveliest woman I had ever met and had already taken me under her wing. She looked after me just as a proper mother would, and I appreciated and loved her for it. She had helped plan the wedding without being intrusive and had attended my dress fittings, crying tears of joy the first time she saw me in my gown. Knowing how deeply her son loved me and how much I adored him, she was the happiest woman in Geelong. She, too, was a woman unimpressed by wealth or status and made me feel comfortable to be myself around her.

'I love being around your family, although your brothers have started to tease me a lot more now,' I remarked. He chuckled again.

'That's 'cause ya fire back at them when ya get mad. They love it when ya stamp ya foot with ya hands on ya hips an' ya sweet little chin pointed out before ya make ya opinion known—whether people want to hear it or not. They keep tellin' me I've chosen a fiery sheila who'll keep me on me toes. I won't tell ya what they said ya would lead me around by as it's not for ya ears.' He continued to laugh as he turned onto his back. 'Speakin' of which, don't we have to see ya solicitor sometime today?' I nodded reluctantly. Mr McPhee had recently demanded Aaron sign a contract relinquishing any right he would have as my husband to claim my inheritance—or the profits from its companies should we divorce. I didn't want Aaron to sign it, as I found it distasteful, but that bloody lawyer insisted on it. 'Stop worryin'. If I didn't wanna sign the contract, I wouldn't. I want ya to know I'm not marryin' ya for the money. I wouldn't care if ya was poor as a church mouse. When is money at the forefront of anythin' for us? It's always about friends an' family an' spendin' time together. We don't attend any social functions or mix with anyone with large amounts of money. I don't need money, Abi, as I have you,' he reassured me, sensing what was bothering me without my saying a word. I kissed the side of his neck in appreciation.

'After today, I don't want to think about this again, so let's put it behind us.' He nodded, taking my hand in his. 'I don't want money hanging over our marriage. You're right, we think little about it, but that's only because we have it. It pays for everything we need, but there are so many people without a penny to their name, Aaron. I know what it feels like to have nothing. That's why I don't spend a lot on myself and try to give others a helping hand. I would rather go through life without thinking about money at all, as I find the responsibility of wealth far too overwhelming. But I don't want either of us to ever take it for granted.'

'Then let's not focus on it anymore,' he suggested. 'We'll go an' sign the papers, an' that'll be the end of it. What do ya wanna do afterwards? Do ya need to do anythin' in town?' I shook my head.

Everything was ready for the wedding, the honeymoon was organised, and I had nothing left to do but put on my dress and walk down the aisle. 'We'll think of somethin'.'

We sat side by side in Mr McPhee's dreary office while he looked for the contract, which, for some reason, he had misplaced.

'I know where it was, but someone has been cleaning my desk, and now I can't find anything,' he snapped, his frustration clear as he roughly slammed papers around on the large desk. Aaron and I silently waited until he located the document for which he had been searching. 'Here it is, filed under your name. That's not where I had it.' He shook his head in disgust before sitting down behind his desk.

I narrowed my gaze at him in disbelief and wondered again how efficiently he was looking after my trust fund. The more I met with this strange little man, the less confidence I had in him; however, I had no other option at present and was forced to leave him in charge of managing my finances. He shuffled the papers in front of him, then looked over at Aaron, his face stern.

'I have the contract here, Mr Cavanaugh. You are welcome to read through it, initial every page, sign the last one, and I will witness it—if you consent to the conditions.' He handed the papers to Aaron, who didn't bother to read them, signed as instructed, then handed them back. Mr McPhee sat straight as an arrow in his oversized padded chair, then turned his attention to me.

'Now it's up to you, Miss Delmont.' He shuffled the signed papers before him, appearing satisfied. 'Would you like Aaron to stay for the next part of our meeting? As he will soon be your husband, you haven't instructed me if I am to continue to speak with only you in confidence once you are married?'

'I am happy for Aaron to stay and be made aware of all my business dealings.' I smiled at Aaron, who took my hand in his.

'All right, then, we can begin. You are already aware you own four Delmont Hotels in London, Paris, New York, and Melbourne,' he began, and I raised my hand to interrupt him.

'I was not aware of that until recently. It seems you are drip-feeding information to me. One lawyer could, and should, have handled this whole thing,' I told him crossly. He grimaced before looking away.

'Well, I told you at the first available moment; however, it was probably during one of your regular hysterical tantrums when you cannot be rational and end up forming opinions on issues of which you have no knowledge.' He waved his hand dismissively as I felt my anger rise. Aaron squeezed my hand discreetly and smiled, preventing me from verbally assailing this snippy little man. Mr McPhee looked at me inquiringly. 'May I go on?' he asked abruptly, and I nodded while forcing a smile. 'As I said, you own the four Delmont hotels, the property so named as Willow Grove, and there is your primary trust fund, which is held in England and managed by your lawyer, Mr Malcolm, until you attain the age of thirty-years. There is a trust fund held here in Australia, and it is substantial due to the fact your great-aunt once owned a very successful shipping company here. One of the largest in the country at the time. A percentage of the interest in this fund you have so very fortunately inherited is released into your bank account each month. At the same time, all profits from The Delmont Hotel, Melbourne, are directed into this fund's principal sum. This ensures the trust fund grows significantly over the next fifteen-years, which you will then be able to access and decide for yourself how to manage your fortune. Am I making myself clear?' he asked, evidently assuming we didn't understand or comprehend the English language. We both nodded, and I forced a smile.

'As clear as mud,' I mumbled under my breath before he continued.

'You've inherited a parcel of land in Gippsland spanning one thousand acres. It says here it is a bush block with a large river running through it. Then there's thirty acres with beach frontage in Brighton, a suburb of Melbourne, that is also yours—along with a parcel of fifty acres on Phillip Island. In addition, a large, prime parcel of land on Flinders Street, Melbourne, was also left to you. Your aunt earmarked this city plot to build the largest theatre in Melbourne in the next two-years. All these properties were purchased over fifty-years ago, and there are no dwellings on any of them. Except for the theatre, building on them is up to you. All of your servants' wages are paid through our firm, as are the costs of running the house. I understand you want the income Willow Grove earns managed by your future husband? Do you think that wise at this early stage? We have been running that side of the business for fifteen-years quite efficiently. Given what profits the stud alone earns, the property more than pays for itself, so I guess it is your choice if you decide to remove that responsibility from my office. I heard on the grapevine you continue to pay your servants a bonus of a pound a week from your own money on top of the wages I distribute. Is this true?' he asked, glaring across at me while shaking his head disapprovingly.

'Yes, it is, and it's nice to see they don't have to worry about money and have enough to save a little every week. It provides a sense of pride being able to buy a luxury item here and there, as many people such as yourself take for granted.' I felt myself blush and fury rise in me. He dared to question what I did with my own money? Aaron was amused but said nothing, although I could see he was enjoying this exchange.

'I am completely opposed to how you treat your servants, Miss Delmont. There is no need for it. You pay them decent wages, and they should only receive what they have earned. You are not a charity, and you owe your servants nothing other than their weekly wage. I have also heard they eat the same food served at your own dining table. You may as well throw your money in a pit and burn it, in my opinion, for all the appreciation you will receive from that lot.' He grunted to himself, while I could feel myself becoming angrier the more he spoke.

'Well, I have a different opinion, and you won't change that, you conceited little man—and please stop calling them servants. The bonus stays. It comes from my own money that you have no control over once transferred to me. I never wanted staff to begin with. My heart goes out to them having to bow and scrape to us just because I had the good luck of inheriting money from someone I have never even met. I did not earn a penny of this money, nor am I any more deserving than any of those who must work to survive. I don't like your attitude one bit and strongly believe you need to take your head out of your arse and remember just who the employer is here.' I crossed my arms against my chest while Aaron threw his head back and roared with laughter. Mr McPhee sat back in his chair as if I had punched him in the face, but said no more. He was not the fatherly figure Mr Malcolm had been to me, and my dislike for him intensified the more I got to know him.

'There is no need for such crude language, young lady. I will not respond to such vile accusations and will remain professional, despite everything in me wanting to put you over my knee and give you the strap for behaving like the obstinate child you are. I believe you need someone to care for you as a parent would, being so young and having no life experience. Look upon me as the father you never had and let me guide you.' He smiled ingratiatingly, and I scoffed, my eyes wide in disbelief, at which point Aaron leaned forward and cleared his throat.

'With all respect, Mr McPhee, I will be Abi's husband in a matter of days, an' I believe if anyone will be there to guide her, it will be me. I'll be meetin' with you once a month to go over the accounts an' profit-an'-loss figures for the farm. I'll also be lookin' at your figures regardin' her businesses to ensure Abi's money is looked after an' all is as it should be. We wouldn't want any mistakes to be happenin' or to find the books didn't add up with no explanation now, would we, Sir?' Mr McPhee stared at Aaron for a long time before sitting back in his oversized chair.

'As you wish, Aaron. Should Miss Delmont consent to handing all of her business dealings over to you and allowing you to run everything, believing I have done nothing of benefit for her all this time, it's at her own peril,' he snapped, his face like thunder. I tried to smother a smile but failed miserably as I watched Mr McPhee's left eye twitch.

'Now, that is not what Aaron is saying, Mr McPhee,' I advised him sharply, having pulled myself together. 'We will run things together as a partnership, and yes, I do want Aaron to take over as much as he feels comfortable with. I trust him, and he is wonderful with numbers and bringing out the best in people. I know the decisions he makes will always be in my best interests.' Mr McPhee raised his eyebrows at the implication; however, he forced a superficial smile.

'I apologise if I have caused offence. I am agreeable to report my dealings to Aaron each month to reassure you everything I do is legitimate and honest.' He had made it clear we had wounded his feelings by questioning his integrity.

'Is there anything else, Mr McPhee?' I asked him briskly. I'd had quite enough of the little tarantula for today and wanted to leave his dark and dusty office.

'No. Nothing more for now. Have you attended the Mercantile Bank next to the Post Office to sign for your new bank account I opened for you? The first payment was transferred to your account over three weeks ago now, and your second payment is due on Monday.'

'No, I haven't been there.' It was none of his business once the money had left his firm and deposited into my account. What I did beyond that, he could keep his large, reptilian snout away from. I hadn't needed to go to the bank yet, as I took any money we required from under the house. There were so many small bundles stacked neatly to the ceiling, and I believed it would last a lifetime, spending as freely as we liked. There were tens of thousands of notes—not their total value, but actual notes—far too overwhelming and time-consuming to count. I could only guess what the real value held in that room would amount to, again piquing my curiosity how my great-aunt had accumulated such wealth—and why she would hide it rather than keeping it in the bank, as she had done with the rest of her fortune.

I planned to let the interest from my allowance build in the bank for a rainy day and continue to purchase our necessities while spoiling ourselves occasionally from the secret room under the house—nothing outlandish but things we enjoyed. Comfortable keeping everything as simple as possible, I enjoyed living like this very much. I didn't skimp when it came to the monthly budget spent running the house, providing Leo with the best ingredients money could buy, among the other items he demanded regularly. Mr McPhee had been unhappy with the amount I allowed Leo to spend on his imported and local goods, but I had stood firm. Finally, he had reluctantly agreed and doubled the budget for food and staples.

Mr McPhee stood to dismiss us. Aaron shook his hand, and he bowed slightly to me, which only irritated me further. I wished again that Mr Malcolm was here looking after everything for us, as this man didn't give two shits about doing his best for anyone. I despised coming to this office and couldn't wait to leave. Mr Malcolm was like family to me, and I knew I could trust him with anything—even my life. However, this little man with the grey aura left me with no doubt he was only interested in managing my trust fund and businesses because of the money it brought him. Aaron grabbed my hand and hurried me out to the carriage, shoving me in before I could open my mouth. He quickly closed the door behind him, then shook his head in amusement.

'That condescending little prick!' I screamed, before an outpouring of expletives filled the carriage as Aaron chuckled loudly. I could hear Harry laughing uproariously as he sat at the front on his box seat, obviously able to hear my tantrum. Finally, Aaron called out his instructions to Harry, who continued to chuckle as he moved the horses forward. 'Seriously, Aaron. Surely you can see how ineffectual the man is. He doesn't give a fat rat's arse about my fund—only what he can get out of me by having control of it,' I griped, just as he leaned across and kissed me full on the mouth. I wasn't sure if it was because something suddenly overwhelmed him with passion or he only wanted to shut me up.

When the carriage stopped at the Black Bull Hotel at 22 Malop Street in Geelong, Aaron lifted me down and swung me around in the street, much to the amusement of those passing by. He invited Harry to accompany us; however, he politely refused, calling out he must continue on to run some personal errands. Aaron bid him farewell before he determinedly guided me towards the tavern.

'We're goin' in here to celebrate puttin' today behind us with one or five bevvies.' He took my hand and led me to the wide wooden door standing ajar. 'The only money we need to worry about is what we earn from our horses an' the breedin' program I'm settin' up.' I was thrilled he was excited about taking over the running of the property. It was far too much for me to manage. I had the house to run and so many people to ensure were healthy and happy in our employ.

We stepped inside the warm room, the fire in the corner burning furiously, and made our way to the polished wooden bar. Aaron offered me a seat before taking a stool and placing it next to mine while we murmured between ourselves. No one else was in the place, and the barkeep had his back to us. Aaron made himself comfortable, politely clearing his throat. When the young man turned around and saw me, his eyes went wide, and he adamantly shook his head.

'No women allowed in here, cobber. There's a room out the back just for you ladies where you can sit together and gossip while taking a lemonade,' he advised us politely, pointing to the door with an unwavering finger. Aaron smiled at him, then leaned across the bar, and offered his hand.

'G'day, mate. Surely there's no harm done when there's no other patrons here to witness it.' They shook hands before he continued, reaching into his pocket. 'How about allowin' me future wife an' I to drink to a special occasion, an' we'll depart if a soul comes in who's offended by her presence?' Aaron slipped a five-pound note across the bar, the barkeep's face breaking into a wide grin—unfortunately exposing two missing teeth—before tucking the money into his back pocket. They smiled knowingly at each other, the barkeep immediately relaxing and appearing friendlier than when we first arrived. It never failed to surprise me how money opened any door you felt like knocking on.

'I suppose you're right, cobber. It's no hurtin' anyone,' he agreed with a smile. We ordered two pints of ale, with shots of whisky in tiny glasses. By the time an elderly man entered an hour later, I was fairly drunk. Aaron took me by the shoulders to steady me and thanked the barkeep, warmly calling out goodbye as Aaron guided me outside. He lifted me into the carriage as Harry teased me for being drunk at this time of the day. Inside, Aaron pulled me onto his lap, and I slipped my arms around his neck. He gently kissed my face. I felt so relaxed and happy, as if my body was floating.

'Abigail, me love. I'm goin' ta have ta watch ya around the whisky. It knocks ya off ya feet, *mo anamchara*,' he remarked, kissing my nose and making me giggle.

'But I like it. It makes everything better. There is not a problem in the world I can think of that could bother me at this moment,' I slurred, and he chuckled. I had never tasted whisky before today. I found if you drank it fast and then followed it with a mouthful of ale, it didn't taste so bad. It made you drunk really quickly, and I liked the feeling it gave me. I vowed I would drink whisky every day for the rest of my life from now on. It was a potion of happiness and cheer.

Once we had arrived home, Aaron carried me from the carriage to my bedchamber. He placed me on the bed and looked down at me, his eyes twinkling in amusement.

'Come, lay by my side. I need you to hold me,' I slurred again. It seemed I could not tolerate alcohol as well as most people I knew. When I drank the same amount as any of my friends, I would end up twice as drunk as them in half the time. Aaron took off his outer clothing and slipped into bed. I kissed him passionately, and after a time, he stopped me and turned away.

'With only three days to go, we're not ruinin' it now.' Instead, he held me in his arms and stroked my head until I fell asleep in a drunken stupor, dreaming things that left no imprint on my memory.

I woke with a start, the room silent. I tried to focus on the clock sitting above the fireplace on the carved mantle. After several failed attempts to focus my gaze, I discovered it was late afternoon. I felt like I was dying. My head pounded in rhythm with my heart, and I made a new vow—I would not drink whisky every day for the rest of my life. Bessie had left a jug of water beside the bed—her cure-all for those who'd imbibed far too much. I drank it, despite my lurching stomach. After I had finished the entire jug, willing the water to stay down as I lay back and tried not to move, she entered the room with another one in her hand.

'Oh, the dead has arisen, I see,' she snapped at me. 'Mistress, I am so disgusted with you, coming home drunk in the morning hours. It wasn't even luncheon when you stumbled in. What kind of lady gets herself into a position like that? You have behaved like a wanton trollop, flouncing around Geelong town drunk. I will die of shame should anyone have seen you frequenting that tavern.' She shook her head as she stood over me, her face flushed and her hands on her hips. 'Don't you worry, I have had a stern talking to Mr Aaron and how irresponsible it was of him to give you whisky. Straight, too.'

She shook her head again before waving her finger at me. 'Ladies partake in lemonade or a weak shandy at most.' I tried to nod. I enjoyed shandies, but they consisted of only a small amount of beer topped up with plain lemonade—not strong enough if you sought oblivion—although I found them excellent in summer to quench my thirst. She glared at me, waving her finger disapprovingly as I refilled my glass from the jug and drank.

'Yes, get this jug down, too, and you will start to feel much better. A letter has come for you today. It was forwarded on from your solicitor's office.' Her tone softened as she reached into her apron and pulled out an envelope, placing it down on my bedside table. I felt excitement well up inside me, wanting to rip it open immediately; however, I concentrated on drinking the water, aware I was weak as a kitten and didn't have the strength even to reach over and pick it up. I had talked to Bessie last night about the new rules regarding my bedchambers once Aaron and I married, and she understood completely. She felt we deserved our privacy and agreed to attend only at the agreed-upon times unless I called her. The rope that rang the bell on the large board down in the kitchen—a feature of the house I certainly hadn't expected or seen before—still amazed me.

When we were at meals or carrying out our tasks on the property, she would attend to the many chores she did daily, ensuring my wardrobe was in order, my clothes washed and pressed before being put away, and my belongings were in place. Poor Bessie also bore the responsibility of supervising the housemaids when in my bed-chamber. She would advise them of their duties for the day, whether it was cleaning the windows until they sparkled, or laundering the drapes occasionally, along with dusting and beating the carpets out-side. They would also change my linen before making the bed in the morning, then return in the evening to fill the clawfoot bath so I could bathe before bed. She believed it would give her more time to spend with Danny, whom she was drawing even closer to, finding him a joy to be around.

Bessie helped me sit up, propping me back on my pillows before hurrying out of the room. I reached over, groaning to myself as I picked up the envelope, the first letter I had received in my new home, filling me with excitement and anticipation, despite how dreadful I felt. Recognising the handwriting immediately, I quickly broke the thick, red wax seal and slit it open with my fingernail, unfolded it, and began to read.

Dear Abigail,

You have only just departed, but I wanted to be the first to congratulate you on your new home and to tell you how much I miss your friendship already. I have less than two-years left until I graduate, and, as I promised you, the first thing I will do is take ship to Australia to visit you all.

I hope everything has turned out as you wanted and you are healthy and happy and might even have met a man?

Please do write back and tell me everything that has taken place since we last saw each other. I imagine all sorts of things that may have occurred to you since you departed, knowing what a free spirit you are and the trouble you get yourself into without even trying. I will be at peace in the knowledge you are well, safe, and happy in your new land once I receive word from you.

As I said, I do not have anything much to report because you have only just left—and I have only just arrived home from the docks after waving you off. The first thing I did was sit at my desk to write, just so you know even if things are not as you imagined or wanted them to be, you still have a friend in me no matter what your circumstances.

Congratulations on your new home. I hope you and Polly, Catherine, and Bessie are all content and thriving in the Australian sun. My parents send their love and best wishes and are eager to hear from you, as am I.

With much love and friendship,
Richard.

How lovely of him to think of me receiving my first letter, and the fact it was from him made it even more special. I hoped the time would go quickly so he and our group of friends could reunite, only it was a larger group now. Aaron strolled in to enquire how I was feeling. He smirked as I closed my eyes, grimacing at the pounding in my head.

'Last time I was here, ya were passed out like death had claimed ya, so I left ya to sleep it off.' He crossed the room and closed the heavy drapes. 'I went out on the farm with Angus, talkin' to the workers an' checkin' on the construction projects. I told Leo we would take our tea in here tonight 'cause I was certain you'd be sick when ya woke. He agreed to send it up on trays an' said to tell ya you'll never be a lady—traipsin' 'round Geelong pissed as a mute—an' apparently, I'm not much better.' He laughed out loud as he lay down beside me and kissed my throbbing temple. I didn't feel like sitting through dinner with everyone tonight. Not only was I hungover, but I had been feeling I wasn't getting a minute to myself lately. With the wedding coming up, I felt I needed some time alone. When Bessie returned, I asked her if she would mind getting me ready for bed.

'Of course not, Mistress. Come with me.' She gently helped me out of bed and guided me into the dressing room, where she stripped off my clothes and slipped a fleecy, clean nightgown over my head. It felt wonderful. I could think of nothing better than snuggling up in it and falling asleep later with a full belly once I was alone. 'I think we will forgo the bath tonight, Mistress.' She guided me back to the bed, finding Aaron sitting at the table reading the Geelong Advertiser.

'There are some Jersey cows advertised for sale in here, Abi,' he called out. 'Leo an' Miss Pickerin' have been complainin' to me for weeks now they're runnin' out of milk, cream, an' butter every day—an' they don't have enough to make cheese—so I'll shoot off in the mornin' to have a look see. Do ya wanna come with me?'

'Yes, I would love to. Jerseys are my favourite cows in the world—with their beautiful, caramel-coloured hides and their big, brown eyes—and those long, long lashes. They remind me of Bessie's eyes.' She smiled at me lovingly, ensuring I was comfortably propped up on my pillows before bidding us farewell and quietly closing the door behind her. Aaron stood and stretched, groaning loudly before crossing the room to my side.

'I've hired a lad to be solely responsible for milkin' the cows mornin' an' night, an' separatin' the cream an' churnin' the butter now we're gettin' more workers movin' in here. Miss Pickerin' an' Leo are strugglin' to keep up with the meals for the farmhands' an' stablehands' once the house staff have eaten. They all have large appetites, an' rightly so workin' from sunup to sundown. It should sorted by tomorrow if these are any good.' He removed his shoes, then lay down next to me on top of the heavy quilt. I snuggled underneath, feeling a lot better thanks to Bessie insisting I drink jug after jug of water. 'I'm not stayin' overnight again till after the weddin'.' He sighed deeply before continuing. 'It's too difficult, Abi. We're so close, an' I would hate meself if anythin' happened.' I carefully nodded in agreement, my head still throbbing. 'I'll leave after tea each night leadin' up to the weddin', so please don't encourage me to stay. Me willpower is non-existent when it comes to you, an' I find it hard not to give in to anythin' ya ask of me.' I heard Leo singing an Italian love song as he carried our dinner down the hallway. Although my head still pained me, my stomach had settled, and I couldn't wait to eat.

'Hello, dirty birdy. I knew Aaron would be back in your bed when he disappeared with no warning from the kitchen.' Leo placed a large tray on the table before straightening up and poking his tongue out at me. Jonathon entered the room and placed another tray down beside it before bowing to me and quickly departing.

'Why don't ya behave like Jonathon, Leo?' Aaron asked as Leo threw himself down on the bed in between us.

'Because I don't have to.' He smirked as he flirted with Aaron, stroking his bicep before he shrugged him off. 'I can't imagine having to bow and scrape to Delilah here. She thinks she's a princess when she can't even behave like a lady. Who else would go into Geelong just after breakfast and come home falling down drunk on whisky before lunch? She acts like she's a man and can do anything they can do. I can't get it through her head. She cannot behave that way just anywhere, or there will be scandals swirling at our door constantly. Maybe you will have more luck controlling her once you are her husband. I'm sure when you're married, you can try to make her behave in ways we will not discuss in front of her.' He paused, lifting his hand to his head to smooth his already perfect hair. 'I will say—you are partly to blame for today, Aaron. You know you can't take her willy-nilly out in public. I hope you have learnt to keep her away from whisky in the future. That is all I will say, other than this—if word got out you were even near her bedchamber, let alone sleep in here with her, she would be disgraced. For some reason, everyone here likes her, so they keep their mouths shut.' He took Aaron's hand in one of his and mine in the other. 'Isn't this wonderful? The three of us, just so in love with each other. I believe one day, hundreds of years from now, you will be able to marry as many people as you like, male and female, with no threat of gaol or the death penalty. I would love to be around to see those changes.' We laughed at him before Aaron kicked him out of bed, much to his disappointment. He made his way over to the small table and sat down heavily, crossing his legs while resting his chin thoughtfully on his hand. 'You know, I should have asked Abigail to marry me. You don't have to snigger like that. I love her just as much as you do, Aaron,' he called out, picking up the newspaper and opening the front page.

Aaron got up and brought my tray to me, placing it on my lap. I was delighted to see Leo had made Moussaka for us, with a Greek salad and creamy rice pudding for dessert. I loved how Leo cooked dishes from so many countries where he had lived and worked. Aaron and I ate hungrily as Leo filled us in on all the gossip from the passionfruit vine. As I finished my rice pudding, he hurried downstairs, returning a short time later with a plate of baklava and fresh, creamy coffee. Afterwards, Leo took the trays away and left us to our privacy. I lay down so full—I felt my stomach would burst.

'I love ya, Abi girl,' Aaron whispered, kissing me on the forehead.

'I love you, too,' I replied, kissing him on the mouth before closing my eyes in bliss.

Chapter Twenty-Three

IT WAS THE DAY before the wedding. I relaxed outside with Amelia on the manicured lawn, watching Mathew kicking happily while laying on a blanket in the sunshine. She had fully recovered and become so strong since turning up here what now felt so long ago—beaten and broken—both physically and emotionally at the hands of George. She had followed through on her demands and hired a ladies' maid and a Nanny—easing my mind only slightly.

Her new maid was in her fifties and possessed a powerful personality—exactly why Amelia chose her. Mathew's Nanny was a lovely girl—no more than eighteen—who was gentle and kind. She had immediately taken to the sweet, blonde-haired, blue-eyed infant, leaving Amelia feeling more than pleased with herself, and rightly so. I couldn't believe how brave she was and how far she had come, and I told her so. She sat up straight on the blanket, caressing Mathew on his tiny foot, and smiled.

'It's all thanks to you, Abigail, and the support I have received from Aaron and all your friends.' The leaves of the gumtree rustled gently above, the smell of eucalyptus filling the air. 'I now view them as my friends too, as they have treated us so kindly. I must thank you again for allowing me to stay and think through what I wanted to do. Having you all around me whenever I needed someone made such a difference—and the talks I have had with you all have made me strong. Where do you think I got the idea to make those demands?

I talked to you all individually and realised I was holding the cards and possessed more power than I realised. I just had to figure out what I knew about him that could ruin his reputation and destroy his credibility. Once I did that, everything went in my favour. It helped Aaron beat him.' She looked directly into my eyes, challenging me to deny it. It still surprised me how assertive she had become in such a short time.

'Why do you think Aaron was responsible?' I asked, trying to show no emotion. She started to giggle as my mouth twitched.

'I saw the way George looked at Aaron, and the things he said were practically accusing him outright, but no one said a thing. I also noticed Aaron's hands were bruised and cut in the days after George was assaulted. What he did—well, I appreciate it very much—although I can't thank him, as I don't want him to know I am aware it was him. Besides, he would tell me if he thought I should know. If it ever comes up between you, please tell him no one has ever done anything like that for me before, and I will never forget it and always appreciate his kindness.'

I smiled at her and squeezed her hand. She was leaving Monday with little Mathew, and I hoped everything turned out well for her. I thought she was courageous going back to such a shite of a husband, but it was entirely her decision. I would be her friend no matter what she chose to do.

I had just swallowed the last mouthful of my lunch, a delicious beef pie Leo had spent all morning making. Aaron stepped into the kitchen and crossed the room, bending down to embrace me.

'Any last-minute doubts?' he asked, looking deep into my eyes, causing my heart to flutter. The kitchen was empty, bar Leo, who rummaged around in the pantry out of sight and earshot. The maids left five-minutes earlier to eat their lunch in the staff quarters around their large dining table, where they could relax and be themselves without worrying about our presence.

'No, of course not—you would know about it by now,' I replied, smiling up at him as he gently kissed my lips. Leo walked past the table and paused behind Aaron, staring down at his backside before sighing deeply and resuming his work. Aaron was oblivious to the number of times Leo would look him over salaciously—or maybe he just chose to ignore it—I wasn't sure. Leo began beating eggs in a large ceramic bowl for a cake he was about to make.

'Well, if I were you, my little chocolate tart, I would have every doubt there was to have,' he called out to Aaron. 'Look at who you have chosen. She's certainly no lady, and although I hold out hope I might be an example to her, I doubt very much she will ever change. She chews with her mouth open—even worse, she speaks with her mouth full. However, I'll admit she is attractive enough for a woman—what with all the boys around here in love with her—obviously for reasons I clearly cannot comprehend. It's got me baffled by what you all see in her, although I, too, do like her boobies very much. They're like gin, when you think about it. Once you have touched them, you cannot stop.' Aaron chuckled as he picked up a glass of apple juice and drank deeply before replying.

'I'll find out tomorrow night.'

Leo's head snapped around toward him, his eyes wide as he stared at him in astonishment. He placed his bowl down on the bench and hurried over to us. Aaron kissed the top of my head before sitting next to me as we returned Leo's stare.

'Are you telling me you haven't touched her there once in the last two-months? Despite sleeping in bed with her and even going away for a weekend together?' Leo demanded to know, appearing horrified. Aaron nodded.

'Yeah, that's right. Not one feel.' He smirked across at me as Leo groaned loudly, shaking his head in disbelief.

'How can you not just grab them? They are the most amazing breasts I have ever felt, even on a chook.' Leo rolled his eyes before taking a seat next to Aaron. 'Not that I have anything to compare them to. Now I think of it, I must ask Polly if she will let me feel hers, just so I know the difference. Abigail's breasts might not be the best in the world, after all. Hold that thought until I can get more experience with boobies. Abigail, you are stingy with your affection, you little prude. How could you not let him even have one feel? He has no idea what he is getting tomorrow when he marries you. You are likely to be hopeless in bed because you won't listen to any of my instructions.' He took Aaron's hand in his and gently placed it on my right breast, over the top of my bodice. He gazed down at me, his eyes sparkling mischievously. I could feel the warmth of his hand through the fabric. It sent tingles throughout my body as he left it there for what seemed like the longest time, waiting for Leo to let go of him.

'Well, it's a little more complicated than just saying "your turn" as you instructed me, you idiot,' I replied darkly.

'There you go, my poor prince. She already isn't treating you well by being mean to me, given we all know you love me more than you love her. But, Aaron, you do have time to change your mind and possibly fall in love with a world-class chef who would adore you. Not that I know anyone who fits that description,' Leo remarked before returning to the bench to continue beating the eggs. Aaron let his hand drop from my breast to my waist before kissing me passionately. 'Oh, please. One feel and you can't keep your tongue to yourself. I told you they were good,' Leo teased. Aaron said nothing, took me by the hand and led me from the kitchen. Leo called out for him to come back, but he just waved goodbye and kept on walking.

To celebrate our last day of freedom before hitching our wagon—as Leo would say—we decided to go horseback riding. When I entered Delightful's stall, she whinnied and walked over to me for a carrot. I gently stroked her long, elegant neck—so soft and shiny—while admiring her lovely, dark eyes. Staying far longer than I intended to, I reluctantly left her to find Aaron as I planned to give him his wedding present today.

I walked through the stables, saying hello to Harry as I passed, still not understanding my feelings toward him. I liked him as a man, but had no conscious feelings of love or desire for him. Baffled by how each time I saw him, I had the urge to embrace him and never let him go—a feeling of pure love welling up inside me—only leaving me more confused. It was the most absurd emotion I had experienced when in the presence of someone with the golden glow. I always had an immediate connection with anyone who the mysterious aura surrounded; however, I couldn't explain or rationalise the connection I felt with Harry. I continued walking through the clean, sweet-smelling stables until I found Aaron. He was saddling up one of the horses we kept for guests, so focussed on his task, he failed to notice me standing at the stall door.

'Hello, my beautiful man. Would you come with me, please?' He appeared surprised but followed without question. I could hear his stallion inside a closed stall kicking the wall as we moved through the large stable, passing horse after horse—all seemingly happy and content in their enclosures as they chewed hay from the string bags tied to the wall. Most of the stalls had a half door you could see over, but several were fully enclosed for the more spirited horses. I had asked Harry to place Aaron's horse in such a stall so he wouldn't see him and ruin the surprise. Finally, we stopped outside the stall that held his wedding present. Aaron stood motionless in front of the closed door, appearing puzzled.

'What are we doin' here?' he asked, a slow smile spreading across his lips.

'Open the door and look inside.' I stepped back, allowing him to open the upper part of the Dutch door. The enormous stallion, a handsome and robust horse that suited Aaron perfectly, munched on hay in the corner. 'This is Goliath, your horse. He's a wedding present from me to you with all my love.' I stood on my tippy toes and kissed him on the cheek as he stared down at me in disbelief before turning to the door and casting an expert eye over Goliath. He reached out and opened the lower door and entered, flashing me a brilliant smile.

'Strewth, Abi. I can't believe I've somethin' as magnificent as him as me own. Thank you, me darlin'. Ya gift means more to me than ya know.' He held out his hand and slowly walked forward, making soothing noises. Goliath stood tense, his head up and nostrils flaring as Aaron approached him. I could smell Goliath's sweat and manure and found it quite pleasant mingled with the fresh hay, the aroma filling the stables, only adding to the warmth and comfort I felt when here. The more time I spent around the horses, the more at ease I became—even starting to find some enjoyment in their company. Aaron raised his hand to the stallion's nostrils to allow him to become familiar with his scent before stroking his neck and whispering to him. Goliath was noticeably more relaxed and allowed Aaron to continue caressing him. 'He's a beauty. He's much bigger than Delightful, isn't he?' He continued to look him over with a practised eye.

'I think he's the biggest horse Willow Grove has ever bred. He is only three-years old, so he needs a lot of work,' I warned him, thinking about what Harry had told me. Aaron appeared too excited to care. He saddled him up while I returned to Delightful to prepare her for our ride.

I attended lessons every day, riding in the paddocks with Aaron, while slowly becoming more confident. I felt in control of her now and could even trot and canter with her by myself. It was true it was easy to sit these horses because their paces were so long and smooth. However, I felt I was getting better at it with each passing day. Finally, Aaron, leading Goliath, stopped in front of Delly's stall and lifted me off the ground into a passionate embrace.

'Thanks, Abi. No one has ever given me anythin' like this before. I'll breed a long line from him that'll go on for centuries,' he promised. It thrilled me how delighted he appeared with his gift. He appreciated even the most minor things and took nothing for granted. He had experienced a comfortable upbringing—but not a wealthy one—so we had a lot in common when it came to our opinions of money and how to spend it.

We led the horses out to the yard, and Aaron lifted me onto Delly's back. I followed him through the back paddock and into the larger part of the property. We cantered towards the beach, and Aaron seemed like he was thoroughly enjoying Goliath, taking him through his paces and using his legs to control him. Finally, we arrived at the beach, and I looked out over the bright blue ocean, the sounds of the waves crashing below. Aaron slowed Goliath to a walk and waited patiently for me to catch up.

'Follow me,' he called out, kicking Goliath forward. 'I wanna show ya somethin'.' After riding a short distance, we came around a bend to find a cottage I had never seen before. Pulling Delly up next to

Aaron—who glanced across at me and smiled before returning his gaze to the sweet little house built entirely of stone—my eyes went wide. 'I call it the honeymoon cottage. I built it for ya when ya agreed to marry me. Polly an' Leo helped arrange the decoratin' an' furniture, but I designed it meself for when you an' I want time alone.' He dismounted before helping me down. Tears pricked my eyes as I watched him hobble the horses. No one had ever done anything like this for me before, and my heart melted as I looked up at him when he returned to my side.

He took my hand, raised it to his lips and kissed my knuckles, leading me to the small entrance as I watched him unlock the door with a key he took from his pocket. Ushering me into a cosy sitting room overlooking the ocean, he looked so proud as he led me into a small kitchen with a combustion stove and icebox, along with a small wooden table and chairs to seat four people. Through the kitchen, a door led to a large master suite, also overlooking the ocean. A four-poster bed stood in the centre of the room, while a large lounge sat near the fireplace. The bed looked comfortable, covered in the most luxurious quilts and pillows I had seen.

Lovingly decorated with the finest materials money could buy, the furniture was simple but beautifully crafted, while shades of blue and white filled each room, reminding me of the sea. It was small and cosy compared to the main house, and I was excited to have such a beautiful place to spend time alone with Aaron. It looked as if it had come straight out of a storybook.

'I think it's the most special thing anyone has ever done for me.' My heart felt as if it would explode—the love I felt for him was almost unbearable as he smiled proudly, gazing around at his handy work.

'It turned out better than I thought it would. The blokes helped me when they could spare some time so I'd have it finished before our weddin'. Would ya like to spend our honeymoon here?' His beautiful blue eyes shone brighter than I had witnessed since our first meeting.

'More than anything, Aaron,' I replied, embracing him for the longest time.

I reclined on a lounge in the back garden, enjoying the sunshine while listening to my friends talk between themselves. Aaron had left for the day, not wanting to bring bad luck to us or risk any misfortune, which had amused me no end. He would remain at home with his family until it was time to meet me at the church in the morning. I laughed when I realised he appeared more nervous than I did about the ceremony. Angus and Polly sat together on a bench near the swimming pool, while Amelia and Leo lay near me on their sun lounges as they chatted about tomorrow.

'I hope I have enough for everyone. The last thing I want to do is have hungry guests. I would be so ashamed in front of all those people,' he whined, then listed all the things that could go wrong between now and tomorrow, including Aaron changing his mind and leaving me at the altar. I sighed deeply as he lay with his arm draped dramatically across his eyes.

'Leo, you are the best chef I have ever had the good fortune to come across. You make meals out of ingredients no one has ever thought of, and the flavours are the most amazing I've ever tasted. Please have confidence in yourself. You are a wonderful chef,' I reassured him. He moved his arm, opened his eyes, and smiled at me gratefully.

'Thank you, Abigail. It means a lot to me you have so much faith in my talent. I know I do this every time, but I can't seem to stop myself, so I will breathe deeply and clear my mind. I will be all right, I promise. It's nice to see you give credit where it's due and realise I am a fabulous chef, and you could do no better.' I squeezed his hand, leaned over, and kissed him. Amelia, sitting up straight in her chair as Mathew lay beside her on the sun lounge, echoed my sentiments.

'I can't wait until tomorrow—for the wedding, of course, but especially for the food if it's anything like I have been eating every day here for weeks now,' she remarked, to which Leo smiled. She was finally at peace and the most relaxed I had seen her since we met, now knowing she didn't have to share her husband's bed or meet his demands anymore. She was now confident Mathew would have a respectable upbringing with a mother and a father of impeccable social standing. I was happy she was moving forward with her life in the best way she knew how. Although it didn't make up for her lost love, at least she had a son who gave her life meaning. Since staying with me, we had become closer, spending some nights in bed talking until the wee hours before falling asleep. Other nights, we would go to the kitchen at midnight and eat leftovers while chatting at the kitchen table. We confided our deepest secrets to each other and promised we would never utter a word to another living soul of what we shared.

'If I tell you something I've told no one, do you promise you will keep it to yourself forever no matter what?' she asked me quietly as the others argued about Australian football.

'Of course, Amelia, I give you my word.' She moved to my side and lay next to me, our heads close, so we were not overheard.

'George is not Mathew's father. Tommy is,' she whispered, tears in her eyes. 'I was having a secret affair with Tommy when I was promised to George.' She looked across at her placid little boy, who was smiling and making noises as he lay on her sun lounge, kicking his feet in the air. I remained silent, not knowing what to say. 'I tried to finish it with Tommy so many times, but always ended up back in his arms. He was the gardener at my parents' estate, and we would often talk while he worked—all very innocently at first, until I felt a growing attraction to him.' She sniffed, wiping away a tear that had slipped down her cheek. 'I was so sick of the upper-class idiots who were trying to court me—and I liked the fact Tommy was a regular man who worked hard and was upstanding and strong. Of course, it helped that he was handsome, too.' I nodded as she turned and lay on her back, gazing up at the clouds. 'We met at night by a big oak tree some distance from the house; then it progressed to Tommy sneaking into my bedchamber at night. Oh, how I miss him, Abigail.' She began to cry as I wrapped my arms around her.

'Were you betrothed to George when you fell in love with Tommy?' She shook her head, sniffing loudly before wiping her face with her handkerchief.

'Oh, no. I fell in love with him long before that man was forced on me. When my parents told me I must marry George, I pleaded with them without success to let me be with Tommy, but they refused.

Finally, two nights before the wedding, he snuck into my bedchamber to beg me not to go through with it and asked me to run away with him. I was foolishly concerned about what my parents' reaction would be and refused him, but I allowed him to make love to me one last time. Six weeks later, I discovered I was with child and didn't know for certain who the father was. My parents found out about Tommy after a servant saw him enter my bedchamber and reported back to my father, who ordered Tommy to leave the property immediately. They dragged him away during the night and would not tell me where he was or how to contact him.' I held her as she sobbed, her body trembling as she grieved her lost love. She went on to tell me George departed for Australia not long after the wedding, leaving her miserable and lonely at her parents' estate. When Mathew was born, she immediately knew Tommy was his father—who also had hair so blonde it was nearly white—contributing to why she was so miserable on the boat. As soon as George saw Mathew, she thought he would instantly know he wasn't of his blood, but since he did not know of Tommy's existence, he had accepted the boy without question.

She had resigned herself to the fact she would never see Tommy again and was determined to make her life as good as she possibly could for Mathew's sake. I admired her newfound strength. Her ability to turn the tables on George had impressed me, too. One thing she did have was a piece of Tommy with her every day. She only had to look at her son.

Amelia excused herself and went inside to change Mathew. Polly waited until she closed the door behind her before making her way to my side and sitting down next to me. It pleased me greatly we saw each other every day; however, Angus was always by her side unless he was working—and she would spend her free time following him around when he was. They still took their meals with us in the main house—except for breakfast—but I still missed her. I understood she was newly married and wanted to spend as much time as she could with her husband, but it would be nice to spend some time alone with her. She leaned over and took my hand in hers.

'How do you feel about tomorrow, Abi? Are you anxious?'

'I'm starting to feel a little nervous about standing in front of all those people. I hate strangers looking at me. But I'm not worried at all about the marriage part.'

'You always hated being the centre of attention from as far back as I can remember. You got worse as we grew older, and people in the village singled you out to the Sisters, commenting on your remarkable beauty,' Polly recalled, causing me to blush at the memory.

There had been an artist by the name of Patrick Adam, who owned a small shop in the village near the orphanage. When he first laid eyes on me at the age of thirteen, he asked every week for permission to paint my portrait; however, the Sisters always refused his requests. I had wanted a small picture of myself to leave with Sister Josephine and had thought a painting would have been lovely. Still, Sister Monica continued to refuse him right up until the Sunday before I turned fifteen and left the orphanage behind. Despite offering to pay for the privilege and to allow a Sister to be present to protect my reputation, nothing he said would budge Sister Monica. So, to compensate for what that mean spirited troll had robbed me of, I planned to send photos of my wedding to Sister Josephine, so she always had something to remind her of me. I secretly hoped Sister Monica got to see them, as I knew it upset her to even lay eyes on me.

My wedding was becoming very real as I listened to Polly talk of the bridesmaids' dresses, reminding me Catherine and Dana would arrive shortly, as they were staying the night to accompany us to the church in the morning. I stared intently at Polly, who was the happiest I had ever seen her.

'Were you anxious the night before?' I asked, worrying that tomorrow I would be a bundle of nerves and fall in a heap before I even made it to the church.

'No, I was excited and couldn't get down that aisle quick enough. I didn't care who was around because I didn't see anyone but him.' She sighed, looking very much in love as her eyes lit up at the memory.

'By the way, how is married life?' I asked softly, taking her hand.

'Oh Abi, it's better than I ever expected or dreamed. All those things we learnt from Dana are paying off.' She smiled, telling me of several private moments occurring in their bedchamber, making me smile. I was glad she was happy—she deserved it more than anyone I knew after all she had suffered.

'How are you settling into the new job?' I called out to Angus, who rose to his feet and stretched before joining us on the lounges.

'I'm enjoying it very much—especially workin' with the farmhands an' alongside Harry an' the grooms. Married life is even more enjoyable, though, an' I'm hopin' to hear the patter of tiny feet in our cottage as soon as possible. My mother is naggin' me already to provide her with grandchildren.' I nodded, thinking of my dear friend Harriett, who would be a loving and kind grandmother to any offspring Polly and Angus had in the future, despite her husband being a complete bastard. Angus' expression changed, and I raised my eyebrows questioningly. 'Have you seen Hamish lately?'

'No, not since the engagement party. Why?' I was surprised he would bring Hamish up with me at all, especially the night before my wedding. He leaned back, appearing to ready himself for a long chat. Polly hung on his every word as I rolled my eyes, but waited for him to go on.

'As you know, he is courtin' Charlotte. She's head over heels in love with him an' would do anythin' for him—an', in fact, is doing everythin' for him—if you know what I mean?' I nodded and rolled my eyes again.

'And your point?'

'It's obvious his heart isn't in it. He treats her poorly, lettin' her down frequently an' not acknowledgin' her most of the time. I know yer friends with her mother. He's only behavin' this way because he is out of his mind with jealousy an' can't accept he's lost you. Abigail, is there some way you can warn Charlotte off him for her own sake? She seems like a nice girl, an' I know yer close friends with her. Unfortunately, he is goin' to break this young girl's heart.' I let out a deep sigh and struggled to sit up before gazing across at him.

'Angus, I'm not the right person to be warning anyone off Hamish. You're right that Charlotte is a lovely girl; however, the problem is she is so infatuated with him it wouldn't matter what anyone said to her, including me. It would cause a rift between us. She would think I wanted him for myself. So, no, I won't do it. I mean, have a good think about it. Given the circumstances, do you really believe I should be the one to say anything?' He smiled weakly and shook his head.

'Aye, you're probably right when I think about it like that. Who should I ask to intervene?' he asked, clearly tormented by his brother's behaviour.

'If you feel that strongly about it, why don't you talk to Charlotte yourself? Even though you are his brother, I doubt she would listen, but it might be worth a try,' I suggested. He looked at me, his eyes widening in horror.

'Abigail, how could you even suggest that? If I went behind his back an' spoke out of turn, it would be a complete betrayal of Hamish.' He appeared mortified at the mere suggestion. I smiled at him, attempting to contain the laughter bubbling up inside me.

'So, it's fine if someone else does it to him, but not you? You two make no sense to me at all. I will never understand the twin thing.' A broad grin slowly spread across his face, and his shoulders slumped as he relaxed and spoke no more.

I stood at the bench, watching Leo prepare the ingredients for tonight's dinner—my last as a single woman, he had declared. He had baked a red velvet cake with cream cheese filling for a special dessert on my last night of freedom. He had also made some cupcakes, which I ate while I chatted with him.

'So, are you scared about doing the dirty deed with Aaron tomorrow night?' he asked, a young maid scurrying away, covering her ears as her face turned red.

'A little. I'm worried it will hurt,' I whispered, seeking a comforting word that all would be fine.

'Of course it will hurt, you twit.' He spread more cream cheese icing on the large cake, not taking his eyes from it for a moment. 'It will feel like someone is murdering you down there. Look at the size of his body—especially his hands. I can't imagine his python would be a carpet snake, given everything else on him is enormous. It will probably be a hundred times bigger than your quim. I imagine it won't be screams of pleasure we will hear tomorrow night. Look at the size of your body. He is over three times bigger than you. If you don't bleed to death when he takes your cherry, he will crush all your major internal organs, so you will die either way. Why couldn't you have picked someone more your own size so I could have had Aaron? You know I adore him, and it was only the fact you saw him first I did the polite thing and let you have him. We agreed that was the rule. Whoever sees him first gets to keep him.' I heard several of the maids gasp and quickly leave the room as Leo straightened up and admired the finished cake before placing it up on a shelf in the large pantry.

'Thanks so much for the support, friend.' I continued eating my second cupcake, helping myself to more icing. 'Here I am worried sick, and you tell me I will inevitably die, whatever happens. Do you really think he has a big one?' I asked, chewing my cake thoughtfully. He smacked me on the hand sharply with a wooden spoon.

'Stop talking with your mouth full. Do you have any idea what red velvet cake with white cream cheese icing looks like being chewed up in your mouth? No, of course, you don't. Well, it's not attractive, Abigail. I cannot understand how half the men in the district are in love with you. They obviously haven't met you or been forced to share a meal with you, you bushpig.' I burst out laughing, spewing crumbs from my mouth onto the bench. 'Nice. Attractive. Beautiful behaviour from a so-called lady.' He rolled his eyes as he wiped the bench with his cloth before smacking me on the shoulder with his spoon. 'As for your penis question. Yes, I do think he would have a big one. He does in my dreams, anyway.' Leo giggled uncontrollably, holding his stomach as I joined in until we were both laughing hysterically, tears running down our faces.

'There is someone here to see you, Mistress,' Mr Masters interrupted. We hadn't seen him enter the kitchen; we had been laughing so hard. Neither of us had ever seen Aaron's dangly bits, but we'd discovered we both dreamed about it regularly. I straightened myself up and brushed down my skirts, trying to pull myself together.

'Who is it, Mr Masters?' Most of my friends knew to come straight through to the kitchen when I was there.

'It's Mr Makenzie,' he replied, appearing worried. Leo gasped in delight as I placed my hand over his mouth, the smile instantly gone from mine.

'Do you mean Hamish?' I asked, feeling panicked. I took a seat and placed my head in my hands.

'Yes, Mistress. I have put him in the sitting room, given it's unfit to bring him into the kitchen,' he reminded me ever so politely. I smiled weakly at him before reluctantly pulling myself to my feet.

'Thank you, Mr Masters. I will find my way there in a moment—please offer him some refreshments. Oh, and ask him to stay for dinner so he can visit with Polly and Angus,' I added as an afterthought. He nodded, turned on his heel, and returned to the sitting room.

'Do you want me to come with you?' Leo enquired, clapping his hands in excitement. 'You know I love gossip, and to be there and hear something first hand for once would increase my credibility among my servants when I spread it around later.' I rolled my eyes before kissing him on the cheek.

'No, I should be fine, Leo, but thank you for only wanting to come along to support me,' I remarked sarcastically as he giggled. 'I can't imagine what he wants, but I doubt he will misbehave. I'm certain your ears will be flapping somewhere near the sitting room, so if I scream, you can come in and rescue me. Otherwise, stay out.'

I took my time to leave the kitchen to learn what I had done to deserve today's visit, feeling no different from if I were being held on a pirate ship and forced to walk the gangplank while ravenous sharks circled below.

Hamish stood when I entered the room, and I walked over to the opposite lounge. I sat down and forced a smile, unable to forget what he had said to me when I had told him of our engagement. I was still deeply hurt and in no mood to even look at him.

'To what do I owe this pleasure?' I asked, my voice calm. Inside, though, I was shaking. He stared at me the way he used to as he studied my face intently.

'Is it a pleasure to see me, Abigail?' He looked like he hadn't been sleeping properly, and his eyes were bloodshot, while there were black shadows underneath.

'Of course, as a friend Hamish, always.' Despite everything that had happened, I still loved Hamish. I had made my choice and chosen Aaron; however, part of my heart would always remain with Hamish, whether I liked it or not. I had such a strong connection to both of these men that somehow kept us close, even when we were physically apart.

'So, have you come to your senses yet and called this whole thing off?' he asked me intrusively.

'Why would I do that? I'm happy with Aaron, and I hope you are just as happy with Charlotte.' He rolled his eyes, then fixed me with a hard stare.

'I have thought long an' hard about this, Abigail, an' if you call it off now, I may be willin' to have you back—damaged goods or not.' I could feel anger rising in me. I straightened up in my seat and looked him squarely in the eye, furious he had the nerve to even call on me, let alone the night before I would marry.

'How dare you, Hamish! Who do you think you are to imply I am damaged goods?'

'Well, you would be by now. I know what it was like with us, an' we wouldn't have waited much longer,' he spat bitterly, watching my face intently.

'That's what you think. It's none of your business what Aaron and I may or may not have done,' I sneered, crossing my arms against my chest as my fists curled into balls.

'You can stop pointin' your chin out at me an' stompin' your foot, Abigail. Your reply was confession enough,' he roared, obviously angry with me again. There was no point in quarrelling with him; he would just argue and persist until he wore me down, to a point where I gave in to keep the peace. 'So, what do you think? Get rid of him, an' we can start again?' I looked at him wide-eyed, shaking my head in disbelief.

'Hamish, I am getting married in the morning. You must understand it's not Aaron's fault you and I are not together. It wasn't him I found in bed with Charlotte, was it?' He averted his gaze before lowering his head to hide the shame that was clear in his eyes.

'Look, I told you that was a mistake, an' it wasn't my fault, but you refuse to listen. I've tried so many times to tell you how I feel about you, Abigail, but you won't let me discuss anythin' personal with you anymore.' I could see he was becoming agitated and shifted in my seat, preparing to leave.

'Hamish, what do you expect? Seriously? I don't want to get into a blame game with you now. Let's just leave the past where it belongs and move forward, and try to retain as much of a friendship as we possibly can. We were friends once. Genuine friends,' I whispered, not wanting to upset him any further. He stared at me for the longest time. A deep sadness crossed his face, and he rose to leave, picking up his hat from the table.

'As you wish, but you're makin' the biggest mistake of your life, an' I won't be there to pick up the pieces when you realise he is wrong for you on every level. As long as you know that, Abigail.' He strode towards the door before pausing. 'I will be your friend, but I'm not waitin' around for you. I am goin' to get on with my life without you.'

'I thought you already were, Hamish.' My voice was barely audible as he turned and walked out without another word, leaving me alone with my thoughts.

Angus, Polly, Hamish, and Amelia played cards in the sitting room while little Mary cared for Mathew. Dinner wasn't far away, so they played a few hands while waiting. Hamish had agreed to eat with us only for Angus and Polly's sake; he was family, which was something we couldn't get away from. We would always be in each other's lives because of our love for them.

I was required to attend my weekly conference with Mr Masters, so I left them to meet with him in his office. He appeared brighter than usual, I noted as I walked in, acting like a proud father seated behind his beautiful wooden desk. The fire was burning in the hearth, and the room was cosy and warm.

'How are you, Mr Masters?' I asked, genuinely wanting to know.

'I am well, thank you, Mistress. Are you excited about tomorrow?' He opened the comprehensive book before him. He recorded all the house business in it and brought it to every meeting to update me on the progress and events happening in the house.

'Oh, yes, more than anything.' He gave me a rare smile, delighting me.

'We, as your servants, are all prepared to make it a wonderful day for you—a celebration you both deserve and will never forget.' He smiled again, and I couldn't help but smile back, given he rarely showed any emotion, good or bad. 'Mr Aaron is very well thought of by everyone at Willow Grove, and they are looking forward to having him here full time.' I thanked him profusely as he waved his hand, as if all their hard work meant nothing.

'Tell me what's been going on with the servants? I prefer to call them by their Christian names or at the very least staff or workers; however, I am aware you strongly disapprove.' He nodded but remained silent, allowing me to continue. 'Who's been doing what to whom?' He gazed at me like a patient father forced to simplify information for his child, so they understood it.

'Where to begin?' He smiled again before looking down at the open book on his desk. 'I caught one footman wandering the corridors during the early hours of the morning. He said he was sleepwalking, but I don't think he is telling me the truth. I caught him in the main house, Mistress, which makes little sense to me. But, I will get to the bottom of it, as all I need is one maid with child and no father in sight.' He shook his head in frustration. 'The farmhands and stablehands have commented on the standard of the food being the highest they have ever had. Miss Pickering does most of the cooking for them with help from the kitchen maids. We have a good stock of beef hanging that are, of course, our own beasts—and several pigs and sheep have also been slaughtered and hanged—along with a kangaroo a poacher shot. He was caught red-handed, so the worker confiscated the carcass and kicked him off the property with the threat of involving the police if he does it again.' He shook his head, his mouth twitching slightly. 'Kangaroo will not be on the menu at your wedding.' His mouth twitched again as I smothered a smile. 'The kitchen servants kill the birds and rabbits as we need them, so they are always fresh. They have killed and dressed our entire supply in preparation for tomorrow.' He cleared his throat before continuing. 'Chef Leo comes in and prepares the meals for the main house and leaves, which is how I think he likes it. I know I prefer it that way. It has been a hectic week, of course, but a harmonious one, nonetheless. Other than the antics we are forced to tolerate from a cook I will leave unnamed out of respect for you—and the fact you share a close friendship with the most painful man ever born on this planet.'

As he snapped his book shut, I wondered just how far Leo would push him until he exploded—my lips twitching at the thought of this very proper man expressing anger or rage—and I hoped I was there to see it if the day ever came.

'How is it between you and Maisie?' He appeared slightly confused for a moment before his face flushed.

'Well, now you mention it, there has been some progress. I'm far too old for her, but she will not hear of it or accept the fact—or any excuse I have thought of so far—so I have given in and am now courting her.' He appeared as surprised at the news as I did, causing me to giggle softly.

'That's wonderful. I do hope it works out for you both. Let me know if you need those married quarters in the future.' He nodded, and I took my leave.

Catherine arrived for dinner just as we were all sitting down at the table. The staff had filled the long rosewood table with white roses in dainty crystal vases that sat under the solid silver candelabras, casting a romantic glow throughout the room. She hurried into the dining room, apologising for her tardiness.

'Hello, lovely lady,' I called out as she came to my side and embraced me. She sat down next to Dana, who had only arrived an hour earlier. I had seen the surprise on Dana's face to find Hamish here, let alone the fact he was staying for dinner. Polly sat to my right with Angus by her side and Hamish next to him, chatting between themselves. Catherine and Dana sat to the left of me with Amelia and Leo. Tonight was my last dinner as a single woman. As of tomorrow, I would always have someone else to worry about, look after, and ensure he had what he needed and was happy.

'How are you feeling, my dear Abigail? Have your nerves overwhelmed you yet?' Catherine asked, patting my hand sympathetically. Mr Masters and the footmen circled the table as they served the entrée; large mushrooms collected from our property stuffed with cheese and baked until golden.

'I am nervous, but not about the marriage part. I feel self-conscious and worry everyone will look at me.' She nodded understandingly. Catherine was very much like me and didn't like attention solely focused on her, so she completely understood my concerns. While we ate, everyone chatted about the wedding tomorrow and how much they looked forward to it, although Hamish avoided the topic altogether. The main meal was served and looked delicious. I piled my plate full of vegetables covered and baked in a cheese sauce, along with a thick steak, smothering it in a rich onion gravy full of flavour and complementing the tender meat perfectly.

'I think we should make sure Abigail gets to bed early tonight, so she is well-rested for the morning,' Polly told them all as if I weren't in the room and sitting right next to her.

'More importantly, she will certainly need to be well-rested for tomorrow night,' Dana chimed in, laughing loudly as Hamish gave her a dark stare. I looked around at the three girls who were officially my best friends and who each gave such joy to me in different ways. They each had their strengths, which I cherished. I saw Dana return Hamish's stare and felt my stomach clench.

'Where's Charlotte, Hamish?' Dana asked sharply, screwing up her nose in disdain as she glared across the table at him.

'At your home, I assume. We made no plans for today,' he replied casually and continued to eat.

'So, she doesn't know you're here? And why are you here, by the way? It seems convenient the night before Abigail's wedding you show your face. You're not here to change her mind or have one last tryst with her, are you?' she asked suspiciously. I saw him flush slightly as he grimaced. He shifted in his seat, appearing uncomfortable.

'No. First of all, I am here to see my brother an' wish Abigail well. Second, we have decided to be friends.' She snorted loudly, openly mocking him.

'If I find out you are playing with my daughter, Hamish, I will find you, and I will hurt you in ways you have never been hurt before,' she snarled, her voice low, although dripping with venom. He dismissed her threat with a wave of his hand.

'Now, now, don't be like that, Dana. We're only courtin', an' it's early days. There is nothin' official, an' no promises have been made. It's not as if I've asked her to marry me.' He glanced sidelong at me, and I quickly averted my eyes. Dana gave him an evil glare, then turned to me, completely dismissing him. He looked relieved, picking up his glass of wine and drinking it all without taking a breath before striking up a conversation with Amelia. Dana turned to me and lowered her voice.

'It's not as if he had the respect or good manners to even come to me and ask permission to court her, the swine.' She stopped and cleared her throat, her eyes starting to sparkle mischievously. 'Anyway, enough talk about him. I heard something last week about Willow Grove and Lady Isabelle Delmont. Do you know there is another home built exactly like this in Werribee? There is apparently quite a scandal behind it.' I shook my head, waiting for her to go on. 'I heard Thomas Chirnside stole the plans to this house and built a replica—even the tiles in the entranceway are the same—much to your aunt's rage. She designed this down to the last detail, based on her own home in York. I'm uncertain of their consociation—or even if they were friends at one time—but I do know there was bad blood between them.'

'I was unaware; however, I do know who the Chirnside family are, and I saw his brother's widow at Tamara and Brian's engagement party. Unfortunately, I was not introduced to her and did not make her acquaintance.' I was immensely grateful Mrs Chirnside had not crossed my path. I had no interest in meeting her. Ever. She nodded slowly, her brow furrowed.

'Mary Chirnside has a few scandals of her own from what I know, but that is better left unspoken. I know little more, other than Thomas took his own life three-years ago out in the laundry house. Maybe your aunt haunted him and drove him to it.' Her mouth twitched as I tried to smother a smile, dismissing the Chirnsides from my mind. 'Is there anything special we must do for you tomorrow?' Dana enquired thoughtfully, smiling brightly, her usual cheer appearing to have returned.

'No. Just help me into the dress and make sure it doesn't get stuck on anything, and I will be happy.' I smiled at her gratefully. To have my three best friends standing up with me tomorrow had already helped calm my nerves. I knew I could get through anything with them by my side.

Polly, Dana, and Amelia sat on the foot of my bed while Leo and Catherine lay sprawled across the quilts, talking about my wedding night and wondering out loud what it was going to be like. They were all teasing me and laughing so hard I soon left them alone to wonder about it without my involvement. Seated at my dressing table, I rubbed my favourite elixir into my face and neck as I wanted my skin to be soft for tomorrow. I had discovered this oil always made my skin glow the next day and had used it every night after my bath since I found it in London. I brought an ample supply with me, finding I only needed a small amount to get the results I wanted so it would last me forever.

I felt wonderful having had my bath for the night, with Bessie taking special care when she washed my hair and put the conditioner through. I had then smothered my body in the coconut oil Leo had managed to get from the Pacific islands. He used it himself to keep his skin soft and smelling delicious and, to my amazement, even cooked with it. I dressed in a comfortable nightgown, with my hair wrapped in a towel as it dried. I lay back down on my bed with them all lazing around me. This bed was so large I was confident ten people could fit—not that I had ever tested my theory.

'This time tomorrow night, you will be laying naked in that beautiful man's big, brawny arms—if he hasn't accidentally killed you,' Leo reminded me. The others laughed, having already heard of the numerous things that could go wrong on my wedding night, resulting in my slow and very painful death. Catherine had been checking all the dresses to make sure they were perfect and had made everyone try on their new shoes to ensure they were comfortable. The shoes reminded me of the Cinderella story I had heard as a child, the crystals covering the entire shoe and sparkling like genuine diamonds in the light. I didn't know how Catherine had made so many dresses and suits in such a short amount of time, but she had achieved it with time to spare.

I was ready for bed, and they moved over so I could climb under the covers. They remained sprawled over the bed, gossiping about the men in their lives and the trials of love. I drifted off to sleep, listening to their voices. Aaron's face filled my mind, disappearing after only a moment; then Hamish stood before me, taking my hand in his as we floated above the clouds towards a strange planet named Hiriarni—all thoughts of Aaron erased from my memory.

A Word from the Author

THANK YOU FOR TAKING the time to read my series 'Samsara-The First Season'.' It's been nearly a decade since I wrote the first sentence of Abigail's story, and it is a privilege to share it with you.

If you have a few moments, I would be deeply grateful if you left a review on your chosen platform or website. It will help other readers find books that they may never have discovered otherwise. Your feedback means the world to authors and we cannot thank you enough for your support! Thank you for investing your valuable time and money in this story and I hope you enjoyed reading it.

If this series was not for you, that's perfectly okay. We all have different tastes as readers and we can't please everyone all the time. Thank you again for your support and I wish you well in finding novels that bring you joy. Much love to all xx

To find out more,

go to www.jlmartinauthor.com

SAMSARA

THE FIRST SEASON

Torn in Two

Volume One Book Three

What if you could remember a past life?
Or worse, what if you couldn't?

ABIGAIL MAKES HER CHOICE *and marries the love of her life, leaving heartbreak behind and consequences that she must face in the future. Basking in the glow of her newfound life, a life so different from her time spent in the orphanage, it is unrecognisable to her as she tries to adjust to situations she has never encountered before. Polly's past unexpectantly haunts them in this new land, leading to secrets being exposed and ending in murder. Abigail experiences a pleasant surprise, one that will change her life in ways she has never known, providing her with a sense of security and contentment she has never experienced. However, unfavourable events soon unfold, leaving some of her friends, especially Dana, grieving and wishing they had never immigrated to Australia.*

Continue the journey alongside Abigail and the cast of characters she calls friends through the first season of 'Samsara' and find out what thousands of readers are talking about.

Want to stay up to date and be the first to hear about Samsara? Go to jlmartinauthor.com to sign up for her newsletter and receive alerts and updates, along with bonus content. Links to social media and bookstores available here too.

www.jlmartinauthor.com